THE ACCOUNTING

THE
ACCOUNTING

WILLIAM LASHNER

THOMAS & MERCER

Text copyright © 2013 William Lashner

Published by Thomas & Mercer
PO Box 400818
Las Vegas, NV 89140

ISBN-13: 9781611099355
ISBN-10: 1611099358
Library of Congress Control Number: 2012920550

I took a piss at fortune's sweet kiss,

It's like eating caviar and dirt.

Bruce Springsteen

"Better Days"

I. VEGAS, BABY

—————❖—————

"Las Vegas. If we can't get in trouble there, boys, we're not trying."

—Augie Iannucci

.

1. Silence

WE TALKED EVERY WEEK, AUGIE AND BEN AND I. WE GREW up together, closer than brothers, and though we went our separate ways, and barely saw each other anymore, we stayed forever in touch. Every Tuesday, by phone. At least that was the plan. We didn't say much, most of the time there wasn't much to say. How's it going? How are the kids? Same old, same old. Sometimes we'd call just to say we were rushing somewhere and couldn't talk. Augie didn't want to hear the details of my suburban life, and I didn't want to hear the details of his self-destruction, and neither of us wanted to hear Ben whine anymore about his ex-wives. But it really didn't matter what we said, so long as we said something. We were each other's canary in the mine shaft. As long as we were talking, it meant we had still gotten away with it.

Which was why I was flying into Vegas out of Philly International. It was a Wednesday morning and the day before, Augie hadn't chirped.

"I wouldn't worry about it," said Ben from his home in Fort Lauderdale. "He's probably just stoned or shacked up with a whore. The problem isn't that he hasn't called, the problem is that he didn't invite us to the party."

"I suppose you're right," I said. "But my call went straight to voice mail. He always has his phone."

"Remember that time a couple years ago when Augie had us sweating for a week and a half before he finally called from a Mexican jail?"

"He blamed it on the worm."

"It's like you always say, J.J.: anything that happens to Augie, he'll have done it to himself."

"He does love his pornography," I said.

"Let me know when he finally rings up, hungover like a buzzard, with some new tattoo he doesn't remember getting," said Ben. "So, how are the kids?"

I didn't tell Ben I was flying out to check on Augie, but Augie hadn't called, and so there I was swooping down toward the gaudy Vegas strip in a 757 with my seat back up and my stomach clenched, not knowing what the hell to expect. Though with Augie, it was always safe to expect the worst.

I didn't much care for Las Vegas. I went there only to see Augie, and there wasn't much fun we could have together anymore. Augie liked to gamble, could play poker in the casinos for days at a time, and was pretty damn good at it when he was sober, but I never took to the tables. For me the pain of the losses always outweighed the charge I got from winning; heaven knew my money had been too hard earned. And Augie liked to end his nights with a lap dance at his favorite stripper joint, but as far as I was concerned, if I wanted to see a naked woman who wouldn't screw me at the end of the night I could just lie in bed and watch my wife undress. We used to play golf together, Augie and I, but after that crank dealer in Reno shot off his ring finger Augie didn't much play anymore, even though one-handed he could still bludgeon me on the course. And frankly, online pornography is not something one forty-year-old man wants to share with another. When I visited Augie we mostly drank, watched sports on TV, and ate at the Applebee's by his house.

Vegas, baby.

We landed with a jolt. I put on my sunglasses and my game face as the plane slid into the gate. The Vegas airport was a party I wanted no part of. The slot machines whirred, the bartenders poured, hawkers hawked their wares as the great screens high above the baggage carousels advertised the production of the year, the comedian of the decade, the sexiest showgirls on the strip. If Vegas didn't exist, you wouldn't be able to dream it up, and if by chance you did, before you could tell anyone about it a white rabbit would have chewed off your face.

All I had was a briefcase, so my journey through the airport was mercifully brief. I took the shuttle to the rental car center, checked in at a kiosk to avoid any face time with a clerk, picked the most generic-looking midsize I could find in the garage, and followed the arrows to the highway. No GPS, thank you. It's not that I knew my way around, it's that I didn't want to leave a record anywhere of where I'd been.

"Mr. Moretti, yes, how good to see you again."

"Thank you," I said to a bank clerk I had never seen before. I suppose obsequious customer service is better than no customer service, even in a strip-mall bank branch not far from Augie's Applebee's.

"Just show me your key and your identification and sign here," said the clerk, "and we can get your box for you right away."

It took me a moment to remember which signature I had used when I first rented the box. An oldie but goodie. Two looping Js, each followed by a period, before a scrawled, half-legible *Moretti*. I showed her the key and a license that had me living at Augie's house in Nevada, the same license I used for the flight and to rent the car.

"Very good," she said after she compared my signature with the one in the file.

She put me and the box in a room smaller than an airplane toilet and left us alone. I sat there for a moment and felt nothing, felt dead. My son had a ball game that afternoon that I was missing, my daughter had a choral concert at the high school that night, and I was booked on the red-eye back, which meant my next day would be a sleep-deprived mess, all to fly out to a city I hated to make sure an old friend, with whom I no longer had anything in common, was okay because he hadn't phoned, even though he was a drug-addicted drunk, which might have had something to do with the lapse. And all of this was in service to something that happened almost a quarter of a century ago. I closed my eyes for a moment, fingered the scar on my neck, and thought what it would be like to be done with it all, to be finished, to let the fear bleed out of me one last time. What would it be like to be normal?

I let the weakness overtake me for a moment, let it pass through me and out of me. And then I opened up the box.

No surprises, nothing popping out like a stuffed clown atop a Slinky, just the same stuff I grabbed from the box each time I came to Vegas to check on Augie. There were the keys to his house. There was the wad of hundred-dollar bills bound in a purple-and-white wrapper, a little pillow of security if things went wrong. There was the automatic wrapped in newspaper and stuffed in a plastic bag so that it wouldn't rattle in the box, something that scared the hell out of me but that Augie insisted on. And oh yeah, there were a couple boxes of condoms.

I jammed the keys in my pocket, along with the money. I removed the gun from the bag, unwrapped it, checked that the clip was loaded and the chamber empty like Augie had taught me, and put that in the briefcase. I was about to close the safe-deposit box, when I thought better of it and grabbed one of the condom boxes. Augie always told me, with a jaunty voice over the phone, that when I stopped by I shouldn't forget the jimmy hats. The condom boxes were old already and still unopened, but I took one anyway in case he needed a few; dealing with Augie meant it was always better to be prepared.

Look at me there, leaving the bank with my sunglasses on, a wad of cash in my pocket, my briefcase holding condoms and a gun. Look at the swagger, at the hint of a smile, like I have the world beat, look at the utter fatuousness of the middle-aged suburbanite playing at being a torpedo. If any man was ever in need of a punch to the face, it was he, me, and it was coming, yes, it was. Sometimes the aardvark imagines he's a lion, but the hyena always sets him straight.

Before returning to the car I slipped inside a drugstore next to the bank and bought a box of chocolates, the biggest they had, bound with frills and goofily shaped like a brontosaurus heart, a deranged greeting-card magnate's idea of a romantic gesture. Then it was back to the sun-drenched morning as I steered the rental across West Sahara to South Rainbow Boulevard.

The residential parts of Vegas are lousy with walls. Every development is surrounded, every backyard. If Robert Frost had ever seen Vegas he would have had a breakdown. I was stopped at a light on West Twain with walls all around me, when a motorcyclist pulled up beside me and revved his engine. At the sound, my blood fizzled like I was mainlining Alka-Seltzer and I felt a throb at my throat.

I tried not to look, but I couldn't help myself. The rider was older, with a gray beard and a denim vest. He seemed to be ignoring me, and I turned my face to the windshield so it seemed I was ignoring him, too. But I wasn't, with all my concentration. I was always jumpy when I saw a biker, felt the twin urges to run away and to run the bastard over. When the light turned, my foot stayed on the brake as the motorcycle zipped away.

After a few bleats from behind, I started up again down South Rainbow. A hundred yards on, I turned into a gap in the wall to my right. SPRING VALLEY, read the dusty old sign. Why, if I didn't know any better it might have sounded like the sweetest little place on earth. Spring Valley. Where the sun always shone down softly and pussy willows waved in the breeze. But I wasn't entering Spring Valley for the scenery.

An old friend hadn't called, and I was paying him a visit to see if I still had a life.

2. Spring Valley

ALL THE HOUSES IN AUGIE'S VEGAS DEVELOPMENT LOOKED alike, sunbaked squat boxes offering nothing to the street but drawn curtains and garage doors. The place was as amiable as a rock. For a time Spring Valley had been hot, prices had more than doubled, fancy cars had been parked in the driveways, lawns were green and shrubs were blooming and SOLD signs sprouted like desert flowers after a rain. And then the bubble burst.

Now the development was littered with forlorn FOR SALE signs and every other house seemed to be abandoned to the bank. The cars on the street were old, battered, a few draped with pale covers like the furniture in haunted houses. The street signs were so caked with red dust it was impossible to read them. It looked like the place had been hit by a neutron bomb. And it had.

Is anything more destructive in this world than easy money?

Augie lived on a road that ended in a cul-de-sac. When I reached the mouth of Augie's street I slowed for a bit but kept going. I didn't see any motorcycles parked at the entrance, or anything at all suspicious, but still I sure as hell wasn't pulling into his driveway. When I asked him why he had bought on a cul-de-sac, he said it was great for kids. He also mentioned something about the schools, and the park a few blocks away. The whole thing made me laugh, considering that Augie had been fixed years ago. It was obviously part of the real-estate agent's spiel as she sold him more house than he needed when the market was rising, houses were selling at above the asking price, and every mortgage seemed like a license to steal. It was only later that everyone realized who was actually doing the stealing. Augie was repeating the patter to convince me of the quality of his purchase, which was sweet and all, but frankly I didn't care. Truth was, I didn't mind him blowing his cash on more house than he needed—hadn't we all done that?—I just thought he should have been a bit more careful in his choice of location. One way in means one way out.

I turned left one block past Augie's cul-de-sac and backed into the empty driveway of the eighth house, a small ranch with its windows curtained and a patch of dead sand in the front, like an ironic comment on the very idea of a suburban lawn. I knocked at the door with the briefcase by my side and the heart-shaped box of chocolates clutched to my chest. I had to knock twice before I heard the shuffling.

"Who is it?" came a rasp of a voice from inside.

"Is that you, sweet Selma?" I said.

The peephole darkened for a moment and then the door opened. The woman standing in the doorway with the help of a metal cane was short and thick, with skin supple as jerky. A cigarette drooped from her lips, her eyes were squinting from the smoke, her hair was so jet black it would have looked false on a Chinaman. "What's that nonsense in your hand?"

"Chocolates," I said.

"Are you trying to seduce me with bonbons?"

"Would it work?"

"Thirty years ago, with a little charm, maybe. Now, honey, it's liquor or nothing. But since you're here…" Selma grabbed the box, gave it a shake, opened the door wide. "Get on in if you're getting in. I don't want to lose the air-conditioning."

Selma's house was dark and cool, overstuffed with over-stuffed furniture pushed against the walls of her tired little living room. Along with the couches were piles of magazine and books, a television on a folding table, a broken chair, a statue of a mermaid in fake stone. The whole place was as cheery as a waiting room at the Port Authority, but the photographs on the wall of Selma as a perky showgirl circa 1962, along with Joey and Sammy and Dean, bespoke a jauntier history. I once asked her where Frank was. "Between my legs, honey," she said with her hoarse smoker's croak. I didn't come to Vegas to make friends, but once I saw where Augie had bought his house, I had made friends with Selma.

When we were both inside the living room, she plopped down in the lounger marked with cigarette burns, ripped open the frills on the box, took a bite out of one of the chocolates. "Where'd you get this crap?" she said.

"I had it shipped from Paris."

"It tastes like it came from a drugstore," she said, dropping the half-eaten piece back into the box.

"A drugstore in Paris," I said. "You don't want it?"

"I didn't say that."

"Then quit your whining. How are you doing, Selma?"

"Oh, I can't complain."

I laughed. "That doesn't mean you won't. So how's Augie? Any suspicious strangers lurking about? Any wild pool parties?"

"Not since you were in last."

"That, I want to explain, wasn't my doing. For some reason Augie felt compelled to show me a good time."

"And you boys had it, too, by the sounds of things."

"He did, at least. Where he finds those girls, I'll never know. They had more tattoos than the Sixth Fleet. I prefer quiet nights spent with distinguished elder ladies with jet-black hair."

"You won't get much of that, honey, if all you've got is drugstore chocolates."

"Has he had any visitors?"

"Not enough. I'm worried about him, J.J."

10

"How so?"

"I wanted to call you, but I couldn't find your number."

"Go ahead, Selma."

"He's been crying."

"Excuse me?"

"Sometimes he sits by the pool late at night and cries. And it's not quiet either. Quiet desperation I understand." She took a long inhale from her cigarette, let it out slowly. "But this is something else."

"Augie goes through things."

"He needs a friend, J.J. He needs help. He needs to get sober."

"That's nothing new."

"But he's at the point where he needs it now. I've been there, I know. It's not enough for you to just fly in for a day and then fly out. He has no family that visits, no one who he cares about, just you. You need to be a friend."

I looked to the kitchen, as if I could see through walls. "Have you heard him crying in the last couple of days?"

"Haven't seen hide nor hair of him."

"Anyone knocked on your door looking for him? Or for me?"

"Who would be looking for you?"

"I think I owe a parking ticket from my last visit."

"And they're hot on your trail? No, sweetie, nothing."

"Okay, thanks, Selma. Mind if I go the usual way?"

"You're a certified kook, you know that?"

I leaned over, kissed her on the forehead. "I like to make an entrance."

I picked my way through her living room, into the kitchen, and out the back door. When I stepped outside I was blinded by the fierce noon light before I put back on my sunglasses.

Selma's small backyard was as dead as her front, just a gnarly plot of stone and sand and a few dead bushes, all surrounded by a wall about six feet in height. At the base of the wall were two cinder blocks piled one on the other that I had put there a couple years before. I stood on the blocks and peered over the top of the wall.

Pretty much the whole of Augie's backyard was taken up by the pool, a sparkling blue surrounded by cement and sand. But the water in the pool was low, it had evaporated beneath the level of the skimmer, and something small was floating in the middle of the expanse. It took me a moment to figure out what it was.

A bird, a species brown and small, facedown and dead.

3. Message from the Past

I HOISTED THE BRIEFCASE TO THE TOP OF THE WALL AND PULLED myself up with a grunt until my belly was resting beside the briefcase on the wall. Slowly I jiggled my legs over and across until I fell awkwardly onto Augie's side.

A lounge chair, a lawn chair, a small row of empty liquor bottles, a net on a stick that could have been used to fish out the dead bird but hadn't. I took the briefcase down and slipped around the pool to the door that opened off the master bedroom. The shade was drawn tight. Why is it that everyone who moves out to the desert for the sun does everything to keep it out once they get there?

I knocked and waited. Even past noon it was still too early for Augie to be up. I knocked again. Then I thought about Augie sitting in the lawn chair with a bottle, looking up at the imperfect darkness of the Vegas sky, and crying. And I thought about that bird floating facedown in the pool. And I caught a whiff of something ugly and suddenly I knew I could wait all day and the next and Augie wouldn't be answering the back door. I slipped the key into the lock and gave it a turn.

When I stepped inside, the scent I had caught just a whiff of through the door slapped me in the face, something oily and thick and sickly cloying. I didn't recognize the odor from personal experience, but something deep in my genetic code knew exactly what this was. I stepped back outside, took a deep clear breath to fight the nausea that had blossomed in my gut, shielded my nose in the crook of my arm, and waded back into the dark mucky air, closing the door behind me for privacy. I gagged loudly twice before finding Augie naked and spread-eagled on his bed.

His body was strangely swollen, his skin was strangely marked, his flesh was strangely green, his jaw was strangely elongated, his eyes were strangely open.

My old friend was strangely dead.

And yet the most surprising thing about it all was how unsurprised I was. As a boy Augie had had the quickness and daring of a pirate, but his addictions had stolen his youth and now his life. Drugs and alcohol, prostitutes and pornography, gambling and violence and the adrenaline of fear—Augie became addicted to anything that pushed him closer to death. Too bad he never became addicted to success. He would have played the hell out of it; that would have been a party to remember. And Augie was smart enough to have pulled it off, too. I wouldn't have been shocked if Augie Iannucci had ended up as the smarmiest politician on television, or a professional surfer, or a pitchman for ShamWow!, or even the dentist he talked about becoming, and not just any dentist—a dentist to the stars. Instead he let his hungers chew him up from the inside; his tragedy was that no matter the hunger, he could always afford to feed it.

When the smell and sight and, yes, the reality of my bloated dead friend became too much to bear, I lurched past his body and into his bathroom to throw up the breakfast I had snatched before takeoff. I turned on the water in the sink, put my hands under the faucet, splashed my face over and again. When I looked up at the mirror, I expected to see a sadness in my wet, red eyes, and I did, but I saw something else, too, something that shamed me in its calculation.

I saw relief.

It was over now, the whole Augie part of my life. No more long-distance entreaties for me to come out and party with him, no more inconvenient visits to Vegas, no more worries when Augie didn't call, no more fears about the brilliant young boy who had turned out to be the weakest of the three of us, no more guilt about how our great coup had ruined him. I was relieved that my best friend in the whole of the world had finally died. What had happened to him? What had happened to me?

I could get into a metaphysical wrestling match with the untrammeled remnants of my once-young soul some other time, and I would, I was certain, when I got back to my basement, where I did all my best thinking. But now was the time to clean things up and get the hell out of there. I knew Augie's secrets, and his secret places, and it was time to empty them all.

The kitchen was an unholy mess; Augie's last days were obviously spent in squalor. Or maybe the final party had gone on a bit too long. But I wasn't in the kitchen to judge his housekeeping. There was an unglued floor tile in the corner by the stove. It was hard to see because there were no gaps in the grout. I spent a few minutes grappling at the wrong tile before I found the right one. With the help of a kitchen knife, I levered up the tile. Beneath was what appeared to be the usual base of glue on cement, but it was really only glue smeared across a board, and that too could be worked up. Beneath the board was a hole, hacked out of the slab and the dirt beneath it. And in the hole was a familiar leather gym bag. I pulled out the bag, looked at it for a moment, remembering, and then zipped it open.

Cash, loads of it, packed in wads $10,000 strong, old stuff, original lucre, untouched over the years. I had figured Augie had blown through his stake and was now living a desperate financial existence, hand-to-bottle-to-gut, but here was a small fortune. He had been more careful than I thought. I opened my briefcase and threw in the stacks, one after the other. Eight. Half for me, the rest for Ben, after I took all that I had loaned Ben over the years.

I put the leather satchel back in the hole and closed it up as tight as I had found it.

There was another hiding place, in the living room, in the stuffing of an old easy chair. Augie said he always stashed some cash there in case he was being robbed and needed to give something up to the gunmen. I suppose those are the crazy kinds of precautions you take when you live the kind of life Augie lived. I saw no reason to leave anything for scavengers, so I headed through the kitchen to the living room, which was in worse shape than the kitchen. It had been trashed, completely. The final party must have been a doozy.

And then I noticed that the chair was overturned, and the lining of the bottom was slashed, and the hiding place within the chair was exposed and empty. Suddenly the potent combination of sadness and relief that had been flowing through me was replaced by raw fear. And I knew, as I should have known from the start, that it wasn't his addictions that had taken Augie down, and that the ruined state of his house was not the remnant of a final wild party.

Back in the bedroom, a quick examination of Augie's body confirmed the diagnosis. Bloated and green, yes, and covered with his tattoos, yes: birds and dice, tribal markings, Chinese letters. And, on his shoulder, just as on my shoulder and on Ben's, three skulls with a banner beneath holding the words *Still Here.* No longer, old friend. He was dead cold, and his joints were loose, which meant he'd been gone at least two days. But there were other things I had skipped over the first time I saw his corpse, maybe because I wanted to. Bruises. Burn marks. A small, jagged wound on his breast. I wondered for a moment who else could have killed him: a drug dealer, a loan shark, a pimp? Actually I was hoping like hell it was a drug dealer, or a loan shark, or a pimp.

But there was something about Augie's jaw, its strange elongation. I had thought that was merely from the rigors of rigor mortis, but now it did look truly strange to me, weird. I leaned over Augie's body and, grimacing, pulled his lower lip back. There was something in his mouth.

Jesus Christ, there was something in his mouth.

With two fingers I pulled it out, a wad of paper, wet with the stinking slime of his festering fluids. Something cold brushed against my neck as I pulled the wad apart to get a look at it.

A hundred-dollar bill.

I dropped the bill as if it were burning my fingers. I didn't need to figure out what it was there for, I knew. It's amazing how fear quickens the thought process, even as it quickens the pulse. It was a message, a message to me, a message from the distant past, as clear as if skywritten in the cloudless Vegas sky. And what it said was that my life, as I now knew it, was over.

The first thing I did was open my briefcase and take out the gun and look about me for a target, any target. I was jumpy enough that I would have killed the television if it had winked at me. Hell of a torpedo I was. Then I took my phone from my pocket and called Ben. He didn't answer, which was a relief, I didn't want a long conversation when a voice mail message would do.

"They found Augie and they killed him," I said. "I'm disappearing. Take care of yourself, pal, and have a good life."

And that was the end of Ben, too, as far as I was concerned. My two oldest friends, snap, gone just that fast. I had shrugged off much of my past already; it wasn't much of a stretch to cast away the rest.

"Good-bye, Augie," I said to the corpse.

And that very instant, as if Augie were returning my sentiment from some dark place in the ether, the cordless phone on his bedside table rang.

4. A Little Rough

I SHOULD HAVE LEFT AUGIE'S HOUSE WITHOUT ANSWERING THE damn phone. I should have just nodded one last time to my old dead friend, let the handset ring itself off the hook, and gotten the hell out of there. But I suppose I still had hope, hope that my suppositions were all wrong, hope that I wouldn't have to do what I knew I had to do once I stepped out of the house, hope, foolish blind hope. Because maybe I was jumping to the wrong conclusion. It had happened so long ago. Maybe this actually was the doing of a dealer, or a loan shark, or a pimp. Weren't those the most likely possibilities? And maybe this ringing phone could set me right, maybe it could be what we all most desperately desire when facing our inexorable fate, a reprieve from the governor.

So with gun still in hand, I took a chance and picked up the phone. "Hello?"

"Well now, so you finally answered," came a voice I didn't recognize, a man's voice, acid sharp but calm, with drawn-out, flat Midwestern vowels. "I've been calling and calling, hoping I'd eventually find you in."

"Who's this?" I said.

"Never mind that. The question is: Who are you?"

"Augie."

"Is that right?" A rustle in the background, a draw from a cigarette. "How's it going there, Augie?"

18

"A little rough," I said as I took the phone to the front of the house. With the muzzle of the gun, I nudged open the edge of the curtain and checked as much of the cul-de-sac as I could see. Nothing.

"A little early in the day, hey, Augie?"

"You could say that."

"I guess so, considering I watched you die two days ago."

I opened the curtains wider, pressed my head close to the glass, felt a new jolt of fear. There, on the other side of the street, two figures emerging from behind what appeared to be just another deserted house. They had thick heads and big bellies and were dressed in black slacks and print shirts that hung loose over their belts. Their sunglasses had the terrifying emptiness of an insect's eyes. I spun around and pressed my back against Augie's front door.

"Why'd you do it?" I said to the bastard on the phone.

"You know why."

"No, I don't."

"That's the second time you've lied to me within the last minute. I'm going to get a complex. We've been looking for you."

"Not me."

"You are precious, aren't you?"

"What do you want?"

"The rest of the money."

"It's gone."

"Not all of it, I'd bet."

"A bad bet in Vegas," I said. "How unexpected. So what tipped you?"

"It was only a matter of time."

"But why now?"

"No time like the present."

I checked the window again, watched as the men got closer. They had no guns in their hands, at least not yet. I had an opportunity to take the initiative, to smash the glass and start firing, to let both bastards have it. Rat-a-tat-tat, baby, just like the hardest scar-faced torpedo in Nevada.

But I wasn't a torpedo, I was a middle-aged salesman with a family and a lawn and a gun he was afraid to use. I let the curtain swish closed as I backed away through the living room, down the hall, into the bedroom.

"You know we could make a deal," said the man on the phone. "We're not averse to a deal."

"Like you made a deal with Augie."

"Augie was stubborn. It was as if he wanted to die."

"And you obliged him, you sick son of a bitch." I jammed the gun into my belt and grabbed the briefcase.

"We couldn't talk to Augie. But you, I can tell, are a reasonable man. With you we could work something out."

"There is nothing to work out," I said. "It's all gone, I told you."

"You could take out a loan."

"Who the hell are you?"

"Just think of us as your friendly neighborhood collection agency. Your life is in foreclosure, boy, and we want to help you find a way to save it. If we sit down together and have an accounting, I'm sure we could come up with something. What do you say?"

"I'll think about it."

"Don't think too long, Frenchy. One way or the other we're going to sit down together."

The sound of the old and hated nickname resounded like a shot over the phone. I stopped for a moment, felt the fear fill me and bubble over and coat me with its molasses, leaving me stuck as if glued to the floor. Glued to the floor until I heard glass break from the front of the house.

Suddenly I was out the door and skip-hopping around the pool. As footsteps thundered along the side of the house, I tossed the phone into the water and charged heedless for the wall. No middle-aged heaving struggle to get over it this time. Fueled by adrenaline, I tossed the briefcase to the other side, planted my hands, and leaped, swinging my legs high as a gymnast on the pommel horse. Who the hell needs steroids? Point a pistol at a baseball player's face and watch the homers fly.

I landed with a thud and stayed low on the other side as I heard something crash through Augie's back door. Hoping they hadn't spotted my mad leap, I grabbed the briefcase and scooted like a chimpanzee toward Selma's house. I opened the rear door slowly, spun myself inside, closed the door softly. I stood just high enough to peek through the blinds at her empty backyard.

And then I heard something behind me. I jumped like an electrode had been placed on my scrotum. I grabbed for the gun but it was gone, it must have slipped out when I leaped the wall. Hell of a torpedo I was. Defenseless now, I turned slowly, expecting the worst, and saw Selma, leaning on her cane, staring at me with something hard and unfriendly in her eyes.

"What in the barnyard's going on?" she croaked.

"Someone killed Augie," I said. "And now they're coming after me."

"Not in here, they aren't."

"They have guns, Selma."

"Guns?"

Selma's eyes widened and just that quickly she turned around and scooted away. To lock herself in the bathroom, no doubt. Smart lady. I was taking another look out the window when I heard Selma behind me once more. When I glanced back, I found her standing there with a huge shotgun in her hand.

"This is Vegas, honey," said Selma. "Everyone has guns. I'll watch the back door."

"Augie needs a funeral," I said as I pulled out the wad of hundreds I had jammed in my pocket, laid it on the top of the washing machine in her mudroom.

"I'll take care of it."

"Try to run it through someone so they don't know you're paying. He'd like something simple, I think. Pine, maybe."

"Pine's nice."

"And just a name on his headstone. No fancy sculpture of a naked lady, even though I don't think he'd mind that so much. His family was Catholic, whatever that means. He was a good friend. And he always wanted to be a dentist."

"A dentist?"

"Yeah." I shrugged. "It was what his mom wanted for him."

"Why are you telling me this?" she said.

"I thought someone ought to know."

"Get the hell out of here already."

"I won't be in touch," I said.

"Is that a promise?"

"You're a marvel, Selma," I said. "Frank had good taste."

"He was the goddamn chairman of the board, honey." She let go of her cane and gave the shotgun a pump. "Now get."

I kissed her on the forehead and I got.

I expected shouts and roars, I expected the bullets would be whizzing about my head like bumblebees. But as I hustled to the rental car from Selma's front door there was only the hot, quiet Vegas afternoon, where the sun seemed to knock senseless everything in its path with billy-club force.

I didn't look around—what could I gain by looking around except for a bullet in the neck? I simply slipped into the car, started the engine, attached my seat belt, pulled carefully out of Selma's driveway, and turned to head deeper into the development. By now the killers might have spied the phone at the bottom of the pool, the gun that had slipped from my belt, they might have surmised my exit route over Selma's wall and through Selma's yard. They might at that very moment be hopping the wall to search for me. I certainly hoped not, I had never intended to get Selma involved in my mess, but then whenever did my good intentions matter one whit?

I kept my speed low and my eye on the rearview. I can't say I saw nothing suspicious because everything I saw was suspicious: that parked truck, that dog on a rope. But I kept on driving, well within the speed limit, giving every stop sign more respect than it deserved.

Where Selma's road ended I turned left and smoothed my way around the park, past the ball field and the basketball courts, the unbroken line of backyard walls to my right. This wasn't an unfamiliar route, I had practiced my departure in earlier visits, but I had never had to drive it when I wasn't playacting and so this felt completely different. This felt like tiptoeing on eggshells filled with razor blades.

Still I felt a surge of relief roll through me as I approached the end of the park. I checked my rearview again. Nothing chasing, nothing firing bullets into the air. The development's exit—and my escape—was just down the curving road, and I sped toward it like a horse heading toward the barn, when I spotted something coming at me from the left, charging right at me like a demon from hell.

5. Flamingo Road

T HE DARK BLUE CAR SHOT THROUGH THE STOP SIGN, ACCEL-
erated as if it were leaping, slammed bang into my side.

My hands flew off the wheel as my car flew off the road. Air
bags and glass exploded around me, something smashed into my
head as the seat belt dug into my neck and the noise of the collision splintered my ears. The car spun and flipped at the same
time, spun and flipped and spun...when some son of a bitch
slammed into me from the exact other side.

I might have blacked out for a moment, or maybe just closed
my eyes as glass and plastic flew all about me, but when I came
to, or came to my senses, my car was shockingly upright. To my
left was the street and beyond it the park. Directly to my right,
peering in through a shattered window, was one of those backyard walls that lined even the interior streets of the development.
It was the wall that had kept me from flipping fully over, that
wonderful wall. In front of me was the curving road that led to
the development's exit. Behind me was the dark blue car, a stolid
sedan, its face now accordioned into the selfsame wall.

Something was stinging my eye and when I wiped at it my
hand came away slick and red. Something was ringing in my ear
and I couldn't hear anything else but the ringing. Something was
pinching my shoulder and I realized the whole left side of the car
had been caved in. Even as I wondered how my luck could be so

rotten as to get into an accident while trying to get away from a pack of murderers, I noticed a movement behind me.

My neck screamed in pain as I twisted around and saw a man climb out of the blue car. And reach beneath his loose print shirt. And there was no good intention in his eyes. And like a dolt, I figured out only then that it wasn't an accident.

The man might have been saying something, too, it seemed like he was, but I couldn't hear a thing except for the damn ringing.

I pressed the gas to get out of there. Nothing happened, I had stalled. Crap.

I grappled for the keys, found them, tried to turn the ignition. No turn, locked tight. Crap, crap.

In the rearview mirror the man was closer, a gun now magically in his hand. Crap, crap, crap.

I slammed the gear into park, tried the ignition again. Locked still, still, wait, no. I pressed the brake and the key spun and I felt the sweet vibration of the engine turning over.

I eyed the development's exit, pulled the gearshift down, jammed the gas as hard as I could, and felt my head jerk forward as the car jumped. Backward. A thump and then a smash. The wheels spun uselessly as the car ground further into the car behind me.

I pressed the brakes, put the gear in drive, shot forward. I could feel a scraping from the rear of the car even as I shuddered down the street toward the exit. I expected something to come at me from the side and slam me into another wall. I expected something to rip through my rear windshield. I expected the worst, as if that hadn't already happened. I tried to check the side-view mirror, but it was gone.

In the rearview mirror I could see something ugly and shapeless smashed up against the smashed-up car. Before I could make any sense of the shape, I hit Flamingo Road.

I barely slowed to make the turn. There was no traffic light, just six lanes directly perpendicular to me, with enough cars whizzing by that there was no way I was hopping across three lanes to take a left. I spun my wheel to the right and somehow the traffic parted for a moment, as if I were the Moses of Flamingo Road, and I slipped right into its stream. The first light I hit was green and when I passed that intersection I let out a breath I had been holding since the collision.

I didn't drive evasively. I stayed in my lane, let faster cars pass, kept my eye out for anything chasing me, stopped at the lights when I had to, kept driving, driving. That was my getaway strategy. To just keep driving, until I could figure out what to do when I stopped driving. I certainly wasn't going to stop right there on Flamingo and check out the car; the thing still ran, that was enough, though the going was neither smooth nor speedy. As the ringing in my ears weakened, I could hear the rackety noise of my car bouncing off the walls that bounded the street, the whistles and scrapes, the strange bellyaching roars. People stared at me as if I were atop a parade float as they passed me on the left. I wiped more blood off my face, tried to look like it was an everyday thing for me to drive such a wreck.

A cop approached from the other direction and I maneuvered so that I was hidden from his view by a white van to my left. I didn't want to have to explain what happened to the car, to Augie, why I left the scene of an accident, who I was or why the hell I was in Vegas. At one point a guy pulled up beside me in a battered Dodge, his windows covered with plastic and the paint mismatched on his doors. He stared over at me. I gave him a thumbs-up, like we were just two guys with bad wheels in the middle of a recession. He smiled back, showing off a bright gap-toothed grin.

When Flamingo Road finally reached the highway, I slid into the left lane and, at the light, took the entrance and headed east. It was a snap decision, I didn't think it out. I saw the sign for 215 and I chose east because east was where my home was and, like a base runner rounding third as the throw came in from the outfield, home was where I wanted to go. How to get there was the problem.

At highway speed the car shook like a milkshake mixer. I realized I was heading to the airport, and for a moment I felt the calm respite of actually having a plan. Return the car—ignoring the startled stare of the check-in guy when I left the battered Impala in the rental-car line—take the shuttle, check in at a kiosk, find an airport bar, and down a row of something, anything, mixed with vodka while waiting for my plane. It was a plan, sure, sit at the bar like a sitting duck, waiting for a bull-headed man in a loose print shirt to knock-knock on my skull.

A few miles down the highway I saw the signs for the airport exit and I passed them by.

I kept driving, and thinking what to do, what to do, letting my panic get the best of me for a longer time than I'd like to admit. For a few moments I considered skipping airports entirely and driving all the way home. I was more than tempted; it seemed both a lame-brained and romantic notion. Road trip, baby. Twenty-five hundred miles, nothing to it, really. And then I came to my senses. The car would never make it in the shape it was in. And how sweet a target would I be in a wrecked car they could so easily identify?

As I drove through a long stretch of desert I thought maybe I should just ditch the car completely and make my way on foot, hitching rides, keeping completely off the grid. No calls, no credit cards. It would take me a week or so to get home, more maybe, but I'd be completely lost, unreachable by everyone. Including my family. But what if the guy on the phone went after them, how then could I help? And wouldn't I be flinching at every car that passed, expecting the worst?

My mind was reeling as I headed down toward some sort of bridge. I desperately needed a place to sort it all out. And then I realized with a start that this thing I was crossing was not just any bridge but the goddamn Hoover Dam. On my left was The

Narrows of Lake Mead, with the art deco intake towers rising out of the water like some evil design by Dr. No. On my right was the huge cement arch.

And in my car, as traffic slowly moved across the narrow rim, I could feel the great dam heave and roll beneath me from the unimaginable pressure of all that water. And I sympathized with the concrete beast. How long had it been holding back the river? As long, it seemed, as I'd been running, not just this one day from Augie's killers, but for years, for decades, running from my past. Wasn't the dam tired? Wasn't it ready just to give it up and let the whole Colorado wash through it?

And where was it coming from, all that water, where was the root of that pressure? The Grand Canyon, of course, which was pretty much right on the way. And I knew then, immediately, that's where I was headed, too. I was in a hole, the deepest of my life. I needed a place to disappear and figure things out. Where the hell else would I go?

6. The Big Ditch

I NEVER MADE IT.

It was dark already when I hit Route 40 at Kingman, and the car's temperature had spiked precipitously. The Impala and I both needed to cool down. So, instead of the awesome spectacle of the Grand Canyon, I settled for a Motel 6, which, when I came to think on it, considering my situation, was a place far more apt.

I parked what was left of the car in the lot behind the wide, low motel so that it was hidden from the main street. I sat there for a long moment with the engine running and then pulled back, shining my brights on the asphalt. A small puddle of something viscous and dark. My rental car wasn't going very much farther. I pulled forward again, killed the motor, dragged my briefcase into the motel office, and paid cash for the room. When the clerk asked for identification, I showed him my Nevada license. I didn't make chitchat with the guy, but when his back was turned to get my key, I snatched a copy of the bus schedule that was in the rack along with pamphlets for the rest of Kingman's wonderful attractions.

There is little more impersonal in this world than a motel room off the interstate. There is no past, no future, and the present is skeevy enough that you don't want to look too closely at the bedsheets. My life writ small, with dusty curtains and a sign over the toilet, SANITIZED FOR YOUR PROTECTION.

Once in the room, I showered off the last few hours. In the fluorescent bathroom lights I looked green and ill and beyond hideous, but the bleeding wound was above my hairline, which was good. With the cut covered, I could fake normalcy; I had been doing that anyway for the last twenty-five years.

Wrapped now in a towel, I started pacing the room, rubbing my sore neck and trying to come to grips with what just had happened to my life. All the deepest fears that I had been carrying for a quarter of a century had suddenly blossomed true; the past was hunting me, I was on the run, and there was no safe refuge. If I didn't play it smart, the rest of my life would be an endless stream of foul motel rooms just like this, one after the other. The cheap TVs with remotes that didn't work, the scent of ammonia and urine, the stained sheets, the stridor of illicit sex banging through the thin walls. I felt bone tired, I felt deep terror, and yet also, quite strangely, I felt the lift of happiness.

Think of the militiaman in his bomb cellar, praying for the apocalypse because he knows how pathetic all his feverish preparations would be if the apocalypse never came. When you prepare for the worst, the worst that can happen is nothing. All my paranoia over the years, all my obsessive planning, turned out to be exactly necessary. Augie and Ben hadn't taken the same precautions; they had assumed they were safe. Augie was now dead and Ben was in the deep latrine. But I had options. It was if my life had been given a government-approved jolt of meaning.

But there was something else, too, giving me a lift. It was the way I had handled myself through the afternoon's violence. I hadn't been able to pull off the gunfight thing—I'm not a torpedo after all—but I had leaped Augie's back wall pretty damn nimbly. And after the bastard had rammed me into the wall by the park, I had taken care of him all right. Did I intend to put the car in reverse to squash the bastard bloody? I wasn't sure, it surprised the hell out of me, but reverse it was, even if it was my subconscious pulling the gear. And I certainly didn't brake after the first thump. The last time I had faced such danger, twenty-five years ago, I had fallen into a pathetic jag of wails and tears, but this time I had risen to the challenge. Over the years I had purposely constricted my life, doing everything I could not to be noticed, not to be too successful, not to achieve all of which I was capable. But suddenly I had an inkling that maybe I was capable enough. Which was good, because I sure as hell would need to be.

It was time to take the next necessary steps. I had turned the cell phone off right after I had called Ben. It was a phone I had bought in an office-supply store with the minutes purchased in bulk. Now I turned it on and booked a Northwest flight from Las Vegas to LA for J.J. Moretti, and paid for it with a credit card in that name, the same card I had used to book my flight to Vegas. Then I lifted the toilet tank and dropped the phone inside to kill it dead. The credit card, I cut into fourths. The card was paid out of a bank account I had maintained with a post office drop box in North Dakota. They could keep what was left in the account. I took my Nevada driver's license and cut it up as well. In the bathroom, with the fan going, I crumbled up some paper and put it in the sink with the cut-up cards on top, set the whole thing on fire, and watched the last of J.J. Moretti melt and turn black.

Frenchy was dead.

I looked at the bus schedule, found something leaving for Phoenix dead early in the morning. I checked the address of the bus station and got a break: it was just down the road, so I wouldn't need a cab. Everything was setting up nicely. A bus to Phoenix, a plane to Chicago, another plane ride, purchased separately and leaving the next morning, to Philadelphia. With the five-hour drive south from Philly, I could be home by early afternoon the day after next.

I knew my precautions hadn't been perfect, there were a thousand details that could have gone wrong, but if the bastards had been waiting for me at Augie's that meant the secret life I had created for myself must have held through Augie's torture.

If they were as sharp as I feared, they would glom onto the truth soon enough, but by then, if everything went as planned, I'd be gone again.

I set my alarm to give me plenty of time and then lay down in the bed and closed my eyes. Tomorrow was a big day, tomorrow everything had to go just right. I needed to be rested, I needed to sleep, I needed to prepare.

Tomorrow I would need to start deconstructing my life.

II. MY THREE SUBURBS

"I only just realized it, J.J., but you are the most boring suburban asshole in the world."

—Augie Iannucci

7. East of Eden

I F YOU WANT TO BLAME IT ON ANYBODY, THE MESS I FOUND myself in, you might as well blame it on my father; I always did.

My father left when I was nine. To say he fled would be more honest, but who the hell wants honesty when dealing with family? Certainly not my mother. First my father was on a brief business trip. Then the brief trip turned to a lengthy assignment in another town. Eventually his absence was barely noted as my mother and I ate dinner together in the large, empty dining room, with a pot of flowers placed directly between us so I wouldn't see all that she was drinking and she wouldn't see me gagging on her tuna casserole.

My father's leaving left a hole in my life, but it wasn't his actual presence that I missed. My father was one of those men whose power was expressed in his absences, an absence of care and concern, an absence of humor, an absence of a personality more dynamic than a cardboard box. My father's leaving would hardly have been noticed if it wasn't followed by concomitant losses, losses so dire that I spent the greatest portion of my life thereafter trying to make up for all that vanished when he vanished, too. Think of the kiwi bird haunted by a hawk floating free across the sky—that was me, haunted by what I once had been.

We lived in a big stone house in a leafy suburb on Philadelphia's Main Line. We had a pool within the gardens in the backyard, a purebred bichon frise named Rex on the leash, and a family membership at the Philadelphia Country Club. My father was a Willing. One of those Willings. It doesn't mean much in Omaha, admittedly, but being a Willing meant a great deal in the dining room of the Philadelphia Country Club. Old society ladies who had known my great-grandmother used to pat my head as they walked by our table; waiters brought me Cokes and addressed me as *Master Willing, sir*; mothers pushed their young girls my way. *Say hello to Jonathon, sweetie, don't be shy.* I wore a blazer and tan pants in the dining room and I ordered the filet from the adult menu, well done, with french fries, hold the spinach, please.

That was the before.

Much later, my mother told me the details of what happened to all that grandeur. The telling came when I was in college in Wisconsin and had flown down to Florida to watch her die. There was a period between the final operation and her death when she was filled with an unnatural energy, like a sun becoming a supernova before collapsing into a black hole. In those few days she told me more about my history than she had in the entire twenty years that had come before. By then the cancer from her lungs had wrapped like a cobra around her heart and bowels, but her disposition was surprisingly cheerful because she had lost so much weight her figure approximated that of the slim beautiful secretary who had unexpectedly won my father's heart. Her dreams had been simple before she met my father, typical of the South Philly girl she had been: a modest house in the neighborhood, summers down the shore, maintaining her size four. But when she married a Willing her life exceeded her dreams, and therein lay the seed of my downfall.

Her troubles with my father, my mother told me from her hospital bed, began shortly after I was born. The delivery had been difficult and my mother hadn't healed well, making conjugal relations unpleasant. And the medications and alcohol she consumed for the pain made it difficult for the weight to come off. And so, as was inevitable, my father found himself a whore. (This is vintage my mother. Notice how the root cause of the problem is her weight, notice how her weight is out of her control, notice how the other actor in the drama is a low-down slut. If you asked my mother about the origins of the American debacle in Vietnam it would all begin with a few extra pounds she gained in 1964 and a Ho.) My father's affair lasted for years; in fact it was less an affair than a secret life. The other woman had a child with my father, she set up house, he played the doting husband with her Tuesdays and Thursdays and every other weekend.

When my mother belatedly caught wind of what was happening, through an offhand remark slipped into the meaningless babble of club conversation as neatly as a knife in the ribs, she had a choice. She could choose to ignore my father's secret and keep our lives intact, along with my stature as a Willing at the club, or she could put her well-heeled foot down and imperil it all. And my mother reacted exactly as one would expect of someone who hadn't ever angled for all she was risking: blindly, foolishly, with no regard for my present or future prospects. A midafternoon visit to the offices of my grandfather, who then stood at the pinnacle of all the far-flung Willing enterprises, started the process of ending my father's secret life. A short time later, after weeks of haggling and anguish, the lawyers paid off the mistress. And my father, after a thorough upbraiding by my grandfather, returned full time to our happy home in the leafy suburb.

I was in the third grade when all this occurred. Generally ignored by my ever-present but often inebriated mother and my absent father, I was used to spending my days at the posh private school where they stashed me, or eating dinner at my schoolmates' houses or at the club, living a life of delicious freedom. But suddenly my now-dour father was home every night, as I was expected to be, and every evening the three of us ate dinner together, chewing our food silently in the dining room, staring at the walls so as to avoid staring at each other. And then one night my father went on his brief business trip.

It wasn't too much later that the lawyers came for us.

My mother's lawyer was supposed to be pretty good, but the lawyers at the Willing family firm were better, and by the time it was over, whatever my mother ended up with was not enough to maintain the lifestyle to which we had become accustomed. Still, she kept us in the house as long as she could. She cried, she yelled into the phone, she fired the servants and cooked economical dinners with execrable results. Things changed, of course. We were no longer included in the family membership at the club. Or invited to my grandparents' house for Sunday supper. And I wouldn't be back at my posh private school for the fourth grade. And my schoolmates suddenly stopped calling. And the lawn went unmowed and algae turned the pool green. But my mother and I shared the strange delusion that as long as we had the house and the dog everything would remain as it was.

Until all we had was the dog.

It was late in the summer, just before the start of the school year, when we moved into our new neighborhood. I was no longer a Willing, my mother had made me take up her maiden name, Moretti, for our new life. She wanted a clean break, her old name, and, yes, a new neighborhood, on the other side of the city as well as the tracks. She said she didn't want to bump into anyone from our other life in the supermarket, and if that was her goal, then Pitchford was the exact right place.

I remember driving onto Henrietta Road for the first time, the moving truck behind us and Rex on my lap. A gang of kids stared sullenly as they shifted their hockey nets to let us pass. A mangy collie barked at Rex. The split-level houses placed cheek to jowl all along the street were shockingly small, the postage-stamp lawns were unkempt, outdated cars were parked at the curb. When my mother pointed out the tiny house that she was renting for us, I burst into tears. I was ten years old and I already knew the best part of my life had passed.

When the moving men left, my mother searched among the boxes for one in particular. She fell to her knees as she opened it, pulling out a bottle and a cut-crystal glass. While still on the floor, she poured herself a stiff drink.

"Go outside, dear," she said, the liquor sloshing in her glass as she motioned me to the door, "and maybe you'll find yourself a little friend to keep you busy while I unpack."

***

See me there, sitting on the front steps with my dog, a lost boy surveying his new world. This was not the shallow yet idyllic suburbs of the American imagination, executive manses one next to the other with tennis courts and pools, or country estates linked by the train line into the city. That was the land I had emigrated from, the land I loved, a rich and fertile land that still seizes my imagination. Pitchford was a different type of suburb entirely, close and tired and overgrown already even though not more than two decades old, the demon spawn of Levittown, but without the charm. Some of the lawns had chain-link fences, some of the cars on the curb were rusted hulks. Garages were turned into makeshift bedrooms to house outsized families, driveways were littered with rusting toys.

Split-level hell.

I tried not to draw any attention to myself as I sat on the steps of my new house and watched the spectacle of the hockey game. I imagined I was invisible, but even so I felt like a mackerel at a tuna convention. I was wearing tan pants, a white button-down shirt, and a tie—my mom had dressed me for moving day—while everyone else was wearing jeans or shorts and a T-shirt. My hair was floppy and stylishly long, while everyone else had buzz cuts. And my dog was small and white and fluffy. I tried coming up with names that might impress if someone asked me what kind of dog it was. He was a Prussian Warrior, he was a purebred Chinese Throat Slasher, he was anything instead of the prissy-sounding bichon frise.

The kids playing in the street were all ages, some in my grade, most older than I was. There were even some black kids. Whoa. They were a scruffy crew, and loud, knocking each other with violent thumps into the parked cars on either side of their makeshift rink. This was just after two Stanley Cups for the Broad Street Bullies had turned even the most tenderhearted Philly kid into a hockey hooligan. One boy, after a particularly vicious check, spit out a tooth, smiled a gap-toothed smile, and then decked the checker with a right to the jaw. And nobody seemed to notice. The game just kept going. Until the next car came through and the nets were glumly moved.

I was watching the game, while trying very hard not to look like I was watching the game, when a slap shot wide of the goal sent the red plastic puck skittering along the street until it died right in front of me.

"Little help?" someone shouted.

I was invisible, there was no way anyone could have been talking to me, so I just sat there while the players all stared. Finally, one of the black kids, big and pudgy, made his way toward me, his stick dragging like a caveman's cudgel on the street behind him. He stopped at the puck and looked up at me.

"That a dog or a r-rat?" he said in a soft voice that sort of slurred through the consonants. "Looks like a r-rat."

"It's a dog," I said. "He's a Portuguese Water Shark."

The boy looked up at me and blinked. "Does it swim?"

"Like Mark Spitz. And its teeth are sharp as a piranha's." Just then I pinched Rex's hind and he snapped at me and growled. The boy took a slow step back.

"You m-moving into the Bernstein house?" he said.

"What's the Bernstein house?"

"You're sitting in front of it."

"We're only staying here until my father comes back and we get our new house."

"Where'd he go?"

"China."

"Why are you dressed for ch-church on a Wednesday?"

"We just came from a funeral."

"Who died?"

"My grandpop."

"That's what they do, all right. You want to play? We need a goalie."

"So you can shoot pucks at my face?"

He looked at me and smiled, like he had caught some glimmer of something he might like. "You can wear a p-paper bag over your head for a mask if you want."

"Does it stop it from hurting?"

"Not really, but that way you don't bleed all over your sh-shirt."

"I'll pass."

"Okay. But whatever you do, don't stay too long in the Bernstein house."

"Why not?"

"B-bad luck," said the kid as he started away, the puck now being slapped back and forth by his stick. "Just ask the Bernsteins."

See me there, walking my dog along the pitted pavements of my new street. Rex pranced like a prince as I slumped along behind him in my tie and loafers. In this strange new place, women sat on the front stoops of their houses in flowered shifts, smoking and frowning at Rex as he sniffed their lawns. Babies in blow-up pools laughed at me. Dogs tied to stakes hammered into the ground gnashed their teeth. Rex barely gave them notice as he continued on his regal way, back arched and tail high, sniffing here, sniffing there. Finally, Rex circled a specific spot of earth, nose pressed into the grass. He was on the front lawn of a dark split-level catercorner to our new place, the dark house's wide picture window curtained tight, the paint peeling off its siding, its garage bricked up. A hulking motorcycle was parked in the driveway.

Just as Rex started his squat, a kid zipped up to us on a skateboard before kicking to a stop. "I wouldn't if I were you, bub," he said.

"You wouldn't what?" I said.

"Let your little chipmunk do whatever he is about to do, at least not on that lawn."

"Why not?"

"That's the Grubbins lawn."

"So?"

"Trust me, bub," said the kid.

He was slight, thin, sharp-faced, with the front of his buzz cut standing straight up, and he spoke from the corner of his mouth as if one side of his face didn't want the other side to know what he was saying. With his manner and his sharp voice, he sounded like one of the kids in the Bowery Boys black-and-whites that played Saturday mornings on UHF. Still, there was something about his manner that made me indeed want to trust him. Rex was just easing into his squat when I pulled him away. And just that moment I heard a shout directed my way from the hockey game.

"What the hell you think you're doing?"

A blond kid, a year or so older and twice my size, charged toward me with a hockey stick in his hands. He wore jeans and a Harley-Davidson T-shirt, his head was shaved close as a convict's. He threw down his stick as if dropping his gloves on the rink. The sound of the stick slapping onto the asphalt resounded like a shot and the hockey game halted immediately, as all the other players turned to stare at me. A skinny kid with round glasses and a runny nose came up behind the big kid like a pilot fish following a shark.

"I'm not doing anything," I said.

"But your little piece of dog was," said the big kid.

"He was just walking."

"I saw him," said the pilot fish. This kid's eyes were beady and small behind his glasses and his two front teeth were twisted like twin doors opening. "He was about to go right there on your lawn, Tony. Right there on your lawn."

"Butt out, Richie," said the kid on the skateboard.

"I saw it."

"It's just a dog," I said.

"Just a dog." Tony turned to the kid on the skateboard. "Are you with this fool?"

"No way, Tony. I don't even know the kid. He just moved into the Bernstein house."

"The Bernstein house?" said Tony Grubbins. "Good luck living in that hole. It didn't do them Bernsteins no good, that's for sure. What is that you got there on the leash, one of those Mex Chihuahua things?"

"It's a bichon frise," I said, too flustered to come up with anything but the truth, and immediately regretting my mistake.

"Ooh la la, a little French dog."

"I thought only girls in pigtails had little French dogs," said Richie with the glasses.

"He's not French."

Tony peered down at Rex, Rex yipped back.

"He looks French. And he sounds French."

"You're right, Tony," said Richie, laughing like a good little suck-up. "He does."

"And you don't sound like you come from here neither," said Tony. "You talk like you got a screw in your jaw. Where you from?"

"Gladwyne."

"Where's that, France?"

"America."

43

"I bet he's a Frenchy, just like his dog," said Richie.

"This is my lawn," said Tony. "My brother makes me cut it and take care of it and pick the crap off it. I hate picking crap off the lawn. It makes me want to throw up. So if I see either one of you Frenchies on my lawn again, I'm going to kick both your asses back to Paris."

Richie snickered.

"I'm not French."

"Like I care where you're from," said Tony.

I could feel myself being stared at by the whole street, the hockey players, the ladies in their shifts, the kid on the skateboard, a host of dogs, mine included. Under such scrutiny I thought of holding my ground, making my mark in this new neighborhood. But I didn't want to make my mark in this new neighborhood, I just wanted to leave it, in one piece and for good. And I had never been in a fight before. And while I might have been able to take the pilot fish, this Tony Grubbins looked like he was already shaving. So, like the Frenchy I was accused of being, I retreated, with some dignity and much haste, pulling the yapping Rex across the street to the Bernstein house amid laughter and catcalls from the hockey players.

See me there, sitting again on our stoop. I hadn't run inside, I wouldn't give that bully boy the satisfaction. Instead I sat on the steps and peered out through watery eyes at my new neighborhood. It had to be an aberration, this brutal dislocation that had happened to me. My dad would come back, my grandfather would rescue me. I belonged in the leafy suburb on the other side of the city. I was the kid at the country-club pool, the kid in the blazer ordering filet mignon. I wasn't a Moretti, I was a Willing, dammit, I was made for better things. It is funny how certain we are of our places in the world when we are all of ten. Only later does it become an utter mystery. But at that moment there was no mystery. I didn't belong here, in this house, on this street, in a place like Pitchford.

But I was wrong, I did belong in Pitchford; it was my country-club past that was the mirage. When I look back at the teary-eyed boy on the steps with his yabbering dog, the whole of the boy's life to come will be determined by what he sees just then through the tears. That hockey game would soon become his hockey game, or his football game, or his stickball game, depending on the season. The morose stutterer who had come over to retrieve the puck and the boy on the skateboard would turn out to be his two great friends Ben and Augie. Tony Grubbins, as big as a barn, would end up chasing him not just on that street but as a specter through the decades.

And that house, the Grubbins house, with the peeling paint and motorcycle in front, with the sense of something foreboding behind its bricked-up garage and curtained windows, that house would be the furnace in which his life after Pitchford was forged.

I didn't know any of this then; all I knew was that something terrible had happened to me, and nothing in my life anymore was certain, except for one thing and one thing only: my dog Rex was going to turn that lawn into a toilet.

8. Philly International

PHILADELPHIA INTERNATIONAL AIRPORT ALWAYS GAVE ME the willies. Being a mere twenty miles from my boyhood home of Pitchford left me feeling exposed, as if at any moment Tony Grubbins would emerge from the crowd and start chasing Frenchy down airport corridors. When do shallow adolescent terrors disappear? I was hoping at least by death; I had no desire to carry the hump of my Tony Grubbins fear through all of eternity.

But just then, two days after I found Augie's bloated corpse, as I passed through the morning airport crowd with an outfit I had picked up in Chicago—a loose T-shirt, a pair of baggy jeans, a white baseball hat with its flat brim low over my eyes, the exact opposite of anything I normally would wear—I had fears more real to contend with than the ghost of a tormentor past. I could pretend it was over, that having missed their shot at me in Vegas they would just shrug their shoulders and let me be, but I could also have faith in the goodness of my fellow man or my wife's fidelity, and where the hell would that get me?

I kept my head down as I strode through the terminal. I had flown in as Jon Willing—I had reverted to using my real name after leaving Pitchford—and the last thing I could afford just then was an old high-school classmate calling out for J.J. Moretti, you old son of a gun, you haven't changed a bit. In a gift shop I bought

46

myself a souvenir of my journey, a pin-striped Philadelphia Phillies license plate, before heading with a show of hurry down the exit corridor, a man in a ridiculous white baseball cap with a crucial appointment to keep.

No one stopped me, no former Pitchford acquaintance called out my old name. As I kept walking, I glanced quickly behind me. Except for a pregnant woman, no one was following. Unless she had an Uzi beneath the fake pillow on her belly, it was looking pretty clean.

I bypassed baggage claim and headed right for the garage, taking the elevator up to level four, and kept walking until I reached my car, a sweet little BMW sedan. The 3 Series I'm talking, nothing too big or too luxurious, nothing to call too much attention to itself, but still a step above the expected. That was how I rolled now, that described perfectly my car, my house, my life, at least what was left of it. I pressed the fob, opened the trunk, threw in my briefcase. From the little tool kit by the spare tire, I took out four adhesive magnets I had put there just for this eventuality, along with a screwdriver.

I headed back toward the concourse as if I had forgotten something, but instead slipped into a line of parked cars. I kept moving until I saw what I needed, a huge black SUV parked with its back to a wall. Not as private a spot as I would have hoped, but private enough. After a furtive scan to make sure no one was near, I scooted to the rear bumper, knelt down, stuck my screwdriver into the first of the screws holding on the license plate.

By now they would have found the car behind the motel in Kingman. I imagined them surrounding it with their print shirts and bullheads, kicking the tires and leaning over the rear fender to examine the blood of their fellow thug, whom I had crushed into pulp. They weren't the mangy meth-crazed cycle gang I had been expecting all these years, tattooed and instantly recognizable, without the resources to track the Byzantine trail in which I had directed my life. Instead they were apparently real-deal torpedoes from the Las Vegas chapter of the goddamn mob, with its tentacles reaching all across the country and deep into the nation's databases. Imagining them kicking at the tires of my rented wreck made me realize how threadbare had been my precautions.

I thought I was being slick flying to Vegas out of Philadelphia instead of the airport closest to my home, and I thought I had covered my tracks out of Phoenix, but I should never have flown as J.J. Moretti out of the city where I left my damn car.

I edged my BMW now to the long row of payment booths at the exit of the airport's parking garages. Affixed to the rear plate was a valid PA license. Because cars in Pennsylvania have only rear plates, my front plate was covered with an abject show of devotion for the Phillies. I didn't look around for someone looking for me as I stopped to make my payment, I simply smiled at the lady in the booth as I took my receipt and waited for the bar to rise. When it did, I pulled slowly into the lanes of traffic. I kept my moderate pace even as I fully expected a couple tons of metal to come hurtling at me like a cannonball.

But nothing shot out in front of me. Nothing came careening from behind.

I followed the signs to I-95 North, skirted Center City Philadelphia, and headed toward New York, checking the rearview all the while. I didn't see anything suspicious behind me, but that didn't mean there wasn't anything suspicious behind me. Cruising in the left lane, I veered suddenly hard right, slipping onto a North Philadelphia exit ramp just in front of a storming truck, spun left at the light at the bottom, and wended my way through a warren of tight city streets.

Nothing following.

I turned into an alleyway between two rows of row houses and parked beside a beat old pickup. I waited for someone to pass. Nobody did. I got out of the car and pulled the two magnetized license plates off, revealing my two Virginia plates. I put the covering plates into the briefcase and drove a few miles south, through the hard urban landscape, still watching behind me.

Nothing following, nothing suspicious.

Maybe I had given the bullheaded bastards too much credit. Maybe they had given up after all. For a moment I let a shard of hope slip into my emotions and fill them with lift, as if the shard were a hypodermic loaded with hop. But then I gained control of myself and spit it out. The hell with hope—it wasn't going to do a damn thing for me except get me killed. If I knew anything in this world, I knew this: those bastards weren't done with me yet.

I sometimes played golf with this guy named Joel. He had a nice swing, a pretty blonde wife, he wore a red plaid vest when he mixed drinks at his annual Christmas party, and he had the best damn lawn in the neighborhood. He lavished his lawn with fertilizer, spoiled it with water. Every Saturday he rode his mower across his yard like a frontier cowboy riding the prairie, and he edged with the clean savagery of a surgeon. What I mean is that if his name wasn't Joel Steinberg, you wouldn't ever have known he was Jewish. But after 9/11, when everyone in the neighborhood was going on about how shocking it was that we had been attacked and how everything had changed, Joel simply shook his head.

"What's changed, really?" he said, a glass of chardonnay in his hand. "They've always been after me."

And I now understood how he felt, because no matter how safe had seemed my life in recent years, what had happened to Augie wasn't a total shock. I had always known they were after me, and though it looked like I had slipped out of Vegas with my skin intact, I knew they still were. But I hadn't sat idly by all these years, I had gouged a route to safety out of the hardscrabble facts of my circumstance. And now all I had to do was follow the simple steps I had laid out for myself.

First I had to make it out of Philly. Then I had to die.

After one last look behind, I punched the buttons on the car's GPS.

WHERE TO?

MY LOCATIONS.

GO HOME.

Which for me meant the place that put the *über* in *suburbia*, and where I had spent the last fifteen years of my life: the Grande Estates at Patriots Landing.

9. Anyone Home?

━━━━━━━━━━━━━※━━━━━━━━━━━━━

THERE IS AN INFINITE VARIETY OF AMERICAN LIVES FOR US to inhabit, from urban living to off the grid, from bohemian rhapsody to rush-hour grind. Usually we don't end up choosing, we just stumble into something and let sweet inertia sweep us along. One of our greatest freedoms is the freedom to simply fall into a life.

But I was never free enough to let utter randomness select the details of my existence. While it might not have been necessary for me to live underground, moving from safe house to safe house like a Weatherman on the run, the great choice I made as a youth determined to a great extent the life I was forced to live. I couldn't place myself at the forefront of public events, I couldn't allow myself to slip into a life of accidental celebrity or make a name for myself in business or the arts. I needed a certain anonymity, not the celebrated anonymity of the Unabomber in his shack, but the anonymity of the man so often seen as to disappear into his landscape.

What I was searching for was a place where with one glance anyone could know all they cared to know about me. A place where I would be judged not by the content of my character— what kind of crackpot would ever want that anyway?—but by the contents of my garage. Where I could strike up a friendship and talk for hours on end, for years even, without ever getting deeper than the secrets of lawn care or the quality of a certain micro-brewed beer. Where I could be defined solely by impersonal yet definitive numbers, my zip code (23185), my handicap (14.6), the series of my BMW (the 3, yes, or did I mention that already?), the Btu's put out by my backyard grill (fifty-five grand, baby, and not a unit less).

What I was looking for was the Grande Estates at Patriots Landing, set nobly on the banks of the James River in Williamsburg, Virginia. Seven different models selling from the mid-threes, financing available.

I remember sitting with my new wife, Caitlin, in the model home slash sales office, built just within the development's imposing entranceway, with its bold brick wall, its twin white lions, the name spelled out in bright golden letters. We were going over the designs of the models, trying to imagine our future from floor plans and idealized drawings. Caitlin was seeking a house in which to raise a family, to celebrate holidays and joyous events. I was looking for genteel anonymity. As we pored over the choices—that gable, that vaulted ceiling, cherry or oak cabinets—we were both finding exactly what we wanted. Caitlin was pregnant at the time with Shelby, and I had just nabbed a promising sales job in Richmond; this seemed like the time to take a leap and buy a home. We could have lived right outside Richmond for less, and my commute would have been shorter, but a home in Williamsburg seemed like a better investment and I assured Caitlin that we could swing it, even if our income didn't yet match the suggested guidelines. Funny how we were always able to afford more than our salaries seemed to warrant. Thrift, I told her, and canny investing.

Caitlin thought the modest Carter Braxton model looked nice, with its three bedrooms and butcher-block countertops, coming in at a cozy 1,700 square feet. Or maybe even the George Wyeth model, a similar size but with a jazzed-up front entrance. The salesman was trying to talk us up to something a little more ambitious, four bedrooms and 2,200 square feet, like the Patrick Henry, with its lovely brick front, or the Peyton Randolph, with its stone entranceway.

"What is this one?" I said to the salesman as I stopped paging through the model booklet and pointed a finger at a wide house with a spire rising from the roof and a porch that wrapped across the whole of the front like a bright ribbon.

"That might be a bit overwhelming for your situation," said the man, smiling kindly, like an indulgent uncle, even as he brought me back to the page he had selected for us. "The Patrick Henry is quite a popular model, and it fits perfectly within the price range you said you were looking at."

"I like the brick on the Patrick Henry," said Caitlin. "Is it real?"

"No," said the salesman, "but you can hardly tell."

"Let's get back to this one," I said, flipping to the page I had been on before.

"That," said the salesman, "is the George Washington."

"It has a ring to it, doesn't it?"

"It is not quite our most regal model—that would be the Thomas Jefferson—but the George Washington is still quite sturdy and handsome. Five bedrooms, a great room off the kitchen in addition to a formal parlor and a cherry-paneled home office, forty-five hundred square feet of gracious living, with a front porch modeled on the rear portico at Mount Vernon." The salesman sighed the sigh of the disappointed dreamer. "It is grand in every way, including, sadly, the price. Now, the Patrick Henry has quite a few nice options, such as granite countertops for the kitchen or even a cupola for the breakfast nook."

"Ooh, a cupola," said Caitlin.

"I could put you on a nice lot on a beautiful and secluded cul-de-sac not far from the entrance." The salesman pointed at a tiny trapezoid on a map of the development. "Chandler Court, right here."

53

"I think we would prefer to be closer to the river," I said.

"Those lots are reserved for our more expensive models," said the salesman.

"Nearer the entrance would be more convenient," said Caitlin. "And maybe we should stay within our price range."

"Very sensible," said the salesman, "so let's talk again about the Patrick Henry. You have your choice of color on the vinyl siding, but I would suggest the off-white, quite classic, and goes beautifully with the faux brick."

Now, at the end of the long journey from Vegas, as I turned into Patriots Landing and drove past the twin white lions, the fearful clench of my stomach finally eased. I glanced at the rear-view mirror and let out a breath of relief at what I didn't see as I passed the very model house where my wife and I had made our choice. The roads were lined with examples of all the houses we considered that day, each looking neatly squared away on its suitably sized lot, the Carter Braxtons, the George Wyeths, even the insipid Patrick Henrys with their fake-brick fronts.

There is a certain unreality to a place like Patriots Landing. It is at the same time both a living neighborhood and the idea of a neighborhood. Driving through the development, fresh from the travails of Vegas, I could see both aspects at once. Kids playing on small front yards, kids biking on the wide streets, men and women gardening and mowing and coming back from running errands, all the indicia of a normal drowsy Saturday in the real world. Yet the trees were all the same size, and the lawns were maintained according to neighborhood code, and everything in sight had a naturalistic artificiality, as if built by a film crew to evoke a nostalgia for something that had never before existed. The whole thing was a conspiracy between developer and home-owner to pretend to create something real, even though the only thing being created was a real piece of artifice. And it was exactly that quality that drew me to Patriots Landing in the first place. Where better to hide in plain sight than within a shared delusion?

Yet as I drove through my lovely neighborhood, I now felt the exact pang of nostalgia the development's designers intended. The entire scene was so lovely and rich with meaning that it thickened my throat. Every fertilized stretch of lawn, every strip of vinyl siding, I was seeing it all with new eyes, the eyes of the exile. For my hours at Patriots Landing were now numbered. This place had been my life, my refuge and my sweet revenge, but whatever it had been, it could be no longer. Augie's murder had seen to that.

Hard by the river, a stone's throw from the development's harbor and in sight of the imposing golf clubhouse, I pulled into a circular driveway before a well-maintained George Washington. My George Washington. The wide lawn was mowed, the wooden pillars holding up the porch roof were freshly painted, all was as neat and well-ordered as the feathers on a duck serenely floating on the wide James River as, beneath the surface, webbed feet pedaled hysterically against the inexorable current. I hopped out of the Beemer, grabbed my briefcase from the trunk, jogged up the steps, and patted one of the wide pillars, so warm and solid, on my way to the red front door.

"I'm home," I called out once inside the center hallway, with its huge mirror and wonderfully pretentious French furnishings.

Silence echoed.

Suddenly the assurance from all my precautions flitted away like a charm of flighty finches. I had visions of my family tied and gagged by a bunch of bruisers. I dropped my briefcase and ran to the soaring stairwell.

"Anyone?" I yelled up, my voice echoing off the marble floor and domed ceiling. "Someone?"

10. Shelby

===■===

"WHY ARE YOU SHOUTING?"

A voice, cold and sneering, like a hardened terrorist's. My daughter, Shelby, leaning on the door to the kitchen to my left, stared at me with her customary air of disdain. Short black hair, too much eyeliner, tight T-shirt, pierced nose, short shorts, cell phone in her hand. I was so relieved I almost ran right over and gave her a hug. But I restrained myself. Shelby didn't let me hug her anymore. I have to admit here that no matter how much those thugs in Vegas terrified me, in her way this small and pretty sixteen-year-old with her punk black hair and tragic eyeliner terrified me more.

"I was just wondering where everyone was," I said, trying to sound as if everything was normal.

"What are you wearing?"

I looked down and checked out my garb anew, the baggy jeans, the faded T-shirt, so unlike anything she had seen me in before. "You don't like it?"

"And what's with that hat?"

"I bought it at the airport for your brother."

"It's all white, Dad, like Eric would ever wear something that G. You look like a pathetic middle-aged wannabe."

"How sweet, Shelby, that's just what I was going for. Especially the *pathetic* part."

"You're the one who's dressed like a creep."

"Here, take it," I said as I took off the hat and tossed it at her. She avoided it as if it were Oddjob's bowler as it spun onto the kitchen floor. "Where's your mother?"

Looking down now, speaking as she texted, "At Eric's game."

"Who are you texting?"

"Mom's mighty pissed at you, you know."

"What's new?"

"You were supposed to be home yesterday morning."

"I got hung up."

"And your phone wasn't on."

"The battery went dead."

"And you didn't call."

"Yeah, well, stuff happens." I glanced around, tried to pick out if anything was out of place. "Was anyone asking for me?"

She looked up from her phone, tilted her head. "You mean, like, a friend?"

"I guess, yeah."

"Don't be ridiculous," she said. "You don't have any friends. But if you keep dressing like that, you can maybe find some in Jackson Ward."

"Cute."

This was normally Shelby's cue to spin and stalk away. She had been my sweet little girl, but something had come between us a few years ago. I liked to attribute it to the general moodiness of the American teen, but I worried it was something darker. No one can look through you like your teenage daughter and I feared that was what she had done, looked right through me and not liked what she had seen. And it felt exactly like that right now as she stared at me without stalking away, stared at her father as if she was staring at a goggle-eyed alien.

"How are things, Shelby?" I said, suddenly realizing this might be one of the last times I ever saw my daughter.

"They suck."

"I mean really."

"They really suck."

"Are you and Luke still—"

"We're not talking about Luke."

"I was just trying to—"

"What's going on with you, Dad? You're kind of freaking me out in those clothes and with your sudden concern for my emotional welfare."

"I love you."

"So? What's that got to do with anything? You're still acting like a weirdball."

"I had a tough weekend."

"What, the strippers in Las Vegas had a hard time unhooking their bras?"

"How did you know I was in Vegas?"

"Mom."

"It was business, not pleasure, not that I go to strip clubs for pleasure. I mean…I don't…"

"Whatever," she said. "The whole idea is gross. Middle-aged men with tongues hanging out for half-naked skanky teens."

"Half?"

She gave me one of those disgusted eye squints that were her specialty. "You're a bigger whore than Luke."

"Ahh, now we're getting somewhere. Can I give you some advice?"

"Please don't. Please please please don't."

But I would—it might be my last chance to impart fatherly wisdom to my daughter, it might be one of her last memories of me. What to say? What gift of wisdom to leave her with?

"You know, Shelby, men are pricks. Don't trust a one of them."

"Us."

"You?"

"No, you. It's an us. Don't trust any of us."

"Oh yeah, right."

She stared at me as if I had just pleaded guilty to an indictment I didn't know had been handed down. "I'm going out tonight," she said, her attention back to her phone, her thumb dancing on the keyboard like Baryshnikov. "I need money."

"Who are you going out with?"

"Does it matter?"

"Yes, it does."

"Micki and Pam. We're meeting up at Doug's."

"Who's Doug?"

"Doug. Doug. I've only gone to school with him since fifth grade."

"Oh, that Doug," I said, still having no idea who Doug was. "Talk to your mom."

"What, you left all your cash inside some G-string?"

"You know, Shelby, there's more to do in Vegas than go to strip bars."

"Like what?"

"Well, there's an Applebee's," I said.

Shelby used to like my jokes, but all I got now was a stone face as she turned and headed back to the kitchen, her attention all the while on her phone.

I thought of going after her, of tossing her phone at a wall and wrapping her in my arms, telling her again that I loved her and this time making it stick. But from prior experience I knew that would only make things worse. Life with Shelby had become an emotional minefield, which left me doubting that I ever said or did the right thing. My life in microcosm. The only solution was time, waiting for her to grow out of whatever she had grown into, but time with Shelby was the one thing I no longer had.

I stood in the hallway, feeling helpless and hapless, and then beat my own retreat up the stairs. Seeing the way I looked in my daughter's eyes made me feel like a clown in a costume. As soon as I hit my bedroom, the pants and T-shirt hit the hardwood floor. I took a moment in the shower to gather my thoughts. Back in the bedroom, my hair still soaked and a towel around my waist, I made a call.

"It's Harry," came a voice over the phone, rough hewn and salty, like an old piece of salt cod. "I'm not here now. Leave a message."

"Harry?" I said.

"Just leave that there message."

"Harry? Why are you pretending to be an answering machine?"

"Who's this, Johnny?"

"Yeah, it's me."

"Oh, Johnny. How you doing there, son? I don't owe you nothing, do I?"

"No."

"Then you don't need to leave no message."

"What's going on?"

"I've been getting calls. You know."

"How much do you owe?"

"Not too much. But the bastards have been threatening to take the *Left Hook*. Can you believe it?"

"But you own your boat outright."

"Yes I do. Or I did. But remember when my engine went on the fritz?"

"You mean when it blew up."

"And then I got those twin 120s."

"I told you that was too much power."

"Oh, Johnny, engines is like tits: there's no such thing as too big or too many."

"Three would be too many."

"I knew a girl in Fresno once that—"

"Harry?"

"But I only got the two there, Johnny. And they were offering a sweet little loan. What was I going to say? No?"

"Exactly. That's my new advice for anyone being offered a sweet little loan."

"You're going to put yourself out of business."

"I've been out of business for a year. You busy tonight?"

"I got plans, sure. I'm getting drunk at Schooners with the Koreans."

"That's a surprise."

"If something works, Johnny, stick with it, I always say."

"Why don't I join you there, say, about ten-ish?"

"No good. Too much running, I was never no good at running."

"Not tennis, ten-ish. Ten o'clock. I need to talk to you. Remember that thing we worked out a couple years ago?"

"What thing?"

"That thing."

"That thing?"

"Yeah."

Pause. "What the hell's happened to you?"

"Let's just say I have creditors of my own. We'll talk about it tonight at Schooners. And if we move, we're going to have to move fast, all right?" I thought about the scare I had felt at the front door. "I think I may be going fishing tomorrow."

"Tomorrow?"

"There's no reason to wait."

"Good thing I got them twins, then, isn't it?"

"This goes through, I'll clear up those calls for you, Harry."

"I'd rather stick around and dodge the damn calls."

"Me, too, but what are you going to do?"

I hung up and sat on my bed with that towel around my waist and let a wave of fear flow through me. It wasn't going to work, I could feel it. I had a plan, and it might have been a pretty good plan, too, if it didn't depend on Harry. But what other option did I have? This was the life I had chosen all those years ago in Pitchford, even if I hadn't known it then. I sat on the bed a moment longer, my legs crossed, my body propped up with one arm as I stared at the paisley swirls on the bedcover. I loved those paisley swirls, their jaunty richness. How was it that a paisley pattern my wife had picked out at the Macy's in Newport News could suddenly send tears to my eyes? And then I thought of Augie, lying dead in his own bed. Lucky bastard.

When I looked up, Shelby was staring at me from the doorway.

"Are you okay, Dad?" she said.

It took me a moment to snap back to the present, and my presence in the bedroom. "Yeah, sure," I said. As I wiped my eyes with the back of my hand, I added a false note of heartiness to my voice. "Good as gold."

"You left these," she said, raising my briefcase and the white hat into the air.

"Thanks, princess."

"What did you do in Las Vegas, Daddy?"

"Nothing much. Just business."

"Okay," she said, but there was something in her face, something different than her default hostility, something frightened.

I glanced down at the towel to make sure I was covered.

"I'll just put them here." She put the hat on the bureau, placed the briefcase beside it, gingerly, as if it contained a bomb, and turned to leave the room.

"While I was in Vegas, I said good-bye to a friend."

She turned around again. "Where's he going?"

"He died."

"Was he a good friend?"

"The best I ever had," I said.

"Did we know him?"

"No. He never came and visited us here."

"I'm sorry."

"Thanks."

"I'll go now."

"Okay," I said. "How much money do you need for tonight?"

"I'm fine, Dad. Don't worry about it."

"Good," I said. "I'm glad."

When she left I sat there a moment longer. I wanted to slip under these paisley covers, to put my head beneath a pillow and disappear into sleep, to Rip Van Winkle it and wake up when everything had passed. But it wasn't going to pass. I needed to keep my cover, for one day more; I needed it to look like everything was normal in my normal suburban life, for one day more. I had been pretending for so long now, what was one day more? So I resisted the urge to hide and instead rose from the bed and put on my usual—khaki shorts, golf shirt, shiny brown loafers—stuck the horrid white hat safely in the briefcase, hid the briefcase in the basement, and went off to see my son fail miserably at Little League.

And the whole time I dressed and drove I couldn't stop thinking about how I had let my life spiral so out of control. There is always a moment when the course is set, always a moment after which the journey toward disaster is as inevitable as death or laundry. When I looked back, I realized maybe I was wrong to always blame my father, maybe I should have blamed my dog.

11. Spirals

"THEY SAY DEREK GRUBBINS K-KILLED A MAN," SAID BEN, when I still was only ten and my life had not yet developed its malignant complications. The Derek Grubbins of whom Ben spoke with quiet awe was Tony Grubbins's mysterious older brother.

"Only one?" said Augie.

"At least one," said Ben. "Maybe five. But this one he killed by sticking a fork in the guy's neck. Blood spurted out in f-four different directions."

"That sounds like the pork roast my mom made last week," said Augie.

Augie, Ben, and I were sprawled on the front steps of my house, idly flipping baseball cards but really just passing time so we wouldn't miss the show. And it promised to be a doozy.

This was only a few months into my new life and already I was looking like a full-fledged Pitchford brat: plaid shorts and white T-shirt and high-top Keds bought at the Sears on Easton Road, my hair buzzed quick and neat at Fred's Barbershop, right next to Milt's Five-and-Dime. If you had walked down Henrietta Road you wouldn't have been able to pick me out of the crowd slapping wildly at the puck. The country-club kid had morphed, on the outside at least. But even though I now lived in Pitchford, and looked like I lived in Pitchford, I still didn't belong in Pitchford.

I was a spy behind enemy lines, watching everything I said and did, so as not to be caught out for what I really was.

And what was I, really? An outsider, thank God. It was the one thing that made everything else bearable, which was good, because it was looking more and more like we were here for the long haul.

My mother had roused herself to take a refresher typing course and then find a secretarial job at some machine shop in Horsham. She was drinking less and cooking better—she couldn't have been cooking any worse—and with her new salary our family life had lost its sense of abject doom. My mother was settling into our rental house, settling into her job, settling into the couch in front of the television at night with her glass of comfort, settling into the pale un-Willing leftover her life was becoming. As for me, I was hanging out with Augie and Ben.

I don't quite know how we became a gang of three, but in the weeks that followed my sad entrance into Pitchford, as I kept my distance from the rest of the neighborhood, first Augie started keeping me company, and then Ben joined in. I suppose each of us was an outsider in his own way and that was what drew us together. I was a filet-mignon boy in an olive-loaf suburb, Ben was the big black kid in a mostly white neighborhood, and Augie was just your average kicked-out-of-Catholic-school troublemaker. If you wanted to smoke, Augie would sell you the cigarettes he stole from his mom. If you wanted to stare slack-jawed at naked women—and, really, who didn't?—Augie would sell you time with the *Playboys* he slipped from his father's workbench in the garage. Later he would graduate to selling concert tickets and pornographic videos and drugs, yeah, but even in those early days he was the supplier of our darkest dreams and as such was always on the periphery. We were, all three of us, on the periphery. All we had was each other.

"They say Derek Grubbins buried two b-bodies in the crawl space of his house," said Ben as he flipped another card and placed it on the pile.

"Only two?" said Augie.

"One was his older brother. One day he was hanging around, then there was a f-fight, and the next day he was gone."

"Didn't he join the army?" I said as I flipped a card.

"They said he joined the army," said Augie. "But have you ever seen him hanging around in his uniform?"

"No," I said.

"There you go, bub," said Augie, turning over a card of his own.

"What about the other body?" I said.

"No one knows who the other one is," said Ben, "but every night Derek goes down to the crawl space and spits on the graves."

Augie hacked up a loogie and spat it onto the scraggly lawn next to the steps.

"Funny," I said.

Tony Grubbins's mother had died years ago and his father had been killed in a construction accident just the year before, when a steel beam shifted unexpectedly at a job site, smashing flat his chest. The accident had left Tony in the care of his older brother, Derek, who had moved back into the Grubbins house to take care of his sibling. Derek, a member of the notorious Devil Rams Motorcycle Club, was a bearded madman who roared onto and off of Henrietta Road on his chopped-up Harley, scaring little squirrels and potbellied war vets at the same time. And each afternoon, right about that time, as he barreled home from work, he inspected his lawn before parking in the driveway and stomping up the cement stairs to his front door.

"And the things I heard about them D-Devil Rams," said Ben. He flipped a card and took the entire pile with a bright smile. "Evil things."

"Like what?" I said.

"Like how if you just look at one of them wrong they tie you in chains and drag you on the street behind their b-bikes until your skin peels off."

"Ouch," said Augie.

"How d-do you think you'll look, J.J., without any skin?"

"Lay off him, you pantywaist," said Augie. "J.J. took a stand. He's not going to let himself get pushed around for the rest of his life. Right, bub?"

"Right," I said.

"He's standing up for himself, just like I told him to."

"That's the mistake right there," said Ben, shaking his head. "Never listen to Augie. He's what my mom calls an instigator. You should have forgotten all about it. It can't end good."

"Maybe not," I said, feeling sick to my stomach, knowing he was right, "but you didn't get a football thrown in your face."

This whole thing started in a chaotic netherworld of violence and mayhem, where all civil rules are suspended and the law of the jungle is the law of the land. I'm talking now of grade-school recess. At Pitchford Elementary, recess was a madhouse. Kids played snap the rope, when the only thing snapping was bones. Kids played six inches, pounding each other relentlessly on the shoulder until tears flowed. Kickball was a sadist's dream, where any advance from base to base invited a big red welt on the jaw. And football was always tackle and always merciless.

Unused to such savagery at my private school, I determined early on to avoid it all. While pandemonium broke out about me, fights and chases, squeals of pain, I sat on the swing, hoping to be ignored until the bell rang and I could retreat to the relative safety of the classroom. And that's exactly where I was, on the swing, minding my own damn business, when I looked up and saw a football whizzing through the air, coming right at me.

I decided to duck, but before my mind could send the message to my body the ball hit me smack in the face.

Knocked too senseless to actually cry, I simply fell backward off the swing. The earth spun like a top, my cheek felt like I had been stung by a swarm of wasps, a sob of bitter indignation rose up my throat. And then I saw Tony Grubbins standing over me, grinning down as he spun in his hand the football he had retrieved from the ground. Behind him, in his usual position, was the skinny kid with the round glasses, the pilot fish, Richie Diffendale.

"I told you to keep your dog off my lawn," said Tony Grubbins.

"He told you, Frenchy," said Richie Diffendale.

"My brother saw a little pile of your crap," said Tony, "and almost put my head through a wall."

"How do you know it was my dog?" I said, my voice thin with whine.

"A little pile of French dog crap, that's what it was. You're the only weenie with a dog that small. And Richie said he saw your rat nosing our lawn."

"And I did, too," said Richie.

"Your dog does it again, it will be more than a football in your face, Frenchy. You'll catch my fist and you'll be missing teeth."

I waited until he strode back to the game, with Richie Diffendale following, looking back every other step and sneering at me, before I climbed slowly to my feet. I was still rubbing my cheek, fighting the tears, when Augie sidled up to me.

"I warned you not to let your dog near his lawn, bub," said Augie.

"How is everyone so sure it was my dog?"

"Are you saying it wasn't?"

"No."

"You look like a chipmunk with half a case of the mumps. You learn your lesson yet?"

"I don't think so."

"Atta boy."

This wasn't only the second time I had been humiliated by Tony Grubbins. He had begun to take an especial interest in me in our street games, checking me hard into parked cars at every opportunity, throwing the pimple ball at my head in stickball, touching me into a broken heap in two-hand touch. Now, Tony was indeed a brutal bully, and I wasn't the only kid to feel his wrath, but I suspected even then that his special distaste for me might have been well earned. He sensed all along the way I felt about him, and his friends, and his neighborhood, the way I felt slyly superior, yes, like a Frenchman. I was prideful and arrogant, I thought I was better than Pitchford, and in truth, if I were in his place I would have checked me extra hard into a parked Buick, too. But even so, for me Tony Grubbins had become an emblem of all the indignities imposed upon me by my new home.

Which was why I had led my dog to purposely crap on his lawn at every opportunity. And why three days after the football met my face I spent the day picking through the neighborhood with a bag and a small plastic sand shovel, following any dog I saw roaming around, leashed or not. I needed a pile large enough, and with pieces thick enough, that there could be no thought it came from my little Rex. I found a nice-sized pile, shoveled it into the bag, and kept looking. Later, in a quiet moment when Tony Grubbins was inside and Ben and Augie played lookouts on either end of street, I emptied the bag smack on the Grubbins lawn.

Holy Peter, it was perfect. It looked like a brontosaurus had made its way onto Henrietta Road.

"They say one guy who overheard something the Devil Rams didn't want him to overhear," said Ben on my steps, "they c-cut off his ears and sewed them onto his ass."

"Whenever he sits down," said Augie, "he goes deaf."

"What's that you say?" said Ben in his famous old-man's voice. "What? What?"

"Stop it," I said as the other two giggled. I tossed a baseball card onto the step to start a new pile. "Let's play."

"You'll be sorry," said Ben. "Yes you will."

And I didn't doubt it. But the son of a bitch had thrown a football at my face. I wasn't going to sit back and take it. I was still at that age where consequences more serious than a schoolyard tussle were not within my consciousness. I figured maybe I'd end up with a bloody lip, a swollen ear, maybe I'd lose a baby tooth a few months early. I never thought the whole thing could spiral so far out of my control it would endanger everything I ever loved. Though, to be perfectly honest, I was the kind of kid that would have done it anyway.

"Here he comes," said Augie.

I cocked my head and heard nothing, nothing, until the clamor of a motorcycle engine in the distance squeezed at my bowels. "Maybe we should go inside and look out the window," I said.

"Maybe we should all j-just go home," said Ben.

"Maybe you girls should change your diapers," said Augie. He tossed a card on top of mine. "He won't even notice us."

The sound of the engine grew louder, the individual piston-churning explosions came closer. Until he appeared, at the very end of the street: Derek Grubbins, helmetless on his Harley. Broad shoulders, brown beard, biceps bulging from his T-shirt, tattoos shining as he roared down Henrietta Road.

He cruised toward his lawn and then right past the pile as if it didn't exist. He pulled into the drive, killed the engine, yanked the bike back on its stand, stomped up the steps to the front of his house, banged the front door open before disappearing inside.

"Nothing," said Augie. "A bit fat nothing."

I was simultaneously relieved and disappointed. It was as if a roller coaster I had been dreading closed before I could hop on. "I can't believe he missed it," I said.

"His eyes must be failing," said Augie, "considering that the pile is as big as his head."

"And it l-looks like him, too," said Ben.

"Now what?"

"Now we go home," said Ben.

"What about finishing our flip?" said Augie, gesturing to the baseball cards between us.

"Okay," said Ben, settling down to finish flipping when—

Bam.

The front door of the Grubbins house blew open and Tony Grubbins flew out headfirst, landing splayed on the lawn. Derek Grubbins strode out after his brother. When Tony tried to scramble to his feet, Derek cuffed Tony hard enough to knock him to the ground again.

"Pick it up now," said Derek.

"I don't have a bag," said Tony.

"I don't give a fuck," said Derek. "I told you to keep the damn lawn clean."

"It's not my—"

Before Tony could finish, Derek kicked Tony in the ribs, hard enough to send his brother spinning, and then stormed back into the house, slamming the door behind him, leaving Tony Grubbins on the grass, clutching at his side as if shards of bone were poking through the flesh.

The beating was quick enough that we might have missed it if we weren't sitting on my steps, waiting just for it. But we didn't miss it, we caught it in all its ugliness, the flash of violence and submission, a glimpse into the dark heart beating inside that house.

What do you feel then, when you realize you've stumbled carelessly into something dreadful and made it worse? You feel shame, and remorse, and pity, of course you do, and I could see all those emotions reflected on the faces of my two best friends. But that's not what little J.J. Moretti felt, as he watched this beating unfold from the steps of his prison in split-level hell. Instead he rubbed the side of his face, still bruised from the football, and felt the taste of victory, bubbly, cloying and rich, like an ice-cold bottle of Coke pulled straight from the cooler at Milt's.

Tony scavenged around the neighbor's garbage cans until he found an old brown paper bag and then, with his hands, he started shoveling the dog crap, handful by heedless handful, into the bag. And in the middle of his shoveling, there was a moment when he looked up from beneath his brow, to my house, to my stoop, right to me. As if he knew.

Of course he knew.

I waited for him to hit back. I kept hanging out with Augie and Ben, listened to their laughter and warnings, and grew ever more terrified. I tried to steel myself for Tony's revenge. Would he do it himself or would he tell his brother what had happened, sending that tattooed monster my way? I tried to guess how many teeth it would cost me, how much blood. And then I didn't have to guess anymore.

I found him outside in our backyard, my sweet little dog, curled into a fluffy ball beside his still-full water bowl, calm and quiet when he was never calm and he was never quiet.

And at that moment Tony Grubbins was no longer just another street bully, he had become a mortal enemy, which might have been exactly what I needed at the time. Whatever Pitchford threw at me in the years to come, I could handle it because I had an enemy. The more Tony Grubbins beat on me, the stronger I would become. And he did beat on me, continuously over the years, and I did strengthen. And it was sweet, my hatred, deliciously alive, it was something I could hold close in my darkest times and watch with joy as it grew, until I was ready, finally, to make Tony Grubbins pay its full freight.

But such empowerment was still far in the future. All I had now, along with my weakness and overweening pride, was the mere seed of that hatred for Tony Grubbins. It wasn't much, but it was enough to keep my shovel clicking into the dirt as I dug a grave in the woods behind the park, under a dying cherry tree.

12. Eric

THERE HE WAS, STANDING IN THE OUTFIELD, LOST AND bored, staring off into the ether as the game trundled on without him, about the same age as I was when I buried my dog Rex in the woods at the end of Henrietta Road.

My son, Eric.

It is no crime to hate baseball, except maybe in Patriots Landing, where the only legitimate excuse not to play baseball is lacrosse. But Eric hated lacrosse even more than baseball. He hadn't wanted to play Little League anymore, had wanted to give it up for video games and comic books, but I, the all-American dad, wouldn't let him.

"A boy needs to play baseball," I said. My wife, Caitlin, flapped her arms in frustration but let me have my way.

Now, as I approached the Little League complex—three diamonds, each with stands and lights and hard green fences plastered with advertisements, along with rows of batting cages hung with netting—I grimaced at the sight of my boy looking so out of place. A short and slight eleven-year-old, his wire glasses on and his oversized uniform hanging off him in loose folds, he was like a tiny lamb among the raging beasts in the field. I wanted to yell out at him to pay attention to the game, but I stifled the urge. My son played the outfield badly, batted last, stood ungainly at the plate as the coach clapped his hands and called out to him to wait for his pitch, hoping he would wait himself to first base. The whole thing was a humiliation.

For me, I mean.

Caitlin, standing by the backstop, saw me approach and gave a blank stare that barely acknowledged my appearance before turning away. She was undoubtedly mad at me for coming home late from Vegas, or mad at me for not calling, or still mad at me for forcing Eric to play baseball and her to show up at the games. These days my wife seemed always to be mad at me. Whether it was a suburban thing or a longtime married thing I wasn't sure, but it was endemic in the marriages of Patriots Landing, at least those still extant. Our wives' anger was a main topic of discussion at the clubhouse bar, the butt of our jokes on the third tee. Yet Caitlin's anger seemed fiercer than that of the others, which I never quite understood.

I didn't drink to excess, didn't torture cats or pick my teeth with a knife. And I didn't cheat on her. Men who cheat, men like my father, need to keep alive some secret splinter of their existences, something totally their own, separate and apart from their marriages. I already had that. And truth was, even though I found my gaze sometimes wandering over the lithe bodies of the Little League wives, like Carl Spackler in *Caddyshack* ogling the lady golfers on his course, I was in the peculiar position of being married to the prettiest of them all. So no, I didn't sleep around. I was one of the good guys; all I was doing was doing all I could to keep our lives intact in difficult times. Which made it all the more peculiar, to my way of thinking, that Caitlin had let me know that she was leaving me, which meant that I should start thinking about moving out.

She was now in a pack of Little League parents in their plaid shorts and wide sunglasses, like a pack of wolves, talking about their kids' private coaches, their kids' tournament teams, their kids' upcoming trips to Cooperstown to play against the best teams from all over the country. Caitlin nodded patiently through it all as her son was swallowed whole by the expanse in right field. In Pitchford we had had Little League, sure, but it was of far less import than our street games. And parents didn't seem to care so much, only occasionally making it out to the scabby little field to watch us play. It was a working-class neighborhood and the parents were usually, well, working. But just as I felt it was obligatory for Eric to play, it seemed obligatory for the parents in our neighborhood to show up to cheer, to cajole, to berate the umpire, to bitch at the coach about their kids' not pitching or playing shortstop.

Little League baseball in Patriots Landing: fun for the whole family.

I was putting in an appearance, I was trying to look like everything was normal the day before I disappeared, but I didn't think I could handle the whole wolf-pack thing, so I bypassed the bleachers and stood a bit down the line and watched as Eric meandered in the outfield, oblivious to the events going on in front of him. When he gazed down at his feet and kicked at the grass, I again restrained myself from yelling a heads-up to my boy. I had been calling out to Eric to pay attention in the field since T-ball, and it never worked to prick his indifference, it served only to embarrass him. To get him to play this year I had promised to keep my mouth absolutely shut during his games. So I stood silently along the third-base line and did what I always did when Eric was in the field: hope that the ball didn't get hit to him.

"Where have you been, buddy?"

I turned to see Thad Campbell, tall and handsome with lank blond hair and a chin like a cartoon hero. His kid was the star player on the team facing off against Eric's. Thad and I played golf most every Sunday, we shared beers after golf, had dinner together occasionally with our wives. He was about as good a friend as I had at Patriots Landing, which was sad, considering I didn't like him much.

"I was away on business," I said. "How are we doing?"

"You're up by three in the fifth, but we've got the bases juiced."

"What about Eric?"

"He struck out a couple times, I think. Good swings, though. You playing tomorrow?"

"I don't know." I spotted Caitlin looking at the two of us, her eyebrows suddenly rising in concern. I turned to Thad and stared at him flatly. "Only if we start early. I'm thinking of going fishing in the afternoon."

"Really?"

"The blues are running," I said without blinking. I wasn't much of a fisherman, and never really knew what the hell was out there to be caught. I either relied on Harry or, when I was alone, just sat in the water and drank beer and thought about things. But if you wanted to explain a sudden fishing trip in Patriots Landing, all you needed to say was that the blues were running, and the understanding nods would follow.

"Blues, huh? Want to cut me some nice fillets for the grill?"

"No problem."

"Great," said Thad. "We're still on for tonight, right?"

"Tonight?"

"Dinner. At Sal's. With Charles and June."

"Oh yeah, that thing." Caitlin's attempt to keep up appearances. "Sure."

"It will be terrif to get together with everyone. We haven't seen you and Kate in a while."

"It's been a little crazy."

"Is everything okay with you guys?"

"Sure," I said. "Peaches."

At Patriots Landing, there were appearances and there was reality, and it was hard to say which was more important: in that way, I suppose, suburbia is like the US Senate, without the sex. There would be a moment when it would all go to hell, and then everyone would know everything, but until then Caitlin and I were as perfect a couple as every other.

On the field, our pitcher was slinging it in there, and the batter was having a hard time catching up to the speedball. On two late swings he barely got enough of the ball to foul it back. But he was a big kid, and if he connected his late swing would wang the ball to right field, straight to Eric, who was gazing now intently up at the clouds. I clamped my mouth shut and fought the impulse to coach from the sidelines, but one more late-swing foul as Eric stared into the sky and I couldn't bear it any longer. It's not like I expected Eric to make the majors, I just wanted him to do well. Catch a fly ball to save a trio of runs, or at least not screw up too badly. For his own sake, I mean, for his own self-image.

"Heads up, Eric," I yelled, finally unable to stifle it any longer. "He makes contact, it's coming to you."

The coach's head snapped up at the sound of my voice. "Hey, Willing," he called out for all to hear, "come on now, pay attention out there."

When the batter finally caught hold of one, Eric was staring at me, his hands at his hips and his mouth agape even as the ball sailed like an artillery shell over his head.

"That's a shame," said Thad, dropping his palm on my shoulder as Eric turned to trot after the ball while the runners whipped around the bases like greyhounds after a hare.

13. Caitlin

Y OU PROMISED," SAID ERIC, AS SOON AS I STEPPED INTO OUR
kitchen.

I had followed Caitlin's black Lexus RX10 from the complex
to our house, but had waited a moment in the car to steel myself
for the inevitable drama. This was not how I wanted to spend
the last day in my current life, defending my stupidity, but in
a way it was fitting, for this was how life had been playing out
for me lately. I couldn't anymore make a move, no matter how
well intentioned, that wasn't wrong. When I finally built up the
courage to enter the house, Caitlin was leaning on the Sub-Zero
refrigerator with arms crossed, while Eric sat at the granite-
topped island, eating ice cream from a bowl, staring at me with
hard black eyes. Is there anything colder than the angry eyes of
an eleven-year-old boy?

"I was just trying to help," I said. "That guy was never going
to pull Jake's fastball. The only place he was going to hit the ball
was directly to you."

"But you promised never to call out to me when I was in the
field or at bat. Didn't he, Mom?"

"Yes he did," said Caitlin.

"You need to get into a ready position with every pitch," I
said, clapping my hands together and then spreading them open
like an infielder ready to make a play. "That's one of the first

things I ever taught you. Watch the way Derek Jeter does it on television."

"He plays shortstop. I never play shortstop."

"You might if you played with a little more get-up-and-go. I could talk to the coach."

"Oh God. Mom?"

"Daddy won't talk to the coach," said Caitlin.

"I'm not good enough to play shortstop," said Eric. "I'll never be good enough."

"Not if you don't work at it," I said. "But nothing's impossible, if you're a Willing." That was my little catchphrase, and it used to get a laugh when my kids were young and cute and adored their father, but it got no laugh today.

"I'm not good enough to sit on the bench. I stink."

"You don't stink, you just have to pay more attention to the game."

"I don't want to pay attention. It's baseball, it's stupid. Watching worms is more interesting than watching baseball. But at least I don't have to do it anymore. You promised and then you broke your promise."

"I did it this one time and I'm sorry," I said. "It's not a big deal."

"It wasn't the first time," said Caitlin, helpfully.

"You broke your promise," said Eric, with the utter calm that he could summon in the most fraught situations, "and under the terms of our agreement, now I get to quit."

"You don't want to do that," I said.

"Sure I do. I hate baseball, I always have. It's dangerous. People get hurt."

"No they don't."

"Then why do we have to wear helmets? Skydivers wear helmets, motorcycle racers."

"Oh, stop it."

"Marines."

"It's just a game."

"Then you play it. I only played because you made me. But since you broke your promise, I'm allowed to quit. That was the deal, wasn't it, Mom?"

"Yes it was," said Caitlin.

"So I quit," said Eric.

"There's no quitting in baseball."

"There is now," said Eric.

"You don't want to be a quitter, son."

"Why not? I love quitting. It's, like, my favorite thing. Remember when Mom got me to try out for that stupid play and after two rehearsals I quit? That was great. And that time you signed me up for that series of golf clinics with that goofy lady?" He raised the timbre of his voice to absurd warbling heights. "'Today we'll learn all about chipmunks.'"

"Chipping is an important part of the game."

"That was the only time I ever had fun at golf, when I walked away. How long did I last at lacrosse?"

"A week or so?"

"Three days, which was two days too long. I thought quitting lacrosse was pretty cool, but now I get to quit baseball, which has been, like, a dream of mine for years. You always say we need to make our dreams a reality, don't you, Dad?"

"Quitting gets you nowhere."

"But I'm not going to be a mediocre quitter. I'm going to be the greatest quitter of all time. I'm going to make the *Guinness Book of World Records*. In fact, I'm going to find more stuff I can sign up for just so I can quit. Dance class. Accordion lessons. In fact, let's go to Dick's and get a squash racquet right now so I can quit that tomorrow. Quitting squash will be one of the highlights of my life, next to what happened today, of course, because today I quit baseball."

"You having fun?"

"I wasn't before but I am now."

"We'll talk about it later."

"But we had a deal. Mom?"

"You had a deal," said Caitlin.

"You're encouraging him," I said.

"If you want to quit baseball, Eric," said Caitlin, staring hard at me, "I'll call the coach."

"He'll be relieved," said Eric. "He'll be thrilled. The only one happier than me will be him."

"You're not quitting," I said.

"Watch me," said Eric, before throwing his spoon at the bowl. "And I still want a dog."

"So you can quit on that, too."

"I'd never quit on a dog, Dad," said Eric, staring right at me, his gaze as sharp as a dart, "but today I'm quitting on you."

Caitlin let a twist of victory raise the corner of her mouth as Eric disappeared from the kitchen. "Isn't it nice to see that our son has goals?" she said.

"I know we have our problems, but you can still support me in front of the kids."

"I won't support you when you're wrong. You were wrong to force him to play Little League this year, and you were wrong to make him look bad in front of his friends. He knows what he likes and baseball isn't it."

"Everyone loves baseball."

"Not Eric. And frankly, I've always disapproved of it myself. Young boys just standing around in the outfield, picking their noses while pitchers struggle to throw strikes. At least in soccer they get to run around."

"Soccer is the leading edge of a plot to turn us French. I won't have my son eating snails for breakfast. And I don't want him to be a quitter."

"He devours books, he finishes all the video games he starts, he's a genius at that computer, and he gets all As in school. The kid is not a quitter, he's just not a ballplayer."

"Maybe we should sign him up for football."

"Are you listening to yourself, Jon? I mean, really."

"You don't understand," I said. "Boys need sports."

"Not your boy," she said.

Caitlin and I met in an Intro Philosophy class our sophomore year at the University of Wisconsin. Back then her good looks were hidden beneath limp brown hair, round glasses, the whole shy-intellectual kit. I fancied that I was the only one deep enough to see through the unremarkable and find the beauty beneath. I wasn't a jock or an activist with vivid political stripes, I didn't write for the school paper or act in the school plays, I didn't do anything to attract attention to myself, which, let me tell you, didn't really draw the chicks. But Caitlin with her baggy sweaters seemed to be right within my wheelhouse.

The first iteration of our relationship started with sex on a beery night and continued in a hang-out-together-with-other-friends-until-we-hooked-up-at-night sort of way. We didn't have deep discussions about what we were doing together, we just did it, and in the doing it was as if we were creating a new type of relationship, free of the bland expectations that society imposes upon the real thing that exists between two people. Whatever it appeared we were to others, and whatever we did while we were apart, we had an understanding that we were together and that we cared for each other even if we were too cool to show it. I thought our relationship was Zen-like in its perfection—as per my Religion 463 course: Buddhist Thought—freedom and sex, attachment and nonattachment. And did I mention the freedom and the sex?

Dude.

Our understanding lasted until the beginning of the next school term, when, with many tears and much anger, she told me to get the hell out of her life. Something about my inability to open up, my inability to share my deepest feelings. She said she was tired of knocking her head against a brick wall, that we were so cool together she was getting frostbite.

"But at least the sex is good," I had said.

"Not that good," she said.

We went our separate ways on relatively good terms and I just assumed, in the way the young often assume, that I'd eventually find someone better. But as I churned relentlessly toward the calamity of graduation, I slipped into a series of short-term relationships that always floundered on the shoals of my personality, variously described in the breakup confrontations as remote, guarded, selfish, detached. One well-meaning waif even sang Simon and Garfunkel's "I Am a Rock" as she broke up with me. It was a bloodbath. Then, at some open house or other during my senior year, I again ran into Caitlin.

When I spied her across the room for the first time in well over a year, I froze, startled at the deep and despairing regret I felt. She was laughing at something someone said, her teeth caught a bit of light, and I remembered the way we were together, the comfort, the tacit understanding, the coolness of her touch. I knew full well what had happened to us, why I always seemed distant. It was the secret, the thing I kept from everyone. For the first time I felt like I was cursed by what I had done, and what it had done to me. And then she turned and saw me staring, and smiled with real delight at seeing me, and it felt as if she was smiling at me from a more innocent and promising time in my life. My mother by then had died in that Florida hospital room, and I had lost contact with everyone from my childhood except for Augie and Ben, whom I only kept up with in our weekly calls and the occasional bawdy outing. In truth, I had more history at that moment with this woman across the room than I did with almost anyone else in the world.

I don't know if I had loved Caitlin in our first go-round, but I loved her at that instant with an eviscerating force. There have been two moments in my life when I saw a brilliant possibility and seized it with all the power of my being. The second was when I saw Caitlin that night and swore to myself that I would never do anything to lose her again.

But somewhere over the years, without exactly knowing how, I had.

Now, as she leaned against the pristine stainless steel of the refrigerator and stared at me, it was like she was staring out with the eyes of a stranger. And maybe she was, since she had replaced her glasses with contact lenses tinted blue. In fact, her whole look had been given a slick suburban burnish. Her limp brown hair was now glossy and gold, with the perfect streaks of a teenager, the specialty of Chez Rochelle on Highway 31. She no longer wore baggy jeans and sweaters, but white capris and a navy sleeve-less top she bought at the Ann Tyler Factory Store off Route 64, an outfit that showed off her tight body and lean, muscled arms carved at the Nautilus Fitness on Route 321. She was prettier than she'd ever been, more beautiful than I had ever imagined she could be back in college. And the gap that separated us had never been greater.

Between us lay all the moments when, instead of confiding wholly one in the other and placing our hearts on the line, we had settled for less. Between us lay routine and habit and the taking of one another for granted. Between us lay the years of our marriage. That those years had become a barrier instead of a lovely shared connection was a tragedy, and the fault was mine. For all the times I had held back a truth here or a fear there, for all the years I had played a part until the acting became the real-ity, the fault was mine. And there was nothing now I could do to make it right and no time now in which to do it. I looked at her and felt something slip inside and I went slightly unhinged for a moment and my eyes filled with tears.

"I'm sorry," I said.

"Don't tell me," she said, "tell your son."

"No, that's not it," I said, wiping at my eyes with the back of my hand.

"Jon?"

"I'm just sorry."

"For what? For staying in Vegas for an extra day of debauchery?"

"No, that couldn't be helped."

"For not calling?"

"My phone went dead."

"And there was no phone in the hotel?"

"At those prices?"

"Then what?"

"For whatever happened to us."

She looked at me coolly, as if it were all a trick, which maybe it was. "What are you trying to say?"

"I don't know, I'm a little out of sorts. It was a tough trip."

"Why? How's Augie?"

"Not so good," I said.

I had never told Caitlin the truth of what Augie, Ben, and I had done in Pitchford all those years ago, but I had told her of the dissolute life Augie was living in Vegas. She admired that I flew out to check on his health and welfare now and then, though she also admitted that it puzzled her. She didn't see me as much of a caretaker, and yet there I was, winging off to Vegas every time Augie had so much as a cold. He's more like a brother, I had told her, and she seemed satisfied with that.

"Is he sick?" she said. "Is he depressed?"

"He's dead."

"Jon?"

"Yeah."

"Oh, Jon. You poor thing. How?"

"How you would expect."

"I'm so sorry."

"So am I, but it was inevitable, wasn't it? It just gets you thinking about things. I never got a chance to tell him that I loved him. That I was sorry the way things turned out. That I wish I had been a better friend."

"But you *were* a good friend to Augie. Surprisingly, shockingly good."

"Not as good as I could have been. I let things get between us. I saw him more as a burden than as a crucial part of my life. Something to be handled. As things got messier I pulled away when I should have been stepping up. I let the detritus of life get between us, and I'm sorry for that."

She pushed herself off the refrigerator, stepped toward me with her arms out. "Jon, sweetie, come here."

I stepped toward her and I let her hug me and it felt good, letting myself be hugged, just standing there with my tears while my wife hugged me. I felt small just then, a little boy being hugged by his mother—not my mother, I don't remember her ever hugging me, but some idealized figure of a mother. I felt safe, loved, cocooned.

"We don't have to go out tonight," she whispered. "We can stay in. I'll call Denise and cancel. We'll stay home and talk it out. About Augie, I mean."

But she meant more, didn't she? Something had cracked in the barrier of habit between us and there it was, a final gift from Augie, an opening toward my wife. For what? Who knew, but it was there, for an instant. What scared me more, the thugs from Vegas or that opening? But what could I do? For everyone's benefit I had to disappear, I had to meet Harry, I had things to plan, there wasn't enough time.

"No, it's okay," I said. "We should go out. Thad's been looking forward to it."

"Is that what he said?"

"Yeah. We'll go out, we'll laugh, we'll forget about things. We promised."

"All right, sweetie, if you insist. But we can leave early, come home, spend some time together, talk."

"That would be nice, really nice," I said, enjoying the last hug with my wife before I pushed myself away. "But I can't. Maybe Thad and Denise can drive you home from the restaurant."

She stepped back, stepped away, stared at me.

"I have to leave a little early," I said, missing the hug, but plowing on like a plow horse. "I have to meet someone at ten."

"Who?"

"Harry."

"Your boating friend? Why?"

"He's having trouble with a loan."

"Why tonight?"

"He's desperate."

"And he thinks you can help?"

"He's grasping at straws."

"He's not the only one," she said.

An instant before, the atmosphere in our kitchen had crackled with opportunity. Now it was suffused with our usual brew of bitterness and suspicion. Caitlin had opened herself to me and I had kicked the opening back into her face so that, as far as she knew, I could get drunk with Harry. And there it went, my last chance to win back my wife, gone, another sacrifice upon the altar of what I had done with my two best friends twenty-five years before.

14. Stems

IT WAS AUGIE'S IDEA TO BREAK INTO THE GRUBBINS HOUSE, A matter of fairness, he said. Augie, our bent wheeler-dealer, talking about fairness was like...well, yeah, exactly. And the whole thing was a harebrained scheme from the start. I mean, of all the houses in Pitchford to break into, only a drug-addled fool would pick the Grubbins house, which explains how Augie came up with the idea.

We were seventeen, still hanging out together, bonded like brothers, a crew of our own, the immortal three. We had found a place for ourselves in the woods behind the small playground at the end of Henrietta Road, within the ruins of an ancient stone structure where stood a single twisted cherry tree, old and barely hanging on to life, the same tree, in fact, beneath which I had buried my dog Rex. When we wanted to get away from everything it was to those woods that we went, where we could lounge and dream, drink beer, write our names in paint on the stones of the ruin, plot, and, most of all, pursue our newest hobby. Almost every night now we got wasted, we got trashed, we got bombed or hammered or Kentucky fried, we got petrified, paralyzed, ripped up, shitfaced, torn down, wiped out, tweaked or toasted, starched or steamed, twisted or bagged, laid out, stretched out, killed, absolutely murdered.

Good times.

We smoked dope like it mattered, but we each of us reefed for our own special reasons. Augie had decided early on to live his life on the other side of whatever line he saw painted on the earth, and drugs were the quickest route there. Ben, who had become an all-county offensive tackle, smoked to take the edge off the pain in his knee and the pressure he was feeling to rise into a superman pro. As for me, hell, from the time my mom had first driven me into Pitchford, like one drives a stake into the dirt, I had been looking for an escape. But I always thought the language was just as seductive as the high. If we were getting "poodled," it wouldn't have felt half so fine. For what seventeen-year-old doesn't want to get wasted, whether with drugs or alcohol, sex or a skateboard, or just by vegging in front of the television? All teenagers are nihilists in their hearts—it's why you can never get them awake in the morning.

And here was the funny thing about our part in the national pastime of rampant drug abuse: our supplier was none other than my own sworn enemy, Tony Grubbins himself.

Things had changed at the Grubbins house over the years. It was still curtained up and locked down, but it was no longer dark and quiet. People were going in and out at all hours of the night; packs of motorcycles were parked along the curb, accompanied by corresponding packs of motorcyclists with their scruffy beards and denim vests, replete with a fierce skeleton ram's head on the back. When they came, they came en masse, hoisting coolers of beer and bottles of liquor, keeping the neighbors up late into the night with their backyard revels. And Derek, with his hard eyes and huge biceps, was no longer working regular shifts at a construction site; instead he came and went with no discernible pattern. But he was doing okay, whatever he was up to, even more than okay, if the gleaming Corvette now parked in his driveway meant anything at all.

And then suddenly Tony Grubbins, a senior while we still were juniors, started making like a mini-mart, selling everything a good little head could ever want: weed, 'ludes, uppers, downers, coke if you could afford it, acid if you had the guts for it. His pilot fish, Richie Diffendale, tall now, and surprisingly good looking even with the same round glasses, made his way through the halls of Pitchford High in a long black leather jacket that hung off his bony shoulders as if from a hanger, taking requests, keeping the ledger, filling the bags and filling orders, and slipping free samples to the prettiest girls, all while Tony supplied the drugs and collected the debts.

"We've been ripped off, boys," said Augie one night by our cherry tree as he picked through a bag of weed he had just bought from Tony.

"Pipe down and roll," said Ben. The years had stripped Ben of his stutter, but his slurry voice was still soft as a whisper.

"No, man. Look at this crap, all stems and seeds, the bottom of his stash. I'm telling you, he kicks us in the face on quality every time."

"So find a new seller," I said.

"Who? Tony's chased out every other dealer at the school, including me. Before I bought this shit, I gently asked him if he could maybe make sure the quality was better than the last batch of crap he sold us."

"He took your complaining well, I'm sure," said Ben.

"Let's just say it was nothing I could repeat in polite company."

"When are you ever in polite company?"

"And, come to think of it, J.J., in the middle of his diatribe, your name came up."

"Me?"

"Yeah, you. If we weren't saddled with your sorry ass, bub, we'd be getting his prime stuff."

"So you're the one killing my buzz, J.J.," said Ben, laughing. "Maybe I should be hanging out with the marching band. They always get killer weed."

"I'm telling you guys," said Augie, "Tony's been dicking us for years. But I happen to know where he's got some sweet Mexican buds stashed away. Richie was bragging about a shipment that came in, saying he saw a bag as big as a basketball in Tony's closet."

"Diffendale's a dick," I said.

"True, but that doesn't mean he's lying. And it's just sitting there while Tony sells his trash to us at a premium. Jesus, there's more dust here than beneath my bed."

"Quit the whining and spark it up, Sparky," said Ben. "You're giving me a headache."

"I think we should go in and get it," said Augie.

"Get what?"

"His good stuff."

"Don't be wacked," said Ben.

"He owes us," said Augie. "We'll be in and out before anyone knows anything happened, and we'll only take what we're owed. With all he's got, Tony will never miss it, and even if he does he won't know who did it."

"He'll know," said Ben.

"But he won't be able to prove it."

"He doesn't need to prove it. If his brother even thinks we broke into his house, our asses are not our own anymore. We're not talking a little beating here, Augie, we're talking death. Not metaphorical death, real death. Fork-in-the-throat death. Devil-Rams-pounding-our-heads-into-the-cement-stoop death. No way in hell is J.J. or me going in there."

"You two can stay outside and be lookouts."

"You're an idiot," said Ben.

"How long have you been going through menopause?"

"Haven't we learned by now not to mess with the Grubbinses? How's your dog doing, J.J?"

"Still dead," I said.

"Leave it alone, Augie," said Ben. "A couple of stems is not worth getting killed over."

"Maybe you're right."

"Of course I'm right. Only a total loser idiot would think of breaking into the Grubbins house."

"What do you say, J.J.?" said Augie.

"I'm in," I said, as quick as that.

We waited like astrologists for the stars to align, when suddenly they did. Derek roared off from the house with three other Devil Rams, their saddlebags full and their sleeping bags cinched behind their seats. They were headed for a jamboree in Virginia, we heard, or maybe North Carolina, but someplace south and far away. And then a day later Tony went off with his girl-friend, Denise, and his factotum, Richie Diffendale, to a party in Hatboro that was supposed to last all night. A half hour after Tony's car left the house, enough time to be sure he hadn't for-gotten his bong, and after a quick inhale of courage, Augie and I slithered through a loose window and landed in the pitch black of the Grubbins kitchen.

"We're in," I said into my walkie-talkie, one of three I had received from my mother for my fourteenth birthday and that, surprisingly, still worked. "Over."

"Over what?" said Ben through a cloud of static. Ben had wanted nothing to do with the whole enterprise and agreed to be our lookout only after Augie convinced him that if we got caught he'd be blamed for it anyway.

"Just *over*, Mr. B.—it's what you say."

"No names, remember? Jesus Christ. Just get it done and get the hell out of there."

"Over?"

"What?"

"You have to say it at the end. Over."

"You're making my head hurt."

"Say it."

"Go to hell."

"Say it. You know you want to."

"All right, if it will shut you up. Over."

"Roger that," I said. "Over."

"While you two bicker," said Augie, clicking on his flashlight, "I'm going upstairs and getting our stuff."

I didn't follow Augie to Tony's hidden bedroom stash of prime Mexican weed. Instead I took the opportunity to pop on my own flashlight and look around. This was why I had so quickly agreed to Augie's addled plan. It wasn't about the drugs, though that was a nice side benefit, and it wasn't about notions of fairness, though fair is fair, and it wasn't just about the thrill of an illegal lark with walkie-talkies, though the lark was indeed thrilling. For the last seven years, Tony Grubbins had lived across Henrietta Road from me, his house daily in my vision, and yet in all that time I had never once stepped through the door into that strange and dark place. This was my chance to scope out the lair of my enemy, the kid who had killed my dog. Tony Grubbins was my Joker, my Red Skull, my Kingpin, my Dr. Doom. What self-respecting comic-book hero wouldn't have taken that chance?

"What do you see?" said Ben over the walkie-talkie.

"Some expired milk, a pack of hot dogs, a couple beers, orange juice, something brown. Over."

"What are you doing?"

"Just checking things out. Over."

"Hurry the hell up, I'm having a heart attack out here."

"Roger Wilko," I said, closing the refrigerator door.

With my flashlight I wandered about, taking in the kitchen and living room. All the houses on Henrietta Road were structurally the same, so there was no mystery in the architecture, but each of these identical houses felt palpably different inside. Some felt happily messy, some felt bereft, some felt old, imbued with the smell of cooked cabbage, some felt sickly and wrong, one even felt rich for a time (and yes, there is a feel to rich that I still remembered from my youth) before the owners expectedly up and moved away to a place far better than Pitchford.

What the Grubbins house felt like, as I scanned the rooms with the beam of my flashlight, was charmless and dead, more like a storage locker than a house. There were no pictures on the scuffed and battered walls, no pictures on the beat old coffee table; the area in front of the curtained picture window was bare except for a television, set upon a cart and facing the couch. The place had the personality of a toad. It was all enough to almost make me feel sorry for Tony Grubbins—almost.

"There's a car coming, wait," said Ben.

I flicked off my flashlight and stooped down stupidly.

"Okay, it went past. Over."

"Over where?" I said.

"Shut up."

"It's not where it's supposed to be," said Augie.

"Get out, then."

"Just keep watching the street," said Augie. *"I'll find the damn thing."*

I took the moment to slip down to the lower level, which in most of our houses contained a small laundry room with two doors, one leading to the backyard and the other leading to the garage. But the Grubbinses, like some of the other homeowners on Henrietta Road, had converted the garage into another room by bricking up the wide opening where the rolling garage door had been, knocking out the wall between the garage and the laundry room, and putting drywall up against the cinderblock walls. I had wondered for a long time what was behind that bricked-up garage door, and now I knew.

Crap.

It had once been a den, that converted garage, optimistically paneled with cheap, stained plywood, but now it was piled with overloaded boxes and stuffed plastic bags, with shattered picture frames and crappy furniture, with cracked knickknacks, bales of wire, pots and pans. It was as if over the years all the traces of homeliness placed into the Grubbins house by the doomed parents had bled down into the sea of rubbish in the converted garage. And yet, for some reason, neither Derek nor his brother, Tony, thought of just throwing it all away.

They were sentimentalists, I supposed, keeping the last traces of their parents alive in this pile of useless junk. Who would have thought? And then I wondered if maybe there was another reason for the mound of crap. Was it there to stop anyone from digging up the garage floor, from digging up what was buried there? I remembered all the old stories, and it felt like something huge and awful was crawling its way up my spine. And then I thought of the missing brother buried in the crawl space and I instinctively whipped my flashlight's beam to where the crawl space beneath the kitchen was in each of the houses, a gap just to the left of the stairwell that led down to the laundry room, and what I saw was nothing but a wall.

A wall? What about the crawl space?

"*Got it, the son of a bitch,*" said Augie. "*Why the hell was he hiding it so deep in his closet? What was he afraid of, the ghost of his mother finding his stash?*"

"*Maybe he was afraid of you,*" said Ben.

"*Anyone coming?*" said Augie.

"*Not yet, but we're pushing our luck.*"

"*Calm down, Shirley,*" said Augie. "*Let me just scoop out a couple of bagsful.*"

"Wait," I said.

"*What?*" said Ben.

"Wait, wait," I said, barely able to catch my breath. "Put the stuff back just where you found it. Do you read me? Over."

"*What the hell?*" said Augie.

"Goddammit, put it back now."

"*Why? It smells sweet.*"

"Do you trust me?" I said.

"Sure, yeah, I suppose."

"Then do what I say. Over."

"Okay, okay, calm down, I'll put it all back."

"Good."

"What the fuck is going on in there?" said Ben.

"Shut up and keep your eyes peeled. And you upstairs, get down here to the lower level. You will not believe what I just found. Jesus Fucking Christ. Over."

<hr />

It was just a slight claw mark on the trim edging a stretch of drywall that sat above the rusted washer and dryer. A stranger to Henrietta Road would have passed it by without a second glance, but I was no stranger to Henrietta Road.

You could chalk it up to mere curiosity, I suppose, but as I wedged an old screwdriver into the slight gap between the clawed wood trim and the wall, I think there was something deeper driving me. From my very first day in Pitchford, the first day of my new and inferior existence, I had been terrorized by this house. Maybe I thought if I dug deep enough I could find out what was at the root of it all, and I'm not just talking about Tony Grubbins and his virulent hostility. I was digging for the root of everything that had conspired against me from the moment my father left home, the root of what had happened to my life.

With each pull of the screwdriver's red plastic handle, as I grunted with the effort and the nails shrieked as they pulled from the wood, I felt like I was getting closer. And then the wood trim came free. And when it did, the piece of drywall shifted slightly. I grabbed the drywall's edge with both hands and slid the large sheet out of the slot created by the remaining pieces of the trim. I could smell the crawl space before I could see it, and it smelled fetid and damp, acrid and raw.

When I shone the flashlight into the great dark gap, I fully expected to see something grisly, a family of rats gnawing on a pile of decomposing flesh and bone, maybe, or a grotesque monster, its limbs splayed, its joints swollen, plagued with boils, infested with vermin, gnashing its rotting teeth as it stared at me with a single cataractous eye.

What I saw instead was our future.

"Holy crap," said Augie after he had come down the stairs to see what I had found behind the slip of drywall. "How much dope is that? It must be fifty kilos."

We both were staring at stacks of brick-like packages wrapped in gray plastic tape, sitting on a tarp along with two large plastic paint buckets, five-gallon jobbers at least. It was the kind of stash frequently hauled out for the television cameras by drug enforcement cops when they wanted to blow their own horns for shutting down some huge and nefarious drug ring, but bigger than I had ever seen on the television.

"It's not weed, that's for sure," I said, "packs as small and tight as that."

Augie took hold of one of the packages that were stacked in piles on the tarp laid across the crawl space. He took a sniff, raised his eyebrows like a wine connoisseur.

"What the hell are you doing?" I said.

"Trying to figure out what it is."

"What are you, Mannix? How the hell can you tell by smelling it?"

"It doesn't smell vinegary, but it smells like something." His eyes widened. "Coke. How sweet is that, bub? We finally hit the big time."

"Wipe your prints off and put it back," I said. "Whatever we do, we're leaving that crap alone."

"J.J., man, one packet of this will keep us high for months, years maybe. And if we start selling it—"

"You have to know what we're dealing with, Augie. That's why I needed you to put that weed back. This isn't Tony's shit, or even Derek's. This is gang shit. The Devil Rams stashed this junk here instead of their clubhouse because they figured it was safer in the suburbs. But they'll kill us if they find us selling stuff we stole from them. And if we're getting high on high-grade crap that we wouldn't be able to afford, they'll know we took it and they'll kill us for that."

"But this stuff is probably so primo."

"It gets us nothing."

"Nothing but high."

"Augie."

"Okay, okay. You're right. This whole thing is so far over our heads it's in the clouds. Close it up and let's get the hell out of here."

"Wait. There's more here than just the drugs."

"Where?"

"The big plastic buckets with the lids," I said.

"What about them?"

"Open one and look inside."

"Why?"

"Just do it," I said.

Augie gave me one of his looks, the sly kind he gave whenever I did something colossally stupid of which he approved.

"*What's going on in there?*" said Ben.

"We've got an issue," I said as Augie grabbed one of the buckets and hoisted it out of the crawl space. "Everything still clear?"

"*For the time, but you've been in there way too long.*"

"We'll be out in a second. Keep looking. Over."

Augie lifted the lid off the bucket.

"Oh. My. God." He let out the words slowly, as if one of the hot black cheerleaders was stripping for him. "Oh. My. Jesus. God."

He looked at me and I looked at him and for a moment we stood together in shocked silence. And then we started hopping wildly around the bucket, our arms and legs shooting spastically in all directions, our mouths wide in silent amazement. If anyone had been peering into the basement of the Grubbins house just then they would have seen two epileptic idiots performing a crazed dumb dance of glee.

"It looks to be mostly hundreds," I whispered when we had calmed enough to breathe. "Stacks, some still wrapped from the mint, like a huge shipment was paid for with bills from the bank. It's hundreds of thousands. They didn't know what to do with it, where to put it, no bank would take so much raw cash, so they stuck it in here."

"Oh. My. God."

"What do you think we should do?" I said.

"Take it," said Augie. "All of it."

"We can't. They'll kill us if they find out."

"Of course they'll kill us," said Augie. "But Jesus, I've never seen so much money."

"If we take it and spend a dime of it they'll know," I said. "A new stereo, a new pair of sneakers, jeans, a stinking comic book, anything, and they'll find out."

"Then there's no point."

"But still, how can we leave so much money? And drug money, yet. Someone's ill-gotten gains."

"Do we take it just to screw with Tony? Do we put our lives on the line for that?"

"That sounds about right," I said.

"You're certifiable, man. We'd be better off burning it than spending it. I mean, let's just say for talking that we don't spend it. Let's say we bury it, not just for weeks, but for years. Decades maybe. What if we don't spend a dime until we're all out of Pitchford, and then only a little at a time, nothing to make anyone suspicious. We might get away with it then, but that's just crazy."

"Crazy," I said.

"I mean, who the hell can do that? First time we're short, we'll be tempted to take just a few bills, nothing much, maybe just a stack, and then, bam. They'll be on us."

"Like ticks on a dog," I said.

"And even if one of us can handle that kind of pressure, there's three of us. Over time one of us will break, one of us will screw it up, and that's the ball game."

"End of the ninth," I said.

"All it takes is one of us."

"Exactly," I said.

"Can anyone trust anyone else that much?"

"*Shit*," said Ben over the walkie-talkie. "*Shit shit shit.*"

"What is it?" said Augie.

"*I think it's—goddamn, it's Tony.*"

"He's not supposed to be back for hours."

"*Yeah, well, the party must have sucked. He's with Denise. Get the hell out of there.*"

"How much time do we have?"

"*He's pulling up to the goddamn curb now. Over.*"

"We can go out the back door," I whispered to Augie. "Throw the bucket back into the crawl space and help me slide the drywall back into place. Hurry."

Augie took hold of the bucket, but even as he began to lift it he looked up at me. And what I saw in his eyes in that moment still haunts me to this day. It wasn't greed that I saw, or a hunger for risk, or even an acknowledgment that we were both thinking the same thing, that we understood the opportunity and the risk and we had both come to the same damned conclusion. No, it wasn't any of those things, though all those things were present. What I saw most of all was a sadness, the sadness of a feral creature who can't help but take one step forward into a trap. It was as if he knew exactly how it would play out for him in the end, how it would play out for all of us, and still he couldn't help himself.

And that it had played out exactly as he knew it would makes the memory of that moment only cut deeper, like a scythe through the soul.

No wonder the son of a bitch was sitting by his pool in Vegas, crying into the night.

⸻

Augie and I really didn't have many other places to go in the Pitchford social whirl—with his questionable wheeling-dealing and my brilliant sense of deprivation we had burned enough bridges over the years that we were stuck with each other—but Ben was a football hero who was welcome to hang out with the jocks, the black kids, the band geeks, the heads. Even the pops were always trying to include him, cheerleaders in their short skirts calling out, "Oh, Ben." So it was a mystery why, each night as the moon rose, he ended up by the cherry tree with Augie and me and a hand-rolled reefer. I asked him once why he hung out with us when there were better opportunities for him, and he looked at me like I was talking fish.

"You're the only ones who don't give a shit about my future," he said, as if that answered everything, and I suppose for him it did.

Sometimes I thought he was a sucker, but thankfully he was our sucker. And in a way, he had become the best part of us. He was a natural offensive lineman, more protector than aggressor, strong enough to hold his ground and keep the worst dangers at bay. Whenever Augie was ready to jump off the deep end, it was Ben holding him back; whenever I let my pent-up sense of disappointment lead me into dark pathways, it was Ben who lit my way home. We kidded him about being an old lady, but truth was, we depended on his caution. He was not quite our moral compass, more like a warning sign placed along the road to utter idiocy. His good sense had saved our lives more than once, like the time Augie wanted to play Green Beret off the water tower with an umbrella.

Which was why, as Augie and I lugged the two plastic paint buckets of cash out of the Grubbins house, we fully expected Ben to slap us both upside our heads and order us to put the damn things back. And put the damn things back we would.

We had closed up the crawl space with the piece of drywall, pushed the wood edging back in place, wiped the whole thing down with our shirts all while Tony was heading into his house. But there wasn't enough time to get out of there before he ushered his girlfriend through the front door—he would surely have heard the rear door opening and closing—so we hunkered down beside the washing machine and hoped like hell that he went right upstairs to take care of business.

He didn't.

We could hear his footsteps above us as he tromped into the kitchen and yanked open the fridge, we could hear the clink of bottles as he pulled out a couple of beers. Hunched and breathing as softly as possible, our walkie-talkies turned off so that they wouldn't squawk, we listened as he turned on the television and sat on the couch and started in on Denise with smatterings of "Oh, baby," and "You sweet thing," and "No, wait, watch it. Yowl!" Despite the fear that was choking out throats, we had to stop ourselves from cracking up while listening to him work. There's a reason to leave porn to the pros.

But finally the television was switched off, the creak of footsteps rose up the stairs. A few moments later a blast of music tumbled down. I was ready to head right out, but Augie put a hand on my forearm as I started to stand.

"Wait," he said.

"For what?"

"That Denise, she's a screamer," he whispered.

"How the hell do you know?"

He just gave me a lopsided smile. And then the screaming began.

Under the cover of rapture, we slipped out the back door and hauled the surprisingly heavy paint buckets across the Grubbins backyard, past the Madigan swing set, through the bushes marking the edge of the Digby property, to a scrubby patch of grass just off the patio at the back of Augie's house. Then we turned on the walkie-talkies and called for Ben to come over and hand down, as if from on high, his judgment.

"You guys are morons," he said after we filled him in on everything, including Augie's plan for getting away with it all, as we three sat staring at the fortune that lay waiting for us in the buckets, so close and yet still so distant. "They're going to kill your asses."

"Our asses," I said.

"Even worse," said Ben.

"How are they going to know it was us?" said Augie.

"The moment they find it missing they're going to beat the shit out of Tony until he gives them a name," said Ben. "And what name do you think he'll spit out?"

Ben turned to me, and so did Augie, and I knew then that he was absolutely right, that the money in these pails was a deadly poison aimed right at my heart.

"We'll put it back," I said. "As soon as Tony leaves."

"You're damn right you will," said Ben.

"But it would have been something, wouldn't it?" said Augie.

"We would have been rich as kings," I said.

"Except for the fact that we couldn't spend it," said Ben.

"Not until we could," said Augie. "But when we could, damn, we would have ourselves a hell of a party. There would be so many tits we'd have to breathe out of a snorkel."

"Tits aren't any good to a dead man," said Ben.

"I don't think I'll ever be that dead," said Augie. "I want to have sex on this money. I want to spread it on a bed and grab Tawni Dunlop and lay her on top of it all and screw her until her ears bleed."

"Or Sandra Tong," I said.

"Or Francine Grey."

"Or Madeline Worshack," I said.

"Now you're hitting out of your league, bub," said Augie. "But you know what I'd really do with the money? Buy a car. Something fast and snappy. And just drive off. Maybe south to New Orleans, maybe west to LA just wander around, like a hobo, except with a car and tons of money. Drinking and screwing and seeing the country mile by mile. I bet there's more out there than we could ever dream of, stuck here in this stinking pit of a suburb. I bet there's worlds out there."

"Augie, you surprise me," said Ben. "That actually does sound rich."

"And when it got old, after, like, a decade or two, I'd come home and become a dentist."

"You crapping on us?" I said.

"No, really, that's what my mom wants me to do. Go to dental school. It would make her so happy. A dentist in the family. Nothing but smiles all day."

"Not to mention a ready supply of nitrous oxide," said Ben.

"Not to mention," said Augie.

"I'd buy a house for my mom," I said. "A big white house with a stone patio and a pool. Maybe join a golf club."

"You don't play golf," said Ben.

"I'd learn. Who knows? I might be great. I could be another Arnold Palmer."

"You can play golf now."

"Where? The pitch-and-putt at Alverthorpe? Screw that, I'm talking a real course, a real club, the real thing. And I'll be a club champion, get my name on a plaque. I remember all those stinking plaques with all those stinking names, lining the stinking hallways of that stinking club. I'd put my name right on top of the rest, bigger and bolder and in gold."

"I only just realized it, J.J.," said Augie, "but you are the most boring suburban asshole in the world."

"So says the dentist," I said.

"You got to admit, J.J.," said Ben, "it is pretty lame."

"Maybe," I said, "but there it is."

"What about you, Ben?" said Augie. "What would you do with the money?"

"Give it back," said Ben.

"No, I'm serious."

"So am I, serious as a bullet in the brain. Give it back, walk away, hope no one is pissed enough to still want to kill me."

"You're too big a pussy to even dream," said Augie. "That's just sad."

"I got dreams, son. You know what I would do if I was rich? I'd quit the stinking football team."

"Ben?"

"You think it's so much fun having those animals wailing on your ass every stinking Friday night? You think it's so much fun waking up each morning and having to roll out of the bed because you can't bend your knee without it screaming? I'd quit the team in a minute, go to college like a regular stiff, study math or engineering, find a job, get a wife, have kids, sit in my backyard with a beer and a barbecue grill and get fat."

"Get?" said Augie.

"And not worry about whether the all-state end from Norristown is going to squash me like a bug."

"There would always be room for both of you in my car," said Augie.

"And I'd have you both to the club," I said. "Except for you, Ben, because my club won't let you in without an apron."

"Wouldn't it have been sweet?" said Augie.

"Yeah, I guess it would have," said Ben.

"Get back into position," I said to Ben. "We'll stay here with the buckets. As soon as you let us know the coast is clear, we'll put them back."

"Shit," said Augie.

"Shit is right," I said, feeling suddenly sad, nostalgic even, for the fortune that was slipping out of our hands. Before the night was over, the money would be safely back in the Grubbins crawl space and we would be safe in our beds and all we'd have left would be another story to tell over beers when we were fat and forty.

"Are we really going to give this back?" said Augie.

"We have to," I said. "Ben's right, Augie. There's no way. They'll come after us first thing."

"Yes, they will," said Ben slowly. "Unless..."

That was the word that changed all our lives. Augie and I both turned to him, surprised as hell. And just then I caught something in Ben's eye, not greed exactly, but something else, something like a glimpse of freedom. It was a funny thing—you could spend a decade with a guy and still not understand all that made him tick, his dreams, his fears, the ravaging pain in his knee that promised to derail the rest of his life.

"Unless what?" said Augie.

"It's just a possibility," said Ben.

"Unless what?" said Augie again.

"Unless we can throw them someone else to blame," said Ben. "But first we have to swear. It's nice to have dreams and all, but if we spend even a cent of this they'll be on us before we have a chance to breathe. We have to swear not to spend any of it until we each agree that it's safe. And it probably won't be safe as long as we're living here in Pitchford."

"I'll leave tomorrow, then," said Augie.

"We can't run. What would be more obvious? We stay like nothing happened. We graduate. We only move on when the time is right, like it's the most natural thing in the world. And then, even after we leave, we don't go through the money like maniacs. When we spend it, we only spend bits and pieces at a time. No fancy cars, Augie. No big houses or fancy golf clubs, J.J. No jewels around our necks."

"What about one little diamond in my tooth?" said Augie.

"We need to swear, on our friendship and on our lives, not to be stupid," said Ben. "It's not just you anymore, Augie. We know you can screw up your life, but now we're talking about you screwing up J.J.'s life and my life, too. If one of us messes up, we'll all pay. We have to live like this never happened."

"I can do that," said Augie.

"I can, too," I said.

"We all better hope that's true," said Ben.

"But when can we start having fun?" said Augie.

"Later, much later," said Ben. "But with this in our pockets, we'll always land soft no matter what slams into us. And we'll get laid plenty."

"God, I hope so," I said.

"But not now. Now we just bury this shit and forget about it. Agreed?"

I looked around at my best friends. Ben had his stern face on, like he was a substitute teacher. Augie was nodding like a bobblehead. I couldn't see myself, but I was sure my face was more green than anything else, revealing the raw fear I was feeling, but also the surge of opportunity that was rushing into my veins like a drug.

"I'm with you guys," I said. "All the way."

"Me, too," said Augie.

"All right," said Ben, "let's put our hands together and swear."

And we did. As friends, as brothers eternal, as the immortal three. We clasped our hands over the buckets of money, looked into each other's eyes, and swore to all of Ben's conditions, swore not to be stupid, and most of all swore to take care of each other for the rest of our newly wealthy lives.

"Now what?" said Augie.

"Now we bury this shit someplace dark and deep, someplace that will keep it safe for months, years," said Ben. "And then I'm going to make a call."

We picked Augie's house to hide the stuff at first because he had no siblings and his parents weren't home that night. We pulled the buckets into Augie's crawl space, covered them with old boards, and packed around enough dirt so you couldn't see that anything was there. Then Ben hiked to a pay phone on a deserted part of Easton Road, he held the handset with a handkerchief, he used his old-man voice.

Thirty minutes later, from our separate houses, we watched as the whole of the Pitchford police force poured onto Henrietta Road.

I had the bird's-eye view from my bedroom window as the police busted down the Grubbins door, as they charged into the empty Grubbins house, as the street swarmed with cop cars and dark vans. And then later, as Tony Grubbins came home after dropping off Denise and heading back from the party, limping for some reason and absolutely stoned, only to find a posse of cops waiting for him. And in the darkness, from my bedroom window, I was smiling ever so slightly at the sight of Tony Grubbins, handcuffed, with a cop on either arm, being led to a police car with its lights flashing red and blue, red and blue.

I backed away from the glass and held my breath until the son of a bitch was driven away for good. And I thought just then, in the swell of youthful ignorance, that my life, whatever future shape it obtained, was already made, when the truth of it, as my life itself would later prove, was exactly the opposite.

15. Fighting Harry Conahan

SCHOONERS WAS ONE OF THOSE BARS THAT ATTACHES ITSELF to boat docks like mussels latch on to wooden hulls. It had the usual decor of the seaside sailors' tavern: buoys, fake lobsters, maritime paintings, a great iron bell, fishing nets hanging about the place like cobwebs on a spider farm. But over the years the discoloration that attacked the clapboards and roof shingles on the exterior of the shack had leached inside, so that the buoys, the paintings, even the fake plastic lobsters held the same deathly pallor as the drunken old seamen sprawled about the joint, noisily slurping their well liquor.

I stood in the doorway of Schooners for a moment, as out of place in my tan pants and pink shirt as a cow on a fishing trawler, trying to find Harry in the dank, smoke-filled room. He wasn't at his usual spots: with the hunchbacked old-timers at the bar, in a booth making time with some alcoholic hag, playing dominoes at a table with the two Koreans. I was about to turn around and head for Harry's boat, when I heard a toilet flush.

A few seconds later the bathroom door burst open, slamming against the far wall, and out staggered an old man still hitching up his filthy blue trousers. He was rawboned and bent, with deep crevices around his eyes and a roughly shaved jaw. His nose was busted flat, his hands were scarred and swollen, his eyes were bleary with drink, his shirt was plaid, his pants were held up by a pair of wide leather suspenders. He blinked at me as he stumbled out of the bathroom, smiled his orange checkerboard smile in recognition, and belched.

"Johnny, my boy," said Harry Conahan, "it's good to see you. What brings you to this hell hole?"

"You," I said.

"What I do?"

"Nothing, Harry. But we agreed to meet, remember?"

"To play a game or something, was it?"

"To talk."

"Is that all?"

"Yeah."

"Then, hell, buy me a drink and I'll let you talk my ear off, so long as I don't really need to listen."

"What say I get us a pitcher?"

"Beer? What do you take me for?"

"A drunken sailor," I said.

"And right you are."

"Grab a booth. I'll get the beer."

"And a couple shots to go with it."

"Are you sure?"

"Sure I'm sure. A couple for each of us. Just to lubricate the ears."

I had never much liked fishing, never much liked boats, actually—too much water all about. But even as I negotiated with the developer for my newly built George Washington in Patriots Landing, I already had one eye looking for a route along which to flee if it became necessary. And the river, wide and calm, like a superhighway leading to some tropical refuge, simply was there. A small airport sat nearby, too, I must admit, but the only thing I knew about little planes was that sometimes they went down, fast, so the hell with that. At the very moment I signed the closing papers, I determined to develop a maritime hobby.

I bought a small sailboat to learn on, an eighteen-foot Cape Dory Typhoon, with an outboard just in case the wind handled me instead of the other way around, and I docked it at a marina away from the prying eyes at my development. I had dreams of picking up something more substantial once I mastered the sailing arts, something twice the size, on which, in the event of an emergency, we could sail down the river, through Norfolk, into the Atlantic Intracoastal Waterway south, and farther south, past the Keys, all the way to the Caribbean, where, with my money and my boat, Caitlin and I could live the dolce vita until the heat died down. But I took to sailing like a cat takes to water polo. I couldn't read the wind, I couldn't keep the boat on course, and I was bored to tears by the whole affair. Stuck in my little boat in a failing wind one afternoon, I watched while muscular power-boats roared by, leaving me shivering in their wakes, and decided I had played it wrong. I didn't want to sail, I wanted to cruise.

But when I looked into the prices for the bigger powerboats, a boat large enough to live on in comfort for the years of my expected exile, and the amounts I would have to pay to keep one of those monsters fueled and docked and ready to roll, I realized no matter how much money I had stolen from the Grubbins house, it wouldn't be enough. And by then, in any event, things had changed a bit. It wasn't just my wife anymore, I had a child, and another on the way. I couldn't expect them to go on the lam with me, but I also couldn't just run away on my boat and leave my family at the mercy of Tony Grubbins and the Devil Rams. I would have to take another path. It wouldn't require a huge power yacht, it wouldn't require gobs of money; all it would require would be a little help. And so, even as I floundered trying to tack against the wind in my daysailer, I kept my eye open. I was looking for someone who could guide me and come through in the clutch, someone shady enough to be willing to assist for a price and dependable enough to bet my life on.

What I found was Fighting Harry Conahan, a bowlegged drunk with a high-pitched raspy voice, a beat old wooden fishing boat dubbed the *Left Hook*, and who, in the distant past, was one

Sugar Ray Robinson straight right to the jaw from the middle-weight boxing championship of the world.

"So what's got your cat all in a twist there, Johnny? What are you running from?"

"Someone from my past. It's not important."

"Important enough to the guy chasing you. What'd you do?"

"Only what anyone else would have done."

"Then why is he after you?"

"Because I did it to him."

Harry lifted up one of his clear shots of tequila and tossed it down his throat with a clatter of coughs. "God that feels bad, God that feels just awful. I'm getting too old to drink like this, and too old to stop. You sure you two just can't work it out?"

"It's too late for that."

"And you can't stand up to him?"

"It wouldn't be much of a fight. All I want to make certain is that you and I are set."

"You and me, we been planning about this for years, haven't we? Sure we're set. And tomorrow, is it?"

"The sooner I get away, the better."

"Tomorrow, then."

"Two-ish."

"What does religion have to do with it?"

"Harry?"

"Some of the toughest lugs I ever fought was Jewish. Herbie Kronowitz, with a left as hard as a hammer. And LaMotta's mother was Jewish, though not everyone knows that."

I stared at the old man for a bit. Sometimes I thought he was certifiable, and sometimes I was sure he was just playing with me, and then sometimes I…

"Two, Harry. Two. I'll be at the spot we worked out at two. We'll capsize my boat, spill some blood, and then you'll take me to that fishing shack you have up the Chickahominy. I'll stay there until the story dies down. Does your friend still have that sailboat we talked about, the one that we planned on taking down?"

"Sure he does, if he's still around."

"Harry?"

"I mean, who the hell knows? My friend with the boat, he might not be alive no more."

"Might not be alive?"

"He might have got hit by a van out in Suffolk, a white van coming out of nowhere when he was just crossing the street to an AA meeting."

"Harry."

"I always knowed them meetings were trouble. I don't know why we just can't take mine."

"It's too small and it's too old. And I was sort of counting on a sailboat for going island to island. In any event, if you and your boat disappear right after I disappear, people will get ideas. That's why you're putting your boat in storage and telling everyone you're visiting family in Michigan."

"All right, don't be fretting like an old hen, now. You still got the cash we talked about, right?"

"I still have the cash."

"One thing you can always get around here is a boat. The only thing they got more of in this world than people buying boats is people selling boats. You sure you want to do this, Johnny?"

"I don't want to do this; I have to do this. One man is dead already, and they just missed their shot at me. I stay, my family's in danger. I run, same thing, the message will be relayed somehow: come back or your family's dead. But if I die, Harry, if a terrible accident befalls me when I'm out fishing, then the danger ends. My family will mourn for a bit, sure, but the life insurance will see them through. It's not like I'm doing them much good anyway."

"You'd be surprised."

"I've been out of work for over a year."

"I been out longer than that and damn proud of it."

"And, to be truthful, I haven't been getting along too well with any of them."

"All the more reason to stay and work it out. Don't want to be leaving on bad terms."

"That's the only kind of terms we have anymore. You're not getting cold feet, are you, Harry?"

"Me? I don't get cold feet, except for them circulation issues I been having. I'll be there, just like I promised. After all, you've been paying me all these years. What did you call it?"

"A retainer."

"That's it. So I'll step up like we talked about." He looked around. "But I'll miss it here."

"Schooners? It's a dump."

"But it's my dump."

"We'll find you someplace better with an island beat. When the coast clears and everything's set we'll head on down. To someplace in the Caribbean maybe, or Central America. Or Brazil. I hear the girls are hot in Brazil, Harry."

"I bet they are." He nodded gleefully for a moment and then thought better of it. "And they sure would be hot for me if I was fifty years younger."

"Didn't you tell me that everyone loves an old man on a boat?"

"I told you that, sure, but that don't make it true."

"Just bring your passport, Harry, and we'll have a time together."

"No disputing that," said Harry, as he picked up his second shot and stared through it like it was a crystal ball. "And you never know, maybe even a good time, too."

16. Splitsville

A FTER MEETING WITH HARRY AND PLOTTING MY ESCAPE, I drove slowly back to Patriots Landing, thinking about my sun-drenched future, my blighted present, the disappointments of my past. The failure at the heart of my relationship with my wife was too familiar not to have been solely mine. What had happened between Caitlin and me, twice now actually, was the same thing that had happened with all the girls in between our two stints together, and the girl before ever I laid eyes on Caitlin with whom the pattern had started. As I drove ever closer to my new life, my thoughts inevitably drifted back to her. There is always one lurking in some hidden crevice of a man's heart, the avatar of perfect, youthful love, the one that got away and forever after remains the standard by which other lovers are judged, and for me that one was Madeline Worshack.

Madeline Worshack was the prettiest girl in Pitchford. She didn't have the insistent good looks of the cheerleaders, with their aggressive curves, their bright blonde hair, their lips like glossy cherries ready to be plucked with your teeth. But Madeline's eyes were green and her hair was red and her cheekbones were high and lightly freckled and sometimes when I looked at her my breath caught in my throat. I had been in crush with Madeline since junior high, but had pined at a distance as she went out with a series of boys both older and better looking than I was. As a sophomore in high school she dated the captain of the football team. Compared with the captain of the football team, what the hell was I?

Shit out of luck.

But somehow something changed in me after that night at the Grubbins house. Whereas before, Madeline knew me as just another of the boys who was tongue-tied in her presence, late in the spring of my junior year she looked at me anew and, even though she had a boyfriend at Penn State and a rash of admirers that spanned the spectrum of high-school achievement, when she looked at me she suddenly liked what she saw.

"Hey, J.J. How's it going?"

"Who? Me?"

"Yes, you, silly."

"I'm okay, I guess."

"Have you been working out? You look…different."

"I guess so, yeah. Pumping that iron. Doing those reps."

"Are you going to Francine's party tonight?"

"I wasn't really planning on it."

"Did she invite you?"

"It must have slipped her mind."

"I'll talk to her."

"No, it's okay. I've got something going on anyway."

"I've been thinking about you."

"About me?" I said, my palms beginning to itch.

"What have you been up to?"

"Nothing."

"I bet not. You look like you've been up to all kinds of things. We'll talk at the party, okay?"

I hadn't developed a six-pack overnight, or biceps, or a fastball to blow away the opposition, or even a shining intellect that made the debaters step back in awe, but there was something surely different about me. Nothing is more alluring, I suppose, than a secret. If I could take a stack of cash and bury it in every high-school kid's basement, there's no telling what the youth of America could achieve.

What I achieved—fist pump—was Madeline Worshack.

I'd had other crushes in my life, and by then I'd had sex with a girl I didn't much care for, but you could say Madeline, as the first girl whom I both dated and loved, was my first real girlfriend. Inevitably, having no idea what I was supposed to do as a boyfriend and overcome with that potent combination of desire, cockiness, and fearful jealousy, I ended up spending as much time as possible with her, primarily at the expense of my time with Augie and Ben. It would be easy enough to cast Madeline Worshack as the Yoko Ono of our little gang, she sure had the cheekbones for it, but it wouldn't quite be accurate. Even before Madeline, things had changed between the three of us, and not for the better.

You know how when you're in high school and you have sex with someone one night, the next day you end up avoiding your partner in the hallways? It's not a purposeful snub, it's just that after such raw intimacy, you're not sure how to act in less intimate surroundings, so you punt. That's sort of the way we felt, Augie and Ben and I, the first couple of days after getting away with the money. The three of us had crossed a line together and we weren't sure how to behave with each other thereafter. Maybe it was simple awkwardness, or maybe we were trying to cover our tracks, make ourselves less believable as a criminal crew, but it felt to me like some deeper chasm had opened. It was as if each of us was a mirror for the other's soul and we suddenly didn't like what we saw.

So we were finding fewer reasons to hang out together as the saga of the Grubbins house played out for all of Pitchford to follow. The day after the police swarmed along Henrietta Road, the DA announced a drug seizure of epic proportions and flashed pictures of the haul on all the television stations. Tony Grubbins was sent to juvie in a different part of the state. Derek Grubbins was arrested at his jamboree, extradited to Pennsylvania, and sent to jail, directly to jail, without ever passing home. The Grubbins house was seized by the state and the whole aftermath looked to be as clean as we could have hoped, until the weirdness began.

First, the neighborhood was infested with motorcyclists, Devil Rams buzzing through the streets of Pitchford like wasps, eyeing everyone with suspicion. Whenever I heard the whine of a motorcycle engine I ducked inside the house, hoping to avoid getting caught by one of those maniacs with a guilty look splashed across my face. Then the empty Grubbins house was broken into, not once but repeatedly, over and again, as if something was being desperately searched for. The place would be plagued by break-ins for months, for years actually, as first the motorcycle gang, and later treasure seekers, sought out the missing money.

But the burglaries didn't stop at the Grubbins house. There were rumors that the cops who had found the drugs had stolen boatloads of cash, rumors that spread like wildfire throughout the community and were reported in the press. And the rumors only increased when the houses of a number of cops were broken into and their families violently threatened by gangbangers with bandannas over their faces. No one was seriously hurt, thank God, but we three knew what it was about, that the gang was blaming the cops, just as Ben had expected when he made the call. There was cash in the crawl space, the police showed up, the cash went missing; what other conclusion could be drawn?

Eventually the state police were called in to calm the waters. The cops who found the stash were questioned by the attorney general's office and publicly cleared. At the same time, the press reported an all-out search for an elderly male who made the 911 call to the police. It was all such a mess, no one could figure out what the hell was going on. No one but Augie, Ben, and me. Though we never talked about it, not even when we were alone. It was all too big, too scary, we were too afraid of being overheard, afraid of being seen even whispering one to the other. All we said when we passed each other in the hallway was a soft "Still here," which was both mordant as hell and amazingly comforting.

The first time we lit up after, together, in the woods by the cherry tree, we were all so freaked about the possibility of lurkers that we ended up not talking at all. No snarky opinions about movies, no rude fantasizing about girls. Sitting in silence as our brains got wacked by the weed, it was like getting high alone. Even so, when the drug hit I was filled with such an acute paranoia—every corner of my body screaming in panic—that the whole experience was far more terrifying than sublime. In every brush of the wind through the trees I heard the roar of motorcycles. After a few more attempts, where I ended up curled in a petrified ball as the world rose up high to crush me, I stopped smoking weed altogether, and so did Ben. And Augie, not willing to quit getting high, started hanging out with a different group of heads, using, according to the rumors, far stronger stuff.

And then the newspapers reported that Derek Grubbins had turned state's evidence and was spilling all he knew about the drug operation of the Devil Rams. Half the cyclists were arrested based on his testimony and the other half stopped hanging around Pitchford. The Grubbins house was finally sold to a family named Morris, and Pitchford gossip moved from the theft to more intriguing matters, such as the Madigans and the Digbys switching partners like at a square dance. Everything calmed, leaving the three of us one final task.

"What are you doing?" said Ben.

"I'm counting up my share," said Augie.

"What does that matter?" said Ben. "We're going to be here all night as it is; just help us split it up and get on home."

"I want to know how much we have."

"A heap," I said. "We've each got a goddamned heap of money."

We were in Augie's living room with the doors locked, the curtains drawn, the lights low, the furniture arrayed around us as a shield, and music playing loudly from the stereo to drown out any of our words that might actually reach past the front door. Augie's parents were in Pittsburgh for a couple of nights as his father received treatment for the kidney ailment that would eventually kill him, which would have been a perfect excuse for a party, but that night we three were attending to more serious business. Ben and I were taking scoops of money out of the buckets and dividing them into equal piles of three. Even with all the bundled bills, the job wasn't as easy as you would think. Some of the bundles had a few bills missing that we had to account for, and there were a lot of loose bills, too, hundreds and fifties and piles of twenties and tens, so we had to go through every bill to make sure the division was even. Ben and I figured it was more important to get our splits exact than to get an exact count. We could estimate the thing pretty damn well, and the numbers were boggling.

"I want to know exactly," said Augie. "Unlike you dolts, I've got plans for my share."

Ben lifted his chin and calmly put down the stack of bills he was working on. "What kind of plans?"

"You know, bub," said Augie. "Plans."

"No," said Ben. "I don't know. What plans could you mean other than burying your share back in your crawl space like we all agreed?"

"That would be such a waste," said Augie. "I've been reading up on this money shit at the library."

"You've been in the library?" said Ben. "That's enough of a story right there to make the *Daily News*. What did you do, Augie, ask the librarian for everything she had on what to do with a huge haul of stolen cash?"

"I'm just getting myself informed about handling money, now that I've got me some. Inflation's almost five percent, man, and it was double that just a couple years ago. Do you know what inflation can do to cash? And the market's shooting up like a rocket ship. We're losing value every day this crap sits in a hole. But there are banks in the islands that will keep our IDs safe and pay interest to boot. We can make stock plays from there."

"Stock plays."

"Have you guys ever heard of this guy called Buffett?"

"Jimmy Buffett?

"Don't be stupid."

"But you're the one talking about islands, right?"

"Yeah, man. Aruba."

"And you're going to take your share down to Aruba?" said Ben.

"Or Bermuda," said Augie. "Or the Caymans. We could make a load and at the same time grab a couple days at the beach to work on our tans. You need to think these things through, Ben. You need to be smart. I'll take your split there, too, if you want."

"And what if they catch you at the border with all that cash?"

"They won't."

"And what if it gets in the papers that you had in your possession hundreds of thousands of dollars? What do you think happens to us?"

"It's my money."

"The minute you get picked up, Augie, we're all dead. You can't just think about yourself anymore."

"No one else is thinking about me, that's for sure."

"I hear you've been shoving coke up your nose like it's Afrin."

"Who told you that?"

"Is it true? Have you been taking the money and spending it on coke?"

"No. Ben, man. No. I haven't spent a penny. I haven't even looked at the buckets since we buried them. I swear."

"Then how are you getting the shit?"

"I just am."

"How?"

"What are you now, a fucking lawyer?"

"You took some from the stash, didn't you?" I said.

Augie looked down at the sheet on which he had been jotting his numbers. "Maybe," he said.

"How much?"

"One brick when we were in the crawl space. Jesus, it was just sitting there. It's high-grade stuff, boys. Zoom. And I'm willing to share."

Ben turned to me. "We should never have trusted him."

"He'll be okay," I said.

"As soon as the coke he stole runs out, he's going to buy more and kill us all."

"You know," said Augie, "I'm right in the room with you."

"I don't know if we should divide this or burn it," said Ben.

"Hey, Ben," said Augie. "Fuck you."

"You already have," said Ben, shaking his head. "Every time you snort up with the stolen coke, my asshole hurts."

There was a long silence as Ben and Augie stared at each other, something ugly sparking in the air between them.

"When the hell did we become old farts?" said Augie finally.

"The day we stole a million dollars from a motorcycle gang," said Ben. "From here on in, being old farts is the only thing going to keep us alive."

It took us a couple of hours to do the whole split-up thing, Ben and I working while Augie did the calculation. And at the end, with Augie's money in a leather gym bag, Ben's in a locked wooden chest, and mine in a green metal toolbox, one of the few things of my father's that my mother had taken when we moved, only a final twenty lay alone in the middle of the floor. And we each had, by Augie's count, $424,390.

The new Springsteen was out, and Augie was playing it on his stereo, and just as we finished the split Springsteen called out the "Two, three, four" for "Bobby Jean." Tired as we were from the job, and hyped as we were from what we had pulled off, and scared as we were by the real threat to our lives that still lurked outside, we couldn't help ourselves. First I got up and started hopping around, and then Augie, and then finally Ben struggled to his feet. And together, the three of us, without even thinking about it, started dancing. "Bobby Jean" is a great song about old friends who drift apart, and the chord changes in the tune itself are so classic they radiate a sad nostalgia even as they're rocking out. There is a point where Bruce calls out, "You hung with me when all the others turned away, turned up their noses," and the three of us looked at each other and started laughing.

When the song was over we jumped around some more and looked at all our money. It was a great moment, really, between old friends who had fallen into an opportunity and run with it right off a cliff. The last great moment we ever had together. And it felt, yeah, it felt the way it felt before it all happened, and we were the best of friends, and all we wanted was to get trashed together in the woods and keep the future at bay. And even though Bruce was now singing "I'm Goin' Down," we didn't care. We were back, together again, at least for a moment.

When we fell down to the floor, still laughing, Augie pulled out a joint. Ben and I begged off and watched as Augie lit up, dragged deep, held the smoke inside until it almost smothered him.

"Where are you going to hide your share, J.J.?" said Augie after he exhaled. "In your own crawl space?"

"I don't know," I said. "I haven't decided yet."

"What about you, Ben? Going to bury it in a time capsule, only to be opened when you're ninety?"

"I'll put it someplace safe."

"Where?"

No answer.

Augie took another drag, stared for a moment at the roach in his hand. "What's the matter, boys," he said with that constipated voice that comes from talking without letting the smoke out of your lungs, "don't trust your old friend Augie?"

Neither Ben nor I said anything, which was an answer right there.

"It's better if none of us knows where the others put the money," said Ben. "If one of us gets picked up, the other two are going to have to run for it. This way, we'll be able to run with our nest eggs intact."

"I thought we swore to be loyal forever."

"This just makes it easier to keep our promises."

"So that's the way it's going to be?"

"That's the way it's going to be, son," said Ben.

"And you, J.J.?"

"It's safer," I said.

"I get it," said Augie. "I understand perfectly."

"Don't be a douche bag," I said. "It's safer for all of us."

"Yeah, yeah. If I were you guys, I wouldn't trust me either," said Augie. "All right, no hard feelings, it's all cool. You guys want to do a line to seal the deal?"

"Got to go," said Ben.

"Me, too," I said. "It's late."

"What about this last twenty?" said Augie, pointing to the orphan bill in the middle of the floor.

"Keep it," said Ben as he and I both stood.

"No," said Augie, "fair is fair. I wouldn't want you boys to think I was cheating you." He took the bill, ripped it into three, and gave us each a piece, leaving the last third for himself. "Fifty years from now, we'll tape it all together and buy each other a beer."

"Sounds good," I said.

"Then I guess this is it." Augie stared down at the joint smoldering in his fingers. "Keep in touch."

We should have shared Augie's joint just then, or done a line in solidarity, we should have sworn our fealty one to the others one more time, we should have done something other than what we did, which was just to leave Augie alone with his pile of easy money and his burning joint and what was left of his stolen stash of coke. Was the future inevitable from that point on?

I think maybe it was, because after that night the three of us, we kept drifting further apart. Augie found a whole new group to get trashed with, along with a whole new bouquet of ever-more-powerful drugs. And Ben, strangely, started playing the full jock role, banging down beers with the rest of the football team, acting like a jerk in the hallways. And I had a new landscape to explore, someplace foreign and lush and absolutely intoxicating, the landscape of Madeline Worshack.

I loved Madeline Worshack. I loved her eyes, her lips, the way her limbs draped around me when we had sex in my bed while my mom was at work. She was everything I ever wanted. I began to make plans for our future. I looked teary-eyed at old couples I passed on the street. I felt sorry for the rest of the world. I was besotted, which should have been warning enough.

And then I felt the knife at my throat.

"Where is it, motherfucker?"

I was in my bedroom, in my bed, in the imperfect pitch of the night, pinned down by some foul-smelling monster while another, skinnier bastard pricked my neck with a knife. This was the stuff of my recurring nightmares, and so it took a moment to understand that this was no paranoid bad dream; this was real as steel.

"Whah?" I said. "Huh?"

"Where is it, dirtbag?"

"Who are you?" I said, though by then I had a pretty good idea.

With the streetlights bleeding in the single window facing the street, I could make out some details. The fat guy's hair was gray and wiry as it poured out of a bandanna wrapped around his face.

He had arms like pistons, a gut like a medicine ball, bad skin, bad breath, a scar on his forehead, the smell of a dog. The skinny guy with the knife had a similar bandanna. He looked even older, and yelled at me with the high-pitched screech of an angry crow.

"Tell me where the fuck it is," he said, "or you'll be carrying your head around in a suitcase."

I would learn later that it wasn't just those two that had broken into my house. There was another in my mother's bedroom to keep her quiet. And there were two more going methodically through the house, room by room, top to bottom, pulling up carpets, stabbing cushions, dragging bureaus and cabinets away from our walls, digging up the crawl space, tossing the place as if our Pitchford split-level was rife with hidden corridors and recessed wall safes.

"What are you looking for?" I said, even though I knew. "What do you want?" I said, even as I was certain they wanted nothing so much as my death.

"Our money, motherfucker," said Knife-Man.

"What money?"

"Did you think you could just waltz away with it?" he said. "Did you think we'd just let it go?"

"I don't have anything."

"Too bad, Frenchy," he said as he started sawing.

There was blood and there was terror. I tried to scoot back to escape the knife, but the fat guy grabbed my hair, and Knife-Man gave me another saw, and my blood spurted. Jesus Christ, my blood spurted. And I could feel my life spurting away with it. I slapped my hand over the cut to stop the bleeding and through the slickness of the blood I felt how wide was the wound. Damn wide. I was going to die, I was sure of it. Molten lead poured into my stomach. I wanted Augie and Ben, I wanted my mommy, I wanted my daddy, I wanted to cry.

But at the same time I was holding back the blood and the tears, part of me had floated away into a cloud of angry reason.

The skinny little demon had called me Frenchy. No one called me Frenchy anymore, no one except for Tony Grubbins. That son of a bitch. He had thrown a football at my face. He had killed my dog. He had beat on me and ripped me off and stolen my change at lunch. And now, guessing I might somehow be responsible for his tragedy, he had sent these two maniacs to slit my throat. My anger gave me a shot of calm. It didn't matter that he was right, Tony wasn't getting the money from me, no way, no how. It wasn't in the house, I wasn't that stupid, and I sure as hell wasn't going to tell these cretins where it was.

"I don't have your money," I said with more bitterness than I intended, all the while just trying to gain some time.

"But you know where it is," said Knife-Man.

"The cops took it."

"But you got your share."

"Why would I get a share? Who the hell am I? Whatever Tony told you is a lie."

Knife-Man's eyes narrowed at the name.

"He just wants you to kill me for him," I said.

"Why would anyone want to kill a dickwad like you?"

"Because he hates me. He killed my dog."

"Your dog?"

"He poisoned him," I said. "My little dog."

And then it hit me with the force of truth. My dog was dead, and I was going to die, and my mother was going to die, and so was Ben and so was Augie, and all of it was my fault, my fault, all of it. If I hadn't poked Tony Grubbins like a bear in his cage, if I hadn't broken into his house just for the hell of it, if I hadn't stolen a boatload of hot cash from his demonic brother, if I had been a decent and kind kid instead of a ruthless pot-smoking thief, none of this would have happened. And Rex would be happily bouncing around. And Augie, Ben, and I would still be best of friends. And my mother and I would be facing a tuna casserole instead of death. The tears that I had been fighting suddenly rushed out of me, just as the blood had rushed out of my throat a few moments before, and my calming anger dissolved, and my emotions took me over the edge.

I started to cry, but not quietly, not with the dignity of a partisan facing his death. Instead I wept, I sobbed, I wailed like a kid on Santa Claus's lap. And when I noticed my attackers cringe and step away from my blubbering, I cried even harder, keening as I pulled my legs to my chest, making myself seem smaller, younger, as unthreatening as a colicky babe.

Later, when the cops came and looked over what was left of our house, and questioned me and my mother as we waited for the ambulance, my pride stopped me from mentioning the crying jag that saved my life. I didn't tell them how terrified Knife-Man looked as I continued to sob, how he backed away, how I heard him say to the fat mountain of a man who smelled like a dog that there was no way this kid had the balls to even steal a pair of socks. Instead I simply described my attackers to the cops and detailed the bare facts of our confrontation. And as I repeated the demands for the money, the officers looked at each other knowingly.

"I can't stay here anymore," said my mother to one of the police officers, a cigarette lit to calm her nerves, a steadying drink in her hand. "This neighborhood is going to hell."

"We're doing what we can, ma'am."

"First a drug ring being run out of the house across the street, and then those motorcycle freaks cruising the neighborhood, and now this. Where have you been? Thank God I'm only renting. We're getting out of here. I hear Florida is nice."

"Yes, ma'am," said the cop, before turning to me. "Any idea why they might have thought you had the money?"

"We live across the street from the drug house. I suppose that's reason enough for them," I said, as I pressed a bloodied towel against my wound. "And I wasn't on the best of terms with the Grubbins kid. Is the missing money really more than a rumor?"

"They sure searched pretty hard for a rumor, didn't they?" said the cop. "They take anything of value from you?"

"We don't have anything of value," I said.

"The TV's still here, I suppose," said my mother. "Thank heaven for that. They could have killed us. I don't know why they didn't kill us."

"You were lucky, that's why," said the cop, looking around at the destruction. "You don't have that money somewhere, do you, son?"

"Me?"

"Just asking."

"If I had it," I said, "would we still be living here?"

The cop laughed, my mother inhaled, an ambulance siren cracked the silent night.

They put twenty-seven stitches in my neck in the emergency room. The knife hadn't gone deep enough to sever anything brutally serious; the spurting blood came from minor blood vessels only. The doctors told me how Knife-Man had missed severing the carotid artery by millimeters, that I didn't know how lucky I was. And lucky was just how I felt, lucky lucky lucky. I always feel lucky when a madman is sawing at my throat. My mother made them get a plastic surgeon before she let anyone stick a sewing needle in her son, but they must have dragged the surgeon out of a bar, what with the jagged scar he left.

Back from the hospital, the ruins of our life piled around us, my mother insisted on leaving Pitchford right then and there, getting in the car and driving south on Route 1 all the way to the end. But I convinced her we should wait until I finished my senior year. I told her senior year was supposed to be the highlight of my life. I wanted to party like a maniac with my friends, go to prom with Madeline Worshack, get into a good college. In a comic turnabout, I convinced my mother that staying in Pitchford was crucial to my making something of my life.

"You owe me this," I said to her, which was a bitter thing to say. But that's just how I felt—she did owe me. And after much argument, she agreed. I didn't tell her that running away like a thief in the night could only raise suspicions. I didn't tell her that if we stayed a little longer despite the danger, I could begin to make the preparations I needed to live a life safely hidden from our pursuers.

And make no mistake, preparations were needed.

My attacker had been brutally on point. I had thought we could just waltz away with it, that they would just let it go. I had thought after things had cooled that the three of us would be safe. But the very presence of those thugs in my house was enough to convince me that safety would never be possible.

When we huddled the next day at our cherry tree, me with the thick tape across my neck like some newly formed creation of Dr. Frankenstein, Ben and Augie told me it had been the best thing that could have happened.

"I think we passed some sort of test," said Ben.

"We?" I said.

"They came after us, yes they did, and the saps came up empty," said Augie.

"Us?" I said.

"The lead Tony gave them turned out empty," said Ben. "We're a step closer than we were before."

"Any closer than that and my head would have been lying on the floor."

"You took one for the team, bub," said Augie. "Don't think we're not grateful."

"Grateful it was you and not us," said Ben, laughing.

But I wasn't quite so merry. It was a sweet little fairy tale they were spinning, that we had been looked at and passed over, and it made them feel better, I'm sure, but they hadn't had a knife at their necks.

So I did it on my own, my preparations to start a new life, a life not just miles away from Pitchford, but miles away from who I had been in Pitchford. Even while J.J. Moretti was going through his senior year of high school, taking tests, drinking beer, licking

Madeline Worshack's nipples like each was the tip of a Carvel soft-serve vanilla cone, Jonathon Willing was applying to a host of universities well out of state. A letter from my mother that I forged and a copy of my birth certificate sent to each admissions office was enough to get J.J. Moretti's high-school transcript and recommendations accepted for Jonathon Willing's application. I didn't tell anyone in Pitchford about the name switch, not even Augie and Ben, didn't tell anyone that once J.J. Moretti finally left Pitchford he would disappear completely. The motorcycle madmen had taught me how careful I needed to be.

The only person I was tempted to tell was Madeline, sweet Madeline Worshack, the love of my life. But I decided I couldn't tell her the truth while we were still in Pitchford. Instead I lived like a spy, keeping my secrets, scheming to end up at the same college as Madeline so we could continue to date and then commit our futures one to the other. In an idyllic campus setting, under the leaves of some ancient oak, I would ask her to marry me. And when she said yes, and she would say yes, I would tell her about the money, and about how lovely our lives would be together with the head start the stolen cash would give us. We would be rich, forever, together. Yes, I was that much in love. She applied to Penn State and so did I, though of course I couldn't go there and stay unrecognized. But she also applied to Boston College and so did I. She applied to UVA and to Maryland, to Indiana and Wisconsin, and so did I. How sweet the future would fall upon us, like the dapple of sunlight on the first crisp day of spring.

"We need to talk."

"Why?" I said, as I nuzzled her neck with my teeth. We were parked at the naval air base in Willow Grove a few weeks after my throat was cut. Her skin tasted of licorice, her breast swelled against my palm, I was drunk on her aroma, on the pressing pulse of my own blood. Who the hell wanted to talk?

Which just showed how much I knew.

"I don't understand," I said a few moments later, after my future with Madeline imploded like a dead sun in my chest. "I love you."

"I know you do," she said.

"Then why?"

"Because there's something always coming between us. I don't know what it is, but half the time I'm with you, it's like I'm alone. And the other half you're trying to molest me."

"Like now."

"Stop. J.J., I'm tired of doing all the work in this relationship."

"And yet I'm always the one unhooking your bra."

"I'm serious."

"It's Richie Diffendale, isn't it? He's been sniffing around you like a raccoon in heat."

"It has nothing to do with him."

"Then what is it?"

"It's you," she said. "It's like there's something else in your life that's more important than me. I don't like the competition."

Getting dumped by Madeline hurt worse than the football in my face, than the knife in my throat. But in a way it was a relief, too, because I had my secret and now, with Madeline gone, I didn't ever have to share it with anyone. And I never did, not with any of the girls who left me for the same reasons Madeline left me, not with any friends I ever made other than Augie and Ben, and not with my wife. When it was time to choose, I always chose the secret.

And now, more than twenty years after losing Madeline Worshack, as I headed toward a new and radiant life of unlimited promise, I realized I was making the same damn choice. For I was about to lose all that I loved most in the world, my children and my wife, but the secret, oh, the secret, would forever stay close to my heart.

Old habits die hard.

17. So Long to All That

FINGERED THE SCAR AT MY THROAT AS I DROVE FOR A FINAL time past the illuminated twin lions and into Patriots Landing. The wide streets, the neat lawns and spotless sidewalks, the unbroken white of the curbs that seemed to glow in the night. You don't see curbs like that everywhere, eight inches wide and built to last. They were there before the houses were raised, and they'd be there when the houses tumbled down again. Good, solid, American curbs. I'd miss them.

It had been a good run, the suburban idyll I had created for myself, but it was over now. I could accept that. All along I knew it was a temporary thing. It was my destiny to live my life in phases, with hard curbs between them. There was the Philadelphia Country Club phase, the Pitchford phase, the Wisconsin college-kid phase, and now this. And it had worked out well, the Virginia suburban family-man phase: the house, the car, the wife and kids, golf. Even financially it had worked out well.

At the start, of course, I had been forced to use the Grubbins cash to help pay the outsized mortgage and car payments. But soon after moving to Virginia, and before we actually bought into the development, I quit a low-paying job in the field for which I had trained when a far more lucrative opportunity beckoned. I was offered the chance to become the pied piper of the American Dream, a genie granting wishes on a commission basis, and yes, I said, yes I will, yes. Suited up and buttoned down, I became a broker with the Jefferson Davis Mortgage Company of Richmond, Virginia.

Whatever hand you wanted, I could deal it: low FICO, no doc, interest-only thirties, interest-only forties, pick-a-pay if you will, and the ever-popular ARM hybrids like the classic 2/28. And you needn't worry about any unfortunate adjustment, because before the hammer dropped we could fix your credit rating, tap the growing equity in your lovely new home, and get you into something more manageable, with the not-inconsiderable fees and costs rolled into the refi so out-of-pocket cost was a big fat zero. It couldn't have been easier.

At the same time I was banking my commissions at Jefferson Davis, Caitlin had traded the kindergarten classroom for her real-estate license, earning commissions of her own as she led others into realizing their own slick suburban dreams. Together we were quite a team, she providing the inspired settings for a gracious new life, me providing the easy money that allowed almost anyone to pay for it. We churned our way from development to development, making more money than the Pitchford kid had ever dreamed. With our new incomes, and by tapping the spiraling value of our own house with a series of ever-larger mortgages, we were able to live appropriately beyond our means without recourse to the stolen cash.

But that was all over now. Times had changed, the real-estate market had dried up, I had been downsized, my family life had soured, Augie was dead, and the bullheaded thugs were on their way. The mortgage on my life had adjusted and my equity had turned negative. It was time to check out of Patriots Landing and enter the next phase of my life.

I could see it all so clearly, the mellow expat existence. Moseying through the Caribbean with Harry, sailing from sunset to sunset, drinking rum, grooving to the island beat, combing through the island women, dark-skinned natives, young working women on vacation, wealthy divorcées looking for a second chance, or a third. Margaritaville, baby. All I needed was to hold on for another twelve hours and I was on my way.

As I drove through the development I couldn't help but notice the FOR SALE signs sprinkled among the lovely lawns bordered by those solid curbs, not as conspicuous a presence as in Augie's development, but there nonetheless. I had brokered the mortgages for many of those houses, I knew the stories behind those signs. Layoffs, depleted savings, 401(k)s in the crapper, maxed-out credit lines and negative equity in homes that were sold as the most secure of investments. Far too well I understood the emotions those signs represented, the pain and anguish, the embarrassment, the uncertainty and fear, the outright sense of failure. I wasn't the only one at Patriots Landing entering a new phase in my life, I was just doing it with a little more panache.

Though the tasteful accent lighting was all aglow at our house, the lights inside were off, the doors locked, the family tucked in for the night. I edged my car into the circular drive and was careful in closing the car door, to keep from waking the kids. I patted one of the pillars as I walked to the front door; it no longer felt warm and solid beneath my hand, more like a hollow piece of artifice than something firm enough to keep the very sky from falling. I slipped my key silently into the lock.

The last night of my suburban life. My mind had slipped already into the next phase, the escape, the hiding, the sail south, the sweet life of rum and sex. My future was more real to me than my present. Now it was like I was walking through a ghost mansion, something cold, from the air-conditioning or from its newly spectral quality I couldn't tell, something already dead and vanishing. I put my keys and wallet in the kitchen, as I always did. I rose up the stairs and slid along the long hall without making a sound. I was as much a ghost as the house.

I looked in on my daughter, asleep in her room, still painted the same purple as when she was six, still plastered with pages torn out of *People* and *Teen Beat*, even though she had outgrown the tween icons years ago. She had been the cutest little girl, Shelby, hugging me when I came home from work, dancing on my shoulders in the club pool. But that girl was gone, replaced with this hostile thing who texted her disdain for me with her dancing thumb. We had no idea how to talk to each other anymore, and she was running so hard from me she was bound to hurt herself. She'd be better off without me.

I stepped in, leaned over, gave her a kiss on her cheek. She barely stirred, as if my lips were already vapor.

"Good-bye, sweetheart," I said before the closing the door behind me.

I looked in on my son, a mere hump of bone beneath his blanket. We had rolled on the lawn when he was a toddler, we had tossed the pigskin back and forth on brisk fall days. But Eric had grown and grown distant, he had turned from sports, and the things that bound us together had fallen to zero as Eric vanished into the screen of his computer. I was for him now merely a symbol of all the expectations he couldn't, or chose not to, meet. I was a test he would never be able to pass. He'd be better off without me.

I took a step inside to give him a kiss but then stopped. He didn't like it when I kissed him, or hugged him, or showed him any affection.

"Good-bye, champ," I said, simply, before closing the door.

I looked in on my wife, asleep on our bed beneath the sheet twisted like armor around her body. In the rise and fall of her side, the swell of her hips, the long line of her legs, it was like I was staring at a memory. I had the urge to crawl in beside her, to pull her to me, to put my lips on her neck, my leg over her hip, my hands upon her breasts, to try to stir something that hadn't been stirred in too long a time. Like the old wedding toast: *May you live as long as you want to, may you want to as long as you live.* At one point in our lives it would have ended with the two of us reaching for each other, pulling each other closer, letting our lips and tongues and hands explore one the other. But I knew how it would end now, with her pushing me away, letting the indignation rise in her voice as she told me what I already knew, that she was sleeping and she was tired and I was an inconsiderate jerk. *If I'm asleep, wake me, if I don't want to, make me.* Whatever we had been together once, we weren't anymore. She wanted me out, she wanted her freedom, she wanted a chance for something more than I could give her, and she was right to want it all. She'd be better off without me.

I stared a little longer, then I left the bedroom and headed back down the stairs, through a door in the foyer, and down another set of stairs to our finished basement. A pool table, a bar, a flatscreen, the ubiquitous dartboard, a couple of movie posters picked by Eric (*The Dark Knight Returns* and *Watchmen*).

Through another door lay the unfinished portion of the basement, where the furnace and twin hot-water heaters shared space with a small worktable, a rusted green metal toolbox (yes, that same toolbox), and a heavy wooden chair. I switched on the light, closed the door, retrieved the briefcase from where I had hidden it, and tossed it on the workbench. I opened the toolbox and rummaged around until I found the right kind of screwdriver.

In the back of one of the hot-water heaters was a white metal plate. I took out the screws one at time, carefully placing each removed screw into my pocket, until the plate came loose. Behind the plate was a square of pink fiberglass insulation. I removed the square, leaving a gap between the opening and still more insulation. I rolled up my sleeve and reached down into the warm gap. One by one I pulled out the bundles, baked hot, one by one by one. When they were all out, I placed the square of insulation back into the gap and screwed on the metal plate.

I put the bundles of cash on the workbench, along with the cash I had taken from beneath the floor in Augie's kitchen, and went through it all quickly once, then twice. Something over $260,000. Even after taking out the money Harry would need to buy the boat, I could live quite well in St. Thomas on that, live like a king in Jamaica with that, live like a fucking maharaja in Mexico with that.

From the metal toolbox I lifted out the top tray, loaded haphazardly with screws and nails and small tools. Beneath that was a scattering of larger tools, two hammers, pliers, more screwdrivers, a rasp. I took them all out and stuck a flat screwdriver in a small gap between the floor and the box's side. I wedged out the false floor, revealing a bottom section about two inches deep, empty except for some matches, the pack of cigarettes I had hidden from my kids, a large folding hunting knife with a bone handle, and an envelope with the name Edward Holt scribbled on it. Edward Holt was to be my new name in paradise, and in the envelope were Edward's birth certificate, social security card, passport, driver's license, and a checkbook for a checking account I had set up in Edward's name at a bank in Maryland.

I took out the cigarettes, the matches, the knife, and the envelope, and then placed the money in an even layer about one inch thick across the bottom of the case. It was amazing how something looming so large in my imagination could fit in so little a space. Atop the layer of money I placed the condoms that I had brought home with me from Vegas, the license plates with their magnets still attached, the knife, and the envelope. I then replaced the false bottom, the tools, and the top tray. The latches shut with a satisfying clack.

I sat in the chair facing the water heater, crossed my legs, lit a cigarette. This had been my spot for the last fifteen years, the place I went late at night when everyone else was asleep. I was not a religious man, didn't ever go in much for prayer, but still, somehow, this patch of unfinished basement felt to me as sacred as a church. I would sit here and stare at the hiding place for my stolen cash and commune with my past, plot out my future, play accountant and tally up the gains and the losses. And this was where, lately,

I had taken pencil to paper and tried to figure a way out of my financial mess, adding up my fading assets and growing liabilities, our expected income and outflows, tracing month by month the inevitability of our fall into the financial abyss, even with the cash in the water heater.

But now this phase of my life was over, and this would be my final session in the basement. I was leaving my life for good, tomorrow. I sat, and smoked, and remembered the last time I had left my life for good.

———————✳———————

The U-Haul was loaded, ready to take my mother's stuff down to Florida. She had rented an apartment in Cape Coral, sight unseen, and was already on her way down with the car. She didn't know much about the place, had never actually been there, but it sure sounded good, Cape Coral, like a launching pad to retirement paradise. It had been hard work, throwing boxes and sofas and bed frames onto the back of the truck, but at least I didn't have to lug it all alone. Old friendships might wither and die, but they sure are handy on moving day.

"That's the last," I said.

"Thank God," said Augie. "One more box and I would have had a heart attack. I'm sweating like an Eskimo in Arizona."

"Where'd your mom get so much crap?" said Ben.

"From her crappy life," I said. "I've locked up and slipped the keys in the slot. Time to get the hell out of Dodge."

"Florida sounds sweet," said Ben.

"Not in July."

"Maybe I'll retire there," said Ben.

"Not me," said Augie. "Have you ever noticed, boys, everyone who finds themselves living in Florida ends up dying?"

"But at least they get buried without an overcoat," said Ben. "When are you heading up to Boston, J.J.?"

"Orientation is at the end of August," I said, looking away so they couldn't see my eyes. "I'll probably take the train up or something."

I had told the world of Pitchford I was going to Boston College, but that was just a cover story. If everyone knew where I was going, what good would the name switch have been? Madeline was headed for the University of Maryland and for a moment I imagined going there, too, pressing my case and winning her back, seizing again the future I had glimpsed when our limbs were entwined. But she actually did go to the prom with Richie Diffendale—what secret hoard did he have buried and what did that say about her? With my little stash of cash, I figured I could do better. So when a thick letter from Madison, Wisconsin, arrived at our house addressed to Jonathon Willing, my future was set. That I hadn't told Ben or Augie the truth gnawed at me some, but not enough to blurt it out. *Incognito* meant exactly that.

"What about you, Ben?"

"Training camp starts in two weeks."

"Good luck with that," I said.

Ben winced. Because of his knee, which cut his senior season in half, the top Division I schools had stopped calling, but he had still pulled a scholarship from Lehigh. The pro dreams were gone, thank God, but he would still have to play college ball, at least until his knee gave out for good.

"What about you, Augie?" I said.

"I've got some things working," said Augie.

"You were talking about Penn State Ogontz."

"Next year, maybe. For now I need to stay around my dad for a bit."

"Yeah, I understand," I said.

"I couldn't do school right away, anyhow," said Augie. "I was so sick of high school I almost puked every time I stepped through the doors."

"That's because you were drunk," said Ben.

"How else could I stand it? But you suckers enjoy taking your tests and writing your papers."

"I'm a football player," said Ben. "We pay someone else to write our papers."

Augie patted the side of the U-Haul. "You ever coming back?"

My hand instinctively rose to my neck and I rubbed the scar. It wasn't red and raw anymore, but it was still raised and obvious as hell. I rubbed it constantly, a reminder of what awaited me if I failed in my precautions.

"I don't think so," I said.

"So this is it."

"Yeah," I said, kicking at the cement. "Good-bye, Pitchford. If you ever see me back on Henrietta Road, you have my permission to hit me on the head with a baseball bat."

"Even if you're gone for good, J.J., we can still get together," said Ben. "Why the hell not? It's not like we won't be able to afford it. Maybe New York, maybe Mexico."

"Mexico," I said, nodding.

"Or Las Vegas," said Augie. "If we can't get in trouble there, boys, we're not trying. And the whores are legal, too."

"Some of us don't need to buy it," said Ben.

"Talk to me after your knee explodes and the cheerleaders stop jumping your bones," said Augie.

Ben thought about it for a moment. "Vegas, then."

I glanced at my watch. "It's a long drive and I want to make some distance before dark." I opened the truck door, hopped up into the cab. "We'll get together for a celebration when we can."

"Next week, boys?" said Augie.

"Not quite," I said. "It's still too soon to start spending, don't you think?"

"We need to keep in touch," said Ben.

"Sure," I said.

"No," said Ben, lowering his chin in seriousness as he lowered his voice. He leaned toward the open truck door. "I don't mean, like, saying we'll have lunch and then letting it pass. I mean keep closely in touch."

"I don't know, man," I said. "It might be hard."

"I'm not talking long heart-to-hearts. Just check in, until we're certain everything is over. Just to know that there have been no more break-ins and that we're all doing okay."

"Like saying, 'Still here,' right?" said Augie.

"Exactly," said Ben. "And so we can pass on anything we see or hear that worries us."

"I get it."

"The thing is," said Ben, his gaze scanning back and forth across Henrietta Road, "we're connected by what we did. It's like a cord between us. We'll always be connected."

I looked down at my two friends and was startled to realize that I was sad. We had gone our separate ways in the last year, but still I sensed even then that I would never have better friends than these two.

"Okay," I said. "We'll keep in touch."

"Since Augie's sticking around, J.J., why don't you and I call him? Once a week, just to say hello. You'll be our intermediary, okay, Augie?"

"You guys sure you want to trust a dopehead like me as the middleman?" said Augie.

"Sure we do," said Ben.

"Absolutely," I said, and Augie beamed at the responsibility in a way that made me feel like a creep.

"Okay," said Augie. "Once a week. You can get me at home, at least until my old man kicks it. Then I think I'll scope out Vegas."

"Just don't start having too much fun without us." I shut the door, leaned out the open window. "I've got to go. It's a long drive."

"We did it, didn't we?" said Ben softly.

"Yes we did," I said.

"Jesus," said Augie. "I don't know if it's the best thing I'll ever pull in my life, but if it is, that's okay with me."

I looked at them both for a moment and my eyes grew teary as I found myself overwhelmed by sorrow, not just because I was leaving them, the best friends of my life, but also because I was leaving my childhood, leaving Pitchford. Figure that out if you want—I still can't. But I opened the door and jumped down and gave them each a hug, Ben huge and solid like a great brown bear, and Augie thin, nervous, wriggling in my arms like a fish on a hook.

And then I hopped back into the U-Haul and drove off, away from Henrietta Road for what I knew would be the very last time, waving once as I made the turn like a goddamn movie hero on his horse. And quick as that, I was gone. But not heading straight for the highway, not yet, at least.

I took a left, and then another, and then I weaved along until I pulled into a small, barely used road that ran along the far edge of a grove of woods. I parked by the side of the road, opened the back of the truck, took out a shovel I had slipped into the corner, and headed into the trees.

I was walking through our woods, just hitting them from the other end. It wasn't long before I found our clearing, surrounded by oaks, with the ruined stone walls and the cherry tree that had miraculously grown within the old building's perimeter. The tree was sickly even when I first came upon it; now its bark was split, the wood peeking through was a drawn gray and infested with ants, its limbs were as leafless and dead as the arms of a corpse. All around the tree, on the stone remaining from the structure, was the ragged graffiti we had scrawled over the last eight years. AI RULES. TG SUCKS COCK. BP—89. GOD MADE WEED/IN GOD WE TRUST. JJ ♥ MW. FUCK THE WORLD. I found a rock at the base of the tree with its own rough lettering: REX—RIP. I shoved the rock aside and started digging.

The dirt was softer than you might have expected. It wasn't long before I found the blanket I had buried there eight years before. The blanket was filthy and tattered but still intact. Inside was a bundle of bones and pale white hair. I pulled the bundle out and kept digging. A few minutes later I heard the lovely scrape of metal on metal.

With the bones of my dog back in the grave, and the stone marker back in its place, I gripped the handle of my father's green toolbox, encrusted now with dirt and rust, and headed back to the truck. J.J. Moretti was as dead as his dog; it was time for Jonathon Willing to begin his life anew, free of the past, free of the fears, with nothing but glorious opportunity ahead of him, and rich as a goddamned king.

As I took a deep, satisfying drag from the cigarette in the basement of my George Washington at Patriots Landing, I remembered the emotions that had coursed through me then, relief and hope and possibility pure, like a clean bright light had washed out all the imperfections of my life. That my future had turned out not quite so rich didn't diminish the power of that moment. And I was feeling some of those very same emotions now as the remainder of my stolen cash rested in the hidden compartment of my father's green metal toolbox and I faced another escape that would save both my life and my family's financial future. But I was also mourning the inevitable losses that had stacked up over the years: a failed marriage, an estrangement from my best friends, Augie's murder, and now, worst of all, the necessary abandonment of my family. And so considering all I had gained and all it had cost me, the question had to be asked:

Was it worth it?

Was it ever.

And it wasn't about the money, or only about the money. That moment when Ben and Augie and I had seized our opportunity was the bravest of my life, the boldest, and, in its way, the truest expression of the dark anarchy at the root of my soul. Everything before was as if it never existed, everything after paled in comparison. As my life deteriorated here, as my marriage crumbled and my kids turned hostile and my business disappeared and my equity cratered, the only thing that stayed solid and reliable was that moment.

And it hadn't just changed my life, it had guided it, too. I had learned to trust it and in that trust it had given me everything. It told me to change my name and go to Wisconsin because Wisconsin was safely away from anything Pitchford, and it was in Wisconsin that I met Caitlin. It led me here, to Patriots Landing, because here I could be anonymous and safe and it was here that I raised my children and found a profession that kept me in the lucre until it didn't anymore. And now it was telling me to change directions again and to seize the life for which everyone secretly yearned. To be free and tanned, living on a boat, living where the rest of the world could visit only on rare vacations. And there would be opportunities for me there, too, I had no doubt: new women, piles of money, adventures that would thrill me to the bone.

The opportunity I had seized twenty-five years ago was leading me now to paradise.

I took a deep drag, felt the smoke expand in my lungs, like the hot, fragrant air of the tropics. Caitlin and I had vacationed in Jamaica before Eric was born. The jungle there was too fertile to control, towers of mahogany and rosewood marching across dense mountainsides, greenery spilling down the cliffs in luxuriant waves of orchid and fern, vines reaching across the rugged roadways and past stands selling breadfruit and plantains, pineapple sliced before your eyes with heavy machetes. The verdant riot fell through the valleys, collapsed alongside breathtaking waterfalls, twisted beside still lagoons before again tumbling down in a great uprising of life toward the brilliant turquoise of the Caribbean Sea.

You know what they could have used down there? Good curbing. Like the curbs we had at Patriots Landing, meaty and thick, impervious to the wild imperfections of the lawns they restrained or the random weight of a badly parked truck.

With the back of my hand I wiped a tear from my eye.

God, I would miss those curbs.

18. Last Sunday

I COULDN'T DO IT.

"Well, of course you couldn't," said Harry. "I knew it from the start."

"That makes one of us."

"But that's always the way, isn't it? The last thing any of us ever sees clearly is his own reflection in the mirror."

"So what do you see when you see me?"

Harry was leaning over the rear of the *Left Hook*, holding my boat fast to his with a grappling hook, speaking a little too loudly, which was his way. He appraised me for a moment, as if I were a piece of beef in a butcher's counter. "A bleeder, with slow hands and sloppy footwork. A tin can full of tomatoes, sure. But not a runner."

Which meant only that Harry was a hell of a lot more perceptive than I had been, because I saw me as a sprinter, pure and simple.

At the time of my planned demise, we had met up in the secluded cove on the James, sheltered by overgrown gorse and thick rafts of pine, the spot I had chosen to take the first steps of my escape. I would slice my arm, spill gouts of blood over the wood and cushions of my boat, put a dent in the boom with a coconut covered with my blood and bits of my hair, capsize my daysailer, and push it out into the main current of the river. The boat would flow downstream, an accident scene waiting to be discovered, while I rode upstream aboard Harry's old wooden fisher.

I hadn't known for sure exactly what I would do when Harry finally showed, but as soon as I saw his boat, with its filthy blue hull, its cramped white cabin, the orange rubber bumpers hanging off the side like huge versions of the red pimple balls we played with on Henrietta Road, I knew I couldn't simply leave it all behind. The tears over the wondrous curbs at Patriots Landing were only the first clue. That very morning, with every step I had taken toward my escape I had felt ever more rooted to my life, ever more possessed by it, even with all its flaws.

Caitlin was already at the table when I entered the kitchen, the coffee was already brewed, the *Times-Dispatch* was already spread out on the island with the sudoku completed, the air was already thick with hostility, well earned and strangely comforting in its familiarity.

"When did you get in?" she said without looking up.

"Late."

"You solve all his problems?"

"Not really."

"Par for the course, right?"

"Are you blaming me for the recession, too?"

"Thad drove me home."

"Good old Thad," I said.

"Thad says you're going fishing this afternoon."

"Maybe."

"Just be sure to explain to the kids why you keep running away from them. I'm taking a class at the gym this morning."

"Good idea," I said.

She looked up at me, finally. "I'm sorry about Augie."

"Yeah."

"But it doesn't change our situation. You know what we talked about, that thing."

"That thing, yeah."

She looked down again, as if it had been the most casual of references. "Maybe sooner rather than later, okay?"

"Sure."

That *thing*. Such an impersonal word to apply to separation, divorce, financial desolation, a cheap apartment at the rathole off the highway dubbed Divorcé Estates for all the kicked-out, locked-out men who lived there, Swanson frozen dinners, every other weekend looking for something, anything, to do with the kids, the soporific comfort of ball games on TV, the fruitless hopes of Match.com. My wife lifted up her mug and took a sip, still looking down at the paper, and in that simple gesture I saw the whole arc of her life with me: the young and insecure college girl she had been, the girl who had loved me truly, and the beautiful and confident woman she was now, the woman who finally had no more use for her husband.

I could win her back, with enough time and enough roses, I was sure of it. It would be hard, impossible almost after the inevitable damage of a seventeen-year marriage, but I would have liked to stick around and try. I stared as she hopped off the stool, put her mug in the sink, grabbed her purple yoga mat from off the table.

"If the kids get up, feed them," she said before heading out to the garage without so much as a wave. As the door closed behind her, I was surprised to find myself tearing up again.

I gained a grip and finished the coffee, glanced at the paper, and then ran off to the club for a quick round of golf. The last thing I wanted was to smack a golf ball around, but Thad and Charles were expecting me and I didn't want anything to seem out of the ordinary on Jonathon Willing's final day on earth. Thad, Charles, and I played golf most every Sunday. We weren't overly competitive, but we knew what was what between us. Charles, a mildly successful painter supported by his lawyer spouse, had the best golf game; I had the prettiest wife; Thad, with Campbell car dealerships all over the peninsula, had the most money. All of which meant that Thad, no matter what we shot on Sundays, was always the big winner of the three.

As my finances had deteriorated, so had my game, and golf had become something to be endured. But standing on the tee of a difficult par three that overlooked the wide James River, I imagined myself sailing down that selfsame river with Harry, sailing down that river for good, never to return to that course, that neighborhood, that life, and I felt my eyes getting wet all over again.

"Are you okay, Jon?" said Charles. "What's going on?"

"Nothing," I said. "Something flew in my eye."

"You just sobbed," said Thad. "What flew into your eye, a bat?"

"I didn't sob."

"Yes, you did," said Thad. "Didn't he?"

"He's two down and slicing like a ninja," said Charles. "If I were Jon, standing on the tee with all that water on the right, I'd be sobbing, too."

"Maybe you ought to use a range ball, Jon."

"It's just so beautiful," I said.

"What?"

"This hole."

"It's gorgeous, all right," said Thad. "Simply breathtaking. Now hit the fucking ball."

And I did, right into the water.

"Good," said Charles. "Now you have something to cry about."

Later, back at the house, after I had looked around a final time and loaded up the car with my fishing gear and the green metal toolbox, I called out for my children.

"Anyone want to go fishing?"

No answer. It wasn't a surprise; in fact, I was fully expecting their silence, counting on it, actually. Though at one point they had each looked forward to their little trips on my little boat, that point had long passed.

"Eric?"

"Forget about it," he shouted down from his computer.

"I promise not to talk."

"Will you promise not to breathe?"

"I guess you're still mad," I said. Then I called out, "Shelby?"

"You've got to be kidding," Shelby said as she passed me on her way from our vaulted family room to the kitchen.

"Why?" I said, following her. "Come on. It will be fun."

"You're going fishing, Dad. I don't eat meat, and I don't approve of one living thing killing another living thing for food."

"Like a tomato?"

"I won't ever participate in the barbaric hunt for a living sentient creature just so you can fillet it and fry it."

"You don't have to worry, I never catch anything anyway."

"Wouldn't it be fairer to fish for sharks while swimming? That way they could hunt you while you hunt them."

"But not as tedious and unrewarding. Come on, sweetie, keep your old man company as he flails around on his boat."

"I'll find something a little more entertaining," said Shelby, her attention now on her phone, "liking sticking pickles in my ear." She gave me a dismissive wave of her hand, and then she stopped her texting and looked up at me. "Dad, are you crying?"

"No," I said, quickly wiping my eyes.

"Jeez, Dad," she said, giving me a strange look as she passed me. "If it means that much to you, make Eric go."

But I couldn't, could I? That would ruin everything. So I simply gave Shelby a final, lingering look (oh, how lovely at that moment) and went out to my car, drove out of the development, and headed to my boat. I loaded my fishing gear and the toolbox, pulled the engine to life, took the boat out on the river, and headed upstream, to my spot, and waited. And waited. Harry was late, but that was okay. I lit a cigarette and the smoke rose to my eyes and I teared up as I waited.

And then I saw the *Left Hook* power into the cove and it hit me like a fist in the face. I wasn't going anywhere on that battered old boat. My life had gone into the crapper and I was in mortal danger and still I wasn't going to end up on a sailboat in the Caribbean. For the first time since that night so long ago in the Grubbins house, I wasn't going to let the money shove me around. I wasn't going to be chased away from my wife, my kids, my family, my life, at least not without a fight.

"That's the spirit, Johnny," said Harry, lighting up a cigarette of his own. "Give 'em heck."

"I'll try."

"You'll do more than try," said Harry. "It's always the pug with something worth fighting for that wins it in the end. Like that ham hock Braddock with the wife and kids. He had nothing but need going for him, and he took down Baer. But look at all you got, Johnny: your family, your kids, that house you're so proud of."

"Don't forget my boat."

"I was being polite. But the wife and them kids, no one could desert a family like that."

"My father could," I said.

"But not you, Johnny."

"No, not me."

But it wasn't because I thought Caitlin and Shelby and Eric needed me that I was staying. Just then, with all my problems, both psychological and financial, not to mention the peril I was exposing them to with my very presence, they truly would be better off without me. And the million dollars in insurance sure would come in handy come college time. And yet still I couldn't leave them. I loved them all: my lovely wife, despite all that had come between us; my sweet daughter, despite her piercings and hostility; my boy, especially with that swing of his, flailing like a flounder at the plate. They were my anchor in the meandering sea of existence. I couldn't imagine living my life without them, no matter how free and seasoned that new life might be.

And it wasn't just my family that I couldn't bring myself to leave, it was Patriots Landing, too. Make fun of it as you will, but this strange existence of mine, built purposely insipid to act as a shield, this almost-satire of the American Dream, was not just a costume I was wearing to keep the bastards off my track. I had played at being the bland suburban dad for so long that what had started as a cover had become my core. And I loved it, every bit of it, the house that was too big, the lawn that was too green, the cars that were too expensive, Little League, Bermuda shorts, lawn mowers and surround sound, a gin and tonic on the back deck with the next-door neighbors as we listened to the crickets and complained about the neighbors on our other side.

Have your say and tell me it wasn't the real world and all I can reply is that it was real enough to me. Was the water in Calcutta wetter than the water that rose like graceful waves of art from my lawn sprinkler? Were the granite faces of the Himalayas any harder than the granite on the island in my kitchen? Patriots Landing may not have been the leafy Main Line suburb of my youth, but it was a pretty good simulacrum of precisely that, and the emotions it pulled out of me were undeniably potent. And however you might self-righteously scoff at my suburban land-scape, don't scoff at those emotions—they were as real as any-thing felt by any landowner in the so-called real worlds of New Delhi or New Orleans.

I loved the wide streets of my development. I loved the smell of Scotts Turf Builder with Plus 2 Weed Control in the morning (it smells of victory over dandelion, chickweed, knotweed, and spurge). I loved the way passersby waved as they passed by, a lit-tle wave expressing perfectly that we had nothing to say to each other and we each were thrilled not to say it. I even loved the stilted chitchat during block parties, the tedious flirting with the unattractive wives in their tennis outfits, the fighting with my children, the complaining about my wife, the slicing of my tee shots, the coaching of my daughter's soccer team. Well, maybe waxing rhapsodic over the soccer thing was going a bit too far, but the other stuff, all of it, had become the warp and the woof of my life and God help me, I loved it.

"Why wouldn't you?" said Harry, still keeping my boat close with the grappling hook. "Of course you would. Why, to think that you'd leave everything behind was pure nonsense. A man needs his home like he needs his family."

"What about you?"

"Alls I got left is my boat and a sister down near Kitty Hawk."

"You need her?"

"I need her like I need a typhoon. I keep telling her being born once is more than enough to suit me. But if I had what you had, Johnny, you couldn't pry me away. That's why all along, all these years, I knew when push it came to shove you'd end up staying."

"And yet you've been taking your retainer each year just so I could rely on you when the moment came."

"A man needs to eat."

"And drink."

"I got a boat, don't I? But tell me one thing, Johnny."

"Okay."

"What the hell's a simulacrum?"

"A dream world," I said.

"Sounds pretty damn good, *simulacrum*, like a coffee cake. So what now? Are you going to fight?"

"I hope not."

"'Cause I can help you there, Johnny. I'm a fighter, you know that. I ever tell you how close I came with Robinson?"

"You told me."

"I had him reeling, the great Sugar Ray. With a couple hard lefts I had him on his heels, and just as I was loading up for one more hook that would have sent him spinning, the son of a bitch—"

"You told me, Harry."

"I guess I might have already. But the point being, you and me together…" He flicked his nose with his thumb.

"Maybe we won't have to," I said. "They're looking for me, sure, but they don't have my name or they would be here already. And I've taken precautions. Maybe they'll give up before they find me."

"Maybe they will."

"Maybe I'll just play it cool, wait and see."

"That's always a good plan, the old wait-and-see when trouble's brewing. I done that a lot myself when things got tight."

"How'd that turn out for you?"

He rubbed the back of his neck. "Not so good, actually."

"Yeah, well, there's always a first for everything. Hold on a bit." I stepped forward on my boat, lifted up one of the seats, pulled out the rusted metal toolbox. "Do me a favor, Harry, and hold this for me. Can you keep it safe?"

"'Course I can."

"It's my life. And I'm trusting you with it."

"You can count on me, Johnny."

"The amazing thing, Harry, is that I know that I can." I hoisted the toolbox over to his boat and watched as he weighed it in his hand for a moment before disappearing to stow it below-decks.

"Done," he said when he climbed back up. "Now what?"

"Now we wait and see if those sons of bitches can find me."

We didn't have to wait for long.

19. A Mr. Clevenger

MR. WILLING?"

"That's right."

"It's Steph? Over at Jefferson Davis Mortgage?"

"Oh, Stephanie, hello. It's nice to hear from you. What's up? Are you guys hiring again?"

"Not yet, Mr. Willing. It's still like a pirate ship here, everyone hunkered down waiting for the next victim to walk the plank. They let go of two more secretaries, Miss Thompson included."

"No."

"Yes. And she's been here longer than anyone. They had a guard walk her out. A guard."

"That's not right. If you talk to her, please give her my sympathy."

"I will. So how are you, Mr. Willing? Did you find anything?"

"Not yet."

"Then I might have some good news. You know how you used to get all kinds of calls from headhunters before everything fell apart?"

"The good old days."

"You just got another call, I think."

"You think?"

"A Mr. Clevenger. He didn't ask for you personally, but he said he was looking for a broker who had a background that seemed to fit you perfectly."

"Fit me?" My ears pricked back like on a horse smelling snake. "How so?"

"He said he was looking for a broker who had been born in Pennsylvania and had gone to the University of Wisconsin. And I seemed to recall you matched up, so I checked your file, and sure enough."

"What did you tell him?"

"I told him we had just the man he was looking for."

"You didn't give him my name or tell him where I lived, did you, Stephanie?"

"I wouldn't do that, Mr. Willing, not without getting in touch with you first. I don't give any personal information over the phone. Especially now. Next thing you know, a client would be showing up at one of the brokers' houses with a gun, and no one needs that."

"No one indeed."

"It's just that he mentioned some Italian name and I told him that wasn't you at all. But this Mr. Clevenger didn't seem discouraged by that. In fact, he seemed pretty excited about getting in touch. He said he had a golden opportunity for you. Maybe it will lead to something, you never know. He left a number." She gave it to me. "Good luck, Mr. Willing. I hope it works out."

"I expect it won't, but thanks," I said before I pressed the END button.

I looked at the number I had scribbled as she talked. A 312 area code. Chicago. The land of the flat, Midwestern vowel. Stephanie was right about one thing: it was a headhunter for sure.

⚌ ✷ ⚌

One winter's day when I was in college, Augie and Ben drove up to Boston to visit me unannounced for some ribald fun. When they found out I wasn't in the city, had never in fact registered at BC, there was a shitstorm, the whole wounded-hearts-and-no-trust-between-old-friends thing. Men do it differently than women: we work it out with fistfights in seedy bars, arguing over our favorite albums. But at the end of the fight, I told them the truth about my college career in Madison, minus the name change. We assured one another we were past it, and that was the night we each got the identical *Still Here* tattoos to prove our undying bond, but the truth was we never truly got past it. We had all gone our separate ways and this was just another wedge.

But the point is that Augie had known I attended the University of Wisconsin. So I understood how this Clevenger, undoubtedly the bastard who had placed the call to Augie's while I was inside, might have known about it, too—the marks on Augie's body had indicated that Augie had received the whole Dick Cheney treatment. And Ben and Augie both had also known I was a mortgage broker. So none of this was totally unexpected, but somehow Clevenger had narrowed his search to somewhere near Richmond.

Except that was as far as it went. This Clevenger was clever, and thoroughly thorough, and scarily swift, but he was still looking for a Moretti, he didn't yet know me as a Willing. I was pretty sure I had severed any link between my two names. I had even scrupulously kept my face out of my college yearbook—Jonathon Willing was listed as "Not Pictured" on the back page of the *Badger*. So he could know about the job, and know about the alma mater, but as long as he still didn't know about the name I was okay.

Which is why Clevenger was sitting lost and lonely by his phone in Chicago, waiting for me to give him a call. Fat chance of that.

"Johnny? Is that you, Johnny?"

"Yeah, it's me, Harry. What's up?"

"Nothing. Probably nothing."

"Well, is it nothing, or probably nothing?"

"Probably nothing."

"Then it might be something."

"It might be at that."

"All right, let's have it."

"I was at Schooners last night, with the Koreans. Nothing out of the ordinary there. And who comes in but a fellow named Prolly, got a commercial fishing boat, docks down in Shipps Bay now. Old Prolly and me, we got into some piles in our day. There was this one time, we was busting on this waitress up there in Ocean City—Maryland, not Jersey, I'm talking. We had gone there on a charter for these business types from Ohio, and the—"

"Harry?"

"Prolly, right? Remember how you asked me to keep my eyes open for anything that might not be on the square."

"I remember."

"Well, when Prolly and me was having drinks, I asked him if he seen anything out of whack and he says it just so happens a fellow came into Prolly's usual joint, a sailors' bar not far up the road toward Virginia Beach, and the guy was buying beers and flashing a picture, offering a hundred if anyone recognized the face."

"A picture?"

"Yeah, a picture. Said it was a guy who owed him on a boat somewhere out of Richmond. Prolly said the picture was black and white and fuzzy. Of a guy walking through a metal detector at an airport."

"What did the guy in the picture look like?"

"It was hard to say. But he was white, tallish, in his forties."

"What about the guy showing around the picture?"

"Well, all Prolly said about that was there didn't seem to be much to him but his smile, but there was something in the guy's smile that made Prolly damn glad it wasn't him he was looking for. And Prolly was a fighter, too, in his day, an amateur and a lightweight, but even so. Still it could have been anyone in that picture, right?"

"Right."

"Like I said, probably nothing."

"You're probably right."

"Though Prolly, he said the guy did mention something about a scar."

Clevenger, that devious son of a bitch.

How the hell did he know about the boat? The scar I under-stood, and the picture, too. The bastards had combed through the photographs automatically taken at the Phoenix and Philadelphia security gates and somehow found a picture they assumed was me. Whether it was or not, who could tell, maybe they had the complete wrong guy, though I suspected they didn't. But how had they learned about the boat? Whatever they did to Augie, however medieval they got, he couldn't have told them about it because I made it a policy to keep anything about my escape hatch from Augie and Ben. Even though I trusted them both, the less they knew about any of it, the better. But somehow Clevenger had divined the possibility that I had a boat, and was now combing the seaside haunts up and down the coast, looking for me.

Well, let him. His thugs could stake out the docks all they wanted; I sure as hell now wasn't going anywhere near my day-sailer until all this had passed. As long as they were sticking to the water, they weren't getting close enough to bite. As long as they didn't have my name, they had nothing.

Nothing.

"Hey, it's Charles. You coming down?"

"Coming down where?" I said.

"To the club. You had a game scheduled this morning, right?"

"What kind of game?"

"Jon, what's going on? We don't play badminton."

"But we didn't plan to play today, did we?"

"Not us. You and your friend."

"My friend?" I said.

"I was in the pro shop when he called and asked if you were a member there. When Don asked why he was asking, the guy on the phone said that you two had made plans for this morning but that he couldn't make it. And you know, I wasn't doing anything today."

"That's a change."

"So I thought if you were planning to play anyway and he wasn't showing up, maybe I could jump in."

"I wasn't planning to play."

"That's a little weird."

"Must be a mix-up," I said. "Did he give his name, my friend?"

"Cleckinger or something, I think it was."

"Clevenger?"

"That's it. Is he any good?"

"The son of a bitch is a plus," I said.

Even before I hung up on Charles, something cold and familiar raised the hackles on my neck. I leaned forward and looked out the window to the street in front of the house. Empty. But it wouldn't be for long.

He had found me. It had found me. I was fearfully peeking out the windows of my house, just days after I had fearfully peeked out the windows of Augie's house, and the terror was the same. My precautions had been for naught; my lines of obfuscation had been obliterated with an alacrity that stunned. A dagger through tissue paper, a baseball bat to the ribs.

Clevenger, that wily bastard, had gotten my name.

Maybe there was some document somewhere in the University of Wisconsin's admission files linking Moretti and Willing. Or maybe they had compared all the names leaving Phoenix at around the time of my flight from Vegas with names arriving in Philly within the next week, the parked car coming back to haunt me. Or maybe someone had ID'd the photograph. But how he had done it didn't matter. I had hoped to create some barrier with the name change, yet really, how could I have thought it would stay a secret for long once the bastards started looking?

And now not only did they have my name, but they also had my development. Our address was seriously unlisted, but how many seconds would that hold them up?

I needed to run, we all needed to run. But how could I get my family to flee with me? A fake vacation? A cruise, maybe? Yeah, that was the ticket. A cruise to nowhere. A cruise that would last for weeks, months. Some big heavy liner sitting all portly and grand in a Mexican harbor. All I had to do was get Caitlin and the kids to go along. And why wouldn't they? Everyone loves a cruise: the shows, the pools, the midnight buffet. We could all run to Miami and hitch on to a boat. Maybe we would like Mexico enough to stay. And I could pay for it with cash—how convenient.

It was all so perfect, except that the exigencies of our lives made it flatly impossible. Shelby and Eric had school. And Caitlin had a couple of open houses scheduled as her portfolio started its slow recovery along with the economy. There was no way I could get them to go with me short of kidnapping. And even if I did, who would cut the lawn? Who would keep up the house? And how could we run from Patriots Landing while maintaining the crucial appearance of still belonging?

I discarded the cruise idea—what kind of delusional fool was I becoming?—and came up with something a lot more sane.

I would get myself a gun.

20. Trifecta

I HAD BOUGHT A GUN ONCE, YEARS AGO, SHORTLY AFTER WE moved into Patriots Landing, a sweet Smith & Wesson nine millimeter. I didn't take it to the range or spend hours cleaning the thing, I didn't want to be conspicuous in my gun ownership even in a conspicuously gun-owning state, but I liked having it in my closet. With all my secrets and concerns, I felt like it was a prudent part of my precautions. Until Caitlin stepped into our room one afternoon and found Shelby on the floor with a doll and my Smith & Wesson, playing spin the pistol.

When I came home from work Caitlin was sitting in the kitchen, waiting for me. Her mouth was tight, her hands shook with anger. The gun sat before her on the granite countertop, its barrel pointed at me like an accusation. As she told me what had happened, she stared at me as if I was as incomprehensible as a piece of liver.

"I bought it for protection," I said. "For the family."

"From what?"

"I don't know. It's crazy out there."

"It's crazy somewhere, that's for sure. And do you even know how to shoot it?"

"It's a gun. It's not rocket science. There's a trigger. You pull it. Bam."

"Bam. That's good, Jon. That's comforting. Bam. And you didn't think to discuss it with me?"

"I didn't want to worry you."

"Well, I'm worried. I'm worried that my daughter is going to shoot herself in the face with your fucking gun."

"It wasn't even loaded."

"I'm worried that a cat is going to knock over a garbage can and you're going to start blasting anything that moves. Don't you know the statistics?"

"Yes, and I have to say, there are inaccuracies in the numbers that—"

"I'm not having it in my house."

"I'll put it somewhere safer."

"There is no safe place for this in my house."

"I can find one, I'm sure."

"Are you listening?"

"I'm trying, but you're not being reasonable."

"About my child playing with a gun? Who are you? I don't know you anymore."

I had wanted to continue arguing, but that final statement shut me up. *Anymore?* How presumptuous was that? Did she ever know me? Did she ever want to know me, the real truth about me, about what I had done in Pitchford, and what I had done since to protect what I had done? About how she had been able to afford the wonderful house, the wonderful cars, the wonderful hair salon and sparkling tennis club? It was a moment when a real dialogue suddenly loomed, when full disclosure, and all its effects, both putrid and pure, trembled in the gap between us. What would happen to our relationship, to our marriage, if finally I bared it all? The question was its own answer, wasn't it?

The gun went. And, a decade or so later, the marriage followed.

But this was no time to dwell on lost possibilities. This was a time, instead, to look cold-eyed at my options. I had panicked in

Vegas and lost the gun, but the time for panic was over, the time to buy a gun was nigh. For a new and very real threat. It wasn't anymore just a nameless crazy with some fearsome mask, it was death itself with a voice and a name: Clevenger.

Fortunately we lived in Virginia, where the only impediment to gun ownership is forgetting your wallet.

There was a shop in Yorktown, a little family-owned joint on Highway 17 that I had passed dozens of times as I avoided crowded Route 64 on the way to Norfolk. I took one more look outside to make sure the road was clear and then headed out, locking the door tight behind me.

I checked my rearview as I left the driveway and drove to the development's exit and kept checking as I made my way toward Yorktown. A white van held my interest for a bit, then a black SUV, then a green sedan, then another black SUV. Or was that the first? I barely missed ramming the car in front of me as I looked closer. The driver of the SUV was a woman with Jackie O. sunglasses and the full Chez Rochelle haircut. You could drive around Williamsburg and see hundreds of the same woman in the same black SUV with the very same sunglasses and haircut. Like Caitlin, for instance. A sight for sure, but not a threat. I breathed easier as I charged down Highway 17.

The store was a standalone mom-and-pop thing, with the family name on the roof flanked by two words, CIGARETTES and GUNS. A neon sign in the window advertised Budweiser, promising the whole Southern trifecta. A little bell rang when I entered the front door.

Ding-a-ling.

"Can I help you?" said an old man, all bones and sagging flesh, sitting in a rocking chair behind the gun counter. He wore overalls and a plaid shirt, he spoke as slow as poured molasses.

I tapped on the counter with my fingertips. "I need a gun," I said.

"You came to the right place for that, mister," he said without getting up. "What kind you looking for?"

"Something big enough to stop a bear in his tracks."

"You'll be wanting a shotgun for that."

"But not that big. It's hard to hide a shotgun in your belt."

"Oh, I see," he said, rocking back and forth as if in deep thought. "A handgun, then. You got yourself one of them permits to carry a concealed weapon?"

"No."

"Are you an American?"

"Yes."

"Are you an unlawful user of a controlled substance or a habitual drunkard?"

"*Habitual* is a tricky word, don't you think?"

"I always thought so. There was never nothing habitual about my drinking, it was just an everyday thing. If you get yourself a permit, it'll make things easier."

"I might eventually, but I need something now."

"Until you get your permit you can carry but you can't conceal. A holster on the side, like, is okay."

"How about at home?"

"At home you can hide it up your butt hole, all they care. We're talking out and about, like in church. You don't want to be taking concealed guns to church without a permit. You go to church much?"

"Not really."

He winked. "Well, then, it should be all right." He pushed himself off the chair, leaned over the counter, and looked down at the handguns on display beneath the glass. "Revolver or automatic?"

"Automatic," I said, "with an extra clip."

He looked up at me and squinted a bit. "Any experience?"

"With guns?"

"I'm not asking about women."

"Not enough with either, I'm afraid, though I've been married for fifteen years."

He looked down at the display as he considered. "Something simple, then, not too heavy, not too flashy. What about price?"

"I'm more concerned about it going off when I need it."

"That's what we like to hear. Makes things more civilized. No one bargains over taking out an appendix, but when it comes to guns, some all they think about is price. Try this," he said as he reached down to unlock the display case and pulled out a medium-sized olive-and-black handgun. "One of our most popular models. Nine millimeter, steady as a hearse, used all over the world."

"What is it?" I said.

"A Glock. Made in Austria. They know their guns in Austria. Their schnitzel, too, but you can't kill a buzzard at forty paces with a schnitzel. And the magazine holds enough to kill you a sloth of bears."

He handed it over. The gun was sharp and solid, and I liked the smell. It smelled efficient. As soon as I took hold of it, something eased in me. Just the way my hand wrapped around the grip gave me a dose of comfort. Like warm apple pie, with a dollop of lead. I waved the Glock around the empty store to get a feel for it.

"Not as heavy as I would expect," I said.

"They use plastic to keep down the weight—imagine that." He clicked his tongue as he took the gun from me, checked that that it was unloaded, and then cocked the breech. "But still as deadly as a redhead in yellow heels."

I looked at the old man as he gave the gun back to me. "I bet you've got a story."

"Nothing I'm telling with my wife in the back. Five fifty, and I'll throw in the second magazine."

"Bullets, too?"

"Five seventy-five will get you the gun, two boxes of ammo, and a clip holster. I'll throw in a case of Marlboros if you want."

"Oh, I want. And a six of Bud, too."

"Bottles or cans?"

"Bottles."

"Go on, give the trigger a squeeze."

I gripped the gun again, aimed it at a cooler filled with beer, pulled the trigger. The click was as satisfying as a steak dinner.

"Deal," I said.

"Credit card or check?"

"Cash?"

"That will do," he said, taking the gun out of my hands.

As he leaned over and placed my gun back into the display case, I felt suddenly underdressed. The old man slapped some papers on the counter along with a pen.

"This is your form 4473," said the old man. "Background check. Won't take but a minute. And when you're done, I'll need to compare it with your ID." He looked at me like he was sending a signal. "That okay, son? You're not wanted or nothing, are you?"

I looked down at the form. Something federal, like a tax form. That first gun I had, the Smith & Wesson, I bought off a guy named Pete I knew at work. No forms on that one, just the cash. I thought about it for a moment. I didn't like the idea of my name shooting over the computer lines to the feds, didn't like the possibility of some alarm somewhere being flipped. But did it really matter anymore?

"No, I'm clean," I said.

"Good. While you fill her out, I'll go in the back and rustle up your merchandise. Reds okay on the Marlboros?"

As I started in on the form, the door opened. Ding-a-ling. Startled by the sound, I looked up as a man in a ragged black sport coat stepped into the store. He had gray eyes, an unshaven jaw, and a tattoo climbing up the side of his neck. He looked around the place just as I had when I first walked in, as if he were in a diorama at a museum. He caught my gaze for a moment, smiled, and nodded. I nodded back, like a stranger anywhere would nod, and went back to my form 4473.

NAME: I had to think a bit, but the only ID I had on me was for Jonathon J. Willing, so that was it. ADDRESS: I had a post office box in Richmond, but that was specifically barred, so I sucked it up and put down the Patriots Landing address that matched the license. PLACE OF BIRTH: Philadelphia. HEIGHT: Sure. WEIGHT: Okay, so I lied. MALE: Yes. BIRTH DATE: What the hell. SOCIAL SECURITY NUMBER (OPTIONAL): Option denied.

"You buying yourself a gun?" The guy in the jacket was now next to me, leaning on the counter, looking not at me but instead down through the glass at the armaments arrayed there like fruit at a greengrocer: handguns, long guns, knives, brass knuckles. His voice was southern Virginia by way of the Bronx. The part of the tattoo that showed on his neck was the tip of a feathered wing.

"Nah," I said. "Guns they just give away down here, but they make you fill these out to buy the cigarettes."

His smile widened enough to be almost familiar. "If you got a choice, my advice—go for the cigarettes."

"Why's that?"

"First, they don't mentholate firearms," said the man. "I like menthol, it's about the closest I get to a vacation anymore. And then, I've found that people who don't know what they're doing with a gun, they usually end up shooting themselves in the ass."

Something about his smile pissed me off. I gave him another look: short and stocky, with spiky blond hair and those pale gray eyes, dangerous eyes. Suddenly I really really really wanted him to stop talking.

"The owner went to the storeroom," I said, "but I expect he'll be right back."

The man slid a little closer to me. I could smell his cheesy aftershave. Old Spice, the official scent of high-school freshmen.

"Look at that little darling," he said, referring to one of the smaller guns. "Wouldn't that be sweet in some bastard's ear?"

I shifted down the counter away from him and turned my attention back to the form, instinctively shielding my answers with my body like a bratty know-it-all in junior high during a science test. (Of course, at Pitchford Junior High, that bratty know-it-all was me.) After questions about ethnicity and citizenship, form 4473 got to the crux of the matter. ARE YOU THE ACTUAL BUYER OF THE FIREARMS LISTED ON THIS FORM? Yes. HAVE YOU EVER BEEN CONVICTED OF A FELONY? No. ARE YOU A FUGITIVE FROM JUSTICE? That last gave me a bit too much pause. Was I? Had I been running not from Tony Grubbins but instead from justice itself for lo these many years?

"And it's not just your own self you got to worry about," said the man in the Old Spice.

"Excuse me?" I said, still working on the form.

"Once the shooting it starts, you never know who's getting hit. You pay your taxes? Not all you're supposed to, I'd bet. Not a guy like you."

I stopped writing, looked up at the man, felt something slip inside me. "What kind of guy is that?"

"I had a pal that tried to get away without paying his taxes. No big deal, we all try to swing it. But when the IRS came after him, instead of just making good on what he owed, he started loading up. Shotguns, scatter guns, pistols out the wazoo. Before he could turn around, the ATF went Ruby Ridge on his ass. He survived, but the wife and one of the kids weren't so lucky. Things like that happen when you start thinking with the barrel between your legs instead of your brain."

I looked down at the form for a moment and then back at the man's unfriendly smile and hard gray eyes. As pale and as implacable as fate itself. So this is the way the world ends, not with a bang but with an insufferable stranger wearing Old Spice. "You don't know me."

"Maybe I don't," he said. "But I sure seen your picture."

He reached into his pocket and pulled out a photograph, tossed it on the counter. A grainy black and white of a man going through a metal detector at an airport.

"That's not me," I said.

"Close enough," said the man, and he was right about that.

I closed my eyes and took a breath. What I was feeling just then must have been much like the feeling you get when death falls out of the sky and flutters to a landing on your chest. Horror and fear and relief all at once. Whatever it was I had lived through for the past quarter century, it was finally, irrevocably over. Something new was coming hard and fast, and all I could think was that it was about time.

"What do we do now?" I said.

"First of all, we don't buy no gun. I already got enough steel for both of us." He pushed away his jacket to reveal a holstered pistol.

"Okay."

"Then you give me your cell phone."

"Why?"

"Just give it up," he said, reaching out his hand. I took my cell out of my pocket, put it in his open hand.

"BlackBerry, huh? Old school, with a keyboard instead of the touch screen. Nice. How's your reception here?"

"Fine."

"I don't get crap. I'm stuck with AT&T. I want to go Verizon, but with the contract they got me by the balls, you know what I mean?"

"Yes."

"I bet you do at that." The man stuffed the BlackBerry in a jacket pocket. "Now we go outside and I follow you back to your house."

"You'll follow me?"

"What's the Beemer worth, even used, twenty, thirty? No need to leave that here. At your house, we collect what's left of the cash."

"It's gone. I spent it all."

"Yeah, yeah, so you say. But still I got my orders to give the house a shakedown, like we did with your pal in Vegas. And then we'll sit around the dining table with you and your family and figure something out."

"They're not part of it."

"They are now."

"You stay the hell away from them."

His pale gray eyes stayed calm at my outburst, but it was a calm that slapped me into silence. It was all there, in that stillness, not just the violence he was undoubtedly capable of, but also that he just might enjoy it.

"There's a way this can go," he said, slowly, patiently, as to a child, "in which the damage is kept to a minimum. There's also a different way this can go. I don't care; for me it's just a job and most of my jobs are messy. So the decision is yours. How do you want to play it?"

"Clean."

"That's what I figured."

"And if I run?"

He reached over and pulled the form from beneath my hand. "First I'll catch you," he said calmly as he gave the paper a scan. "And then I'll hurt you. And then we'll still head on over to that fancy development where I picked you up. How's the wife, she a looker? If she is, that will make things more pleasant."

"Look, I'm sure you and I, we can work something out. Off the record. How much to walk away?"

"You want to pay me off."

"That's the way it works, isn't it?"

"You see, this is the thing that got you in trouble in the first place. You have no idea who you are dealing with. Go on, now."

He jerked his head toward the door, and I stood there for a moment, my eyeballs spinning as I considered my options. Then my posture slumped, as if my spine had been extracted, and I headed for the exit. I had just opened the door—ding-a-ling—when the old guy in the overalls came out of the back room with a large brown box.

"Mister," he said, "where you going? I got your merchandise."

"He won't be needing that pistol no more," said the man in the black jacket. "But if you don't mind, I sure could use a carton of Newpees for the road."

21. Chandler Court

I T WAS A LONG, ELEGIAC DRIVE BACK TO PATRIOTS LANDING, AS somber as a sprinter's funeral. Our small procession, my BMW and the blue rental Ford following close behind, was marking the death of an era. For a quarter of a century I had been on the run, taking wild gambles, devising devious strategies, plotting exits, racing ecstatically around the whole of the country to keep the wolves at bay. It had become not just a path of prudent precaution, it had become the richest part of my life. My past was painful, my present was confused and disappointing, yet no matter how life batted me about, I always had the warming knowledge that I had gotten away with something, something huge. Now, having finally been caught, I felt bereft, pale, weak, and useless, as if meaning had been bled out of my very existence.

My life as I had known it was over; all that was left was managing the aftermath. And even that was too optimistic a pronouncement, as if there were any managing I could actually do.

A cop car approached from the other direction, and I had the urge to flag him down with my lights. That would put an end to the immediate threat to my life—and with the statute of limitations having passed on the Grubbins caper I wouldn't even end up in jail—but then what? What could the police actually do about my problem? The bastard with the Old Spice would be gone before I even pulled over to the side of the road, and while

I was still trying to explain the whole story to the incredulous officer, Old Spice would be wreaking havoc on my house, and maybe on my family. No, I had to keep him as close as he had to keep me.

I swiveled my head as the cop passed, felt an opportunity vanish, and looked back at the road in front of me. With each mile that passed beneath me I came a mile closer to Patriots Landing, and with each mile my wretchedness rose.

I needed to make a deal. I should have called Clevenger when I had some of my anonymity left still to trade. Now my cover was blown, my location was known. But just because it was too late to make the best deal didn't mean it was too late to make some deal. They could have the cash, they could have the car, hell, they could have the house. But that wouldn't be all Clevenger would insist on. Just as they had killed Augie even after they had gotten the stash beneath the chair, they would surely kill me, too. After all my planning it was ironic that the one thing that wouldn't be faked would be my death.

Yet, if Clevenger would stop there I'd spit on my hand to seal the deal and consider it all well played. I would have called Clevenger right there and made the offer, but the son of bitch driving behind me had my phone. I'd have to bide my time to make that deal a reality. But would the Old Spice thug even let me make the call? The way he leered when he asked if my wife was a looker gave me all the answer I needed. Whatever happened wouldn't end with my death.

My God, it might only begin there.

In the car in front of me a woman threw back her head, laughing. How could she laugh, how was such an act possible? A man with a bucket hat powered past me in a convertible. Where could he be going that was so important? That the whole of the world continued to spin on its axis, blandly oblivious, seemed impossible to me. Somewhere tragedy was striking, a tsunami, an earthquake, an invading army of children with machetes.

That's where I belonged, where everyone felt the despair that was welling in my throat.

Without even knowing how I got there, I was suddenly at the entrance to my development, with its brick wall and lordly cement lions. Patriots Landing, the very anodyne of despair. But not today, not now. I stopped for a moment, not wanting to make the left that would take me home, not wanting to make it all final, when my car lurched suddenly forward.

It took me a moment to realize what had happened. The son of a bitch had rear-ended me.

I had to stop myself from jumping out and checking on the bumper. Did he have any idea what it cost to fix those things? Then I remembered it was his car now. When I looked into the mirror he waved his hand at me, telling me to take the turn. I closed my eyes, felt the car lurch again, along with my stomach. I opened my eyes and drove into my development.

The road in was lined with Carter Braxton models and George Wyeth models, houses that were too mean for my ambitions all those years ago but now looked perfectly lovely, idyllic even. I turned onto a street lined with Peyton Randolph models. What wouldn't I give to safely call one of those precious homes my own. My own George Washington now seemed flatly grotesque, its ostentatious wings a manifestation of my grandest delusions. As I continued I saw a road to the right lined with Patrick Henrys, Chandler Court, the very road the salesman had tried to sell us on when first we visited Patriots Landing. Sometimes I would drive down it just to feel grateful about my splendiferous George Washington. But I wasn't feeling so grateful anymore.

Without even being sure of what I was doing, I turned onto Chandler Court and started down its curved way. The houses with their lovely brick fronts passed by as if in a parade. I could have been so happy in one of them, I thought. I'd give anything to be happy in one of them right now. In the rearview mirror I saw Old Spice with a phone to his ear, looking right and left, trying to catch the numbers, unsure of where he was going. While he was distracted, I pressed the gas pedal and sped forward.

Toward the cul-de-sac at the end of Chandler Court.

It was wide, that cul-de-sac, designed to place a maximum number of homes around its circular edge, since cul-de-sac homes sold at a premium. The cars that were parked were parked in the driveways, leaving me a broad circle in which to make my turn. I zigged left to get the best angle, zagged hard right, banked left again as I whipped around the circle, centrifugal force throwing me and everything else in the car to the right. When my tires slapped back to horizontal I was facing the exact opposite direction, toward the mouth of Chandler Court, heading right for Old Spice in his rental Ford.

His eyes widened when he saw me coming and realized how crazy I might truly be.

I aimed for him head-on, with just enough of an angle that the reinforced corner of my sturdily built German tank would slam into his grille front and center, sending the entire engine, hot and spinning, into his lap. I was closing like a rocket on a string, the space between us tightening with an unimaginable fury, when Old Spice flinched. He thought I was playing chicken. He thought I expected him to turn so I could make my escape, and to save his skin, he did just that, turned to the right, leaving me a gap in which to flee. But he hadn't lived the last quarter century of my life.

I wasn't intending to escape; I was there to end a threat to my family's existence on my own terms. Even if I couldn't make the call to Clevenger to present my offer, I was going to make the most important part of the deal happen on my own. And by flinching, all Old Spice did was turn the soft side of his car toward the hard corner of my own, like a great whale turning its belly to the harpoon.

I leaned forward and gripped the steering wheel tighter. The accelerator was jammed to the floor, my hands were bolted onto the wheel, the BMW jumped forward as if in bloody anticipation. I screamed Caitlin's name into whatever breath of existence remained within the vanishing gap between us.

22. Frenchy Finds a Snorkel

I GUESS I WASN'T GOING AS FAST AS I THOUGHT.

When I came to, there was a loose airbag hanging from the steering wheel, the windshield was cracked, shards of safety glass covered my lap. My face held the swollen numbness you get when you're hammered into submission by a bullyboy's fist. I lifted my hand to my cheek and it came away bloody. Through the car window I could see smoke rising from beneath my creased hood. Beyond that, still with my front corner buried in its side, was the blue Ford, rammed over the curb, its front end bent around the narrow trunk of a maple.

With a panicky start I remembered where the hell I was and what the hell I had done. And for a moment, I admit, I was disappointed to still be alive. Then I got a grip and reached for the keys. The starter screamed like a cat in hot oil; the damn car was still running. Those wily Germans—how'd we beat them twice, anyway? I put the car into reverse. The engine roared, there was the straining sound of metal bending, and then my car popped free. The Ford slapped down onto all four of its tires, and in that motion I saw something bobbing inside the crushed cabin.

I backed away hard, shifted into forward, stopped with a jar when I was parallel to the wrecked Ford, pushed open, with much effort, my door. I tried to jump out of the front seat, found myself unable, and realized I was still belted in. Once out, I examined my car. It was a mess, its side bowed, its front absolutely wrecked, the metal torn, the headlight blown, the bumper sagging.

A dog across the street was barking. An old woman had come out of one of the houses right on the circle, but she was in no hurry to get involved. I snarled at her and she backed away before running inside. With the blood on my cheek, I must have looked a fright. She would justify her cowardice by dialing 911, no doubt. It wouldn't be long before the cops appeared.

I leaned over and peered into the Ford. The airbags hung limp, the man's head was bleeding, his eyes were unnervingly open but glassy with shock, his leg trapped by the twisted steel of the door. A tremor in his hand let me know he was still alive.

Should I wait for the police, and explain? And then what? Wait for what I knew would come after the explanation? Hell with that.

Something sounded from inside the car that made me jump. A phone. With a familiar stupid jazzy ringtone. My phone. Son of a bitch. Old Spice was still staring his blank stare at me. I reached through an opening in the shattered glass of the car's front window, snaked my hand inside his jacket. I could feel the buzzing sensation of his chest rising and falling, but the phone wasn't in his jacket. It kept ringing. I tried to open the door, it wouldn't budge. I ran around to the door on the other side, gave it a pull, yanked it open. And there it was, on the floor, right inside the door, its screen lit with excitement. I grabbed it and took the call.

"Where have you been?" said a voice familiar enough, since it had infected my dreams over the last few days. "You shut off right in the middle. What happened?"

"There's been an accident," I said.

"Holmes?" said Clevenger.

"Someone should have told Holmes not to talk on the phone while he was driving."

"Frenchy? My God, is that you? Tell me it is—that would be so precious."

179

"Don't call me Frenchy," I said.

He laughed. "You are in so far over your head you need a snorkel."

"I want to make a deal."

"Here it is. You give over what you got and we'll talk about the rest."

"What kind of deal is that?"

"The best you'll ever get from me, friend."

"Then maybe I should find someone else to negotiate with. You're just a hired thug, anyway. Who hired you to find me?"

His sharp voice grew snappish enough to confirm my suspicion. "Don't get ahead of yourself, boy."

"I'm ready to make a deal, but not with you. After what you did to Augie, I've got nothing for you but spit. You tell whoever's giving you your orders that he's the one I want to deal with."

"Silly boy, I'm giving the orders."

"Not anymore. When I call back I want to talk to the man in charge. But before we talk, I need to take care of some business."

"My advice?" said Clevenger. "Take care of it quick."

I hung up and closed my eyes and felt something lift me into the air. Not a way out, exactly, it was too early for that, but maybe the merest intimation of a way out, which was a hell of a lot more than I had had a bare few moments ago.

I hopped around the wreck and headed for the still-smoking Beemer, but I stopped for a second when Holmes, his eyes still open, shifted on the seat. I could almost see the comprehension of his situation starting to bleed into those eyes, and with that comprehension I sensed a new danger. I doubled back, reached again through the shattered window, pulled his pistol and holster off his belt.

"It turns out I'm going to need a gun after all," I said to him. And then I had a thought.

My briefcase was still in my car. I jacked the case open, put the gun in one of its pockets, took out a piece of paper and a pen. I scrawled something quick. Just as I stuffed the paper in Holmes's shirt pocket, I heard the sirens in the distance, two of them at different pitches, coming closer. I jumped into the still-smoking BMW and headed out of Chandler Court. Something dragged on the cement beneath me, but I didn't care.

The sirens were to my left; I turned right and started weaving through the roads of the development. I wasn't going to wait around for them, I needed to get away clean, because the phone call had given me a clue to a way out. For too long I had been sitting back, waiting for them to come at me. For years, for decades, even before I woke up to the knife at my throat. But it was time to stop waiting, it was time for me to put a knife at someone else's throat. I wasn't sure yet whose throat or how to do it, but I had cash and a gun and the ghost of a plan. It wasn't much, but it was enough.

The sirens were getting louder, closer, but I was already heading the other way, toward the back entrance of the development. If I had my druthers, the cops and I would pass like ships in the night, one in the Atlantic, one in the Pacific. By the time the police set up shop at the scene of the accident with their cameras and their yellow tape, by the time they found the message I had left in Holmes's pocket, I would be long gone from Patriots Landing. Maybe for good.

23. Pickup

Y FACE WAS RAW, MY EYE WAS BRUISED, MY CHEEK WAS scraped and bleeding, my nose might have broken but it hurt too much to tell. As I stared in the mirror I had a strange case of the déjà vus. Here I was, back in a high-school bathroom, washing off the results of some unabashed brutality. I wouldn't have been surprised to find Tony Grubbins sitting in the back of one of the classrooms, gloating.

I cleaned off the blood, dabbed at the clear fluid rising on the wounds. I put on the white baseball hat that had been in the briefcase to hide what I could, and my sunglasses to cover the rest. I still looked a mess, but better, I am sure, than I did when I pressed the intercom and looked into the camera to be let inside. As satisfied as I was going to get, I left the bathroom and headed for the office.

"I'm here to pick up Shelby Willing," I said to the secretary. "We forgot about it but she has a doctor's appointment that she really can't miss."

"And you are?"

"Her father."

"I'll need some identification."

"Of course."

The woman at the desk looked at me like I was a felon, which I suppose I was, before examining the license. And then she tap-tap-tapped her computer to check Shelby's schedule and, I assumed, for any extant protective orders. "She's in Spanish now. Sign her out and I'll call down to the classroom."

"Thank you."

"And next time, Mr. Willing, try to remember to have your daughter bring in the official form the morning she's to be pulled out."

"We surely will," I said.

As Shelby dragged her backpack down the hallway toward the office she seemed strangely young and out of place, a black-clad sparrow in a meat locker. She smiled when she saw me, which must have been a product of the surroundings, because at home she never smiled when she saw me. At home, for Shelby, I was the death of smiles.

"What are you doing here?" she said, and I realized her smile was nervous only, and that she was worried that something terrible had happened. Which I guess it had.

"We have an appointment."

"With whom?"

"Dr. Reilly," I said, referring to her pediatrician for the sake of the woman staring at us from behind the office counter.

"Why?"

"Come on, let's go," I said, leading her out of the office and toward the entrance.

"What happened to your face?" she said after the door closed behind us.

"Is it that noticeable?"

"A-yeah. What did you do, wrestle a raccoon?"

"Pretty much. Hurry, we have to pick up your brother."

"Why? Does he have an appointment, too?"

"Something like that," I said.

When we reached the high school's parking lot she stopped in her tracks, her jaw dropped, and she stared at me with accusatory eyes. "What happened to the car?"

"A little fender bender," I said. "Nothing to worry about."

"Dad, that is not a little fender bender. You had a massive accident. Tell me the truth now. What is happening? Who died?"

"No one, yet." I walked around the car to the dented driver's door, yanked it open with a crunch of metal, and then spoke over the car's hood. "Get in, we have to go."

"Does this have anything to do with the stuff in your brief-case?"

I looked at her for a moment without saying anything, as if I had no idea what she was talking about.

"All that money, and the rubbers, and the fake license plate," she said. "That was all very shady, Dad. When you came back from Vegas you were acting all weird, so I looked in. That was a lot of money. I didn't take any, but Dad. And what were you doing with rubbers?"

"It's a long story, Shelby. Get in the car."

"I didn't tell Mom, if you want to know."

"You didn't?"

"I mean, if you're cheating on Mom then you're a skeevy ass-hole, but that's your business."

"I'm not cheating on your mother."

"It was a box of rubbers. Not one, not two, a fricking box. What was in Vegas, a stripper convention?"

"It's a long story. But thank you for keeping my confidence."

She smiled at me, for a second time that day, a new record, and then shrugged. "It's no big deal, I don't talk to Mom either."

"Well, maybe it's time you start. While I'm picking up Eric, could you please take out that phone of yours and find out where your mother is?"

When Eric came out of his middle school and saw the car sitting crushed and steaming in the circle in front of the entrance, he stopped walking and stared at the sight with the calm of a calculator.

"Are you kidnapping us?"

"What?"

"Have you and Mom finally split up? Are you kidnapping your children and taking us to some foreign country with a terrific beach where they won't let Mom take us back to America?"

"Don't be ridiculous."

"Why not?"

"Is that what you want me to do?"

"Maybe, but not today. I have a Science Olympiad training session after school. Chemistry. I need the work."

"I'm not kidnapping you."

"Don't you want us? Aren't you going to fight Mom for custody?"

"What are you talking about?"

"I'm just asking. And a nice LCD flatscreen to go with my PlayStation 3 might get you some pretty sweet testimony at the hearing."

"We're not divorcing."

"That's not what I heard."

"Really," I said. "What exactly did you hear?"

"What did you hit, Dad, a truck?"

"A deer."

"A deer with blue paint?"

"Get in the car, please."

"So you *are* kidnapping me."

"Is that what you want, Eric? Do you want me to kidnap you?"

"If it would get me a dog."

"I'm not kidnapping you and I've told you a hundred times, we're not getting a dog. All they do is crap everywhere and then they die and break your heart. I'm doing you a favor."

"Some favor."

Just then the car door opened and Shelby stuck her head out. "Mom's showing a house by Remnick Pond."

"Okay," I said. "Good. We'll head there as soon as Eric gets in the car."

"Don't be a dweeb," said Shelby. "Get the hell in."

"He's kidnapping us," said Eric.

"God, I hope so," said Shelby. "Anything to get out of that fricking school."

Eric thought about it for a moment longer. "Shotgun," he said.

"Fat chance," said Shelby.

***

Caitlin's black RX10 was parked in front of a Prius and right beside the FOR SALE sign stuck into the lawn. The tidy little development house was not far from the lake and in a desirable neighborhood, though not as desirable as Patriots Landing if you were keeping track of those things, though who was? Certainly not me. Anymore. The house's front door was open, with a little lockbox for the key hanging from the doorknob, and the garage door was raised to show off its two-car spaciousness. From the look of the house's curtained windows, its sparse landscaping, and the completely empty garage, the place had been unoccupied for quite a time. It would sell one of these days, but probably not today.

I stopped behind Caitlin's car and, with the engine still idling, told the kids to get into their mother's car.

"Just do it," I told them when they started jabbering their complaints. There must have been something in my voice; they did as I said, and right away, too.

When they were out, I pulled the BMW around Caitlin's car and drove down the driveway into the empty garage. On my way out of the garage, with my briefcase in hand, I pressed the button. The door lowered behind me as I walked up the driveway.

We waited in the SUV for Caitlin to give her little tour, to point out the stainless-steel appliances in the kitchen, the porcelain in the bathrooms, the natural light in the master bedroom, the wonderful backyard space for entertaining.

"Can I go get her?" said Shelby.

"Just wait."

"This is so boring," said Eric.

"What class would you be having now?" I said.

"Social Studies."

"That sounds fun. What are you studying this year in Social Studies?"

"You're right," said Eric.

"Maybe I should homeschool you both."

"Maybe you should get a grip," said Shelby.

"I know, let's sing show tunes."

"Here she comes," said Eric.

"Thank God," said Shelby.

Caitlin stepped out of the house, trying to walk down the front steps in her high heels without tripping, all the while talking to a young couple, unbelievably young, with their whole lives before them, a lovely house, a backbreaking mortgage, ungrateful children, unsatisfying sex, lawn mowers, ridiculous cable bills. I had the urge to run up to the couple like a mad prophet and warn them of all the impending disasters that would inevitably befall them. But then again, they probably wouldn't screw it up as badly as I had. I wished them well and hoped they fell flat on their faces at the same time.

Caitlin, ever the professional, kept up her sales patter even as she noticed the three of us inside her car. She tilted her head quizzically as she finished detailing the advantages of the neighborhood, the quality of the schools, and the motivation level of the sellers. Then she stood on the steps waving as the lovely young couple drove away in their Prius. When they were gone, her hands went aggressively to her hips.

"What the hell is going on, Jon?" she said when I got out of the car to talk to her. "Why did Shelby call, why are the kids here?" She stared at me for a moment, trying to figure something, anything, and then her jaw started trembling. "Oh my God, what happened? Who died?"

"No one."

"My father?"

"No, Caitlin. Everyone's fine. Calm down."

"Then why are the children out of school? And what the hell happened to your face?"

I took her by the arm and led her away from the car so the kids couldn't see us. "We have a problem."

"Jon?"

"I screwed up," I said, catching a sob in my throat. "I screwed up so badly."

I didn't want to cry, I wanted to stay strong, I needed to stay strong, but here, now, face-to-face with my wife, I couldn't help myself. One of my jobs as a father, perhaps my most important, was protector of the family. How had that turned out? My bruised face collapsed slowly, like a building imploding from the bottom up.

"Jon?"

"They're after us."

"What?"

"They're after me."

"Who?"

"And they won't hesitate to go after you and the kids to get at me."

"Have you gone crazy?"

I lifted my glasses to wipe at my eyes and she saw the full extent of the bruises and wounds and she took a step back.

"Augie didn't just die of his addictions," I said. "He was murdered. For something we did when we were kids, long before I met you. I never told you, I wanted to protect you—"

"Protect me?" she said, catching me in a lie. "What did you do?"

"Something. Something stupid."

"And all this time you held it apart from me? For my own good, you selfish son of a bitch?"

"We thought they didn't know who did it. We thought we had thrown them off the track. That's what the tattoo was all about. We each got one, like a defiant kick in fate's face."

"*Still Here*," she said. "Now I get it."

"But fate just kicked back. When I found Augie murdered, I realized they had finally figured it out."

"How?"

"I don't know how. But they knew me only by my mother's maiden name, so I thought we were maybe still safe. I thought it would pass. I hoped, I prayed. But I was wrong. They found me. Today."

"Is that what happened to your face?"

"There was an accident. Not really an accident. With the BMW."

"Jesus, Jon. Where is it?"

"In that garage there."

"Are you crazy?"

"Yes, no, I don't know. But I do know we're not safe, any of us."

"What have you done, you son of a bitch?"

"I screwed up."

And then she slapped me, right there on that suburban street, in front of the kids, on my bruised face, she slapped me.

"Oh, stop crying," she said when the tears started again. "So what are we going to do, Jon? Sit here until they come for us?"

"No," I said, wiping my eyes again. "It's my problem and I'm going to take care of it, one way or the other. But you need to be safe while I do it. I can make a deal, I know it, but I can't make a deal if they have a gun to your head."

"Is this real?"

"Look at me," I said, and she did, carefully, like she hadn't looked at me in years.

"Okay," she said. "I'll deal with you later. Right now we'll go back to the house and pack up. I'll take the kids to my parents' for a few days."

"We can't go back to the house. They might be there already."

She looked at me and blinked a couple of times. "Then we'll just go, right now. We'll drive up right now."

"They're going to look for you to get to me. You can't go to your parents. You can't go to your sister or to anyone they can connect with you."

"Then what the hell are we going to do, Jon? Hide out in a cave?"

"I have someplace."

"Where?"

"You have to trust me."

"Why the hell should I trust you now?"

"Because no one cares about you or the kids more than I do. I love you, Caitlin."

"Screw you, Jon," she said.

24. Kitty, Kitty

'M IN A FIGHT, HARRY," I SAID.

"I can tell that by your face."

"The fight of my life."

"There ain't ever any other kind, when you're in the middle of it."

"And I don't know if I'm up to it."

"Oh, you're up to it, all right, Johnny."

Harry and I were together belowdecks in his boat while my family waited on the dock outside. Water sloshed beneath the floorboards as the boat stirred in the water. The cabin smelled of gasoline and sewage.

"I don't know much in this world," said Harry. "Never had no use for formal schooling, waste a time for a guy with a brain the size of mine, but I do know a little bit about fighting. And what I know is this. When you're looking for the difference between victory or being swept off the canvas with the blood and dust of the world, there's only one thing that matters."

"Heart."

"Heart?" Harry snorted. "Where'd you get an idea so stupid as that? Heart."

"It's what they say. It's in the song."

"Yeah? Who'd the song ever beat? Tell me that."

Harry's boat was tied up at a commercial marina in Hampton, Virginia, just south of Williamsburg. Caitlin's eyes had widened a bit as the four of us wended our way through the marina's docks with their spacious yachts and grand three-tiered fishing boats, all tied up one next to the other in a pretentious display of wealth and privilege. But her eyes had narrowed again as I led her to the battered blue boat waiting for us at the farthest dock. Next to the sleek fiberglass beauties we had passed, the *Left Hook* was an old washtub.

"Don't tell me we're going in that," she said.

"It's Harry's boat," I said.

"Where'd you find him, anyway?" she said, eyeing him from a distance, his filthy clothes, his rough-hewn countenance. "Passed out on the floor of a bait shack?"

"Actually, yes. But he's a good friend. He'll take you someplace safe."

"If we don't sink first."

"Harry's boat has been floating longer than you've been alive," I said. "I'll be right back, I have to take care of something on board." I gave the children what I hoped was a comforting smile before I climbed onto the deck.

I had hopped into the boat before my family specifically to retrieve the toolbox. I wouldn't have been surprised if Clevenger's thugs were already at our house, slashing cushions, turning over bookshelves, trashing whatever they could trash to find my stash. I was grateful I had thought far enough ahead to give the box to Harry for safekeeping; it wouldn't have lasted the first five minutes of a search. But I needed it now if I was going to negotiate my way out of this mess. As I cleared out the box's upper levels so I could get to the hidden compartment, Harry yabbered on about boxing.

"You could see it in their eyes," said Harry, "the ones that was already beaten. It wasn't so much fear as it was common sense. They'd put up a good show, bobbing and jabbing, but if they went up against a bruiser with the right look in his eye, well, they melted like a pat of butter on the griddle. It was them others, the raw winners, that knew what was what. And that's what you need to know there, Johnny. That's what...Oh my sweet heaven."

This last was in response to my wedging out the false bottom of the toolbox. Even in the dim light of the cabin, the stacks of money glowed.

"My nest egg," I said.

"If I'd have known what was in that thing, I wouldn't have come back with it."

"Sure you would have, Harry. Because you might drink too much, and you surely talk too much, and you might have taken one punch too many to the head, but in spite of everything, you're a man of honor."

"You don't know me good enough," said Harry.

"Take this," I said, tossing him a stack of bills. "For expenses."

As he caught the stack his tongue slipped out and licked his lips. "I'm not no good with receipts."

"I'm not expecting change."

"Good, 'cause you ain't getting none."

I took out the hunting knife, put it in my pocket along with another stack of bills, and then closed the box. When I was back on the dock, with the rusted green thing in my hand, Caitlin looked down at the chest. "What's with the tools?"

"I lent them to Harry so he could get his engines ready for the trip."

"Where is he taking us?"

"To his sister in Kitty Hawk. She'll preach at you a bit, but she'll take care of you, too. She has a house not far from the beach."

"What are we going to do in Kitty Hawk?"

"Frolic. Just don't tell anyone where you are. You can call your parents from the boat to say you're okay and that maybe they should take a quick trip somewhere just to be safe, but that's it. And keep your phone off so they can't trace you."

"What about clothes? What about food?"

"Here," I said, pulling the bundle of hundred-dollar bills out of my pocket and trying to hand it to her on the sly. "That's more than you'll need."

She took the money and held it out and stared at it for a bit, heedless of what anyone else saw. She riffed the bills, smelled them even. And then she gave me the strangest look, as if I were someone she had never seen before. As if I were suddenly someone worth seeing. It's funny what cash can buy.

"You can't use your credit cards," I said. "They'll trace those, so use the cash for everything."

"They have outlet stores in Nags Head."

"Buy some clothes for the kids."

"How long will it take?"

"I'll get it over with one way or the other as quickly as I can."

She stared at me for a moment longer. I reached out to give her a kiss, but she pulled away, as if I were indeed a stranger. I supposed then that the pretending had all ended. Ignoring my offer to help her onto the boat, she turned to Harry, who reached out a hand to pull her aboard. She looked at his weathered face, at his proffered hand black with grease, back at his face, which was now awkwardly smiling, and then put her hand in his and climbed into the boat.

"That was quite a slap Mom gave you in front of that house," said Shelby quietly, after Caitlin was safely aboard.

"She's right to be upset. I'm an idiot."

"What did you do, really? Why are you sending us away?"

"When I was your age, I did something, something a little brilliant and a lot stupid, and I've been dealing with the fallout ever since. Let that be a lesson, young lady: choices matter."

"Oh, so that's the way it works. You screw up and then start lecturing me."

"Yes," I said. "That's the way it works. But I'm going to handle it once and for all."

"While we go for a cruise," she said, gesturing toward Harry's boat.

"Exactly. Be sure to try the rock-climbing wall."

"Where are we going?"

"You're going someplace safe. With a beach. But I'm not going with you. And neither is your phone."

"What?"

"Give it to me."

"No. It's my phone. It's personal."

"They can trace these things now, Shelby. Every second your phone is on, it's sending a signal telling anyone who cares enough exactly where you are. Normally it doesn't matter, but right now it does."

"It's not fair."

"It's not about fairness."

"I'll turn it off, okay? And promise not to use it. Promise."

"Sweetie? Give me the damn phone."

She looked at me and saw something in my bruised eyes that caused her to take out her phone, turn it off, and hand it over.

"What will I do?" she said.

"Talk, read, think."

"This is so not fair."

"Take care of your mother, please."

She rolled her eyes. "Are you going to be okay?"

"I hope so."

"Okay, see you," she said with a quick wave.

Her back was turned to me and I expected her just to tromp off to the boat, but she did something strange instead. She backed into me and turned slowly so that, before I knew it, I was hugging her. She didn't hug back, that wasn't her way, but she did bow her head into my chest, as if she were giving me permission to kiss her on the crown. Which I did.

And then she was gone, reaching out and letting Harry pull her up onto the boat to join her mother.

"Are we going fishing?" said Eric.

"Do you want to go fishing?"

"Please God, no."

"Then good news: no fishing. Harry's just taking you on a little trip."

"Where?"

"Kitty Hawk."

"The Wright brothers?"

"Yeah."

"Cool. Maybe I'll build my own plane."

"And fly where?"

"Back to school. Didn't I tell you about the Science Olympiad?"

"I'm sending you off with your mom and sister on a beach vacation. What kid doesn't want a beach vacation in the middle of school?"

"Me." He looked down at the wooden dock. "Why don't I come with you?"

"You can't. It's too dangerous."

"I'll be your Robin."

"My what?"

"You know. The Boy Wonder."

It took a moment for the implication of that comment to sink in, and when it did, something cracked in me and the emotions flooded. Is it too pathetic for such a throwaway moment to be one of the greatest of my life?

"I'd like that," I said. "And you would be a wonder. But you know how when you go up to bat in baseball, you can't bring anyone with you? This is like that, something I have to do myself. For you, not with you."

"Is it as bad as Little League?"

"Worse."

"Wear a helmet."

"What I need you to do is take care of Mom and make sure you all stay safe. Can you do that?"

"Yes."

"Good. Now give me a hug."

"Okay," he said, and he did, a hug so quick and furtive, it was as if he wanted no one to notice, not even us. And then my boy wonder hopped onto the boat.

They were my crew, my family, along with one of my last true friends, and the emotions that had flooded in when I said good-bye to Eric continued rising as the boat finally pulled away from the dock. Eric waved and Shelby waved and Harry waved and Caitlin turned to stare at the end of the harbor. And then they were heading out toward the mouth of the river, away, getting smaller and smaller, and my tears flowed. In the last few days I had become a faucet and it was embarrassing. I was tougher when I was ten. But there I was, tearing up as my family disappeared into the horizon, and I remembered what Harry had said the difference was between winners and losers in the prize ring.

"When you're in a fight, Johnny—a real fight, I mean, where you're both pounding the hell out of each other without an ounce of mercy—you're going to see death in that ring. He's standing there, true as life and ugly as a washerwoman. And if you step away from him, you step into the cross that puts you down. That's just the common sense I was talking about, because there's no safer place than on the canvas with the ref counting six, seven, eight. But the pug who steps up and gives death an embrace, that's the boy what climbs the rope to standing and ends up on top. If you're in a fight like you say, Johnny, make sure you're the one giving death that hug, make sure you're the one most willing to die."

When the boat was gone, while still staring at the horizon, I took the phone out of my pocket and turned the thing on. MENU: OUTGOING CALLS: a Chicago number. I pressed SEND.

"Frenchy," said Clevenger. "I've been waiting for your call."

"I told you not to call me that."

"It hurts your feelings?"

"No, it makes me think of Augie. And then all I want to do is slit your throat."

"Oh, aren't we suddenly feisty. Okay, boy, what's on your mind?"

"A lot, but I'm not telling it to you. I'm telling it to the guy pulling your strings. Put him on."

"No one pulls my strings, pal. The only one you're talking to is me, and you better talk fast because I have an army of collection agents on your trail."

I suddenly felt naked. I looked around at the docks and the boats and the houses along the waterfront. "Is that what you call your goons, collection agents?"

"That's what we are. You have a debt you need to pay, we're here to collect."

"Whatever happened all those years ago, you weren't involved. The guy who hired you was. He's the one I want to talk to."

"He doesn't want to talk to you."

"Does he know you killed Augie?"

"Don't bother me with details."

"That detail is going to cost you your neck."

"Now you're a comedian."

"You hear yet from your boy Holmes?"

"I will."

"You better lawyer up before you do. I left a note for the cops linking him to Augie's murder. They're going to be asking all kinds of questions, and the answer to each of them is you."

"You know, friend, you're turning into a thorn. We're going to have that sit-down sooner than you think."

"What are you in this for, Clevenger? The money?"

"What else? The same as you."

"You willing to die for it?"

"I'm willing to kill for it. Isn't that enough?"

"Not nearly. Put me in touch with the guy who hired you."

"No chance."

"Then I'm going to find the son of a bitch on my own."

III. PHILADELPHIA STORY

"Keep in touch."

—*Augie Iannucci*

25. My Strip

T HE THOROUGHFARES OF THE AMERICAN LANDSCAPE HAVE been sanded flat by commerce. Wherever you go, there are the same bold trademarks fighting for your attention, signs for fast-food joints, casual dining joints, rib joints, steak joints, Walmarts and Kmarts, chain hotels and chain motels. You can hit a strip and not know if you are in San Jose or Santa Fe, in Virginia or Maryland or Delaware. And then you approach a strip as anonymous as all the rest and yet in the curve of the boulevard, in the rhythm of the signs, in the juxtaposition of that McDonald's with that Target with that Sunoco, you feel a vibration in your chest. Because that McDonald's is where you used to hang when you cut lunch in high school. And that Target used to be the Sears where your mom bought that cheap red bicycle you rode back and forth on your street all afternoon. And that Sunoco is where you filled up your mom's Chevy that time you were so wasted you drove off with the hose still jammed into your car and tragicomedy ensued. This isn't just any strip, this is your strip, and suddenly you know you are home.

It should have been no surprise that I was heading back to the old neighborhood. What criminal doesn't have the urge to return to the scene of the crime? But what did surprise me were the emotions that welled as I drove along my old strip. There was fear, of course, and despair at ever fixing this thing, and a lingering nausea that hadn't left me from that moment in the gun shop when I knew I had finally been found. But there was also excitement, a quickening of the pulse. If you asked me what I considered my home, I would tell you Patriots Landing, or maybe the leafy Main Line suburb of my early, prosperous youth, but the emotions I was feeling now would put a lie to all of that. Whatever the word *home* meant, for me, even against my will, it meant Pitchford.

I couldn't resist a quick visit to Henrietta Road.

I expected the suburban slum of my memory, I expected desolation row, but what I found was a pleasant street of split-level houses in a wide variety of colors. The lawns were mowed, the siding kempt, the spindly trees grown lustrous. My old house, forever the Bernstein house, was well cared for, as were most of the others. In fact, the Grubbins house was the only one on the block that seemed in disrepair, as if our ghosts continued to haunt the place. But more surprisingly, there was none of the despondency I felt behind the FOR SALE signs in Augie's old neighborhood, none of the hidden desperation behind the FOR SALE signs in Patriots Landing. In fact, on the whole of Henrietta Road there was not a single FOR SALE sign posted, as if the downturn had missed this small slice of the housing market.

A little slice of heaven?

It was difficult to relate the wholesome scene I was driving through to the hardscrabble street of my memory. Henrietta Road seemed an altogether decent place to raise a family. It was already after school when I made my pilgrimage and kids were jumping rope and playing football in the street, as if the game I had seen on my first day had been ongoing for the last thirty years without interruption. There were more blacks in the game now, in fact it was a pretty large majority, but when they interrupted the game to let me pass they eyed me with the same sly surliness with which we had eyed the cars that momentarily forced us from our playing field. I wondered how different Eric's life would have been if he had grown up on Henrietta Road, playing ball on the street with lifelong friends instead of holed up in his room playing *Call of Duty*. I wondered if Shelby would have been happier had she jumped double Dutch on the sidewalk with the girls on the corner. The wide and well-curbed streets of Patriots Landing seemed suddenly sterile. What had my blighted aspirations as a boy done to my own children?

But I wasn't in Pitchford to see the sights or wallow in regret. I had someone to find and I needed to find him fast. I took a left off Henrietta Road, passed Augie's old street, drove a bit deeper into Pitchford until I took another left. I stopped in front of a split-level with a ragged brick facing and stared for a bit, and as I stared my palms started to itch.

The name DIFFENDALE was painted on a sign above the house number. I wiped my hands on my pants as I climbed the steps to the Diffendale door and waited a beat before knocking. Suddenly as nervous as a schoolkid, I might as well have been polishing my shoes on the back of my pants leg and checking my breath for stink. It is funny how sometimes no matter how far you run, you end up in the exact same place.

"Yes?" said the woman, standing in the shadows as she answered the door so that only her glistening eyes were lit. And when I didn't answer right away she spoke slow and loud, as if it was my hearing that was the problem, or I was French. "Can I help you?"

Then, as if through a haze, her eyes narrowed in recognition.

"Hello, Madeline," I said finally. "Long time no see."

26. Oh, Madeline

OKAY, I ADMIT, I HAD FANTASIZED REUNION SCENES WITH Madeline Worshack over the years. One of the roles for old girlfriends in our lives is to be the raw meat that feeds our fantasies. We'd meet up by chance, by design, on a beach, in a hotel, behind a Dumpster outside a fast-food joint. She'd be married, she'd be divorced, she'd be something, it didn't much matter, and it would begin. To be honest, I had fantasized about movie stars and folk singers, about my kids' teachers and various Little League wives. They say men think about sex every fifty-two seconds, and I was determined to do my share. I've even fantasized about my wife, no matter how pathetic that might sound. But number one on the pop charts had always been Madeline Worshack.

Not anymore.

"I shouldn't have been surprised to see you on my doorstep, J.J.," said Madeline when we were sitting across from each other in her living room. She had brought out beers from the kitchen, had downed hers in three quick snatches before I had even taken a sip. "What with everybody and his sister showing up asking about you."

"About me? Who?"

"The police, for one," she said. "They wondered if I knew how to find you. Something about a suspicious death in Las Vegas. They said it was Augie. Is that true?"

"Yes, sadly. But why would they be looking for me?"

"They said you were a person of interest in the Vegas investigation."

"What did you tell them?"

"The truth. That I thought you were dead."

"Good answer," I said.

Her house was dark. And it wasn't just that the curtains of the big picture window were closed or that the lamplight was dim. There was a gloom hovering within that house, spreading its tattered wings over Madeline, my Madeline.

"And even before the police came," she said, "there was someone on that same doorstep asking about J.J. Moretti. A man."

"Did he give you a name?"

"Something. I don't remember. But he had a tattoo on his neck. And he was trouble, I could tell. One thing I can spot a mile off now is trouble."

"What did you tell him?"

"The same. And when he laughed and said he doubted it, I just told him that I didn't really know and I didn't really care."

"Did he buy it?"

"The truth usually goes over. You want another beer?"

"No, thank you, I'm fine."

"So what happened to Augie?"

I waited a beat before I said, "Drugs."

"He was always headed there, wasn't he? Augie should have been pictured in the yearbook under *Most Likely to Die Beneath a Highway Overpass.*"

Something about that grated. "He died in his bed," I said.

"You want another beer? Oh yeah, you said no already. But I'll have one. To celebrate our reunion." She rose from her chair and turned her back on me as she made her way into the kitchen. "Have you been home since graduation?" she said as she pulled open the fridge.

"This is my first time back in Pitchford. After high school I just wanted to disappear."

"I know you hated this place," she said, now standing the kitchen doorway, twisting open her beer, "but it was like you dropped off the edge of the earth."

I lifted my bottle in salutation. "Mission accomplished."

"You look the same, J.J. Just a little fatter in the face. And your nose grew. And someone beat the hell out of you. But other than that..."

"You look the same, too," I lied. "So Madeline, how's life? Really."

"You've been away for twenty-five years. You don't get to show up on my door one day like a magician's trick and ask that question. How's your stinking life?"

"I've had my ups and downs. And downs."

"You're not just saying that to cheer me up, are you?"

"My wife wants a divorce, my kids hate me, and I owe too much money to the wrong people."

"Thank you," she said. "God, whatever happened to us, anyway?"

"You broke up with me."

"I thought it was you who broke up with me."

"Do you want me to go over it word for word? Because I still remember each and every one."

"That's the nicest thing I've heard in years," she said. "And you're right, it was me. I broke your little heart, didn't I?"

"I got over it," I said, suddenly surprised at how pissed off I was. "But why'd you do it? I was never quite sure."

"Richie had a better car," she said.

"I only had my mom's old beater."

"Exactly. And..."

"Go ahead."

"Forget it."

"No, go ahead. Why?"

"I was young, and I was pretty. Wasn't I pretty?"

"You were pretty."

"And now?"

I peered at her through the murk of time. She was still slim enough, but not a sexy slim anymore, more like the slim of an old battered plank. The prettiness that had captured my breath was roughed down into plainness, the breezy manner was gone, the sexy laugh had turned bitter. I could just make out the curve of her face, more lumpish now than sharp and angular, and there was something slightly misshapen to her features. Her cheekbones had been razor-sharp when she was young, but they had somehow disappeared, beaten down by time or...yeah, that's what I thought, too.

"You don't have to answer," she said. "I can barely look at myself in the mirror. Life's rougher than I ever imagined. But in high school I needed to be the center of everyone's attention. And my boyfriend's attention most of all."

"You were."

"Not when I was with you."

"Then what was?"

"I never knew. I needed you to adore me, but your eyes were always on something else."

"And Richie Diffendale adored you?"

She let that hang there for a moment. "Sophomore year of college I actually went to find you up in Massachusetts. It was in the middle of...let's say a difficult time. And I was thinking about you, and how nice we were together, and so I screwed up my courage and hopped a train to Boston. I don't know what I thought would happen, maybe everything, maybe nothing, at least that we'd fuck again. I figured everyone would know your name, but the surprise was no one did. You weren't even a ghost. I went to the administration office, but there was no record of you ever even showing up."

"Boston College didn't quite work out. I ended up at Wisconsin. It was a better fit."

"And you never called to let me know."

"I'm surprised Richie let you go up looking for me. He always seemed the jealous type."

"I wasn't with him then. We broke up at the end of the summer after graduation."

"I didn't know that."

"You had driven that truck off to Florida already. But I broke up with Richie before I went to Maryland. I wanted to be totally free when I started my new life."

"How'd that work out?"

"Not so well," she said. "I wasn't ready for college academically. I had played around too much in high school. And then I got involved with a lacrosse player."

"Lacrosse players," I said, shaking my head.

"I crashed and I burned. I was flunking out, I was feeling scared, I was totally lost. I needed to be rescued. And the thing is, J.J., I hoped it was you who would swoop down and do the rescuing."

"Me?"

"Funny, huh?"

"I didn't know."

"How could you?"

"Why me?"

"Because of all the boys I had known, you were the nice one. And that's what I needed then, someone nice. It's an underrated quality."

"By the hot girls, yeah. So what happened?"

"I was sitting on the green in front of the library, wearing long sleeves on a hot day—I've gone through bad times since, but nothing is as bad as teenaged bad—needing desperately to be rescued, and I looked up and there he was, like a gift."

"Richie Diffendale."

She took a long swallow of her beer. "And the gift keeps giving."

"I never liked him."

She scraped at the label on her bottle with a thumbnail. "Richie always thought you guys, you and Ben and Augie, took the Grubbins money."

"Is that what Richie thought?"

"Over the years I've told him he was crazy, but when that guy with the tattoo on his neck showed up a few weeks ago asking his questions, Richie just mashed my face in it. It proved he was right all along, he said."

"There's a reason I never liked him."

"Is it true?"

"You're asking if I took the money?"

"Yes. Did you take it, J.J.?"

"I live in a suburb in Virginia. If had the money I'd be living on a beach instead, don't you think?"

"Well, you wouldn't be living here, that's for sure."

I looked at my bottle, took a quick swig, kept looking at it as I said, "I always thought Tony took it."

"Tony?"

"Well, it was his house. He was the only one who might have known something was there. And he was selling drugs all through high school. Maybe he decided to go for the big score."

"It wasn't Tony."

"How do you know for sure?"

"Because Tony actually does live here."

My neck tightened in raw adolescent fear. "Tony Grubbins is in Pitchford?"

"He has a drywall business. I see his truck go by now and then."

"My God, I thought he'd be in jail. I guess putting up drywall in Pitchford beats doing time, but not by much." I picked at the beer label with my thumb. "What's he up to other than drywall?"

"You remember the Stoneway?"

"The stripper joint on the hill."

"Tony works there nights as a bouncer. Dates one of the girls."

211

"Everybody's dream."

"It's Richie's, for sure. He almost single-handedly keeps that place open. But it's sort of funny, J.J., you being suddenly so interested in Tony Grubbins after spending all of high school running away from him. Why the sudden curiosity? Maybe Richie's right after all."

"Richie's not right," I said, "about anything."

"Another beer?"

"No, thanks."

"Getting drunk with you is like drinking alone."

"I didn't know that's what we were doing."

"It's a Wednesday afternoon. What did you think we were doing?"

When she came back from the kitchen with a fresh beer, I was standing. "I can't stay," I said.

"Oh, come on, J.J., stick around, have another drink with me. Don't you want to say hey to Richie?"

"Richie's an asshole."

"That asshole is my husband."

"That's no excuse."

"He showed up, J.J. Where the hell were you?"

"Do you need my help, Madeline?"

"Don't you have enough troubles of your own? What about the guy with the tattoo on his neck?"

"I already took care of him."

"My tough little man. So you're going to rescue me now?"

"Maybe it's time to rescue yourself."

"You're not so nice anymore, J.J."

"I don't hit women."

"You might if you were married to me."

"No, I wouldn't. I loved you."

"I was pretty, wasn't I?"

"Breathtaking."

"You were always so nice. I've wondered what it would have been like if you showed up in front of the library that time instead of Richie. I even imagined what it would be like if you showed up just like this on my doorstep."

"Did it live down to your expectations?"

"Every damn one."

27. The Stoneway

THE STONEWAY, SET HIGH ON A RISE OVER THE PITCHFORD strip, stared down at my old suburb like a Romanian pimp, scarred and hard faced. For a Pitchford brat growing up in its shadow, the Stoneway had been something like a dare. It was the promised land of adulthood, a place to smoke, buy drinks, watch women who stripped naked and licked their nipples just for you. Disneyland for horny teens. The three immortals had each, in turn, climbed that hill and tried to slip inside with an Augie-special ID and each, in turn, had been turned away, and not so kindly either. A slap of the head, a kick in the rear, an arm wrenched if we tried to sneak by while the bouncer's attention was elsewhere. The Stoneway had remained a distant dream, unfulfilled by any of us before I left Pitchford for good.

Augie had eventually made it, though. While he was still living at home and watching his father die, he had become a regular at the Stoneway. From what he told me in our weekly phone conversations, he got drunk there, got high there, sold drugs there, got blown there. I always worried that he was slipping our hot hundreds into even hotter G-strings (and for all I know he was, which might explain the getting blown there), but for Augie the dream never died and the Stoneway seemed to become the very model on which he based the rest of his disastrous life. I suppose the best thing that never happened to me was getting into that joint.

But there has to be a first time for everything.

I dimmed the interior lights of my car as I made the turn up the steep drive to the club. My neck strained nervously as I checked out the bouncer at the solid front door. Huge, and hard, and black. I took a deep breath, pulled the car to the far corner of the half-filled lot, and parked. The bouncer barely looked at my Edward Holt ID as I hunkered down in the collar of my golf jacket, paid my ten-buck cover, and passed through two doors and one bead curtain into the forbidden pleasure palace of my youth.

It was not as big as I had imagined—Hagia Sophia would not be as big as my teenaged self had imagined the Stoneway—but it didn't disappoint in its utter seediness. The walls were purple and plush, the ceiling was black, the music loud, the carpet stained. Running up the entire left side were alcoves, each with its own curtain that could be taken off its hook and spread across the alcove's opening for privacy. A woman in a bikini came out from behind one of the curtains, fixed her top, wiped her mouth with the back of her hand. A woman without a bikini worked the runway to the right, two poles and a disco ball for your viewing pleasure. The runway led directly to the wide bar, where two other naked women danced on either side, panning for dollars. Hot and hot-running girls at the Stoneway, so long as you like tepid.

Inside the bead curtain I looked around for a familiar face, found none, and, relieved, made my way to the corner of the bar, a long strip of wood for drinks raised a few inches above a four-foot-wide dance parquet. The plan was...well, the plan was to come up with a plan. I needed to find Tony, that was what my disturbing visit to Madeline had been all about, and I needed to find out if Tony was behind the bastards who had killed Augie and come after me. He had set the motorcycle goons on my ass twenty-five years before, leaving my throat scarred for life, and he was the most likely to have set Clevenger on our trails. If he was the one, I had to turn the tables or make a deal. And to do that, I needed to learn what I could about his life now.

"What'll it be?" said the barkeep.

"Huh?" I said, staring up at the woman gyrating on the bar just to my left. Black hair, breasts gloriously false, long legs, red high heels close enough that I could have licked them clean if I were so inclined. She looked down and smiled. I bit my lip. She gave me a hip pop and shimmied away.

"A drink," said the bartender. "You want a drink, pal?"

"Why else would I be here?" I said, still staring at the woman.

"No idea."

"How about a vodka martini? Use the Belvedere. And are your olives any good? Do you have Manzanillas from Spain?"

The bartender was kind and didn't laugh, he just stared for a moment as I let the surroundings seep in. I was no longer at the taproom of the Patriots Landing Golf Club. "Use whatever and throw in a twist of lemon."

"Nine seventy."

I pulled out a hundred, slapped it on the bar. The dancer's head snapped to the sound; her eyes focused like lasers on the bill. She smiled broadly at me as she made her way back.

When the change came, along with the drink, it was all in fives. It took three bills, two in a red high heel and one in a G-string, before the dancer slid away again. And suddenly I wished Augie and Ben were there with me. They would have made it a party, Augie egging on the girls, Ben holding cautiously on to his money, Augie ordering a round of lap dances, Ben shying away, Augie pushing us all into going way too far and then one step beyond, the three of us laughing about it all with some reefer back in the woods. *God, I don't think I've laughed uproariously since high school.*

"Is Tony in tonight?" I said when the barkeep came over to make me another drink.

"You a friend of his?"

"We went to school together."

"I didn't know that knucklehead even went to school."

"He sort of checked in at lunch and checked out after study hall," I said, as if Tony and I were the best of buds back in the day.

"I don't think he's working tonight, but he usually comes in anyway at some point."

"I hear he's dating one of the girls."

"For a while now." He nodded toward a tall blonde woman in a bikini and leopard high heels chatting with a man at the far end of the bar. "Chastity."

"I bet she is. She seems sweet."

"They all seem sweet," said the bartender.

"Nice shoes, though," I said. "When you have a moment, can you send Chastity over here? I'd like to buy her a drink."

It wasn't long before she was by my side, her body taut and powdered, her breasts barely contained by a bikini top. She was older than I had first calculated from a distance, almost my age, but with abs like in an infomercial, and she smiled at me as if she had always liked my type, whatever type I was. It always amazes me how attracted women are to me in strip clubs, as long as the women being attracted are strippers.

"So you know Tony?" she said.

"Old friends," I said.

"What's your name? I'll be sure to tell him you came in."

"Augie."

"I like that name."

"He ever mention me?"

"Not so as I recall."

"It was a long time ago. What are you having, Chastity?"

"Champagne cocktail, please."

"Why am I not surprised?" I said as I spun my finger to the bartender and pointed at her. "So tell me about good old Tony. I haven't seen him for a while. Still humping that drywall?"

"For now, but you know Tony, he's always got things percolating."

"He's a doer, all right," I said. "Anything specific?"

"Tell me about yourself, Augie," she said as she took her drink from the bartender, ginger ale in a champagne glass, no doubt, for a mere $12.50. She dipped a long red fingernail in her drink and ran it lightly on the upper flesh of her breast. "What do you like?"

"I sure like that," I said.

She licked her teeth. "You want to find a little privacy? We could rent ourselves one of the pods."

"Pods?"

She nodded toward the curtained alcoves.

"I really only want to talk."

"We can do whatever you want in there, sweetie," she said, running her nail lightly over my cheek.

"How much is a pod?"

"Twenty-five for fifteen minutes, fifty for the half hour."

"I can do the math."

"Plus."

"Plus?"

"You said you wanted to talk, right? We'll talk about the plus once we get in there."

"It's going to be an expensive half hour."

"Oh, it will be worth it, I promise you."

"Go ahead, Frenchy," said a voice from behind me. "It's only money. Better enjoy yourself while you can."

I felt a fission of fear fizzle up my nerves at the sound of my old nickname. My neck tensed and my hand twitched as I turned around slowly. The man who had spoken was leering at me. Tall and sloppy, relentlessly middle-aged, a bad shave, a bad comb-over, owly glasses, his two front teeth dementedly twisted. At the very sight of him I felt an anger rise in me, something old and young, something lovesick and postadolescent.

"Or maybe better yet," said Richie Diffendale, "why don't we talk business before you stain your pants."

28. The Pilot Fish

L ET ME GET THIS STRAIGHT," SAID RICHIE DIFFENDALE,
resentment riding like a surfer along the extended vowels of
his Pitchford accent. "You thought you'd show up after all these
years like a pizza delivery boy and grab yourself a quick piece of
action with my wife. Was that the idea?"

"It stinks to see you, too," I said. Diffendale had sent off
Chastity so we could talk privately, downgrading the view consid-
erably. I was leaning both elbows on the drink shelf now, trying to
control the anger I was feeling while Richie spewed his irate gloat,
along with his spittle, into my ear.

"Boy, did you ever pick the wrong house," he said.

"Let me buy you a drink."

"You want to keep it friendly, is that it? You try to make my
wife and you want to keep it friendly?"

"Do you want the drink?"

"Hell yes. You sure as hell can afford it." He scratched his ear.
"Rum and Coke. The good rum, too."

I waved to the bartender and ordered a Bacardi and Coke for
Richie and another vodka martini for me. The barkeep looked
at me, at Richie, back at me, as if he were offering some sort of
assistance, as if Richie Diffendale were the kind of regular who
often pestered guys at the bar whose only offense was trying
to get quietly soused as they looked at a little nookie. I nodded

to the bartender that it was okay and he went off to make the drinks.

"I knew it was you that did it," said Richie.

"Is that so?"

"I looked around and wondered who were big enough assholes to steal that much money, and the answer was easy. On the asshole meter, you and your two pals were always at the top."

"You're such a clever one."

"Clever enough to cage your girl, huh? I bet that always ate you alive. Maddie was out of my league until she started up with a frog like you. You teed her up for me."

"Another thing I can feel guilty about for the rest of my life. So what are you up to these days, Richie? Still cleaning Tony's ass?"

"I'm in sales."

"Toupees? Gym equipment? What?"

"Plumbing supplies."

"Toilets. Perfect."

"You know what it was that clued me in for sure? You guys always acted as if you knew more than the rest of us, as if you were granted some special knowledge. Those arrogant grins."

"We were high, that's all it was."

"So when the money disappeared and everyone was looking for it behind every damn door, to understand what was really behind those smiles of yours didn't take a genius."

"Which meant you were perfect for the job."

"It was the unfairness of it more than anything that got to me. I was Tony's pal, I was in that house all the time, but it was you guys who ended up with the cash. All I ever wanted was my share."

"What are you complaining about? You won, Richie, you got Madeline."

"Oh yeah? Don't get me started on Maddie. There's a reason I'm here every night, let me tell you. But see, I was never the type to just sit back and get pissed on. I see angles a pool shark would miss. Like when those motorcycle freaks were buzzing the neighborhood after the money disappeared."

I turned and looked at his ugly face. "What about it?"

"I pulled one of the freaks over and made an offer."

"You made an offer?"

"I had my sights on Maddie, and on a piece of the money you assholes heisted, and so I took a combination shot."

Just then the bartender brought our drinks over.

"Cheers," said Richie, lifting his drink in a mock gesture of friendship and gratitude. I closed my eyes and took a sip and let the burn slip down my throat and mix with the something ugly and sick within me. It had been there from my visit to Madeline, had risen when I recognized his twisted front teeth, and it felt just then that it would explode in my chest, as if the vodka was mixing with nitroglycerine.

"It didn't work out quite like I thought," said Richie. "They didn't find the money on you, so I only pocketed one ball, on the rebound, you could say. I thought that maybe I had been wrong about you after all."

"You were wrong."

"That maybe it was the cops that actually scored the cash."

"It probably was."

"So I let it go, but it nagged at me. I had been so sure. And then, all these years later, that guy Holmes with the tattoo appears at the house and suddenly I knew I was right from the first. I mean, why else would a hard case like that be looking for a winkle like you? He put a price on your head, too, did you know that?"

"Dead or alive?" I said.

"Alive, unfortunately. After that I was just praying you'd show up, and I must be doing something right in the Big Guy's eyes because here you are."

"So how much am I worth to you, Richie?"

"See, that's the thing. I figure you can beat his price to keep me quiet. That's my new angle. What with all the cash you took all those years ago, and with the stock market climbing like it did in that time, I bet you got yourself a seven-figure bundle by now. I only want six."

"Six dollars?"

"Six figures."

"That's a lot of money."

"Cash."

"You're dreaming."

"Sure I am, I'm dreaming big. But whatever I get, it will be less than that guy with the tattoo will take off you. By the look of your face, he already started the job. You can bet that next time he'll finish it."

"So it's a bargain is what you're saying."

"Absolutely."

"One I can't afford not to take advantage of."

"You're smarter than I remember."

"You have me in a vise."

"That's right."

"A hundred thousand dollars in cash, just like that. As if I had it sitting there in the trunk of my car."

"A hundred thousand is just the starting point. We'll negotiate the details later." He took out his phone. "I already called the number, said I might have you spotted. The guy on the other end, a guy named Clevenger, said he could have someone on-site in ten minutes if I give him a location. Do I make the call or do we have a deal?"

"What's my alternative?"

"Exactly."

"Other than putting a gun to your head."

Something ugly slipped out of his eyes just then, his unwarranted arrogance fell away, replaced by uncertainty. He looked at me and took a long gulp of his drink and then, as if the rum and

Coke had suddenly increased the size of his balls, tried to smile his way out of the threat. "Don't pretend to be something you're not, J.J. I've known you too long."

"See, that's the thing, Richie, you've never known me at all. Normally I'd just ignore you, like I'd ignore a piece of dog shit in the street. But it turns out you're the one who gave me the scar on my neck, making you a piece of dog shit on my shoe, which is a lot harder to ignore. And then there's Madeline."

"What about her?"

"Do you only hit her on special occasions, Richie, or is it an everyday thing?"

"Why, what did that bitch say?"

"How does it make you feel when you hit her? Like you're finally getting your share?"

"Whatever she said, she's lying."

"She chose you, you son of a bitch. Of all the people in this world, Madeline Worshack chose you. You showed up when she was down and she allowed you into her life, and you should be worshipping her every day for that one act of grace. Instead you haunt a dump like this and complain about the things she won't do. And you hit her to make yourself feel like someone other than the piece of dog shit you are."

"Forget it," he said, looking down at his phone as he started pressing buttons. "I'll take what Clevenger is giving. It comes without the bullshit. Enjoy your death, asshole."

"I'll surely enjoy yours," I said as I calmly pulled Holmes's gun out of the holster clipped onto my belt and jammed the tip of the barrel hard into Richie Diffendale's temple.

"Ow," he said when the metal banged into his head. And when he realized exactly what it was I was pressing into his head, his eyes widened nicely. I took his phone, dropped it into his drink. Beneath the grinding music, I could hear a silence descend in the bar. Even in a strip club, with breasts bobbing all about, you pull out a gun and it will be noticed.

"What do you want?" he said.

"I want to kill you."

"I won't call, I swear."

"See, the problem is, I can't trust you further than I could spatter your brain. Which is only as far as that wall. So really, what choice do I have? You've got me in a vise, all right."

"You'll be in jail the rest of your life."

"No, I won't. I'm two names beyond J.J. Moretti already. For twenty-five years I was a ghost in Pitchford. Once I kill you, I'll walk out of here and become a ghost again."

"You're crazy. You can't just walk out."

"Who do you think will stop me?" I slapped his cheek with the barrel so his head jerked toward the bartender, who was standing stock-still not five feet from us, staring at the gun. "Him?"

"Help me," said Diffendale in a voice as gratifyingly high as a castrato's.

The bartender slowly, carefully, ducked down until he disappeared.

"Her?" I said as I slapped his other cheek so he turned toward a girl in a bikini who had been not three feet from us but was now backing away.

"Oh God, no."

"Him?" I said, slapping his face again so his head swiveled toward a man in a black leather jacket who was suddenly standing by the door.

"He's going to kill me," said Diffendale.

"No, he's not," said the tall man in a hushed gravel road of a voice.

I took a longer look at the man, who had now taken two steps toward us. He wasn't the bouncer who had been here when I arrived. This man was taller and broader, with a hard face, long blond hair, a blond goatee. And there was something familiar in the squint of his eye.

I suddenly swiveled the gun to the huge man's gut. "Do you have next ups, Tony?" I said. "Do I have to kill you after I kill him?"

"You won't have time for both of us," said Tony Grubbins. "You'll only get one shot before Sid behind the bar blows your head off."

I looked to my left. The bartender, who had ducked down, was up again with a shotgun trained at my head. Now I was in a vise for sure. My mind clicked like a baseball card in the spokes of a bicycle wheel through all the James Bond moves that could get me out of this. Maybe, if I dropped down below the bar, I could pop Tony and Richie both, before rolling like an acrobatic monkey out of the club, evading Sid's buckshot. It almost seemed reasonable, excepting the small detail that in a million years I couldn't pull it off.

"Then I guess it's you, Tony," I said. "For what you did to Augie."

"What'd I do to Augie?"

"Don't even try pretending you don't know."

"Alls I know, Moretti, is after a couple decades of never thinking of your ugly face, I come into the Stoneway and here you are with a gun at Diffendale's head. Not that he doesn't deserve it every now and then."

I considered it all for a moment, considered the calm behind Tony Grubbins's hushed voice, considered the way it turned out that Richie and not Tony had sent those Devil Rams assholes into my bedroom the night I got my scar, and then, without saying a word, I turned the gun back on Richie Diffendale.

"Shit," said Richie Diffendale.

"I have an idea," said Tony Grubbins. "Instead of dying today and really messing up the decor of the club, why don't we all just calm down, act like human beings, and have ourselves a couple of beers?"

29. Tony Grubbins

I T WAS A MOVE BORN OF FEAR AND HYSTERIA, MY PULLING A gun on Richie Diffendale. I didn't intend to kill him, but I sure as hell meant to scare the crap out of the twists of his bowel. And it felt surprisingly good, like I was pulling a gun on the bastards who had killed Augie and were chasing me now, like I was pulling a gun on all my fears and frustrations, like I was pulling a gun on my past. But even as I pulled that gun on Tony Grubbins's pilot fish, I knew it was as if I were dumping a bucket of chum into the ocean. And like the shark he had been, Grubbins wheeled around and came for the blood.

Now Tony and Richie and I sat in a ratty back office of the club, a room lined with old file cabinets and piled with empty liquor boxes, a tragic fire just waiting to happen. Being in the same metropolitan area as Tony Grubbins gave me the sweats; being in the same room as Tony Grubbins was appallingly terrifying. He could have been wearing a priest's collar and I'd still be shaking. It was something deep and primitive, this fear, and I desperately missed the security of a gun in my hand, but Tony had insisted I hand the piece off to the bartender before we did any talking and, like my fourteen-year-old self, I had done what Tony ordered. So there I was, facing off against the monster beneath my bed with fear in my heart and only a beer bottle in my hand.

Grubbins leaned back and stared at me from behind an old metal desk, lit a cigarette, tossed the smoldering match into one of the empty cartons. A curl of smoke rose out of the box.

"Okay, this is good," said Tony, his voice a crushed pack of Marlboros. "The guns are put away and we're almost acting civilized."

"He took it," said Richie Diffendale.

"Took what, Richie?"

"The money, man. From your house. The money that the Devil Rams stashed with all them drugs."

"You think little J.J. Moretti here took that money?"

"I know it."

"And that's why he came back to Pitchford and put a gun to your head?"

"So I wouldn't tell."

"Tell who?" said Tony.

"You."

"Me?" Tony stared blankly at Richie. "It wasn't my money. Why the hell would I care?"

I cocked my head at that. Nothing in the last few days had surprised me more. Why wouldn't he care? Why wouldn't everyone care?

"And there's someone looking for him, Tony. Someone looking hard."

Tony took a draw from his cigarette and exhaled slowly, like he was trying to figure something out. "You said Augie Iannucci was murdered, is that right, Moretti?"

"That's right."

"Richie, is this guy you were going to tell about seeing Moretti the same guy who killed Augie?"

"I don't know anything about what happened to Augie," said Richie.

"Don't you think you ought to find out before jumping into the deep water?"

"Right after the police found the drugs," I said, "the Devil Rams stormed into my house, looking for the missing money. They gave me this scar."

"What did they find?" said Tony.

"They found nothing, because there was nothing there. But I always assumed it was you who did the ratting."

"Pretty fair assumption," he said.

"But tonight I found out it was Richie."

"And that's why you pulled the gun."

"Wasn't I justified?"

"They came for me, too," said Tony. "This was after I was sent to that group home for rejects. Two of my brother's old gang pals, Corky and the Fat Dog. They wanted the money, which I didn't have. And then they wanted a name."

"Who did you give them?" I said.

"I wanted to give them you, Moretti. Not because I thought you had the money, just for spite. That's the kind of kid I was. We had that thing between us."

"Yeah, I'm sorry about that."

"I'm not. I had a lot of hate in me and it was a pleasure dishing it out to you because you had hate in you, too."

"Me?"

He let the smoke rise in front of his face. "But I sure as hell wasn't going to let those bastards beat it out of me."

"You protected me?"

"Not you. Something else."

"What about our share, man?" said Richie.

"Our share of what, Richie?" said Tony. "It wasn't your money either."

"But it sure as hell wasn't Frenchy's. If he wants to keep us quiet, he needs to pay."

"Truth is, I don't know if there was ever any money to take," said Tony, looking now at his cigarette as it smoldered. "I always thought my brother made off with it long before, and then called in the cops to arrest his butt and get him off the street. It's something he would have pulled. A few years in jail and the rest of his life to spend like a fool, no matter what happened to me. That would explain why he's disappeared off the face of the earth; he's spending his cash in every whorehouse in South America."

"But the guy who is looking for Moretti offered up a reward," said Richie. "We can split it, Tony. You and me."

"Blood money, dude."

"As long as it's J.J.'s blood," said Richie.

"Guys like that," said Tony, shaking his head. "I been around enough to know that guys like that don't leave loose ends."

"I can take care of myself," said Diffendale.

"Like you were taking care of yourself at the bar when Moretti here put a gun in your face? You get guns put in your face enough times, one of them is bound to go off. My advice, Richie, is to forget all about our friend Moretti here. Anything else won't end well. Now get on home to your wife."

Richie sneered at me before he stomped out of the room; I pointed my finger at him like the barrel of a gun. Tony shook his head as if saddened at the very state of the human race.

Tony Grubbins was nothing like I had expected after twenty-five years. Sure, he was raw and huge and scarred and imposing, the kind of guy if I saw him in an alley I'd throw my wallet at him and run the other way, but there was something in his manner that I found shocking. As if the hate that had been his defining trait as a boy had somehow been burned right out of him. As if he had somehow evolved, evolved in a way I hadn't been able to.

"Richie always had issues," said Tony.

"So why'd you let him hang around with you all those years?"

"Every dog has fleas. What are you doing here, Moretti?"

"Someone killed Augie looking for the money," I said. "And now they're coming after me. And my family. I thought you were behind it."

"And what were you going to do about it?"

229

"I was going to do something."

"Die, most likely."

"Or make a deal."

"With what? That gun of yours? Do you even know how to shoot it?"

"It's got a trigger."

"And a safety, which was on," said Tony. "And a chamber that needs to be primed, which it wasn't. That gun was as dangerous as a mug of milk in your hand."

"Do you really not care about the money?"

He stared at me for a long moment as he finished his cigarette. "Let's just say if someone did steal it, he did me a favor."

"I don't understand."

"Yeah, well, you didn't live with my brother. You kick a dog enough, he just lies down and licks your hand and takes it. But when a stranger shows up, he becomes the most vicious son-of-a-bitch watchdog you ever saw."

"But you're not that dog anymore," I said, not a question, instead a puzzled declaration. "If it's not you, then it's your brother."

"How does that follow?"

"They called me Frenchy."

"Frenchy, huh? Derek would have known you by that name." Tony leaned forward on the desk, let the smoke wash over his face like a veil. "So," he said, his hushed voice wide with apprehension, "Derek's back."

"You look like the scientist in a Godzilla movie."

"I feel like I've been slugged."

"Do you have any idea where he is?"

"None."

"Who would?"

"You don't want to go there, trust me."

"I'm running for my life. My family's in hiding. I don't have a choice. I need to find your brother."

"You're saying all this as if I give a crap. Why on earth would I want to stick a shovel in the dirt and dig my brother up from wherever the hell he's buried himself?"

"Because he's doing to me what he did to you."

"Then do like I did: fix it yourself."

"I need your help."

"What you need to do is to go home."

"You owe me."

He laughed at that. "What could I possibly owe you?"

"You terrorized me, you beat me up, you threw a football at my face, you scarred my life. You owe me something."

"I threw a football at your face?"

"You don't remember?"

"No, but I'm sure you deserved it."

"And you killed my dog."

He looked at me, looked down at the desktop, rubbed his beard. "Yeah," he said finally, "I always felt bad about the dog."

30. Death in Guaymas

I WAS ANGRY AS A SCORPION WHEN IT ALL WENT DOWN," SAID Tony Grubbins in his husk of a voice. We were now in his pickup truck, well south of Pitchford, heading deep into the heart of Philadelphia. For some reason Tony had agreed to help me discover where I might find his brother, and I didn't think it was only because he had killed my dog thirty years before. "I was ripped away from everything I had ever known. For my own good, the judge said. But they couldn't find a relative willing to take me. So they put me in the group home, where Corky and the Fat Dog found me. First chance I got I stole a cycle and roared out of there."

"Where were you going?" I asked.

"It didn't much matter." He laughed a little. "And once I got there I kept on going. All I had was the anger, but it was better than a truckload of Red Bull at keeping me fueled."

There was something about this current incarnation of Tony Grubbins that made me doubt one of my most cherished certainties. I never believed that people changed. Their relationships changed, their luck, the size of their investment portfolios or the value of their real estate, even their habits, but the inner person, the continuing monologue that droned on and on through the entirety of a life, that didn't change—at least mine never did. That's why we could always recognize the kid in the adult. Richie

Diffendale was still the same owl-eyed brat, Augie had always been the same self-destructive sardonic daredevil, I was the same calculating resentful snit. But this man sitting next to me seemed a living refutation of what I had taken for comforting fact. Simply sitting next to him was disorienting. "What the hell happened to you?" I had asked him, a little amazed. This was his answer.

"And it wasn't just the things that had been done to me by my brother that caused the anger, it was also the things I had done. I had become as much an animal as he was. That's what happens when you get beat on every day of your life: you find places to release the pain. In the schoolyard, on the football field, in the backseat of a Chevy with insecure girls. And that's the way I still was, when, in the middle of the desert, I ran into Nat."

* * *

It was in a bar in Nogales where Tony had beaten the crap out of some migrant who had accidentally caused him to spill his beer. Nat was old and gray and missing half his teeth, but his eyes remained sharp enough to see Tony clear. With the blood still drying on Tony's hands, Nat pulled him aside, bought him a drink, made a proposition. They were holding unsanctioned prize fights on the other side of the border—no rules, bare fists— and they were looking for Anglos who could take a beating. The money was good, but for Tony the violence was better. He signed on right then, and was in the ring the next night.

It was a raucous crowd of Mexicans and dissolute Americans, all being worked on by bookmakers and prostitutes, by tequila boys moving through the stands and selling shots. The girls parading around the ring with numbered signs indicating the round were topless, the canvas floor of the ring was stained with blood and urine. Fighters came back into the basement dressing room with their noses flattened, their ears hanging, deltas of blood streaming from their foreheads. This wasn't boxing, this was cockfighting without the birds, pure barbarism untouched by art. For Tony Grubbins, running from something and running to nothing and angry at the world, it was perfect.

If I'm embellishing, humor me. Tony's story has expanded and grown in my mind's eye since first I heard him tell it. I take it out now and then like a golden coin and twist it in my fingers, rub its cold hard surface with my thumb, smile at its shine. For me, it is no longer just this tale I heard in the midst of danger, it is part of me. Every once in a while a story hits so deep it buries itself in your bone.

"Work fast and don't show fear," said Nat before the first bell that first night over the border.

"What's fear?" said Tony.

"Now you've got it," said Nat. His voice was high and scratched with age, the caw of a raven. "Don't play around in there. Start pounding and don't stop until you put him down."

Whatever crimes Derek Grubbins had committed against his brother, he had sure taught Tony how to fight. The first opponent Tony faced was a hard-muscled Mexican with scars on his chest and hate in his eyes. Tony worked him over without an ounce of pity, all while Nat was barking out, "Put him down. Put him down." Tony busted the Mexican's nose, smashed him to the canvas with an elbow to the neck, split his head wide open, and then split the purse with Nat. That night he pissed away most of his share in a brothel with a whore named Lita and was good to go the next morning.

After that, Tony and Nat made the circuit, leaving blood and broken bodies in every hectic city or small village they passed through. The mobs that came to see him fight dubbed him El Rubio Salvaje, The Blond Savage. He used to start slow on purpose, hands at his side, letting his opponents hit him at will. He liked to feel the blows to his face, he liked to taste his own blood, he liked to let the hopes of the crowd rise. It put him in the mood to wreak destruction. Then Nat would yell out in that raven's caw,

"Put him down," and Tony would do just that. It didn't matter if the other fighter was bigger or faster or more experienced. Tony was always angrier. He fed off the catcalls and boos that rained down, along with tomatoes and raw eggs, while he meted out his punishment. "Put him down." Broken ribs. "Put him down." Broken jaw. "Put him down." A nose smashed to jelly. Tony goaded the crowds, spit blood at them in the middle of his fights, cursed them in the crude Spanish slang he was learning from the whores. It was glorious.

El Rubio Salvaje.

And then one night in Guaymas, they matched him with a kid who wasn't a fighter. One look and Tony knew. Nat knew, too. But there was blood to be spilled and a purse to be won. Tony started with his hands by his side, letting the kid hit him, and he barely felt the blows. When Tony finally raised his hands and laid a fist on the kid's jaw, the kid went down like a sack of rice and Tony raised his arms in angry triumph. But the kid climbed back to his feet and took a swing, wild and unbalanced. Tony hit him again and down the kid went. "*Estancio abajo*," Tony said to him. *Stay down.* But the kid had something in him, ugly and fierce, just like Tony had something in him, ugly and fierce. The kid climbed up, smiled a bloodied cracked smile, and took another swing.

"The pug's got heart," said Nat between rounds.

"But nothing else," said Tony.

"Put him down."

"If I finish it, I'll kill him."

"Do what you got to do," said Nat, "but put him down."

When the bell rang, the kid, both eyes already half-closed, came right out swinging. Tony pushed him away and clocked him at the parting and the kid fell. And then got right back up and came again at Tony. And as Nat was yelling at Tony to put him down, the kid punched Tony in the face.

"So what did you do?" I said.

"I murdered him," said Tony Grubbins in the truck that night in the dark heart of Philadelphia. "It was like I had no choice. I held him up on the ropes and I beat him to death. Like I wanted to beat my brother to death, or the judge who sent me away, or the cancer that had killed my mother, or you and Augie and Ben, all of Pitchford, all of Pennsylvania, the whole damn country, anyone who had anything to do with my godforsaken life. And when it was over, when he was on the canvas, one leg shaking, and I had climbed the ropes to bellow at the mob, the crowd wasn't throwing eggs and tomatoes anymore, it was throwing chairs and bottles, knives. And I welcomed it all."

That night in Guaymas Tony didn't get drunk with a whore, he got drunk alone. When Nat came looking for him in the morning to take him to the next fight in the next town, he was already gone.

He didn't know where he was going, he didn't care. He went south from Guaymas, and then south again. He kept moving south for weeks, drinking and whoring away whatever money he had. Finally he found a clot of old hippies camped on some beach and he stayed drugged up with them for he didn't know how long. They slept on the sand, roasted fish on the fire, ate peyote, and fucked in the moonlight. Tony was trying to run from what he had done in that ring, what he had become, even as he was trying to embrace it, too, in some strange way. And the drugs, and the hippies, and the ritual dances around the fire, seemed to let him do both.

Then one night, by the light of a full moon, with a tab of acid under his tongue, Tony stripped naked, dove into the water, floated on his back, felt the press of the night sky on his chest. And he started crying. He cried for the kid he had killed, for the kid he himself had been, for the empty husk of the man he had become. And he found himself sinking, as if his limbs were wrapped in great iron chains. Water poured into his nose and his mouth as the chains pulled him down. Above him, lit by the moon, he saw a raven circling, his death wings outstretched, his caw like an invocation to the ocean itself. *Put him down. Put him down.* And the chains grew heavier, and the water kept pouring in, and the raven kept circling, and he knew he was going to die that night. And he was glad.

Yet even as he drowned in that ocean, he felt at the same time as if he was circling free in the sky, staring down through raven eyes at his dying body. And from that vantage he could see that the chains weren't wrapped around his limbs at all, they were held in his hands, and he was clutching them with a death grip. To become free and save himself, all he had to do was let go. Let go of the chains that were dragging him down and float freely back to the surface. He was a slave and he could be free—all he had to do was let go.

And right there beneath the surface of the water, under the bright silver moon, Tony Grubbins made a choice. He chose to open his fists. It was harder than it should have been, because he wasn't just letting go of the chains, he was letting go of himself, too. What was he without the prison of his past, without his pain or his anger, without his sweet violence? He didn't know, but he was ready to find out. It was the hardest thing he had ever done, harder than he ever could have imagined, but with all the strength he could muster from his soul he pried open his fists and let go of the chains.

Slowly he rose, out of the depths, back to the surface of the great heaving ocean. And as he gasped like a newborn for air he kept rising, right out of the water, his limbs spread, his chest arched, rising like a dream of freedom into the moon-drenched sky.

* * *

I sat there for a moment as we drove through the narrow urban streets of North Philly, a bit dazed, disconcerted by the juxtaposition of the fantastic elements of Tony's story and the hard reality we were driving through. Nothing is as rooted in the facts of this world as the streets of Philadelphia.

"Is any of that true?" I said finally.

"The acid," said Tony, laughing. "I was so wasted I had to piece together the other stuff from snatches of dreams."

"So it's all bullshit," I said, as if trying to comfort myself.

"It feels true," said Tony. "And I'll tell you this: when I stepped out of the water, naked in the moonlight, I was different. I was a free man, for the first time in my life."

"I'm free," I said, a defensive whine in my voice.

"Why did you pull that gun on Richie? Because he stole your girl when you were seventeen? Why did you point the gun at me? Because I killed your dog when you were eleven? Dude, you got more chains around your neck than King Kong."

"You're the one still living in Pitchford."

"By choice. In California I ran into a guy I used to know. Remember Denise? He told me Denise had a ten-year-old kid. She was married in Pitchford, and doing well by the kid, but ten years and nine months before that she was sleeping with me. My parents left me by dying. That was one of my chains. I was strong enough by then that I could choose to come back and take a chain away from the kid. So I did."

"How's he doing?"

"Pretty damn good."

"Why are you helping me find Derek?"

"Because I didn't want to. It's not so easy being free—you've got to keep letting go."

He pulled the truck to the side of the road and parked. We were in a district of worn-out warehouses with their windows boarded, of old factories long shuttered, of dreams murdered in their sleep by some invisible hand. In front of us, between two dead buildings, the only sign of life in the whole decrepit block was a neon sign with a pack of shined Harleys sitting out in front. The sign flickered and hissed into the night: THE DEVIL'S BREW.

"That's the unofficial clubhouse of my brother's old gang."

"Is he in there?" I said, a burp of panic rising in my throat.

"No, but his oldest gang mates might be. They could know where he is. I've been purposely avoiding that place since I've been back. I suppose it's time to stop the avoiding."

"What's the plan?" I said.

"Not to die, how's that?"

"No, we need a plan. We have to know why you're looking for your brother, and why now. We've got to have a cover story."

"A cover story."

"Yeah."

"You know what your problem has always been, Moretti? You think too much."

"Why don't we say that you're in some AA twelve-step program and you need to ask your brother for forgiveness? They might buy that."

"That's my cover story?"

"Your name is Tony and you're an alcoholic. I could be Jon, your sponsor."

Tony stared at me for the longest time, stared at me like I was a dog on the flying trapeze.

"It could work," I said.

"Like pulling a gun on Diffendale worked."

"It got your interest quick enough."

"Just keep your mouth shut and let me do the talking. And leave your gun here."

"I'm not going in there without a gun."

"You pull a gun in that place, they'll make sure you need to use it. And you use a gun in a place like that, you're not getting out alive. Put it in the glove box."

I thought about it for a moment, thought about how I hadn't remembered to prime the chamber, how Sid the bartender had trained that shotgun at my head without my even knowing it. I did the calculation and then did as he said. Not because I was scared of him but because he was right. And then, I don't know why—maybe it was his story, the image of all those chains being released from Tony's hands, or maybe it was the truth of what he said about me, about how I was bound like an oversized monkey to my past—but I did something I'd never thought I'd ever do in ten million years.

"I stole the money," I said to Tony Grubbins. "From your house. You should know that before you go in there. You had been selling us dust and stems at an unfair price, so I broke in looking for weed and I found two paint buckets filled with cash in the crawl space and I took them, both of them. It was me."

He looked at me for a moment, Tony Grubbins, the very face of my nightmares, something unfathomable working across his features, and then he said in that hushed voice of his, "Try not to tell them that."

31. Devil's Brew

As soon as we opened the door, the babble of conversations turned to silence. We were sized up quick and spit out flat, before the babble rose again. There were about twenty bearded motorheads in denim vests scattered about the place with half that number of biker chicks, although to be honest, even with the beards it wasn't so easy to tell them apart. The fantasy of the slim, leather-clad vixen gripping tightly to your chest as you roared westward on your Harley died an ugly death inside The Devil's Brew.

The very name still evokes a sensory overload in my memory. The wafting scent of vomit in an atmosphere already poisoned with nicotine, weed, and exhaust. A jukebox so loaded with heavy metal it could have been declared a toxic-waste site. A ratty pool table with a skinny old man in a ragged gang vest sleeping atop it. And tacked on the wall like deer heads, the vests from a whole host of different gangs, their colors slashed, many of them stained maroon. Seeing them there as we stepped inside, I could very well imagine my whole body hanging among the trophies like a stuffed marmoset.

The bartender stared at us both as we brushed through the hostile glares on our way to the bar, his gaze catching especially on my garb. I was wearing my usual: tan pants, brown loafers, a white dress shirt I had bought at a strip mall on my way up from Virginia. It was a look that wouldn't have batted an eye in Patriots Landing, but sitting at that bar in that hole, I'd have been less out of place wearing a tutu.

"Are you fellows sure you're in the right joint?" said the bartender, a broad-shouldered brute whose shaved head led inexorably to a jaw shaped like the head of a ball-peen hammer.

"You mean this isn't the Elks Club?" said Tony.

"My bet is you're not," said the barkeep. "What can I get you?"

Tony looked at me for a moment and cocked an eye before saying, "Two club sodas."

"Shots to go with it?" said the barkeep.

"No shots," said Tony. "Just a couple of limes."

"This is a funny kind of place to drive your wagon," said the barkeep. "Maybe you fellows should try Woody's on Thirteenth Street."

"We're wearing shoes and shirts," said Tony. "Make the damn drinks."

"Fine, pal, but take my advice and drink fast."

As the bartender spritzed the seltzers I said quietly to Tony, "I guess my plan wasn't so stupid after all."

"I couldn't come up with anything better on the fly."

"Now that I'm here, I could actually use a beer. In fact, right now I could use a Xanax."

"Crutches," said Tony as he took out a cigarette and a lighter and flicked it all to life.

"Two club sodas," said the bartender bringing over the drinks. "With limes." He looked at Tony with his lit cigarette. "You see the sign?"

Behind the bar was a small red sign that read By City Ordinance, Smoking Prohibited in All Public Places. Tony looked at the sign and then around at all the cigarettes burning in the place, their tips glowing like a herd of fireflies.

"I see it," said Tony before inhaling.

"Just checking," said the barkeep. "Give a holler if you guys think you can handle another round."

"Is Flynn around?" said Tony.

"Flynn who?"

"Fat Dog Flynn."

"You knew the Fat Dog?"

"A while ago, yeah."

"Seen him lately?"

"No."

"Guess not, since he's been dead ten years. Died in prison."

"I'm tearing up," said Tony.

The barkeep glanced quickly over at one of the tables and then leaned closer. "You did know the son of a bitch, didn't you?"

"What about Corky? Is he here?"

"Who the hell are you?"

"Someone who used to come around a long time ago."

"You were a member of the Rams?"

"My brother was."

"Oh yeah? Who's your brother?"

"Derek Grubbins."

The barkeep kept his quiet at the sounding of the name. And in a strange way his silence spread like a ripple in a pond, reaching outward along the bar to the tables. Even the jukebox quieted for a moment between songs as everyone in the place stared at the two of us. Tony hadn't been talking loudly, but the very name had seemed to cut through the room's haze of noise like the crystalline ring of a silver bell.

"Now I know you're in the wrong place," said the bartender, before heading out from behind the bar.

Tony and I watched as the bartender made his way to one of the tables at the far corner of the room. There was a big-boned moose at the table, his long scraggly hair falling out of a red bandanna tied over his head. Sitting next to him was a huge mound of a woman with stringy hair and tattoos up and down her billboard-sized arms. A woman so big her shadow had stretch marks, a woman so ugly her pillow cried at night. The bartender leaned over and spoke quietly to the lovely couple. The man nodded and thumbed a signal. One of the other men at the table stood, grabbed a pool cue, and poked at the old man sleeping on the pool table.

"What the hell?" barked the old man.

The man with the pool cue leaned over and whispered in the old man's ear. Like a corpse meeting a cattle prod, the old man shot up to sitting. Skinny and clearly wracked with something, he stared our way for a moment as the man with the pool cue kept talking in his ear. Then the old man rolled off the table and hobbled over, his legs bowed like an old cowpuncher in a black-and-white movie.

"Is that you, Tony, you punk?" said the old man.

His face was drawn, his hair was yellow gray, his beard was scraggly, and there was something familiar in the high screech of his voice that made the scar on my neck twitch.

"Hello there, Corky," said Tony.

"What the hell are you doing here?"

"Looking for you."

"Don't get no ideas, now. I'm nothing but a sack of bones held together by tumors, but I could still gut you afore you saw the glint of my blade."

"Not anymore," said Tony. "And even then you couldn't, not without Flynn."

"That thing what we done, it was business only. Nothing personal about it. I always liked you."

"No you didn't."

"Well, maybe not. But in them days I was so cranked I didn't like nobody. Who's the primp?" he said, indicating me.

"Just a friend."

He stared at me for a bit. "Almost looks familiar."

"I have something I need to say to you," said Tony.

"Not sure I want to hear it. Anyway, Billy wants to talk to you."

"Who's Billy?"

"The new chief."

"The one at the table?" said Tony.

"You got it."

"Looks young."

"Maybe, but rabid as a junkyard rat," said Corky.

"So how's things going with you, Corky?" said Tony. "How's your life?"

"What the hell?"

"I'm asking. For real."

The old man stared at Tony like he was a freak, shifted his weight, looked awkwardly behind him. He was one of those guys who had aged far beyond his years. Ancient and wizened, he might have been only in his early sixties, but the years had been hard. Early sixties put him at late thirties when he slipped into my house and stuck his knife into my throat.

"I'm trying to make a connection here," said Tony.

"What the hell for?"

"What I wanted to say," said Tony, "what I need you to know, Corky, is that I'm sorry. That what you and Flynn did to me that night, it's in the past and I'm sorry I drove you to it."

The old man looked at Tony for a long moment with his wet rheumy eyes and then spat on the floor. "I don't want your stinking apology."

"That doesn't matter," said Tony. "It's not like a blender, you can't give it back. So now you're off the list."

"What list?"

"How was that?" said Tony to me.

"Pretty good," I said.

"What's this list?" said Corky.

"Am I finished yet?"

"One more," I said.

"What the hell is this list?"

"All the people I need to apologize to. I won't be able to apologize now to Flynn, which is a shame. I had a lot of apologizing to do to Flynn. But now I only need to find my brother."

"You want to say sorry to that son of a bitch?"

"He stepped up to take care of me after my parents died, and I treated him like dirt. That's all. There was the time I crashed his car, the times I stole cash from his wallet, all the times I stayed out late and ignored his advice, the grief I gave him. He did a lot for me."

"He beat you like a lazy dog, day after day."

"That he did, but I usually gave as good as I got. I just want to give him a sorry, check him off the list, too. You know where he is these days?"

"That a joke?"

"No sir."

"I ain't seen him since he went off to jail."

"Has anyone here heard from him?"

"Let me tell you, Tony, if anyone did know where he was, he wouldn't be there no more."

"I'm sorry to hear that," said Tony, standing now and tossing some bills on the bar for the soda waters. "But that's all I came for." He put his hand on the old man's shoulder, peered deeply into the old man's eyes. "Thank you for listening. Take care of yourself now, Corky. And I mean it."

A moment later Tony was headed out of the bar and I was scrambling to catch up, grateful as hell to get out of there, when a huge man, like a great block of ebony, stepped in front of the door and shook his head. He was almost Tony's size, but even so his presence wouldn't have stopped Tony without the tire iron he held like a baseball bat. When we turned around, Corky was right behind us.

"You may be done asking your questions, Tony," said Corky, "but we got some of our own."

"I don't have any answers."

"We'll see. Give up your wallet."

"My what?"

"You heard me."

"No way."

"Hand it over," said Corky, pulling a huge bowie knife from behind his back. "Billy wants to talk."

"Is this a robbery or an invitation?" said Tony.

"In this joint there ain't much difference. Billy's waiting for you. Billy Flynn."

"Flynn?"

"That's right. The Fat Dog's kid, and Billy wants to talk about old debts."

32. The Fat Dog's Kid

"FUCK YOU, TONY, ALL RIGHT?" SAID FLYNN. "AND FUCK YOUR brother, too, only harder and in the ass. I ought to shoot you in the head just for thinking we might know where that piece of shit is hiding. And who is this table-faced white-shirt faggot sitting next to you?"

The last of this spew of obscenity from Billy Flynn was aimed directly at me.

Billy was not the man we had thought he was. In fact, he was not a man at all. Instead, Billie Flynn was the woman at the head table, huge and round, with a face like a fist. The man beside her was her so-called old man, even though he looked a decade younger than she, but from the authoritative honk of her expletive-spewing voice and the cold, maniacal blue of her eyes, it was clear who was in charge.

"Drink your fucking beer," said Billie to Tony. Billie had sent Corky over to get enough beers for us to have one in each fist and a boatload to spare. The table looked like an Anheuser-Busch parade.

"I'm off the stuff," said Tony.

"Not tonight you're not. We don't buy that twelve-step bullshit, not in here, not at my table. At my table any man who can't drink doesn't walk away in one piece. Drink your fucking beer."

Tony stared for a bit until Corky picked up his knife, poked it into the table, flicked out a chunk of the wood. Tony drank half a bottle in one swallow.

"How'd that taste, Alkie Boy?" said Billie.

"Pretty damn good."

"You bet it did. I tried the whole Bill's-club thing once under court order and the only way I could stand the meetings was to get shitfaced before them. What about you, Pencil Pocket?" she said to me. "Drink up."

I quickly took a sip.

"What, your husband won't approve? Drink the whole damn thing, you tan-pantsed fuck."

I took a bigger sip.

"Who the hell are you, again?"

I was starting to give her my Jonathon Willing name when she said, "Shut the fuck up."

I shut the fuck up.

"So Tony, how are things on…" She opened the wallet Corky had taken off him, looked at the driver's license. "Buxton Drive in Pitchford, PA."

"Dreamy," said Tony.

"I'm glad you're enjoying your life. My daddy's not enjoying his anymore. He died in that prison your brother shafted him into. Someone shoved his head into a lathe at the machine shop. Needless to say, the casket was closed, which was a relief, really, because even with his face, my daddy was uglier than me, and that's saying something."

"I'm sorry about your father," said Tony.

"No you're not and neither am I. The only two things he ever did for me was ejaculate and die. But he was my daddy and someone's got to pay. Hey you, Mr. Tan Pants, you think this is funny?"

"No," I said. "It's just that my father was a bastard, too."

"Now this is touching. Here we are, drinking beer, swapping stories about our dads. Tell me more, or, on second thought, fuck your daddy. You think I care? I'd as soon have Corky slice your throat than listen to one more word about your fucking family."

"I think I knowed him," said Corky, tilting his head as he continued to stare.

"You couldn't," I said.

"I could swear," said Corky.

"The scar on your throat," said Billie, waving a fat finger at me, "that thing that looks like a caterpillar trying to hump your Adam's apple. How'd you get that?"

"Golf."

"Tough sport," said Billie's old man, nodding.

"Did I tell you to talk, Stoner?" said Billie. "I want your opinion, I'll pull your head out of my cockpit and ask. It looks like your work, don't it, Corky? I mean the scar, not them two bruised eyes."

"Sure does."

"What are you doing with a weak stream of piss like this one, Tony?"

Tony looked at me, shook his head. "He's my sponsor."

She barked out a laugh. "I got my sponsor off my back by getting him hooked on coke, which I was selling at the time, so that worked out well. Drink up, boys."

We drank up. When our beers were finished she pushed two more at us.

"Drink until you puke and then drink some more. That's what I got out of the two A's. It wasn't just my daddy your brother put in jail, he put Corky in, too."

"Six years," said Corky.

"And half the other guys here. Ever since I was ten and my daddy was in that jail, he would tell me about the Rams on my visits, about the rides, the fights, the glorious outlaw life. It's all a girl could ever want. I got myself tattooed like a Chinese sailor in anticipation. But when I showed up here there was nothing left but the chicken bones. Your brother, Tony, he tore the whole thing apart. And I've built it back piece by piece for one purpose. These are our life goals now, in reverse order: to drink, to fuck, to ride, to fight, to fuck, to cut Derek Grubbins's fucking head off his fucking body and nail it to the wall." She looked up at an open spot between two ragged vests. "Right there, actually, so I can stand on the table and hump his face."

"Let me get this straight," said Tony. "What you're telling me is that you don't know where my brother is either."

"Tony, you never was too bright," said Corky.

"If we knew where your brother was," said Billie, "he'd be dead already and we'd have drunk a keg of beer to celebrate and pissed it out on his corpse."

"Do you have any ideas, any possibilities?" I said.

"You're talking? Why are you talking? Tell him to shut the fuck up, Tony, or I'll have Corky cut his throat all the way through this time."

"Shut the fuck up," said Tony.

I shut the fuck up.

"He's somewhere, your brother, in some fancy house probably," said Billie, "living under an assumed name, playing tennis and screwing the neighbors' wives. He thinks he's safe in witness protection? They better protect his asshole with a cork, because when we find him we're going to let Sparky over there stuff it with dynamite." She nodded toward a skinny kid with greasy blond hair at another table, flicking his lighter on and off, on and off. "Sparky likes fire. It's good to have a hobby, don't you think? Mine is murdering your brother."

"I get it," said Tony. "You want to kill my brother. You really want to kill my brother. You want to kill my brother and then bring him back to life with electric paddles so you can kill him again."

"Payback's a bitch and I intend to strap on and pound away until her nose pops off."

"You know what you got, Billie? You got issues."

"You're damn right I got issues. I weigh three hundred pounds, I'm a mean drunk, I bash heads to calm my nerves, and I want to fuck my dead daddy. Even my issues got issues. Anything wrong with that?"

"But think about it," said Tony. "Whatever my brother did to your father, he did when you were ten. And you've been carrying it like a boulder all this time. Isn't it getting heavy? Don't you think it's time to let it go?"

"Then what would I do for fun?"

"Just let it go. Just drop it, like a stone into a pond. Plop. You don't know how light you'll feel."

"I don't want to feel light. I like my hate. It keeps me hungry and horny. Oh, baby boy, I'm going to find and kill your brother, yes I am, but only after he coughs it up."

"Coughs what up?"

"You always was stupid, Tony," said Corky. "But not that stupid."

"My daddy told me that back in the day they were pulling in so much cash they didn't know what to do with it all. They couldn't bank it, invest it, or spend it; the only thing to be done with it was hide it away or steal it. My daddy said he would have done the stealing himself if Derek didn't beat him to it. Then maybe I would have been born a rich little girl, and then maybe I wouldn't have this big fucking stone of hate on my shoulder."

"So it's not just revenge you're after," said Tony. "It's also your childhood."

"Am I on a couch? It's about the money, Sigmund Fuck. And that means you've got a chance here, Tony. You're on step nine, right? And you want to make amends to your brother? What about making amends by saving his fucking life, how does that sound?"

"How do I do that?"

"Didn't I just tell you it was about the money, you dumb shit? Here's a deal. A hundred thou from your brother's stash and I'll promise to drop my hate into your fucking pond. How does that sound?"

"Extortion wasn't what I had in mind." Tony looked at me like Ollie looking at Stan: Another fine mess you've got me into.

"What are you looking at him for?" said Billie. "What does he have to do with anything? Look at me, you fuck."

Tony turned his head to Billie.

"You want to make amends? Find him before we do, find him first, get us the money, save your brother's neck."

"I'll see what I can do."

"You've got a week."

"I can't find him in a week."

"Try."

"You're insane."

"You bet I am. And if I don't hear from you in a week, Tony, I'll be bringing the crazy to Pitchford. Maybe just so you'll know we're serious, I'll let Corky kill my little tan-pantsed man right here, right now."

"You're going to kill him?" said Tony.

"Or maybe we'll let Sparky do a number on him." Sparky was still at his table, flicking his lighter, staring at me through the flame. Flick, flick. "You got a problem with that?"

"Not really," said Tony.

"What?" I said.

"Actually, you'd be doing me a favor."

"What the hell?" I said.

"I understand," said Billie. "Sponsors, like a pimple on your ass. And believe me, I know about pimples on my ass." Billie opened up the wallet, pulled out what cash was inside, and counted. "Twenty, forty, fifty, fifty-five, fifty-six."

"I guess the next round is on me," said Tony.

"You guess right. Now drink the fuck up."

She tossed the empty wallet back, and we drank the fuck up.

33. Rattle Rattle

"YOU WERE GOING TO LET HER KILL ME," I SAID AS WE SPED away from The Devil's Brew, Tony squeezing his truck through the narrow city streets with cars parked on either side.

"She was just barking," said Tony.

"And what if she wasn't? Corky was more than ready to finish what he started twenty-five years ago. And that kid with the lighter. What a bunch of freaks."

"You would have deserved everything you got. They're after my brother because of what you did twenty-some years ago. And now we've got that crazy bitch up our assholes without us getting any closer to finding Derek."

"Just to be precise, she's up your asshole, not mine."

"Oh, she's up your asshole, too, Moretti. What did she call you? Her little tan-pantsed man? You give her half a chance, she'll be sitting on your face."

"Don't," I said. "Just the thought…" I paused as I swallowed a belch.

"Like Fat Dog, like daughter. And there you sit, with enough stolen money to get her off all our backs for good."

"It's funny, isn't it? I've been in Pitchford, oh, six hours now, and you're the third person who's put in a claim for the money. What do you think I have left after all these years?"

"You better hope it's enough. She's threatening me, which means she's threatening you, because if she comes to take me out, I'm taking you out first."

I looked at him and wondered if I should be surprised and then realized no, I shouldn't be. So why did I feel such disappointment? "That's the Tony Grubbins I remember. And it feels good, like the balance of the universe has been restored. Too bad you don't have a football handy to throw at my face."

"I'll find something."

"It's funny how some things just never change."

"You sure haven't."

We stayed silent for the rest of the trip, as the narrow city streets made way for the wider suburban boulevards. I hadn't left my car at the Stoneway; not knowing when I would get back and not wanting to leave it sitting alone in the lot, I had parked it back at my motel, a Hampton Inn on the Pitchford strip where I had registered as Edward Holt. I still had the Pennsylvania license I had stolen from the airport lot, with its magnets in place, and I had slapped that over my plate just in case anyone trolled the nearby hotels looking for a Virginia registration. What with the fake license plate and being registered in my new name, I figured I was pretty well covered.

But when we reached the motel, and I saw my car sitting dark and silent among all the other cars in the lot, something seemed wrong. I surveyed the area. Lines of cars by the building, a white van in the corner, a truck parked by the Dumpster. Everything quiet, everything dead.

"How long are you staying in Pitchford?" said Tony.

"I'll be gone tomorrow."

"No lingering visit to the old hometown, hey?"

"There's not enough Zofran in the world."

"Zofran?"

"Nausea medication."

"Oh, it's a joke," said Tony. "Okay."

"What's up your butt?"

He stared at me for a bit in the glow of his dashboard. "What were you thinking?"

I knew exactly what he meant. "I was seventeen and high," I said. "On weed you sold us, I might add."

"It was your whole little crew, I suppose. Augie and Ben?"

"I shouldn't have said anything."

"You know what you guys did to me, right?"

"You said you were grateful. You said the guy who did it did you a favor."

"Yeah, well, maybe I was blowing smoke up my own ass. I thought I had let go of my hatred of your fucking guts, but I guess some chains are just wound too tight."

"But it's not true that we're no closer to finding your brother. Billie Flynn told us that after Derek testified he was put in the witness protection program."

"So?"

"So someone at the US Marshals Service knows where he is."

"What are you going to do, hack their computers?"

"Something like that," I said.

"From here on in, leave me out of it."

"Believe me, I will," I said. "Does anything look strange here?"

"Where?"

"This lot. Does anything look wrong? It seems weirdly quiet, nothing moving around."

"It's a parking lot at three in the morning."

"Yeah, you're right." I opened the door, climbed out of the truck, closed the door again with a sharp thump. I looked away for a bit, peered into the darkness, saw nothing. Through the open window I said, "Thanks for trying to help. I guess it was good seeing you after all these years."

"No it wasn't," said Tony. "But I really am sorry about the dog."

"Well, to be fair, he did seem to be inordinately fond of crapping on your lawn."

He gave me a half smile before he drove away, Tony Grubbins, the great tormentor of my youth. He gave me a half smile, and he drove away, and I felt a strange sense of loss. And I couldn't tell whether it was because he was leaving, or because I had finally let out my secret and the world hadn't changed.

I shook myself back to the present, shook my head and cleared my senses, before stepping over to my black SUV to make sure everything was in order. It seemed fine, just an anonymous car in an anonymous lot. I looked around, all seemed quiet, dark. Why did I feel so uneasy? Turning back to the car I noticed the something, just a little something, but still my neck seized.

The magnetized PA license plate was a little off-center, just enough that some of the Virginia plate was showing through.

Had I been that sloppy in placing it there? I remembered lining up the edges, I remembered running my fingers across all the sides to make sure it was exact. I stooped down to readjust it and suddenly had a horrible thought. I stood up again, grabbed my keys, pressed the fob to unlock the car. When I slammed open the rear hatch, the cover over the cargo bay opened up as well, exposing the contents.

It was still there, along with the assorted detritus from my suburban life: gardening tools, leaf bags, Eric's baseball crap, a pair of golf shoes, and the green metal toolbox, still locked as if rusted shut, as innocuous as a flower. I let out a deep breath of relief and was just about to close the rear when I heard my name, my old name, its triple syllables rattling together like the tail of a snake.

"Moretti? Yo, Moretti."

34. Rampage

I GRABBED AT WHATEVER WAS IN THE CAR, FOUND ERIC'S OFFI-cial Little League aluminum bat, picked it up before slamming shut the hatch. Only then did I turn around.

Richie Diffendale. Walking calmly toward me, a finger in the air as if signaling for a busboy.

"Get the hell away from me, Richie," I said.

"I just want to talk," he said as he continued approaching. "I was getting greedy in the bar, I admit it. But I'm sure we can still work something out. Maybe five figures, low fives even. Ten?"

"There's nothing to work out."

"Don't do it for me," he said. "Do it for Maddie."

I tilted my head. He came still closer and lifted his finger in the air again.

"She gets a better life," he said, "you get to glide away safe and free, everyone's *gaaak*—"

This last word wasn't a new piece of Pitchford slang—you know, I'm gaaak, you're gaaak, we're all just gaaak—but the sound that emerged from Richie Diffendale's throat when I slammed his face with the baseball bat.

The bat gave off that aluminum ping as his head swiveled with the blow. His body landed with a thump as his teeth rattled along the asphalt like a turn at Yahtzee.

I would have taken the time to admire my handiwork—my shot into the gap couldn't help but improve his smile—but there was no time. The moment I realized it was Diffendale calling my name, even as fogged by drink as I was, it all became clear in a flash. Richie hadn't come back to try again to make a deal, not with the way his last effort had ended. He had waited outside the bar, he had followed my car to the hotel, he had made the call to Clevenger, the opportunistic son of a bitch. Which meant the thugs were already on-site, maybe waiting for me in Edward Holt's hotel room. Richie was in the parking lot just to ensure I didn't simply drive off. Misinterpreting my motives at the Lexus, he had probably already called up to the room with what he was seeing before he tried to delay me. Which meant there wasn't time for niceties or chitchat.

So I did my small talk with an Easton Rampage, minus eleven.

I dropped to the ground and reached for my holster, touched only my belt. Crap. I had left the gun and holster in Tony's glove compartment.

I gripped tight to the bat and scanned the parking lot. All clear.

I grabbed the keys from my pocket, scooted between my car and a Honda, took hold of the driver's door handle, swung the door open, swung myself inside. The car started like a dream. I checked the mirrors: rearview clear, side views clear, clear—clear except for a sprawled leg on the asphalt.

The only way out was right over Richie Diffendale's prostrate body.

Where some see obstacles, I see opportunities, and here was one. Simply by backing out I would free myself from my immediate peril, free Maddie from her abusive husband, and right all past wrongs meted upon me by this creep. He had sold me out tonight, like he had twenty-five years ago when I got my scar, like he had whenever he laughed hysterically while Tony Grubbins pounded on my head. It was all so perfect my unconscious must have set the stage, and all I had to do was put the shifter into reverse. One little act to do so much good.

Yet I couldn't do it. He would do it to me, I had no doubt, he already had, but I couldn't do it to him. Even with all that had happened, what was true in Vegas remained true. I was no torpedo. With the car still running, I opened the door, dashed back out to the lot. Richie was moaning as I grabbed him under the armpits and lifted him enough so I could pull him out of the car's way.

He whimpered as his shattered jaw dragged loosely behind his face. And there was something else sounding underneath the whimper, like the clicking of bone on bone, or something.

"You touch Madeline again," I said to Richie Diffendale as I dragged him, "and I'm going to finish the job."

I dropped him out of my route and ran back to the car. But just as I was about to leap into the driver's seat, the door slammed closed and some bullet-headed brute was standing there, his hands flexing for me. Trapped on three sides, I spun around to get the hell out of there, when another brute slammed me in the gut.

The breath left my lungs so fast the force of it sent me to my knees. A kick into my back finished the job of sending me sprawling.

"Got you," said the second brute, before he clamped his hands over both of my ears and pulled my head straight up. My neck screamed as my body followed. The brute leaned me against my car and slammed me once more in the stomach, holding me up with his other hand so I wouldn't collapse again. I tried to say something, anything, and failed. I tried to swing at him, but my hand was swatted away like it was a moth.

"You're not going to try to give us no trouble, are you? Not like you did to Holmes."

I shook my head.

"Good. Call it in, Ferdie."

The first man slipped away from between the cars and reached for his phone.

"Now we're going to ask you some questions, just like we asked your friend in Vegas some questions. Nice simple questions, like how much you got left, where it is, and where you can get more. And if you survive the asking better than your friend did, then it will be worth your while to give us some answers. *Capisce?*"

"What?"

"Understand?"

"How much...is left...of what?"

"Don't be a clown, I'm not in no mood." He took a handful of my shirt collar, gave it a yank. "Let's go."

My eyes spun as he dragged me across the asphalt, toward the white van in the corner of the lot, sitting alone in the darkness. I didn't have a bat in my hands to smash his jaw to bits. I wasn't in my car to slam-bam into him. I didn't have my gun to put a bullet into his murderous brain in vengeance for Augie. I had nothing, no options, no strength left in my battered body, no way out. They had me, the bastards, and they had the rest of the money, too, though they didn't know it yet. They didn't have my family, which was one bright spot, but who knew what I wouldn't give them under torture. Let's be honest, I was a suburban dad; no matter how tough I acted, threaten my cable and I'd spill my darkest secrets.

There was a gurgle. I thought it came from me for a moment, but no. A gurgle and then a crack.

"Ferdie?" said the man, whipping around as he whipped out a gun. "Ferd-man?"

A bird came hurtling through the air toward us, just bits of its silver wings catching the artificial light of the parking lot. A bird, or a bat, flying straight and hard, like it was flying out of hell. And then it wasn't a bird. And then it smacked into the bruiser's forehead with a thud.

The thug let go of me and his gun at the same time, grappling at his forehead, which was suddenly stained with dark streaks. The gun clattered onto the asphalt next to the wrench that had slammed into his head. I didn't try to figure out what had happened, I jumped away as soon as I was free, falling and then rising, and then tearing the hell out of there toward my car. Still running, I turned back and that's when I saw it.

A man, standing with legs spread and arms outstretched, standing like a superhero from one of the overheated comic books of my childhood, holding in his hands the bloodied bruiser of my persecution, raising him high before throwing him like a sack of recycling to the ground. No, not a man, a legend.

El Rubio Salvaje.

"You forgot your gun," Tony Grubbins said to me when it was over and the second collection agent was collapsed into an unconscious heap. Tony tossed the gun and holster at me, leaned over, and picked up the wrench. "I guess the guy never played dodgeball."

"I was done for."

"Don't forget who you're messing with," said Tony. "Finding Derek might be near impossible, but that's still the easy part."

"I know," I said. Awkward pause. "I guess, you know, thanks for, kind of, saving me."

"Shut up."

"Yeah."

"Now go away."

"Okay. Look, if I actually do find him, do you want me to let you know?"

"No."

"Okay."

"Wait. I don't know. Just the thought of seeing him again turns me into a scared little boy."

"Then maybe you ought to leave him be."

"No, you're wrong. If you do find him, let me know. You ever read *The Tibetan Book of the Dead*?"

"Please."

"It's all about facing your demons. Maybe it's time for me to do just that."

"You've become strangely spiritual over the years, Tony. It doesn't suit you."

"Things change, Moretti."

"Not me," I said. "It was Richie that brought these two thugs here. I think he followed me out of the Stoneway and then made the call. He's over there on the ground. He's going to need an ambulance. I shattered his jaw with a baseball bat."

"Nice shot for the worst baseball player on Henrietta Road."

"I never told anyone else before about the money. No one. I never told my mother, I never told my wife."

"That's a hell of a chain to have wrapped around your neck."

"Yeah."

"And I bet it keeps growing tighter."

"It does."

"Then maybe it's time to let it go," he said, "before it chokes you to death."

35. The Club

WHEN I ROUSED MYSELF FROM SLEEP THE NEXT MORNING in another motel on another trademark-laden strip, I was stiff and aching, lonely and hungover, unsure of who the hell I was anymore or why I was doing any of what I was doing. But then I bought a bag of toiletries at Rite Aid. I bought underwear, a fresh pair of Dockers, and a new white shirt at Kohl's. I had a Grand Slam breakfast at Denny's. I picked up a double espresso macchiato at Starbucks. Whatever the commerce of America had devolved into over my lifetime, it was exactly what I needed to prepare myself. For I was stepping up that day, rising out of the mire, and I intended to look and feel every inch the country squire as I drove into the lush landscape of my early youth.

Impossible mansions with their mansard roofs, developments with lots large enough that each could have swallowed whole blocks of Pitchford, great estates with swaths of priceless pasture where horses leaned down to pick at the pristine grass with teeth so perfect they would make a Britisher weep. It had been decades since I had been back, and I had seen my share of glorious vistas in the intervening years, but still nothing pulled at my heart like the wealthy enclaves of Philadelphia's Main Line. Milton could have written an epic poem about it all. In fact, he did.

And then I found myself before a grand stone-columned entrance, standing like Lucifer before the very gates from which he had been cast down eons ago. The sun burned more brightly upon its vast lawn, its grass smelled cleaner, its air held the crisp scent of new dollar bills. The valet took my keys, the sign said No Tips.

Is this heaven?

No, Jon, it's the Philadelphia Country Club.

I didn't recognize the building before which I stood. The fashionably shoddy clubhouse entrance that had been there in my day had been replaced with this gaudy front, not too different from the entrance to the golf clubhouse at Patriots Landing or any other upscale course. But still, when I handed off my keys and stepped inside I had a knot in my stomach that would have foiled Alexander. I fully expected someone to grab me by the scruff of my neck and toss me out feetfirst, but no one stopped me, no one asked who I was. An older woman standing by the door smiled at me, like the old women of the club used to smile at me because I was a Willing, and, grateful, I smiled back.

I took advantage of the opportunity and roamed among the halls of my youthful privilege, from the great banquet room to the bar to the grill to the Polo Room with its terrace overlooking the verdant fields of golf. I was afraid of being recognized and desperate to be recognized. I didn't belong and yet the place was in my bones. I was a lapsed Catholic strolling along the intricately decorated nave of St. Peter's, ready to be called out and embraced at the same time. It was beautiful, and gaudy, and thrillingly sumptuous, it was everything I had ever wanted, everything I had ever felt deprived of in my life, the place where all my lurching opportunism had led me, and yet...

And yet...

"May I help you?" said a woman who approached me on the Polo Room terrace, as polished as the brass, with a freshly ironed suit that belonged behind the front desk of a grand hotel.

"I'm just poking around," I said.

"Only members are allowed to poke, sir."

"I used to be a member."

"Then you used to be able to poke."

"I might have been a little young in those days."

The woman's smile suddenly widened into officiousness. "How, then, may I help you?"

"I'm looking for Mr. Willing. I called his house and was told he would be here."

"I believe Mr. Willing is in the Grill Room. Is he expecting you?"

"I would think so," I said. "He must have figured I'd show up at some point."

"If you wait on the terrace, I'll see if he is available. Who can I say is here to see him?"

"Tell him it's Jon, Jon Moretti, with two *t*s."

"Very good. Would you like a complimentary drink while you're waiting?"

"That sounds about right," I said with a wide smile.

I sat on the terrace with my gin and tonic, watching the foursomes make their way across the eighteenth fairway and the holes beyond. As a boy, I had seen in these fields a thrilling landscape of heroic deeds and dark adult secrets; now I knew it to be just another golf course. I had sliced my ball out of bounds on better. And the clubhouse wasn't the fabulous Shangri-la of steak, french fries, and Coca-Cola of my youth. After what was apparently a recent renovation, the place looked like nothing more than your usual four-star resort, with its plush furniture, its arranged flowers, its utter lack of mystique. I remembered old chaises where the aristocracy of Philadelphia had lounged, the stodgy locker room with its ancient metal lockers where the richest barons in the world had changed out of their knickers and golfing shoes. I remembered Olympus, not something where all that was required to get past the front door was a credit card.

I took a sip of the drink, quite good, tangy and bracing. The glass was beaded with moisture even as I remained cool in the breeze, which seemed right. In this place the drinks did the sweating instead of the members. I took a longer sip, felt the cold of the tonic wash through me. This could have been my life, sitting here, drinking this, the ice so clean, the limes so fresh. If my father hadn't deserted us, that would have been me leading the caddie along the pristine fairway. That would have been me taking my wedge and neatly splashing the ball out of that deep trap. That would have been me making the six-footer for par. Fat and flushed and pale all at once, in plaid pants with a white belt, that would have been me. Satisfied with all he had been given, married to a Biddle or a Wister or a Chew, with no secret darker than a fudged score on the tricky par five or an awkward tryst with the polished assistant club manager.

Never before had I realized how much I hated the game of golf..

"Mr. Moretti?"

I looked up at the woman in the pressed suit, her hands clasped in front of her, her smile forced.

"If you'll follow me, please."

"Absitooviley," I said, before polishing off my cocktail.

She led me back through the halls of the club, down a set of stairs, past still other rooms into which I hadn't poked, until she led me into an elegant boardroom with a long inlaid mahogany table and a number of overstuffed leather chairs.

"This is the Founders' Room, Mr. Moretti."

"Of course it is."

"Can I get you another cocktail while you wait for Mr. Willing?"

"No, thank you," I said. "I have enough to drink in as it is."

The Founders' Room was decorated with old photographs of the club, pictures of golfers in their plus-fours posing poststrike, of fat men in overcoats and hats smiling next to a horse-drawn carriage, of the crowds on the course for the epic 1939 US Open. Here it was, the grand legacy of the club's history, laid out as if an object lesson placed upon these walls just for me.

The photographs vividly demonstrated the club's primacy in the history of America's aristocracy. And even from its immodest start in 1890, there had always been a Willing at its core. As I gazed at the photographs, one after another, I had no doubt that the pictures were populated with my ancestors, well fed and prosperous, blithely self-satisfied, at ease in their entitlement: William Willing and Montgomery Willing and Peter Willing and Montgomery Willing II, and my great-grandfather Edward R. Willing, and my grandfather Montgomery Willing III. But there would be no celebratory pictures of me. I might be Jon Willing in Patriots Landing, but here, at the Philadelphia Country Club, I was Moretti to the core.

"Yes? Hello? You asked for me?"

A man stood in the doorway, old and lean and ferocious, his gray cardigan buttoned, the pleats of his pants crisp. White hair well trimmed, eyes blue and clear, nose straight, lips thin and turned down in perpetual disapproval. I stared at him and felt my emotions rising. It was as if the knot that had been in my stomach the moment I walked into the club tightened, squeezing out the moisture in my eyes.

"Who are you and what is this about?" the old man said, his voice a snap of impatience. "It better be important for you to disturb me with business at the club. Let's get on with it. What is it that you want?"

And then my ten-year-old self leaped up and grabbed me by the throat, raising the pitch of my voice even as it stifled my breath.

"Grandfather?" it said.

36. UnWilling

I HAD BEEN WAITING FOR HIM MY ENTIRE LIFE.

I never expected that my father would save us when circumstances sent our lives spiraling down from our Gladwyne estate into Pitchford. My father was useless; my father would forget me as soon as he walked out the door each morning and look startled at my presence on the rare nights he came home. But my grandfather was made of richer stuff. He was a man of the world, a man of power. When we visited on those special Sundays he took more interest in me than my father ever did. Tall and stiff in his gray suit and black tie even on the Sabbath, he would stand with his hands behind his back and quiz me on my Latin studies at the same posh private school that he had attended. He was the heir and the patriarch, he was the Willing who mattered, the Willing who would rescue my mother and me.

And so I waited for him. I waited for him to come for us after my father left and the pool grew green with algae. I waited for him in Pitchford to show up on our doorstep, tall and stiff in his gray suit, to sweep us out of our split-level hell and back to the playing fields of the Philadelphia Country Club, where we belonged. And after I took matters into my own hands in the basement of the Grubbins house, I still somehow found myself waiting for him. In Pitchford my last year, in Wisconsin during college, even during my life in Virginia. I had taken his name when I left Pitchford, I was easy enough to find. In some especially delusional part of my delusional brain, I was certain that someday he would come for me, pull me out of my life, hoist me into the very stratum I had been destined for as a youth. Is it any wonder, then, that in the deepest trouble of my troubled life, I looked to him to dig me out?

And now, here he was.

"Don't be a fool, young man," said my grandfather as he made his unsteady way to the board table, leaning heavily on his cane, and took his rightful place at the head. "Using the term *grandfather* as a rote appellation for an older man is rather impertinent." He eased himself slowly into the chair. It was a shock to see him so old physically. His huge presence in my imagination hadn't aged in thirty years; this man was like the shrunken-apple version. "Now, what is it you want?"

"I'm Jonathon," I said.

"Jonathon?" said my grandfather.

"Jonathon Willing."

"But I thought your name was Morelli or something. That's what Denise told me."

"Moretti," I said. "That was my mother's maiden name. I thought it best to keep this between us when dealing with the help. But I'm still a Willing. Here is my driver's license."

I took my license out of my wallet, placed it in front of my grandfather. He picked it up, held it far in front of him, squinted at it.

"Edward Holt?"

Sheepishly, I grabbed it back, found my Virginia license, and handed that to him. He looked at me as if I was an utter idiot and then squinted again.

"Okay," he said. "You have a license, one of at least two, that registers you as Jonathon Willing. Which proves what?"

"That I'm your grandson. Long lost. You're my grandfather."

"You're either badly mistaken or a raving lunatic," said my grandfather. "Based on the condition of your face, most likely the latter. But you are not my grandson. I have four grandchildren and eleven great-grandchildren and that sum is quite sufficient. Now we are at the end of our business together and it is time to conclude this meeting." With both hands on the table, he struggled to standing. "Good day."

"Preston Willing was my father."

"Preston? So that's what this is, a con job." He snorted. "Where did you meet up with him, in some casino? And now, all these years later, you're making your move? Well, your research is thorough, Mr. Moretti, but not thorough enough. My son had no children."

"Of course he did. He had me. And another with his other family. Ask him."

"My son can no longer speak for himself. He died four years ago of a heart attack."

"I—I didn't know."

"In Las Vegas. At an all-you-can-eat buffet."

"I'm sorry," I said, and strangely, sadly, I was. Orphaned, and not for the first time, I blinked and I saw him there, my father, standing in the corner of the Founders' Room, trying to stuff his life to make up for something, stuff it with wives, with lives, with food. The image of him dying at a seedy all-you-can-eat Vegas buffet with its piles of barely warmed-over crap was heartrending. And I was shocked at the bitterness revealed by my grandfather's volunteering of the information to someone he considered a stranger.

"Now, this is a private club, Mr. Moretti," said my grandfather. "Leave the premises forthwith or I'm calling the police. I've heard of this con, long-lost children coming to claim their inheritance. But I've been around the block, I've dealt with my share of scoundrels, and I know one when I see one."

"I used to visit your house every Sunday," I said, still seeing my father's image in front of me. I wasn't arguing anymore, I was remembering, in a reverie for my dead father and all he failed to mean to me. "The big white house with the pillars. The long red dining room. Gloria the maid. Jelly beans in the silver bowl in the living room. Tulips in the spring. The tennis court. Your fruit trees with their branches growing straight across. Roast beef and potatoes. Crystal goblets for Sunday dinner. Your weekly toasts to Nixon."

The old man stared at me. "How could you know all that?"

"I'm Jonathon," I said. "You called me Jon Boy. I was put in the family prep school. I used to have dinners by myself at this very club, swim in the pool out back. I'm your grandson."

And then something happened to him, my grandfather: the cast of certainty on his face, like a plaster death mask that had been affixed there for the whole of his life, suddenly cracked— just a bit, true, but still it cracked. And he collapsed back into the overstuffed leather conference chair. And I could see him trying to remember, trying to remember me. I thought for a moment that it was a dementia of some sort, some failure of his synapses, a spongiform encephalopathy that had burrowed through his brain like a swarm of termites. But then it came, the recognition, it was there in the widening of the eyes, the tremble of the jaw. I was in there all the time, just suppressed, like one suppresses the memory of a motor vehicle accident, the stray hand of a smiling priest, an unwanted child.

"Hello, Grandfather," I said.

This was the moment when the violins would swell and his eyes would grow moist, the moment when the old man would stand and stagger forward into my arms. This was the moment when I would be welcomed back into the bosom of my family. This was the moment.

"You're a fraud," he said, his eyes suddenly clear again and now hard as slate. "My son Preston never married."

"How can you say that? He married my mother. There was a ceremony, a party after."

"There was surely no such affair."

"I've seen pictures of the wedding. I've seen pictures of you at the wedding."

"Pictures," he said with disdain. "Stalin knew what to do with pictures."

"My mother was not a Stalin."

"Preston had no children, which was a blessing, because Preston was a great disappointment to me. He failed at everything he put his hand to, and not just feebly, but disastrously, and the offshoots of his failures continue to threaten our family's prosperity to this very day. We remain ever vigilant to weed out his errors. So I can say, uncontrovertibly, that you are not a Willing."

"I didn't come for your money."

"Then you won't be disappointed."

"My God," I said, my voice wide with a sort of amazement. "Of all the scenarios for our first meeting after thirty years, I never imagined you'd sit there and deny me to my face like this. I thought I might get an apology, or an explanation, or even a tearful embrace, but not this. What is it with you people?"

We stared at each other for a moment, him in his determination, me in my shock. Which was a joke, really. How on earth could I have been shocked by anything that old man did? He had thrown me out of his life three decades before and now here he was, lying baldly about who I was to my very face. How could I have expected any other result? If anything, this journey into my past was really a journey into my naïveté. Something had caused me to stop emotionally dead in my tracks, and I had a good idea what the hell it was.

"I don't need to sit here and be insulted by riffraff," he said, struggling again to rise.

"Oh, you'll sit," I said, standing now, towering over him. I slapped hard on the table and the sound caused him to drop back into his chair. Then I took out my hunting knife.

It opened with a sharp click and my grandfather drew back at the intimation of violence, drew back yet let himself smile at

the same time, as if all his prejudices against me were being justified in the glint of the blade. His smile disappeared when I cut
a slash in my palm. Blood welled from the wound and dropped
onto the table.

"Here's your proof," I said. "Enough to provide a whole new
set of heirs to vie with your precious great-grandchildren for the
Willing estate."

"You're insane."

"Not totally, but I am your grandson, so I'm probably halfway there."

"What are you after, Mr. Moretti?"

"I came here to ask my grandfather for a favor, but it's not
a favor anymore. You want to be rid of me, you want Preston's
heirs to remain erased from your life and the life of the Willings
forever? Then this is what you must do. You were the friend of
senators and cabinet secretaries, you drank with Nixon, you
donated huge gobs of money to both parties, you are more connected than a switchboard. And what you can't get by connec-
tions you can get with your lawyers and your money."

"I knew you were after something," said my grandfather.

I took a folded piece of paper out of my pocket, smoothed it
out, slid it across the table so it sopped up the blood I had spilled.

"This is a name and a number," I said. "The number is my
phone. The name is of a murderous motorcycle thug who turned
on his gang and was put into the government's witness protection program. Now, because of something that happened many
years ago, he's threatening me and my family with serious bodily
harm. I'm a Willing, I will do anything to protect my family. I'm
sure you understand. I need to make this thug stop, but I can't do
that if I don't know where he is. I need his address."

"That's impossible. Even if I wanted, I couldn't do—"

"Nothing is impossible," I said, "if you're a Willing. I'll be
waiting, but I won't be waiting long. I'm so excited to meet the
rest of the family, to tell them everything. About my father and

his secret lives and the way you weeded my mother and me out of the family as blithely as you weed your tulip garden. Oh, the reunion will be so gay."

My grandfather looked at me for a long moment, a ripe anger in his eyes. That anger had terrified me as a boy, and it would have terrified me even as an adult up until five minutes ago. Now I just stared back. When I tilted my head just a bit, he recoiled. Then he took hold of the paper.

I closed the knife, put it in my pocket, sat down, took a tissue from my pocket, and placed it on my bleeding palm. "Good. Now, Grandpop, do you want to know how I'm doing in my life without you?"

"I certainly do not."

"Fine, thank you for asking. I have a beautiful wife and two miraculous children. Shelby is lovely and smart and fully engaged in the world. I don't know what she'll do with her life, but she'll do it with passion and style. She has your blue eyes. And Eric, he's a pistol. Funny and self-assured. Not so good at baseball, but a whiz at video games. You ever read *Ender's Game*? He's my Ender. A pretty decent harvest, if I must say so myself."

"Are you finished, young man?"

"Yes, I'm finished. Get me what I need and then, lucky you, you'll never have to deal with the Moretti side of your family again. But isn't it funny, Grandpop, how sometimes we throw away the most valuable things in life just to safeguard our crap?"

I couldn't get out of that room fast enough. I brushed brusquely past Denise as I climbed the stairs. My skin itched as if I had been infested with lice. When the valet brought the car I left him a hundred-dollar tip—fuck their no-tipping policy—and I shot out of there as fast as the RX10 would take me.

Listen, I'm no Pangloss who believes everything that happens in our lives is always for the best. I happen to think that most of what happens in our lives is for the absolute worst, and my life has pretty much proven that over and again. But racing down the long lovely road, away from the Philadelphia Country Club, when I thought of all that had happened because of my father's leaving, my being defenestrated from that club, being disowned by the Willings, being plunged into Pitchford, all I could think of was that pale-faced golfer and his plaid pants.

Life springs its blessings in the most surprising of ways.

37. Unsafe at Any Speed

MY INTERNAL COMPASS HAD ALWAYS BEEN AIMED TOWARD Philadelphia; that had been my heart's magnetic north. In Wisconsin, I pined for the East. In Virginia, I always considered the sprawl between DC and Boston the center of the world while I lived willingly on the periphery. Whatever place I found myself was always a substitute. And in grade school as in life, no matter how pretty or merry the substitute, it is never the real thing.

But now, as I headed out of the rich western suburbs of Philadelphia, out of my grandfather's domain, it felt as if my compass had been reset. I couldn't wait to get the hell out of there, I couldn't wait to head back to my home. And my route home didn't anymore lead to Virginia, it led through Virginia.

"Harry?"

"Johnny? Is that you?"

"It's me, all right."

"What's been going on, boy? We been worried about you."

"Nothing to worry about," I lied. "Just revisiting some old memories, renewing family ties, that sort of thing. But I'm done up here and coming home. Any news?"

"None that you'll like."

"Then tell me what I won't like."

"Well, you can't say I didn't warn you."

"About what, Harry?"

"My sister. She don't approve of them kids of yours."

"What's wrong with my kids?"

"She says they're not godly enough and so she's taken as her mission to save them."

"Oh, Harry."

"Things have gotten testy."

"I can imagine."

"My sister says your wife's language is a bit salty, too."

"Taking the Lord's name in vain, no doubt."

"Not His, yours."

"But other than the clash of cultures, are they still safe?"

"They're talking about going home, with or without you. Are you almost done?"

"I think so, but they have to stay put for a bit. Look, I'm coming down right now to see them. I've got about seven hours of driving left. I want you to meet me there."

"Do I have to? I told you how my sister gets with me."

"That's what I'm counting on. If your sister has your soul to worry about, she might not worry so much about the collective soul of my family. How's your truck running?"

"Pretty good, now and then."

"Which is it?"

"More then than now."

"Do you have a mechanic that will do some work quickly?"

"I knows a guy what knows a guy, I suppose."

"Do me a favor, Harry, and use some of the cash I gave you to get the thing running as smoothly as possible. Change the oil, lubricate the pistons, maybe a tune-up, change the battery, check the brakes. And how are your tires?"

"Still got plenty of miles on them, I'll tell you that."

"Who was president when you bought them?"

"Bush."

"So they're about five years at least?"

"The first Bush."

"Get four new ones for me, all right? And not retreads."

"What's up, Johnny?"

"They've ID'd my car. I can't keep using it. I'm waiting to get a location on the bastard who is after me, and when I do, I'm going after him, but I'm going to need a car they won't recognize. I'll trade you my SUV for your truck, but it will help if the truck doesn't break down on the way."

"I don't want your car. You leave it with that wife of yours. My sister keeps up her harping, your wife will need it to get the hell out of Dodge. But you're not thinking you might need some backup, are you?"

"Are you offering?"

"I'm just talking here."

"It could be dangerous."

"How dangerous?"

"*Dangerous* dangerous."

"Well, maybe I knows a guy what knows a guy."

"You're a peach, Harry."

———————— ✳ ————————

I've told my kids over and again that texting while driving is suicidal and that talking on your phone while driving is as dangerous as driving drunk. I've made it a point of pointing out all the oblivious jackaloons jabbering on their cell phones while driving like idiots. "Look at her, she's not even looking," I'll say as someone cuts me off. "See that guy on the phone? I bet he rear-ends someone before he gets off the highway." My children know my position on using the cell phone while in the car. They also know my position on fast food (against) and on soda (the devil's elixir).

Still, there I was, barreling down I-95 with a cup of Coke between my legs, a hamburger in the hand holding the wheel, and a cell phone against my ear. But I had an excuse: I was an asshole.

***

"Thad Campbell, here."

"Thad, it's me."

"Who?"

"Willing."

"Jon? Oh my God, Jon. We thought you were dead."

"Dead? Why would I be dead? I mean, as opposed to, like, in Mexico or something."

"Is that where you are?"

"No," I said without being more specific. "Why did you think I was dead?"

"Because you disappeared, all of you did. And the cops have been looking for you."

"Me?"

"They found your car in some garage by Remnick Pond. Pretty mangled. And they connected it to some accident that almost killed a guy on Chandler Court. And then, what with all that's been going on at your house, we were all pretty certain something bad had happened."

"What about my house?"

"It's been ransacked. More than once. After the cops were called the first time, they found the place a wreck inside. They bound it with cop tape and went door-to-door looking for you. Next thing you know it was ransacked again, even worse."

"Is it okay? The house, I mean."

"It's still standing, if that's what you mean. But I hope you're insured. From what I've heard, whoever was inside sure didn't like you much. They slashed every mattress, every piece of furniture, smashed lamps. What the hell is going on, Jon?"

"I'm in the middle of some old business, is all."

"Something to do with your job?"

"Nothing that rough."

"What about Caitlin? And the kids? Are they okay? Where are they?"

"Someplace safe. Has anyone been looking for them or me other than the cops?"

"You mean other than the cops and the debt collectors?"

"What debt collectors?"

"It's about the money you owe."

"What money?"

"They say you owe gobs of money, hundreds of thousands. They say you skipped off with a fortune. They're going around asking everyone where you might be."

"What did you tell them?"

"Nothing. We're pals, remember. But they're offering cash for information. And they want to know about your friends."

"You mean like you, Thad?"

"Yeah, I guess. Or that old rummy you hang out with sometimes. The boxer."

"How do you know about him?"

"Jon, you're my neighbor, my friend."

"Did you tell them about the old boxer?"

"No, Jon, no. I didn't tell them anything. They didn't look like any debt collectors I've ever seen before. But they're offering money for information."

"So who sold me out?"

"No one."

"Are they there now? Are they listening on the other end of the phone?"

"Jon, get hold of yourself. Jon. Come home."

"That's what I'm doing right now."

"Good."

"I'll stop off at your place first," I lied.

"Good idea."

"Just one more thing, Thad, okay? And be honest with me if you can."

"Yes, of course. Anything. Any way I can help."

"Are you sleeping with my wife?"

———※———

Thad had just added an hour to my drive, the son of a bitch.

The fastest route to Kitty Hawk was along I-64, right past Williamsburg. I had thought of stopping home, grabbing some fresh clothes, maybe some things for the kids before continuing on. But with the cops looking for me now, along with Clevenger's collection agents, I wanted nothing to do with the whole damn peninsula. So when I hit Richmond, I didn't take the exit for Route 64 but instead, like Grant before me, I headed for Petersburg. Then I took 460 toward the coast.

The phone I had been using was one of three little units I had picked up at a 7-Eleven on the way to my grandfather. They weren't fancy, but they worked well enough and, most importantly, they were disposable. The bastards had found me in Vegas, they had found me in Williamsburg, they had found me in Pitchford. They had proven quite adept at finding me on their own, I didn't need to help them out with a traceable signal to lead them right up my ass.

Before I threw the first one out, I made one more call.

———※———

"Who's this?"

"It's me. Like it said on the tattoo on Augie's shoulder, I'm still here, baby."

"A new number. You're getting careful in your old age."

"Are you done searching my house? What did you find, a couple quarters under the cushions of the couch? Some dust mites in the mattresses?"

"We found the plate on the water heater, is what we found. We found the gap in the insulation, a hole big enough to bury a fortune."

"And what did you find in the gap?"

"It's only a matter of time, friend."

"Let me see," I said, trying to sound jaunty and hard, and succeeding surprisingly well. Clevenger seemed to bring out the worst in me. "My guess is Holmes is either still in the hospital or maybe transferred to the lockup so he can tell the cops all about you. And your two goons in Philly are probably recuperating now in Pitchford Memorial, with two detectives waiting outside their room to have a crack at them. It's getting dangerous out there for your boys."

"I don't need any help to take care of you."

"That's good, because at the rate you're going, you won't have any."

"So who was the mother's helper at your motel last night? You hire some muscle, Frenchy? You buy yourself some protection?"

"I don't need protection, but let me tell you, your pal Derek sure as hell does."

He took a moment to light his cigarette, to inhale. The little pause that confirmed everything. "Who's Derek?" he said finally.

"Don't kid a kidder, Clevenger, you don't have the irony for it. I just wanted you to relay a message for me."

"I'm not your messenger boy."

"Today you are. Tell him I'm coming. And, Clevenger, you should be there, too. I'd be disappointed if you weren't."

"Don't worry, pal. I wouldn't miss it for the world. For a hooker maybe, but not for the world."

"Good," I said. "Someone's got to answer for Augie, and it's going to be you."

"This is personal, is that it?"

"That's it."

"So no deal, right? You're going to play it out with blood? Because that's what I'm hoping for, that's the way I want it, too."

It took me a moment to process what he had just said. I was driving too fast, I was getting too angry, I remembered the cackle of his voice while I stood over the body of my dead best friend, and as he spoke of blood all I wanted was to see his, spattered over his face. Which is why it took me a moment to get the whole import of his words.

"What kind of deal?" I said finally.

"Curious as a cat, you are," said Clevenger. "So here it is. We'll end it. We'll call off the dogs. You get your life back, your family back. And whatever you've been running from all these years, the ghosts and the demons, it's over. Safety, security, peace, the whole ball of wax, pal. After twenty-five years of running and hiding, we're offering you your freedom."

As I listened to his offer, I slipped neatly into my mortgage-broker guise, as if this was as simple as paying off an ARM before the adjustment became ruinous.

"Terms?" I said.

And then he told me.

It was dark already when I drove along the bridge across the Currituck Sound. I had no clear idea of where exactly I was or onto what street I was headed. I was relying on the RX10's GPS to get me where I needed to go. But in all honesty, even though I had never been to the Outer Banks before, by the time I hit the end of the bridge I believed I could have done the directing with my GPS off and my eyes closed. The new setting on my internal compass was guiding me unerringly.

Right onto the highway, right again onto a street that swiped a golf course. Follow the road around to the far side, to an old, narrow house wedged between two extravagant mansions and backing up upon the woods on the left. An unpaved drive led toward the narrow house and I took it, parking at the end beside a beat old brown pickup, my lights still on to illuminate the house in front of me. A narrow set of stairs angled its way up to the front porch.

And then the door opened and my son came out onto the front porch and peered down at the car and jumped a bit when he saw it was me and called out behind him. And my daughter stepped through the door with a smile strange to me only because I had seen so little of it lately. And then my wife, her face as inscrutable as a politician's. I turned off the car, hopped out, ran up the stairs to hug them. My wife pulled away even as my children allowed me to grip them with a fervor that must have surprised them, because it surprised me.

"Can we go home now, please?" said Eric. "Please?"

"Do you have my phone?" said Shelby.

And then Harry came out, grinning and nodding. "There he is, that's Johnny."

"Hello, Harry," I said. "Thanks for taking care of them."

"It wasn't me doing the caring," he said.

And behind Harry a woman, tall and formidable, her gray hair beehived to within an inch of its life. "About time you showed," she snapped. "I guess them strip bars finally closed."

"I'll have you know," I said, giving Shelby a wink, "I haven't stepped into a strip club since last night."

"Oh God," said Caitlin.

"Come on in, you," said Harry's sister, "we've been saving supper. And I've got some talking I mean to do."

38. On the Beach

HOW MUCH?" SAID CAITLIN.

"A ridiculous amount," I said.

"How ridiculous?"

"More than enough for them still to be hunting us twenty-five years later."

We were alone on the beach, my soon-to-be-erstwhile wife and I, sitting in the sand, our legs stretched out in front of us. Behind us was a row of charming beach cottages lit and cozy in the darkness; before us was the light of a crescent moon skittering along the uneven surface of the sea. We had left the kids with Harry and his sister so we could take our walk and have our talk. The talk. We were facing the water because it was easier than facing each other. As I spoke, she remained mostly silent, staring out at the ocean, and I stared out along with her. And what I saw hovering above the luminescent white at the tip of each dark wave surprised the hell out of me. What I saw was my father.

My father was usually as absent from my thoughts as he was from my life. My mother raised me, if you consider benign neglect to qualify as such, and my grandfather loomed large in my imagination as both tyrant and potential savior. My father, by contrast, was a mere shadow that passed by at a far remove. Yet there it was, that shadow, rising over the great heaving sea, faceless really because I knew not his face anymore, stretching his arms out to me.

I never considered before what it must have done to my father to be the son of my grandfather. When everything you touch is a disaster, what choice is there but to reach for the dynamite? I can see now why he married my mother, a Moretti from South Philly who had never even heard of the Philadelphia Country Club. It wasn't a brilliant love story, because we know how it ended, but it sure was a shove up the old man's gut. And my grandfather shoved it right back by blandly accepting it all, by having us all over for Sunday supper, by playing the contented patriarch to his new clan as he waited for my father to screw it all up. And of course my father couldn't help himself from doing just that.

From what my mother told me, my father's mistress was much like her, his second life much like his first. He was unhappy with his one life, so he re-created it exactly over again and somehow, strangely, was happy with the two. The world trundles on with its morality and its mores, it forces us into molds, and in the end, even if only as rebels, we all succumb. But a secret allows you step outside of the whole damn process. My father's secret life was his ultimate declaration of independence. Winston Smith in Oceana would have understood. Sometimes the life we end up living is not enough, sometimes we need a secret to give it the grandeur an enterprise like living in this world requires, and I know of what I speak.

I loved the money that I had stolen, my too-big house, my too-expensive car, but my secret was an even richer treat. At home I might have been a boring suburban dad, but I was more. At work I might have been just another fiscal huckster, financing dreams on foundations made of playing cards, but I was more. And even after I lost my job and became just another victim of the recession, in the heart of my secret I was no victim. Whatever anybody thought of me, they had no idea. I was free of their assumptions and judgments. My secret meant that I was free.

But while a secret can be a barrier to keep the wolfish world at bay, there is also something lost in its embrace, and I saw it clearly when I thought about my father. He was living in Vegas, he surely was in the town during some of my visits to Augie. We might have been at the very same craps table or at the very same Applebee's and not even known it. And so he died alone among the nauseating excess of the unlimited Vegas buffet. The rebellion of my father's secret life had cost him something, it had cost him me. I might have understood, but I was sick of paying the price.

Through the whole of the dinner the evening I arrived at Kitty Hawk, I was in mourning. Harry's sister, Mathilda, made us hold hands for a good five minutes as her grace invoked the stern God of retribution before she served a shockingly delicious meat loaf with a side of pickled comments. Harry noisily rued the lack of beer in the house. My son complained about there being no computer or video games. My daughter seemed strangely calm and happy, even cleared the table when we were finished eating, which worried me. Caitlin avoided looking at me, as if I had grown snakes on my head. And I was quiet during it all, feeling a strange sadness, not for my dead dad or over my disillusionment with my grandfather, no. I felt sad because I knew my secret was to die that night.

And then on the beach, sitting next to the woman I still loved but had clearly lost, beneath that crescent moon, I killed it dead. I started with my first day in Pitchford and I told her everything. And as I told it I could feel something inside me deflating, like a pin had pricked the bladder of my entire sense of self. What the hell was I without my secret? I guess I was about to find out.

"Ten, twenty thousand?" she said.

"More."

"A hundred thousand?"

"Four times that."

"Jesus."

"Each."

"My God, Jonathon. And the stack of bills you gave me on the dock?"

"Originals, yes. There's probably enough stink of the cocaine still on them to drive a drug dog wild."

She was calm, calmer than I had imagined she would be if ever she learned. But I don't think it was because the secret wasn't big enough, I think it was because she had checked out of whatever we had long ago and this only confirmed that she was absolutely right to do so.

"What did you spend the money on?" she said.

"On us. The family. Whenever we needed something, I took some from my secret stash. A little extra to pay the mortgage, a little extra for the car payment or the vacation. I took what I had to, but only as little as possible to get us the things we wanted, and not enough to draw any attention to us."

"I thought you had investments."

"No, my investments are crap. I don't even have the Midas touch with mufflers. But I had this."

"This," she said, nodding, like it almost made sense. "And you thought it was the right thing not to share all this with me?"

"It was just one thing."

"Oh, come on, Jonathon. It wasn't just one thing, it was everything."

And she was absolutely right, she had seen it right away.

"Don't say you didn't like it," I said, "the house and the sporty cars, the vacations in Aruba, your hair appointments at Chez Rochelle. It hasn't been all bad, the money. It's how we bought our life."

"So let me get this straight: it's not just you who are a fraud and a criminal, you have made our life itself fraudulent and criminal."

"It's not like that."

"Oh, yes it is, on so many levels. I look in the mirror, Jon, and I don't know who I am anymore. All I see is a shell that has been layered onto me, all the stuff I got because I couldn't have the one thing I really wanted."

"And what was it you really wanted?" I said with a touch of bitterness. "What didn't I steal enough to be able to afford to give you?"

"A love affair with my husband," she said. "That's all I ever wanted out of my marriage. But there was always something in you that killed the chance of it. That's why I broke up with you the first time. Because there were too many barriers to get through, with no promise of what was behind them. And then I found a relationship where there were no barriers, where we breathed each other's breaths. His name was François, and I lost myself in him."

"François?"

"Yes."

"French?"

"Canadian."

"Fake French, then, like a Starbucks croissant."

"He was my great love, Jonathon. How does that make you feel, hearing that?"

"Like I'm getting what I deserve. You don't need to do this."

"Oh, yes I do. I never told you about him, but we're telling our secrets, right? Not all of them, but some. Boys like François, they exist to break your heart, and so he did. The devastation, my God. It was like a natural disaster. When you reappeared, I was an invalid, ready for some distance. It was my fault, I admit it. You were about all I could handle at the time. And I thought you would open up at some point. I thought you simply had a trust issue, and if I built the trust, then when you did open up it would be like it was with François, closer than close, without the pain. But I kept waiting, and you kept moving further away. I couldn't figure it out, it didn't make sense. All I knew was that I couldn't bear it anymore. And now I know what was behind it."

"It was just something I did when I was young."

"No, Jonathon. It was something you did every day of our life together. I never even understood the tattoo until now. My God, I have no idea who the hell you are."

"We've been married seventeen years."

"You're a complete and utter stranger."

"It doesn't matter that I told you?"

"You told me seventeen years too late and only because you had no choice. What else don't I know?"

"When they came after Augie I was going to run away. I'd already created a new identity for myself. Edward Holt, with a pretty decent picture on the passport, I must add. I was going to fake my death and run away with what was left of the money and leave you with the life insurance."

"You cowardly son of a bitch."

"It was going to be for your own good. And it's not like you weren't going to divorce me anyway if I stayed around. But I couldn't do it. I couldn't leave you or the kids or our lives. I love my life. I love my kids. I love you."

"Don't."

"And after this is over," I said, "I'll do anything to make it work. Anything."

She turned and looked at me for a long moment, looked at me as if I were an interesting specimen, a dead jellyfish that the tide had deposited onto the moonlit sand.

"Exactly who is after us?" she said.

"A motorcycle madman. The money was hidden in his house. He turned state's evidence when he was arrested. He's in the witness protection program now, but he hired some bounty hunter to go after us."

"How'd he find out it was you three?"

"I don't know. None of us would have given up the others; Augie, Ben, and I, we were brothers. That's the one thing I can trust absolutely."

"What are you going to do about this motorcycle man?"

291

"I'm trying to find him. That's why I went back to my old hometown. I have one chance to get his location. It's a long shot, but it's the only shot I have."

"And if you do find him?"

"I don't know. Maybe I can get the Marshals Service involved or something. I'll figure out what to do when it happens."

"That's a good plan, Jonathon. That makes me feel so secure. And we're supposed to stay hiding out with that woman until you figure it out."

"It's safer, I think, than anything else. Though not as safe as I thought. Thad told me that they knew about Harry."

"Thad?"

"Yeah," I said. "Thad."

"You spoke to Thad?"

"I had to find out what was happening in Patriots Landing. Evidently a lot."

"I'm going to my sister's."

"Caitlin, no. They'll find you there."

"Then I'll figure out something else. I'm not sitting like a stuffed doll, waiting for them to find me here. We'll go somewhere until it all blows over. And it will blow over quickly, right?"

"I'll try. But even if I don't find Derek, there might be another way. I was offered a deal by the bounty hunter. He promised to call the whole thing off for a payment. He's offering to be bought."

"For how much?"

"For more than the money I have left. But I could cash out whatever equity we have in the house, take out what we have in our retirement funds, borrow the rest. It would pretty much wipe us out."

"And you need me to agree. You need my signature."

"Yes."

"And then it would be over?"

"That's what he says. I don't know if I trust him."

"Do we have a choice but to trust him?"

"Not if I can't find the guy he works for."

She stood up, dusted the sand off her legs with a few quick slashes of her hand. "Do what you have to, Jonathon. Do what you have to and get these bastards out of our lives."

"I will."

"And then you get the hell out of our lives, too."

39. Nocturne

I AM LYING NEXT TO MY WIFE, ALONE IN THE NIGHT, BECAUSE that's the way it is now when I lie next to my wife. Outside the wind rustles the leaves, outside a dog barks, outside something ferocious waits. And I have nothing to fight it with.

In the middle of the nameless night there is only a present tense. My wife's back is turned to me, her spine a familiar barbed wall keeping me out. We are sleeping together on a full bed in the tiny second guest room, but not by choice. Back from the beach, Caitlin had wanted nothing more to do with me, I could tell, and I hadn't wanted to taste her angry disdain all night. But by the time we got back, Shelby and Eric were asleep in the first guest room and Harry was sacked out and snoring on the couch, which left us only the other bedroom with the single bed.

But we are long married, we know how to sleep apart on the same mattress.

I lie in bed with my shirt off and my arms behind my head, my eyes open, staring at the darkness that flows like smoke within the atoms of the ceiling, staring at my future. I am in that most frightening of places, the zone between the before and the after. If my life has been guided by the secret for the last quarter century, what will guide it now? I have lost my job, my wife and family, my place in the world, and, if I make Clevenger's deal, I will lose what was left of my money, too. I will have nothing.

Bob Dylan made it sound romantic, but he was only twenty-four when he wrote "Like a Rolling Stone"—what the hell did that pup know? I am forty-two and lost in the darkness. If I thought I was free before, I had no idea of the true terror of freedom pure.

A sound as soft as a breath. "What were you thinking?"

It takes me a moment to realize it isn't my subconscious whispering to me, it is my wife.

"I thought you were asleep," I whisper back.

"I knew you weren't. You breathe differently when you're awake."

"How do I breathe when I'm awake?"

"Like you're hiding something."

She's right. I can remember bouts of sleeplessness where I limited my breathing so she wouldn't know I wasn't blissfully dreaming, so she wouldn't ask me about the abject terrors keeping me up all night.

"That's the old me," I say. "Now it's utter honesty to the end. What I'm thinking about, if you really want to know, is the existential muddle that is my life."

"Is that what your life is?"

"And I'm being generous."

I feel the mattress shift, I feel her turn to me. When did that happen last? A faint heat washes over the side of my body. The size of the bed has forced her as close to me as possible without touching.

"It's brave of you to share your existential anxiety, but I'm not asking about that now," she says, her whisper full of a real curiosity. "I'm asking about then. What were you thinking when you took all that money?"

"I don't know. I was young, and stupid. And quite high, I might add."

"Smoke much?"

"Augie, Ben, and I, we were total heads in high school," I say.

"Really? I can't imagine it, you're, like, the straightest man I know."

"There's nothing so straight as a reformed pot smoker."

"But what was actually going through your brain when you took the money?"

"I had a chip on my shoulder. Through the whole of my childhood, after my father left, I felt like I was living through someone else's bad dream. When you feel like that, the only thing you're not willing to do is play it safe. I stumbled on these buckets full of cash and I saw a way out, a way to get everything I had always felt deprived of."

"It just seems so not you. You're always cautious, careful, you always run from confrontation. It's like I'm lying here next to a stranger."

"That's marriage for you."

"No, this is beyond the usual suburban-marriage-midlife-growing-apart thing. With everything you've told me, I realize I don't know you at all." The warmth on my side gets a little warmer. Something brushes my chest. An accidental touch from her hand? Her breast?

"Do you like it?" I say.

"Like what?"

"Being in bed with a total stranger."

"A little."

I feel her press up against me, I feel her chin on my chest, I feel myself stiffen.

"So the less you know me," I say, "the more interesting I get."

"That's about right."

"There is so much you don't know," I say, laughing.

In the darkness I remember the first time I slept with Caitlin in Wisconsin. She was small and thin, with interesting eyes, but nothing out of the ordinary. I was drunk enough that it wasn't her I was after so much as the sex. It could have been the girl down the hall, or the field hockey player in my statistics class—I was game. But the girl down the hall was studying and the field hockey player was dating a football star and so that night I ended up with skinny little Caitlin from Intro Philosophy. U2 had just put out *The Joshua Tree* and "With or Without You" was playing on my stereo when the vest came off, and the baggy sweater, and the glasses, and the T-shirt, and suddenly all I wanted was the girl I was with. Her arms long and slender, her breasts fuller than ever I had imagined, her thin waist and legs, the shockingly confident jut of her hips. Watching her undress was like opening a small box on Christmas and finding a pony inside. And during the sex itself, it didn't feel like I was getting away with something, the way it felt with Madeline Worshack and all the ones after her, it felt like *we* were getting away with something, which is completely different. And after, after the laughter and the trembling jaw and the riotous chewing of each other's lips, she kissed the sweat off the side of my neck and, in a gesture shockingly intimate, far more intimate than the sex that had preceded it, she placed her chin on my chest, stared at me with those eyes, and asked me if I really believed all that bullshit I had said in class about Kant.

In that instant it was as if I was discovering something bright and new in the world. And now, with her chin resting on the very same spot on my chest, it is as if I am rediscovering that very same thing. Only this time she isn't asking about my warped take on the categorical imperative—more Ayn Rand than Immanuel— she is asking about its fruits.

"How much did you really end up with?" she says.

"I told you."

"The exact amount, I mean."

"Four hundred and twenty-four thousand, three hundred and ninety," I say, "along with my part of a twenty-dollar bill that Augie, Ben, and I ripped into thirds."

"Wow," she says, her hand absently tapping my side.

"Yeah," I say. "We didn't know at the time that cutting up legal tender was a crime."

But that *wow* is real, and hard earned. She is seeing it now as I always saw it, an unimaginable boon. It's what the idea of easy money does to everyone, it was how I made my living when I was still making a living, and it is almost disappointing to see her captured by it. But it is far from disappointing to have her talk to me without aggrievement in her voice.

She draws her chin closer to my face and lowers her voice. "And how much is left?"

"Less."

"No, really, how much do we have left?"

In the ebb of the darkness and in the timbre of her whisper I can tell she is smiling, and the smile in her voice is so entrancing that I almost miss the pronoun and its import. I don't understand anything that is happening, but my erection does, and we—my erection and I this time—both like it.

"We had about one eighty left before I went to Vegas. Augie had eighty hidden beneath the floor of his kitchen, which I took, along with his share of the twenty-dollar bill. Technically some of that eighty belongs to Ben, although I had lent him some over the years. And I gave ten to Harry for helping you and the kids escape, and ten to you, and I spent some. So let's say I have about two hundred and ten left."

"Cash?"

"That's right."

"Tax free?"

"It was all tax free."

"So two forty."

"Ben has to get some—"

"Fuck Ben," she says.

"Whoa."

She rises up on her arms, hovers over me. She is wearing a T-shirt and her breasts are straining the fabric. Her straight blonde hair hangs down close enough to tickle my face. She seems now as strange to me as she did that first night together our sophomore year. How is that possible? And why do I like it so much?

"Where is it?" she says.

"In the car."

"Unprotected?"

"It's safe. Trust me."

"You boys are all the same," she says. "I want to see it."

"No you don't."

"Yes I do," she says, still hovering. "I paid for it."

"You paid for it?"

"It killed my marriage."

"Is that what did it?"

"You don't think so?"

"Maybe we were incompatible. Maybe we just grew apart."

"We never had the chance to grow together. There were hundreds of thousands of us in the relationship and I never knew." She swings a leg over mine so that her thigh is rubbing up against my crotch. "It's time for me to meet the competition."

I roll her off me and roll myself off the bed. Without putting on my shoes, I grab my keys from the top of the bureau and head outside. When I come back, there are tiny pebbles embedded in my soles and the rusted green toolbox is in my hand. I turn on the light. I open the box on the bed. I lift out the top tray, take out the tools, pry up the false floor.

"I thought there would be more," she says, staring at the piles.

"Hundred-dollar bills stack up neatly."

"Can I?"

"Go ahead."

She picks up a stack, hefts it, puts it on the bed, picks up another. It isn't long before all the stacks are lined up on the bedsheet, leaving only the cigarettes and the condoms in the toolbox. I expect to hear about the latter two items, but Caitlin makes nary a comment. What else would you expect to find with $240,000 in cash? The way she's reacting, I don't think she would blink if she knew about the gun locked in the glove compartment of the car.

"My God," she says.

"It is a sight, isn't it?"

"It does something to you," she says. "You spend so much of life thinking and worrying about money that when you see so much of it in one place, it does something to you."

"It's why people go into banking."

"It makes me hungry."

"Now you get it."

She takes a stack and slips the paper wrapper off. She fans the bills in her hand and then tosses them in the air so that they flutter onto the bed.

"What are you doing?" I say.

She does it again with another stack.

"Stop it," I say, but I say it halfheartedly. I'm a stranger to her and now she's a stranger to me. Of all the reactions I ever expected, this was not one of them.

"I've always wanted to do this," she says.

"Do what?"

"Haven't you?" she says.

"Do what, exactly?"

And then she shows me. With the lights on.

It is only after, when the money and tools are packed away, and the lights are back off, and Caitlin is lying beside me again in the quiet of the dark, that I remember being with Augie and Ben the night we took the money, talking of having sex on all the bills with Tawni Dunlop, with Sandra Tong, with Madeline Worshack, all the avatars of our high school lust. And I smile when I think of it, because it was better than I ever imagined. And it was with my wife.

Augie would have never understood. And, frankly, neither did I. But it filled me with something, the hope it brought, something maybe even more powerful than my murdered secret.

40. The Morning After

W HAT'S UP WITH YOU AND MOM?" SAID SHELBY THE NEXT morning. Eric, Shelby, and I were walking on the beach.

"I don't know for sure," I said.

"So are you getting divorced or what?" said Eric.

"What do you want us to do, Eric?"

"I want you to stay together for your kids, live at home together, and be so miserable that you leave us alone."

"That sounds like a plan."

"So it's Mom's fault," said Shelby, "the whole splitting-up thing?"

"No," I said, resisting the urge to start laying the groundwork for our inevitable postsplit child battles. I figured there would be time enough for that when this was all over. "It's my fault, all of it. I've been a jerk."

"But you've always been a jerk, Dad," said Shelby. "That's you."

"Thank you, sweetie. Look, that's not what I want to talk about. Your mom and I will figure things out eventually, but right now that's between us. What I want to talk about is why you've been stuck here for these few days without phone or e-mail."

"It's not so bad," said Shelby.

"Really?" I said.

"I thought I'd go crazy without a phone, but it's so calm. And I sort of like Mathilda in a weird way.

"Speak for yourself," said Eric. "That lady creeps me out."

"She's okay," said Shelby. "She taught me how to make biscuits."

"Biscuits?"

"Yeah, can you imagine?"

"No," I said.

"She asked me if I was a sinner," said Eric. "I told her not yet, but I'm only eleven, give me time."

"Even Mom laughed at that," said Shelby.

"But there has been no phoning or e-mailing, right? You're not doing anything that can give your location away, are you?"

"We're not stupid, Dad," said Shelby.

"I know you're not, sweetie."

"We just go to the library and read."

"But no phones."

"No, I promise."

"Okay, here's the story. A long time ago, when I was just a bit older than Shelby, some friends and I discovered a stash of money. I mean a lot of it. And we took it, just like that."

"You stole it?" said Eric.

"Sort of."

"How cool is that?" said Eric.

"No, it wasn't cool."

"Sort of stealing," said Shelby. "Is that sort of like being pregnant?"

"Well, *sort of* means it wasn't really anybody's money. It was drug money. The guys we took it from made it selling drugs. To kids. In schoolyards. They had no more right to it than we did."

"So it wasn't stealing?" said Shelby.

"It was like *Grand Theft Auto*," said Eric, "where everyone is bad so you can do whatever you want?"

"We didn't shoot hookers and steal cars," I said.

"But you stole something," said Eric.

"Did the people you took it from think it was stealing?" said Shelby.

"Oh, yes. And that's what's going on right now. They're looking for it. And they think I still have it."

"And do you?"

"Not much of it anymore. I spent most of it. On us, I mean. The house, the cars."

"And your strippers?" said Shelby.

"Strippers?" said Eric. "You really are the Batman."

"No, I'm not. And I know it's a disappointment to you, Shelby, but I actually don't like strip clubs. I'd rather go to a ball game."

"So, you bought all our stuff with drug money?" said Shelby.

"Some of it, I guess. Though I didn't make it selling drugs."

"But still," said Shelby.

"Look, I was young and stupid."

"But you weren't young when you were buying, like, cars with it. That was, like, last week."

"No, I was just stupid then."

"This is all pretty cool, Dad," said Eric. "You're an outlaw. I can't wait to tell Teddy."

"No, it's not cool, and I'm not an outlaw, and you're not telling anyone. The truth is, I'm just another idiot who screwed up badly. Everything would have been better if we just left it alone."

"So it *was* stealing," said Shelby.

Here's a new rule to live by. If you can't justify your actions to your kids without sounding like a fool, then all your little rationalizations are nothing so much as puffs of wind dying at the mountain's edge. And it's true whether you're stealing drug money from a basement, or selling subprime mortgages to people who can't afford them, or betting other people's life savings on credit-default swaps.

Fortunately, before I tried to wade again into the untenable, my cell phone rang and saved me from the humiliation.

"Give me a minute," I said to my kids before heading to the ocean's edge, where the surf could drown out my conversation. This call wasn't coming into my original phone, or the phone I had used to call Clevenger on the way south from Philadelphia—those were both long gone. The phone that rang had a number I had given to only one person. I looked at it a bit to steel my nerves, and then pressed the ANSWER button.

"Is this Mr. Moretti?" An older voice, solid and discreet, like a concierge at the Hotel Adultery.

"The name's Willing," I said. "Jon Willing."

"Call yourself anything you want," he said. "I'm phoning from the offices of Talbott, Kittredge, and Chase, Mr. Willing. We're a law firm in Philadelphia."

"You don't need to identify yourself to me," I said. "My mother got the occasional missive from Talbott, Kittredge, and Chase during our darkest days in the wilderness. You're the Willing family firm, specializing in disinheritance and body bags."

"We're just lawyers, Mr. Willing."

"And Al Capone just sold a little beer."

"We have some information for you, but first we're going to put you on a recorded line. Is that acceptable?"

"Do I have a choice?"

"No."

"Then knock yourself out."

"Thank you."

There was a pause, and then a click, and then another pause, followed by the man giving the time and date.

"Now, you claim to be Jonathon Willing, is that right?" said the man.

"It's the truth," I said.

"We won't dispute that for purposes of this conversation, Mr. Willing, though we admit to nothing. And you've been made aware that this conversation is being recorded, isn't that correct?"

"So you said."

"Very good. Now, Mr. Willing, our understanding is that you are intending today to renounce all claims you might have against the estate of Montgomery Willing III or of his son Preston Willing, is that correct?"

"That depends."

"On what?"

"On what I get in return."

"Mr. Willing, you made a request, is that right?"

"That's right."

"And you relayed that request to Montgomery Willing at the Philadelphia Country Club, is that not correct?"

"Yes."

"And now, in full consideration of his efforts to meet that request, and for the payment of one dollar, which will be sent forthwith to your address in Virginia, you are intending today to renounce all claims against the aforementioned estates, isn't that correct?"

"What did you find?"

"What we found is not under discussion at the moment. We have made a good-faith effort to satisfy your request. We are also sending you the dollar. If that is sufficient consideration to renounce all possible claims, please say so on the recording. If not, our business here is at an end."

"You're not going to tell me what you found?"

"Not until this part is clarified."

"Okay, I accept. I renounce."

"And you are renouncing all claims not only for yourself, but also for all of your issue, for all of time. Is that acceptable?"

I glanced at Shelby and Eric clowning in the sand, thought of that old man at the club, and I said, "Good riddance."

"Just say yes or no, please."

"Yes."

"And you admit that your claim to be a relation of Montgomery Willing III is fraudulent."

"No."

"Excuse me? Need we try this again?"

"No, the only thing fraudulent is that old bastard. I don't want his money, but I'm his grandson. And he knows it. And you checked the DNA already, or the marriage records, or something, or we wouldn't be having this discussion, so you know it, too. And let me ask you, how does it feel to so blithely slice off a member of your client's family tree?"

"It's what we do, Mr. Willing."

"So said Al Capone on Valentine's Day. Anything else?"

"There are a few more things we need to go over."

"No, there aren't. I'm done. Give me what I want or I'm coming back to Philadelphia. The press always likes to blat out the scandals of the aristocracy. I can see the headline in the *Daily News*: 'Disowned Scion Ready and Willing.'"

"There is no need for publicity here."

"Heaven forbid."

"We're going to end the recording now, is that acceptable?"

"Let's keep it going. We're having so much fun."

A pause, a click, another pause.

"It's off," he said.

"All right, bub. What do you have for me?"

"We have an address for you, Mr. Moretti."

"Willing."

"Whatever. It's not the exact address of the man you're looking for, but it's the next-best thing. A contact number buried deep within the files of the Department of Justice. It was quite hard to obtain, quite expensive. You should be grateful to your grandfather."

"That's like being grateful to a scorpion. It doesn't matter how grateful you are, he'd still sting you just because he can. Let me have it."

"The number itself won't be much help. It's the number for a local US Marshals Service office, most likely the office charged with keeping tabs on the protected witness. Will that address help?"

"It's a start."

"Good. Two-Ninety-Nine East Broward Boulevard."

"East Broward? What is that, Florida?"

"Fort Lauderdale," he said.

"Son of a bitch," I said. And suddenly, the one thing that had puzzled me through the whole of this mess became clear. "Son of a bitch."

"Is that valuable to you, Mr. Moretti?"

"It'll do," I said. "Now, can you relay something to my grandfather for me?"

"Off the record?"

"Yes, definitely off the record."

"That can be arranged."

I looked at my kids staring at me as I stared at them. The scene blurred, like a film had been placed over a lens to soften the image.

"Tell my grandfather thank you."

"Of course."

"And tell him that I love him, still. That I always have. And that I miss my father."

By the time I left the ocean's edge and reached my children I thought I had gotten myself under control, but that was a mirage.

"Dad?" said Shelby, as if she was seeing an apparition, and I suppose she was. What could be more ghostly than watching your father cry? How could my children know that I was finally mourning my own father's death?

"Is everything okay?" said Eric.

"Of course everything's not okay," said Shelby. "Look at him."

"He's crying, so what?" said Eric. "If I have to spend another day in this pit I'll be crying, too."

"What's wrong, Dad?" said Shelby.

"It's nothing," I said, my jaw trembling still. I reached out and hugged them. "It's just that I love you both so much. And I screwed up so badly. And worst of all, now I have to go to Florida."

IV. EVERFAIR

"Have you ever noticed, boys,
everyone who finds themselves
living in Florida ends up dying?"

—Augie Iannucci

41. The Final Third

I WAS ALONE IN THE ROOM I HAD RENTED IN FORT LAUDERDALE. The refrigerator rumbled like it was still digesting. The faucet in the kitchenette dripped liked a Chinese torturer: drip, drip, nothing, drip. There was a brown hot plate, a mold-stained shower I wouldn't walk into without boots, two beds with stained plaid covers, a television with a picture tube that painted everything a sickly shade of green. This is what I had done to myself, this is what my existence had been whittled down to: scratching my skin raw in the Sea Queen Motel. The way things were going, there was a pretty good chance that this was the first day of the rest of my life.

And I had earned every inch of it.

Outside the traffic poured through the sunlight with bleats and roars up and down Atlantic Avenue. There was an apartment building across the street and beyond the apartment building another, finer motel and then the beach. The lovely beach. If only they didn't have so damn much of it. I sat with the lights off, in a tattered chair, facing the doorway, waiting. When I left Kitty Hawk I had been filled to the brim with a host of emotions, and not all of them were negative, emotions like hope and love and even a twist of optimism. But the positive emotions had been burned out of me by the reality of the situation facing me now, and I was stewing in a toxic mix of anger, fear, and self-loathing as I waited.

The trip down the day before had been sixteen hours in Harry's truck. I had been battered in Vegas, I had been in a brutal collision in Virginia, I had been cracked and beaten like a scrambled egg in Pitchford, where my chest and stomach had been purpled with bruises, and still all of it had been just a prelude to the pounding I took in Harry's truck. We had showed up in Fort Lauderdale well after midnight, cruised the strip until we saw a VACANCY sign, and bought this hole for a couple of nights. Sixty-five a day, snapping bugs included for no extra charge. Harry, though, seemed to like the accommodations. "Living like princes," he had said before collapsing in his bed and snoring gloriously through the rest of the night. I understood, I had been in his boat. But I hadn't slept as soundly, tossing and turning and scratching until the night bled into the bleary morning.

When Harry finally awoke with a snort and a start, we found a diner and ate our hash and eggs as we hashed out our plans. "Any questions?" I said.

"Not that I can think of," said Harry, "though thinking was never my strong suit. You mind I take a couple beers with me while I wait, just for the company?"

I looked at my watch. "It's not even noon."

"Just for the company, Johnny, not for any real drinking."

"Do whatever you want. You're about all I've got left to trust, so I'll trust you'll take care of business."

"You know I will, Johnny. With me, business is business, and beer is still just beer. I'd drink water if it wasn't so damn wet."

"I don't know exactly what he'll look like. It's been a long time."

"I got enough to find him, don't you worry."

"And don't scare him or anything, keep it nice and calm. Just show him what I gave you to show him and don't let him make a call before you bring him back to the motel."

"And if the varmint don't want to come?"

"You show him what I gave you to show him and he'll come."

There was really only one way to play it anymore, which was why I was waiting in the motel room while Harry did the leg-work. It wasn't enough that we had ditched my car. I had made it clear to Clevenger that I was coming for Derek and now we knew that Derek was here. If Holmes had my picture, they all had my picture, and who knows how many of them were trolling Fort Lauderdale looking for me. But Harry, an old beaten-down drunk in an old beaten-down truck, could float through the city as unnoticed as a hyena on Wall Street. He could go to the house and wait, he could follow, he could make contact, he could say just what I told him to say and show what I told him to show in order to lure our quarry to this motel room, where I waited.

"What are you going to do?" Caitlin had asked just before Harry and I left Kitty Hawk.

"End it one way or the other."

"How long will you be?"

"Not too long. Either it happens or it doesn't."

"We won't be here when you're finished."

"I know."

"I went a little crazy last night."

"No, you didn't."

"I'm sorry."

"About what?"

She looked at me and sighed. I had seen that same look before, and that same sigh, from every girl who ever broke up with me. "Just make the deal, Jonathon. Just end it."

"If I trusted the man on the other side, I would. But I don't. My grandfather gave me another option and I'm going to take it. I'll call you when we get down there, just so you know we've arrived."

"We won't leave until you do."

"Are you ready to start over?"

"Yes, I am," she said.

"With me or without me?"

313

"Nothing's changed."

"What about last night?"

"What about it, Jonathon?"

"It was something, wasn't it?"

"Something like good-bye," she said.

"It would be different with us from now on, you know that."

"But that's not enough, is it?"

And she was right, it wasn't enough just to be different. What kind of husband and lover would I be, shorn of my secret? A bigger bore than I was already? Just like every other father at the Little League games, just like every other parent at the choral concerts, just like Thad? Was that what she wanted? Evidently.

And yet still, even in the squalid Sea Queen Motel with its hot- and cold-running chiggers, I was clear-eyed enough to see in this whole brutal crisis not just danger but opportunity, too. With my secret blown, and my whole life at risk, I had the opportunity to re-create my marriage, my relationship with my children, to re-create myself and my future. I had spent the last twenty-five years dreading exactly this moment, and yet now that it was here it felt less like a curse than like a benediction. Augie was crying in his last days, so said Selma, and I understood. How long had he felt trapped by his life? Twenty-five years and running, no doubt. And so had I, in a way I had never seen before, but not anymore. It had all come crashing down at the exact right moment.

But why now? That was what had puzzled me through all of this. They had found us out, fine, maybe it was inevitable, but why at this moment? There had to be a singular event that cascaded into disaster. I tried to learn what I could from Clevenger, but he was just a shade. I had thought Tony Grubbins would have the answer, but the only answers he had were in *The Tibetan Book of the Dead*. It was all a mystery, until my grandfather gave me his gift of information and sent me hurtling down to Fort

Lauderdale. I now knew who could tell me what I needed to know. And that's whom I was waiting for.

The beach beckoned, but I ignored it. I made coffee in the crappy motel coffee machine, drank it hot, pissed it out warm. When my legs grew restless I paced. When my nerves got the best of me I did push-ups. Whenever I heard footsteps approach on the walkway outside my room I sat up in the chair, but they always passed by. Passed by. I sat and stewed and waited. I was ready, I had to be ready, I had no choice anymore. It had moved beyond just wiping out my debt, far beyond.

"She's gone," Caitlin had said through panicky tears when I called her from a pay phone off the beach shortly after Harry had left with the truck.

"Who's gone? What?"

"Shelby. She was at the library. She was using the computers there."

"But I told her not to—"

"Oh, Jon, when does she ever listen? She was messaging on Facebook with that Luke. They were getting back together, that's why she was so happy. And then, yesterday, she never came back. No one saw anything. She left the library and disappeared."

"How could she be so stupid?"

"She's sixteen, that's how. And why should we be running like convicts, anyway, when we did nothing—"

"Call the police," I said.

"Jon, you bastard, what have you done to us?"

"Call the police. Have them try to find her up there. Tell them her abductors might be taking her to Florida and they need to check the roads, put out an Amber Alert, whatever. I'll do what I can to find her down here."

"Jon?"

"They'll be taking her to Florida, I'm sure of it. I'll find her, Caitlin. I'll get her back."

"Jon?"

"They don't want her, they want me. I'll trade myself for her, give over everything I have. Caitlin, I'll get her back. Trust me."

When I hung up I was shaking, with fear, with frustration, with resolve, with disgust at every mistake I had ever made. *Trust me*, I had said to my wife. It's always good to leave them laughing.

I went back to the room in a daze and tried to figure out what to do, how to deal with the escalation, because whatever had been between this Clevenger and me it had suddenly, drastically, escalated. I thought through my options, all the possibilities, and came up with only one that made some sense. Clevenger wanted to see crazy, well, he would see crazy, all right; I'd dial the crazy up to eleven. I went out once again to the pay phone and made a series of calls and then, back in the room, I sat down in the tattered chair, stared at the door, and waited. And waited. Someone was going to give me answers or someone was going to die, and just then I didn't much care which one it was.

Footsteps on the walkway outside, footsteps that approached and didn't pass by, footsteps that stopped right at my door.

Knock, knock, like the beginning of a joke.

"Who is it?" I called out.

"It's me, Johnny. It's Harry. We've got us a guest."

I gripped tight the armrests of the chair, I lowered my jaw. "Let him in," I said.

The door slowly opened. Sunlight streamed into the room through the opening and then, with the blinding light behind it, a silhouette, huge. Its shoulders reached from doorjamb to doorjamb, its head had to duck down as it stepped inside.

"J-J.J.?" said the figure as it leaned forward to peer into the darkness of the room, with that extra *J* thrown in as a bonus. "Is that you?"

"Hello, Ben," I said. "I've been waiting for you."

42. 52 Pickup

M Y GOD, J.J.," SAID BEN, ONE OF THE IMMORTAL THREE, which were, contrary to the name, now down to the immortal two. "I'm s-so glad to see you," he said, his voice soft and slurred like always, but now tinged with a panic evident in his resurrected stutter. He stepped toward me and stopped. "When your friend Harry showed me those two pieces of the old twenty taped together I almost y-yelped. I've been so worried. I didn't know what happened to you after you called me about Augie."

I stayed seated, still gripping the armrests of the chair, as Harry, from behind Ben, said, "You need me to stick around, Johnny? I can, if you want."

"No, thanks, Harry," I said. "We'll be fine."

Ben turned his head to look behind him, puzzled by my purposeful lack of reaction to his presence in that room after all those years.

"I might just head off to the Elbo Room for a jolt, then," said Harry. "You don't mind I take the truck, do you?"

"Enjoy yourself. Just close the door behind you and be back in a couple of hours."

"Will do, chief," said Harry, just before doing it.

With the door closed and the stream of sunlight shut off, I could actually get a clear view of Ben. I hadn't seen him in years, and the years I hadn't seen him in hadn't been gentle. He didn't look so much like Ben as like a bad copy of the Ben I had known. He had gained weight and held his body crookedly, as if the bad knee had ground down to meal. His jowls were pouched, the bags beneath his eyes were well packed, his face was lopsided, with a ragged recent scar on his cheek, and his mouth was a tense pucker.

"J.J.," said Ben. "Wh-what's been happening to you? Where have you been?"

"On the run," I said. "Ever since I discovered Augie's body."

"My God."

"They found my house in Virginia, and they ransacked it. They followed me to Pitchford."

"You were in P-Pitchford?"

"I barely got out of there alive."

"Wh-what were you doing in Pitchford?"

"Trying to find who was after us, Ben. Trying to find out how they got onto us. Trying to find who killed Augie."

"Did you l-learn anything?"

"Yes, I did."

"Then who is it? Wh-who killed Augie?"

"Derek Grubbins."

"That animal? Christ, it's worse than I thought. What are we going to do, J.J.? How are we getting out of this?"

"I don't know if we do get out of this."

"I ran when I first got your c-call. But I had no place to go and nothing left to lose. After two divorces my bank account was empty and my m-mortgage was underwater. What were they going to take? So I figured, the hell with it all. If there was a price to pay I was ready to pay it."

"And they never came after you?"

"Maybe they knew I had nothing left."

"We need to find Derek."

"Are you insane? He's a maniac."

"I know he is," I said. "But that's the only way to play it. Make a deal if we can, take the fight to him if we have to."

"He'll k-kill us."

"Only if we sit back and wait for him. He killed Augie, he's coming after us, we have to make him stop."

"Augie," said Ben, his voice softening. "Was it bad?"

"Worse than you can imagine."

"It crushed me to hear it," said Ben, something trembling inside him. "I hadn't seen him in years and still I m-miss him. More than I thought I would."

And there, just there, in his eyes, was a sadness that I remembered. It's often like that when you see an old friend. First you can barely recognize him within the crust of age. But then something familiar shows itself, a famous smile, a tilt of the head, and the age disappears with every blink until all you see is the person beneath, and the old friend is no longer old, and you can honestly say he hasn't changed a bit over the years. And here, before me, suddenly stood the Ben I had known from my very first afternoon in Pitchford. And he was crushed about Augie, as crushed as I, he couldn't fake that, my Ben would never be able to fake that.

My eyes teared as I pushed myself out of the chair. "Ben," I said. And then I stepped forward because, truthfully, only this man in all the world could understand how it felt to see Augie dead in his bed in that barren Vegas house. And I reached out and I hugged him. I hugged Ben, like I had hugged him on that final day in Pitchford before I drove away in the truck. I hugged Ben, the last of my old friends, my arms barely reaching around his bulk. And he hugged me back, hard. And I could feel the heaving of his sobs, true and earnest, unless the sobs I was feeling were the echoes of my own.

"God, J.J.," he said.

"Ben," I said. "Ben. They have my daughter."

"Who? How?"

"I tried to hide my family, but they found her, they found my daughter, and they took her."

"J.J., my God."

"My daughter, Ben. And all I want to know is, why?"

He didn't say anything, as if the question was rhetorical, but I could feel him tense in my arms, not quite sure.

And then, soft as a breath, I whispered in his ear, "How could you do it, Ben?"

Ben's exhale caught in his throat, his fists behind my back balled, the full weight of his body pressed against the knob of metal at my hip. For a brief moment the air crackled with the prospect of blood, and the bright tang of violence filled my mouth. I bowed my head and leaned into the inevitability.

Ben had always been bigger and faster than I was, always twice my strength, always able to freely pummel me had he so chosen. And even now, in his bloated and deteriorated state, between Ben and me there would be no such thing as a fair fight. And yet I had foreseen the possibility that it would come to this, and not only was I ready for it, but also I welcomed it. I had been battered by strangers in the past week, it would be cleansing to be battered by Ben. And I would get my licks in, too, don't be deceived. It would be ugly and bloody, and all of it would be well deserved on both our parts, but I wasn't wholly unprotected. That knob at my hip was Holmes's gun, safety now off, and if it turned badly enough against me I wouldn't hesitate to kill the son of a bitch who had set up Augie, who had set me up, too, and who now had put my daughter at risk. Even if he was one of the two best friends I had ever had in this world, I wouldn't hesitate.

And then, as I hugged him close so he couldn't get a crisp shot at my jaw, I felt the taut snap in the atmosphere go soft. And Ben's weight sagged into me. And my knees buckled, and I staggered back, still clutching at his huge body. For a moment I was certain that I would collapse backward, and Ben would fall atop me and crush me with his great bulk, and the whole bout of necessary violence would end in my being smothered without getting in even one good blow.

I grabbed tight and lunged to the right and spun Ben onto one of the stained and flabby beds. And he let me throw him down without a fight, like a huge sack of wet towels. And when I backed away he just lay there, as if stricken by something, his hands, palms facing out, covering his face.

"Do you deny it?" I said.

Silence.

"They knew I had a boat, Ben. How could they know that? I hadn't even told Augie about the boat. But I mentioned it once during one of our idle chats, let it slip out when you told me how much you liked going fishing. But I wasn't worried. In all the world the one person I truly could trust was you, right, Ben?"

Silence.

"Tell me I'm wrong, please. Tell me I'm full of shit."

Silence.

I took out the gun, chambered a round, put the muzzle in his eye. "Then tell me why the hell I shouldn't kill you now."

"You should," said Ben softly, without shying away from the cold steel.

"That's not what I asked. I know why the hell I should; tell me why I shouldn't."

"I can't," said Ben, the stutter suddenly gone now along with the lies. "I deserve a bullet for what I did."

"They have my daughter, you son of a bitch."

"Just do it, and you'll be doing me a favor."

"We loved each other."

"Before we took the money."

"For always."

"Not after," said Ben.

I stared at him for a moment, a heaving mass of flab and flesh quivering, not from fear of my anger, but from something else, something deeper and far more devastating.

I took the gun from his eye. It was one thing to pull a gun on Diffendale, one was another to pull it on Ben. Christ, what was I becoming?

I clicked on the safety, ejected the magazine, opened the chamber and let the bullet drop out. In my fevered imagination I had thought I could point the gun and solve everything, point it at Ben, at Derek, at the deranged Clevenger. The gun was my daughter's ticket to freedom, the gun would solve all my problems. But only now, as Ben lay in a heap on the bed, did I know that to be utter bullshit. The gun would solve nothing. It was their tool, not mine, it would only end up killing everything I loved. I tossed the automatic on the floor and watched as it skittered into the corner. If I could end up pointing it at Ben, there was no telling what tragedy I couldn't cause with that damn thing.

I sat down in the chair and put my head in my hands to gather myself. I never knew what that expression really meant before, but I did now. I was all over the place, my anger, my fear, my love, my hate, I was spread about that room like a deck of cards after 52 Pickup. Bit by bit I gathered myself until I was close to whole.

"Tell me why," I said, finally.

"What good will it do?" said Ben.

"Shut up and talk," I said.

And he did. And to God I almost wish he hadn't. Because friends are grand things to have and hold in our lives, but it is our enemies that stoke the fires of our grandest achievements. We need our betrayals to be hard core and deep rooted, to be based on long-seated resentments that have infiltrated the bone, we need our betrayals to be personal as blood to drive us to get even in the worst possible ways. But how could anything as banal as needing to pay the mortgage do the trick?

43. Second Chance

I N THE BEGINNING, BEN HAD BEEN EVEN MORE CAUTIOUS THAN I had been with the Grubbins money. A full scholarship put him through Lehigh without tapping his cash, and as an engineering graduate from a top engineering school he immediately found a job in Florida, as far from Pitchford as he could manage. And to keep prying eyes prying elsewhere, he kept his expenses well below his after-tax income. The Grubbins money was socked away in a safe-deposit box, to be used only in special circumstances. A trip to Vegas with Augie and me, an engagement band for his soon-to-be wife, the occasional outlandish gift for his kids, the occasional whore when his marriage turned stale.

"What really happened with Sylvia?" I asked. "You never went beyond the irreconcilable-differences stuff with us."

"The differences were pretty irreconcilable," said Ben.

"Was it the prostitutes?"

"That was only toward the end, when it was already dead. Sylvia said it was the silences that killed it."

"But that's just you, Ben. What did she expect?"

"She said she expected more than a brick wall."

It was the divorce that set the disaster in motion. Suddenly there was alimony and child support, along with his share of the mortgage payments on the house in which his wife and kids were still living, in addition to his own rent. Ben missed a few payments during the divorce proceedings, which crapped his credit score, but he was able to catch up and then keep things going by using some of the stolen money each month, not a lot, but enough for him to know that the status quo wasn't sustainable. Yet in the heat of the moment he couldn't worry about that; he was just trying to make ends meet. And then there was another marriage, and a new house for the new wife, bigger than he really could afford because she had one kid already and there was another on the way. But the real-estate broker was touting the investment value of holding both properties in a rising market, and the mortgage broker performed a small miracle.

"I bet he did," I said.

"He found us two interest-only loans, one for the old house and one for the new. The rate was slightly higher than we had been paying because of my credit score and the nature of the loan, but the payments were much lower. I fudged my income figures to qualify, and suddenly I was back in the black."

"How long until they converted?"

"Five years."

"Ouch," I said.

"But by then my credit score would have been scrubbed clean, the houses would both have gained enough that I could refinance again, and we could keep it all going with an even lower rate."

"Magic."

"And things were okay," said Ben. "I was making it work, we had the kid and then another. Everything settled down, until the second divorce."

"What happened the second time?" I said.

"She found me cheating."

"With who?"

"Sylvia."

"Jesus, Ben."

"Yeah."

"What happened to you? You were always so careful."

"I don't know, something changed in me. I just never could stop feeling alone, no matter how many wives, how many children. It made me do these crazy things."

I didn't have to ask when that feeling started.

It was with the second divorce that the serious troubles arose. Two houses and an apartment and child support and alimony. He pleaded poverty but neither the wives nor the judges believed him, and the money started draining out of the safe-deposit box as if a hole had been drilled into the galvanized steel. He started hitting up his friends for cash. He borrowed from me, he borrowed more from Augie. But he was pretty sure he would make it through okay. He was up for a promotion at work that could stabilize his finances. And with a bump up in the value of the houses, he soon would be able take out ever-larger loans at ever-lower rates to pay everyone what he owed and get back on his feet. That was his plan, and he had a wily mortgage broker available to make it a reality.

Until everything changed.

When the mortgages were about to convert, with a radically higher rate and a crushing payment of principal and interest amortized over twenty-five years, the mortgage broker wasn't wily enough to refinance two houses that were suddenly worth less than their loans. And Ben's company started downsizing, laying off employees and cutting the hours and pay of those who remained as its business fell flat. Ben was one of the lucky ones who kept his job, but his pay was reduced and the drain of the stolen cash became a sucking swirling wound until it was gone, all of it.

"All of it?" I said.

"I was like the worst loser at the craps table," said Ben, "throwing in that last handful of chips just because it was easier than picking up and walking away."

"All of it?"

"Gone," said Ben. "I guess I was hoping I'd die of a heart attack before it all came to a head. But even with all the weight I gained, no such luck. I thought maybe I should be a little more proactive about dying. And that's when I decided to take matters into my own hands."

A few years back he had spied a man at a shopping center, a man he didn't ever recall seeing before but the sight of whom evoked in Ben a strange, almost existential terror. The man looked like your average Florida businessman, gray haired, clean-shaven, with nice shoes and a long-sleeved shirt open at the collar. So why had the very sight of him struck such a nasty chord? Curious and terrorized all at once, and always on the lookout for danger, Ben followed the man from one store to the next, trying to figure it out. And then he recognized the tattoos.

Ben spun around in fear on the very spot. Derek Grubbins, in Ben's city. It was Ben's worst nightmare come true. He thought of slipping away unnoticed, he thought of running for the hills. But what would that achieve? Safer than running was to learn all he could about what Derek Grubbins was up to in Fort Lauderdale. So he kept following, through the shopping center and to Grubbins's car, a blue Corvette. Ben took down the license plate number.

"How come you didn't tell us you found Derek?" I said.

"What good would it have done?"

"Augie and I should have known."

"You would have panicked and Augie would have done something stupid and everything would have blown to hell. But I lived here. I couldn't have you two screwing it up for me."

"That's crap," I said. "You were saving him for yourself, weren't you, Ben? He was your ace in the hole."

"Maybe, but not like you think."

"You had betrayal up your damn sleeve for all these years."

"No," said Ben. "It wasn't betrayal I was thinking of. But over the years, as everything fell apart, I did come up with an idea of how to make money off the bastard. From what I knew of his story after Pitchford, he was in hiding for his life. There were plenty who would pay to find him. I figured he might pay more not to be found."

"You were going to blackmail Derek Grubbins?"

"I was at the end of my rope, J.J. I was so blinded by my circumstances, I didn't see any other way out."

"You're insane."

"I was, yes," said Ben. "Every night, lying alone in that crappy apartment, the debts pressed down on my chest until I couldn't breathe. And every morning, when I woke to another day of failure, I thought how much simpler it would be if I just killed myself. I figured if it went bad, Derek would just save me the trouble. I had found out he was the general partner of a real-estate development firm downtown. So I drank a few midafternoon Scotches for courage and I paid him a visit."

"My God."

"Yeah."

"How did he react?"

"Not like you'd expect," said Ben. "Not like you'd expect at all."

Derek Grubbins's office was large and rich, with a seating area like in a hotel lobby. Giant maps of a planned golf community hung on the paneled walls. It took Ben a while to get past the secretary, but when he did, Derek Grubbins greeted him with a warm smile and open arms, as if he were genuinely glad to see an old face from the old neighborhood. Derek was preternaturally calm, his rasp of a voice was soft, his weathered eyes warm.

"Of course I remember yous," said Derek, still neighborhood rough in his manner and accent. "Big Ben. The only kid on the street tough enough to stand up to my beast of a brother. And then you played football for Pitchford High, right?"

"That's right," said Ben, perplexed by Derek's utter friendliness.

"You was going to be a superstar, turn pro. How'd that turn out for you?"

"Not so good," said Ben.

They sat in the easy chairs by a wide window and spoke amiably, about their old life in Pitchford and their new lives in Fort Lauderdale. They talked about the two old friends Ben always used to hang out with, the kid in the Bernstein house and that Augie Iannucci with the skateboard. They even talked about Tony. It was weirdly pleasant, like chatting up an old friend, even though it was the first words that had ever actually passed between the two of them. When Ben finally tried to make his blackmail demand, with the hesitation and stammers of the natural-born noncriminal, Derek just laughed him off. "Who the hell still cares about an old broken-down biker like me?" said Derek. And then, most improbably, he started asking Ben about Ben. How was the family? How was the job? How were the finances?

"If there's anything I can do to help yous out," said Derek Grubbins, "you let me know. We Pitchford brats, we need to stick together."

And when Ben, eager to talk to anyone, started in on his money problems, Derek Grubbins gave him a smile and a wink and told Ben that he had some banking contacts that might be able to help. "Get me all the details," said Derek Grubbins, "and your financials. I'll see what I can do."

Four weeks later, after an astonishing appraisal on both houses and a strangely spiffed-up credit report, Ben was ready to close on two new mortgages with rock-bottom interest rates and terms that would lower his monthly payments dramatically while putting $10,000 cash money in his pocket. It was like a gift from on high, it was like a favor from a best friend.

To celebrate the approval of the loan, Derek invited Ben to his house for a preclosing drink. The house was in Harbor Beach, a huge spanking-new Moorish castle right on the Intracoastal. Lucille, Derek's live-in girlfriend, was tall and young and blonde, with a mouth that looked designed by a committee for sucking dick. The cigars were smuggled from Cuba, the Scotch was well aged. Derek Grubbins had hit the jackpot of life. After the pleasant pleasantries, Derek took Ben out back, past the pool, right to his deepwater dock where, floating like a sleeping shark, was his thirty-five-foot Bayliner dubbed the *Second Chance*.

"Yous up for a cruise?" said Derek.

"Sure," said Ben.

Down the Intracoastal, under the Seventeenth Street Causeway, out into the ocean, zooming by boats crawling with bikinis. There were a couple fishing rods, which they didn't use, and a cooler full of beer stashed inside a bench seat, which they certainly did. Feeling the lift of the engines, the heat from the sun, the unsteadiness of his stomach as the boat lurched in a wave, and an unfamiliar optimism about his future, Ben felt like he was floating in a haze. They talked more about the old days, the old friends. Ben told him that he used to have a boat before he ran out of money and that his friend J.J., a mortgage broker, still did. He told him that Augie now lived in Vegas. He told him that they still all stayed in touch. Derek smiled and piloted the boat deeper into the ocean and told Ben to have another beer. And another beer. And that's when Derek made his offer.

"You know, Ben," said Derek, "things is working out pretty swell for me down here. My business is growing like a cancer, and I'm always on the lookout for talent. I can use a man with the guts to take a risk in exchange for a big enough payoff." They were sitting now on the benches at the stern as the boat drifted sweetly far out in the ocean. "I'm working on a new development carved out of the Everglades west of Fort Lauderdale, called Everfair."

"Everfair?"

"That's the ticket. It was tricky and expensive getting the permits, but that's finally been taken care of. We've already begun building and I'm telling you, the place looks terrific. Right now I could use an engineer to help with some drainage issues, entertain the local inspectors at the local strip clubs, that sort of thing.

The pay is twice what you're making now, and you'll have shares in the corporation."

"Twice what I'm making?"

"It's a risky enterprise, now, it's no sure thing. If it was, who the hell would need you, right? We got issues still and the inspectors are making noises. But if we get enough sweaty tits in their faces, if we can keep this deal going like it's headed, we'll all be rich as kings when it's done. You interested?"

"Absolutely."

"Thought so."

"But I have to ask. Why me?"

"You want me to be honest here, right, Ben? We trust each other, right?"

"Sure," said Ben.

"It's not just your engineering smarts we're looking for. There's a boatload of federal money we can tap into if we have sufficient, you know, minority ownership. My partners are whiter than me. We need some color in the boardroom. That would be you. We'd be using you to check off a box. Any problem with that?"

"I've been waiting a long time for my forty acres and a mule," said Ben.

"About time your face got you more than a traffic stop, hey? But I want you in the deal for more than just the obvious reasons. I also want the Pitchford in you, Ben. You're a neighborhood kid, you know what it is to claw your way up the ladder, you know what it is to take unbelievable chances." Derek looked at his beer, downed the rest of the bottle, and then tossed it overboard so that it bobbed in the ocean. "Like you and your pals did that night in my basement, twenty-five years ago."

The alcohol in Ben's blood froze; the haze of the day suddenly sharpened into tacks buried in his eyeballs. His head swiveled. If there was another boat in sight he would have dived and swum to it; if there was so much as a buoy he would have been in the water. But there was nothing around but water and more water, a desert of water.

He tried to speak, but his stutter returned and his denials floundered like a dying fish in his mouth. "Wh-wh-wh—"

"Come on, Ben. You gave me your financials, remember? There's no way in hell you could have made the payments on those two mortgages with only legitimate money. Your salary didn't cover half. You had to have another source. And you're not skinny enough or ugly enough to be a meth dealer. That friend of Tony's, Diffenfuck or something, spread the word a long time ago it was you guys what took the cash. Two of my boys even paid your friend Moretti a visit to check it out. But they came up empty because you guys was too damn clever."

"It's n-n-not true," said Ben.

"Ben, I thought we trusted each other."

"We do, but it's not…it's not…we didn't…"

"Look at me," said Derek Grubbins. He pasted on a wide, comforting smile. "It was long ago, in another life. For both of us, another life. You obsess about the past, you end up lost there, I know. It took me a long time in prison to figure that out. But you see everything I have now, the house, the boat, the girl. What do you think of her?"

"She's something."

"And young, too. You don't get a prime piece like that by holding old grudges. I've moved on, Ben. We're sitting in the *Second Chance*, right? I look forward now, not back. That's been the secret to my success. And that's why I need to know."

"I don't—"

"Everfair. That's my future now. I need a crew of pirates to bring it in. Are you a pirate, Ben?"

"I don't know."

"Ben? Cut the shit and tell me truth. Are you a pirate?"

"It was a combination of everything," said Ben, in my room at the Sea Queen Motel in Fort Lauderdale. He was sitting up now, his eyes closed as he told me the story. "The alcohol, the rocking of the boat, Derek's smile, the relief I had felt when the loan was approved, the mouth of his girlfriend, the chance to be rich. I wanted to believe. And the closing on the loans that would save my life was still a week away; I had no choice but to believe."

"Ben," I said, shaking my head.

"And so I told him what he already knew. I told him that I was a pirate. And that, yes, I had taken the damn money."

"Christ, Ben. What did he do?"

"He smiled at me," said Ben, "and then he stood, lifted up the seat to grab us another beer. But instead of the bottle, he picked up the entire cooler and smashed it into my face."

The next thing Ben knew he was lying on the floor of the boat, blood pouring onto the deck from his busted cheek as Derek methodically kicked the shit out of him.

"Try to blackmail me again, you son of a bitch, why don't yous?" said Derek as the point of his shoe smacked Ben in the ribs. "I ought to cut your balls off and feed them to the barracuda."

Ben didn't cry out, didn't fight back, even though Ben could have given him a fight. He just lay there and let Derek Grubbins do his worst. He felt he deserved everything, for thinking he could get something out that bastard, for admitting what we had done, for losing all his money in the first place. He just lay there and took it all and bled, hoping that the life would bleed right out of him. He thought Derek would throw him out of the boat, he thought Derek would leave him floating bloody in the ocean for the sharks. Maybe he was hoping for it, too.

But when Derek was finished, he coolly picked up a beer that had fallen onto the deck, opened it with an explosion of foam, took a long satisfied drink, and stepped back up into the cockpit. While Ben lay in a puddle of his own blood, Derek steered the boat to shore. At some dock, not his own, he backed the Bayliner to a dead stop and told Ben to get the hell out of his boat, and without argument or complaint, Ben did just that. He climbed out on his hands and knees and rolled onto the splintering wood like a freshly rolled drunk.

And then Derek said, from the boat, "Don't be late for the closing."

"Closing?" said Ben.

"You better show the hell up," said Derek. "I've got my finder's fees to think about. But the cash you was taking away from the table, you're not taking it away no more. Understand?"

And that's the way it went down at the closing that saved Ben's financial hide.

"What about Everfair?" I said while trying to get to the bottom of the sordid tale in my Sea Queen room.

"It's a real deal," said Ben. "It's going up right now on the southwestern edge of the city. But he was never going to let me be a part of it. It was just a way to get me to spit out a confession."

"Why didn't you warn us? Why didn't you let Augie know?"

"I could barely admit to myself what I had done, how could I admit it to you? And at the closing, when Derek acted like we were best friends again, I thought maybe that the beating he had given me would be the end of it. Weeks passed and our weekly calls were unchanged. And I felt like we had all gone through a gate and there was no more fear on the other side. I would have told you both that we were free of it all, except then I would have had to tell you how I knew, and I couldn't. I couldn't. So I kept it to myself. And then Augie didn't call."

"Christ."

"And the next thing I heard was your message that Augie was dead and you were on the run. And I hoped you'd get away, J.J. I so wanted you to get away. Why didn't you run like you told us you always would?"

"Love," I said. "The oldest trap in the book."

"I'll do anything to get you out of this. Anything to get your daughter back."

"You bet you will," I said.

And then I looked at him, this huge bubble of a man, hollowed out by failure and loneliness, and the sight scared the hell out of me. He outweighed me by a good hundred pounds, was taller and wider and black as obsidian, but still it was like looking at a mirror. He was as bruised as I was, as fearful, as yearning for something he couldn't quite identify, as scarred by what we had done together.

"It's not just your fault, Ben," I said. "We all screwed up, the three of us. When I went to check on Augie, one of his neighbors told me he had been crying at night by his pool."

"Augie?"

"She told me he needed a friend, not someone who just flew in for a day here and there to make sure he was still alive and then flew out again. He needed you and me to be something we hadn't been in decades. I didn't see how sad that was until I heard your story. Because we all were struggling."

"You?"

"I've lost my job, I've ruined my marriage, my life is a mess. And I felt like I had no one to turn to. Just like you felt. Just like Augie felt. How was it possible to have no one to turn to when we had each other?"

"We all screwed up so badly."

"We thought there wouldn't be a price to pay," I said. "We thought we could get away unscathed. How wrong could we be?"

"What are we going to do, J.J.?"

"We're going to forgive each other for everything. We're going to be friends like we should have been all along."

"And then what?"

"Tell me what you learned about Derek. What name is he going under?"

"Doug. Douglas Grayle."

"Convenient. He didn't even have to change his mono-grammed towels. What does he do all day?"

"He works," said Ben. "Either at his office or visiting the Everfair development site. But he kicks off about two, goes home to bang Lucille or take out the boat. He's got himself a life."

"That's what I'm counting on. Will the girl remember you?"

"Maybe."

"Let's assume she will. I have to wait for some things to arrange themselves, but tomorrow, while Douglas Grayle is still at work, you're going to take me to the house."

"His house?"

"He sent his goons to Augie's, he sent them to mine. We're going to return the favor."

"You bringing the gun?"

"No gun."

"If we're going up against Derek, you ought to bring the gun."

"A guy once told me that if you pull a gun on a guy like Derek, he'll make sure you need to use it. And if you use a gun against a guy like Derek, you're not getting out alive."

"Who told you that?"

"Tony Grubbins."

"Get the hell out of here."

"He's changed."

"People don't change."

"We have, for the worse. Tony maybe has for the better. If anything happens to me, call him. I'll give you the number. He'll know exactly what to do, he saved my life once already."

"Tony? Jesus."

"So I'm not bringing Derek a bullet, I'm bringing him an opportunity. A chance for us to move once and for all beyond the crap."

"And if he doesn't take it?"

"Plan A is a way for me to get my daughter back without a fuss, for Derek to pocket a hundred thou in cash, and for all of us

335

to live out the rest of our days in serene harmony, with the past buried in the fields of time behind us. Plan A is all about peace, prosperity, and sanity."

"And plan B?"

"The opposite."

44. Derek

THE PLAN WAS TO ARRIVE AT DEREK GRUBBINS'S GARISH, Moorish-style house while he was still at work, bluff our way inside, make ourselves at home on the elaborate furnishings as we waited for the son of a bitch to show, maybe even hit a bit on the girl just for effect. The point was that when Derek finally returned to his mansion and saw us there with drinks in our hands and cigars in our teeth he'd know, viscerally, that we weren't the only ones with something to lose. We wanted him to have no doubt that his house, his boat, his real-estate development, his whole second-chance life here, were on the line. I had spent the night working on the terms, on the threats, on my delivery. After fifteen years of peddling mortgages, one thing I knew was how to make a sale. And once Derek had a truer sense of the risks he was facing, then maybe we could work out an arm's-length deal that would leave everyone alive.

At least that was the plan, until the front door opened.

The girl standing there was so young and fresh I was taken aback: bare feet, short-shorts, and sure, a mouth just like Ben had described, but still, not much older than my daughter. The sight of her made me think of Shelby, bound and gagged in the rear seat of some car, barreling south. So much for maybe hitting on the girl for effect. What I really wanted to do was give her a lecture and send her to her room.

I had called Caitlin that morning and the report was not promising. No word on my daughter. None. And the police were skeptical about the whole abduction story, assuming Shelby had simply run away to be with the boyfriend. She's at that age, they told Caitlin. In fact, they were more interested in me than in my missing daughter. Why was I wanted for questioning by Virginia authorities? Why had I left the scene of an accident? Why was our house being ransacked? Where had I run off to? The more Caitlin relayed the scene in Kitty Hawk, the more I knew that if my daughter was coming home, it was up to me to make it happen.

"We're looking for Doug," I said to the girl at the door. "Is he around?"

"What about?" she said with great disinterest.

"It's a business thing." I tried to look past her, into the house. "He told us he'd be here."

"Are you the ones?" she said.

"Oh, yes, we're the ones," I bluffed.

As the girl gave us a once-over, her blue eyes snagged a bit on Harry, standing ragged and uneasy to my left, before reaching Ben. "Hey, I know you. Ben, right?"

"Hello, Lucille."

"What happened to your face?"

"A boating accident," said Ben.

"The *Second Chance*?"

"Yeah."

"I hate that fucking boat."

"That's two of us," said Ben.

"Which one of you is Moretti?"

"Ah, so we *are* the ones," I said. So much for the element of surprise. "I'm Moretti. Is Doug at home?"

"Uh, why would you be here if he wasn't?" she said with the singsong logic of the young. "I'm only supposed to let Mr. Moretti inside."

"But these are my business associates. Doug told us all to meet him here. For a drink. You want a drink, Harry?"

"I'm a bit parched," said Harry.

"It's been," I checked my watch, "almost twenty-seven minutes since Harry had a drink. He could use a glass of something wet, so long as it isn't water."

"I'm like a diesel leaking oil," said Harry. "Got to top off the well ever few miles."

"It's either get him a drink or call him an ambulance," I said. "I'm sure Doug won't mind my friends coming, too."

She listened without listening, just like my daughter listens, her eyes glossed with disinterest. "It's only supposed to be you."

We could have rushed her, the three of us, forced our way in, and that tactic had the benefit of feeding the anger that was coursing through me. But this Lucille was so young it seemed wrong, somehow, not to abide her. Derek was inside, Derek was waiting for me, which was disconcerting but positive nonetheless, because if Derek had been waiting for me to show, he obviously wanted to talk.

"Okay," I said. "Ben and Harry, why don't you go back to the room and wait on me."

Ben shook his head before pulling me aside. "You don't want to meet him alone," he said.

"I don't have much choice."

"She can't stop us. We'll all go in together. I'll have your back."

"So we barge in and then what? We fight it out?"

"I don't know. Maybe."

"If he's waiting for me, then he wants to make a deal as much as I do. Remember, that's what this is about. Go on back to the room with Harry. I'll call you when we settle up and I'll tell you where to bring the money."

"It's a mistake," he said, and it probably was, but I had been angling for this meeting from the start and I wasn't going to back down now. This was the crucible on which everything would depend and, truth be told, I hadn't doubted that I would have to do this alone. Ever since that night in the Grubbins house, I had always had to do everything alone.

"Go on back," I said. "I'll be fine."

I stood there as Ben and Harry headed to the truck. Harry waved weakly as he climbed in.

"All right, Lucille, let's go see Dougie-boy."

The girl led me through the wide door into the grand foyer of a house so over the top it would give Patriots Landing a complex. A gold chandelier hung from the ceiling two stories up; a gold-flecked medallion lay embedded in the marble floor. I followed her as she floated across the medallion on her bare feet, through a huge living room that looked like it had been decorated by Saddam Hussein, and then down a short flight of stairs into an overdone man cave. A billiards table, a poker table, a flatscreen on the wall, a granite-covered bar with swivel chairs that looked beyond the pool, past the hulking powerboat, into a wide swath of water.

And sitting at the bar, his back to me, was a broad-shoul-dered man with a gray ponytail hunched over a drink. He didn't turn when we came into the room.

"That guy you were waiting for, he showed up," said Lucille, her voice as bored with Derek as it had been with us.

The man didn't move.

"I'm going to Miami for a few days," she said. "I'm taking the Explorer and staying with Lulu."

The man at the bar lifted his right arm and gave his hand a little twist, like a beauty queen waving good-bye.

"You're no fun when you drink, and you haven't been fun for ages," she said before walking out of the room. And still Derek Grubbins didn't turn.

I had assumed if he knew I was coming, which he surely did, he'd have some protection, a few lugs with dead eyes and arms like legs. But there was no protection here. If I had brought the gun I could have killed him right then and there and he wouldn't even have heard the shot until he was already dead. What that meant I couldn't figure, but he sure as hell wasn't scared of me, at least not yet.

"Nice kid, that Lucille," I said, unable to keep the anger out of my voice. "Not much older than my daughter."

"You was supposed to be here yesterday," said Derek, his back still turned. "I hope you don't mind I started drinking without yous."

"I want my daughter back."

"I bet you do."

"We're going to end this once and for all, you and me, here and now."

I expected him to turn around and spit, to berate the hell out of me for what I had done all those years ago. I braced for an onslaught. But when he did turn around he simply smiled at me, a strange sadness in his eyes. "Ending it once and for all," he said as he raised his glass, half-filled with a pale amber liquid. "Isn't that a pretty fucking dream?"

Derek Grubbins was smaller than I had expected, not that he was small, and older than I had expected, not that he was ancient. It's just that after all these years I had expected a monstrous figure right out of the nightmares of my childhood, a terrifying minotaur riding a Harley, not this ordinary older man in black slacks, a long-sleeved silk shirt that looked like a paisley had thrown up all over it, and a poseur's ponytail. His face, shorn of his beard, was the weathered face of anyone who worked outside for a living, a construction worker maybe, or a golf pro. His shoulders were wide, sure, but nothing that would make you blink twice in the free-weight section of the gym. And he had a white bandage wrapped around his left hand as if he had cut himself making cocktails.

"I brought out my priciest Scotch for the occasion." He gestured toward a squat bottle with a stag's head on the label. "You want?"

"No."

"It's a good single malt, not much younger than Lucille. You sure?"

"I didn't come to drink, I came to make a deal."

"A deal?" Derek seemed to ponder that for a moment. "No chatting about the old neighborhood? No telling each other how good we look after all these years?"

"You look like shit."

He stared at me for a bit, startled, it seemed, and then he burst out laughing. "Life's a bitch, or you just finding that out now? So what kind of deal we talking about, Moretti? How about you just give me back my money and we'll call the whole thing even?"

"It wasn't your money," I said, "it was your gang's money. And it was drug money, so even if it was your money it wasn't your money."

"It sure felt like my money," he said, not with anger, but more with a wistfulness at the follies of youth. He turned his head to scan the room and the outside. "Where's the third member of your little crew?"

"Third?"

"I already beat the shit out of Ben, and you're here playing Monty Hall, so where's the third? You know, that kid with the skateboard."

"Augie," I said.

"Yeah, Augie. I thought we'd wrap this all up neat in a bow with the three of you."

"It would have been hard for Augie to put in an appearance," I said, "considering that he's dead."

"Dead, huh?" said Derek. "That's too damn bad. Last I heard he was fat and happy in Vegas."

"He was until your man Clevenger went into his house uninvited, tied him onto the bed, and tortured him to death."

Derek tilted his head and stared at me for a long moment, like a dog staring at a penguin, before downing his single malt as quick as if it were a hot shot of cheap tequila.

"You didn't know?" I said. "Your debt collector didn't tell you?"

"What does it matter?" said Derek as he refilled his glass.

"Who the hell is Clevenger?"

"The absolute wrong guy to have on your ass, I'll tell you that. And you can't say Augie didn't get what he deserved, the snarky son of a bitch. But I'm sorry about this thing with your daughter. I wasn't happy when I heard about your daughter."

"Then call him up, tell him to let her go."

"It ain't that easy."

"It better be. You signed an agreement, didn't you, a witness protection agreement that got you out of jail and offered you protection so long as you told the truth and didn't commit a felony? What would happen if the US Marshals Service learned you sent someone to kill Augie and are now involved in a kidnapping?"

Derek looked at his glass. "It wouldn't be no good, that's for sure."

"And if the feds don't take care of it, then maybe your friends in the Devil Rams will. The Fat Dog died in the prison you sent him to, the Fat Dog's kid now leads the crew. What happens if a call is made to The Devil's Brew and an address is whispered?"

"Is that dump still there?"

"Still standing and still smelling like a craphouse. I know, I was just there, and let me tell you, for some reason your name sends the Devil Rams into conniptions of rage. They want to mount your head on their wall."

"Ah, the old gang. I almost miss the bastards."

"They won't miss if they find you. And in case you're getting ideas, if anything happens to me, the calls will still be made. Ben's been given the numbers and all the information."

"You got me in a bind, don't you?"

"Yes, I think I do."

"You're pretty good, I must say. You sound like you've been practicing that all night. You sure you don't want a drink? What

343

I found is that a drink here or there makes everything just a little easier to take. Which is why I've been drinking a lot lately."

"I don't want a drink," I said.

"Have one anyway." He reached over the bar with his good hand and pulled back a glass. "A drink to seal the deal."

"We have a deal?"

"We're getting there," he said with a wink.

My nerves eased as soon as I saw it, that wink. Things were moving so far outside my harsh expectations that I had a hard time processing it all. Derek wasn't the fierce motorhead I had expected, he seemed instead somehow defeated. Maybe he didn't have the stomach for the fight anymore. Or maybe just by finding him I had won the game and now all he wanted was to end the threat. Or maybe he had changed like his brother had changed. And maybe this vendetta against us had morphed out of his control and he intended now to rein it in and end it. God, I hoped that was it. But whatever it was, I had been in on enough negotiations to know when an agreement was going to happen, and right now, in this room, an agreement was going to happen. I thought of the moment I would hug my daughter; my eyes got a little misty and my throat tightened on me. And then I shut down the emotions and put myself back into my salesman mode: closing, always be closing. And if it took a drink or two to close, bring it on.

Derek poured two fingers of the Scotch into the glass and looked up at me. "A splash?"

"Sure."

He tilted a bottle of ginger ale over the glass, pouring in just enough to loosen the whiskey, and handed the glass to me with a smile. "Tell me that ain't nice."

I took a sip.

"That is nice," I said, and it was, truly, the liquor dark, with hints of vanilla and smoke, alongside the brightness of the sweet ginger. It gave me a sense of well-being, of developing possibilities;

it somehow eased all the tension in the world. A hell of a Scotch. I would have to make sure they stocked it in the taproom at the Patriots Landing Golf Club when I climbed back into my life.

"Dalmore," said Derek. "A hundred and something a bottle, and worth it."

"Yes it is."

The front door slammed and I jumped a bit, but Derek just raised an eyebrow. "Lucille, off to South Beach."

"She's young."

"Tell me about it. I can't keep up with her. She wants to dance all night and screw for hours; I just want to sleep." He burst out into laughter again, like everything about his life was a cosmic joke. "God, when did I get too old for someone that young?"

"What happened to your hand?"

"Fishing accident." He looked at his Scotch for a moment. "So, Moretti, are we talking any money, too? Money always makes a deal a little sweeter, don't you think?"

"Yes, it does," I said, taking another sip. "There's some, I suppose, if you insist on it."

"How much?"

"Not as much as you would expect after all these years."

"Okay, I see, there you are, lowering expectations so you can try to lowball my ass. And then I'm going to have to say it ain't enough. And you'll pretend to be shocked. And I'll pretend to get pissed. And you'll give another fucking speech and throw out another crap number. And so it will go until we're both bored to tears. Let's just get to the meat of it, okay? What's the final number?"

I stood there and made a show of considering for a bit, play-acting a decision not to playact. "A hundred."

"That's a nice number, yes it is. Round. Solid. Are we talking cash or a payment plan, because I don't got the stomach for no payment plan."

"Cash."

"Neat. And then, after you hand it over, we each go our separate ways forever and ever."

"That's the deal. Ben and I get off the hook, you stay safe in your happy home, and I get my daughter back."

"Pretty good. You built an attractive package. And what about this Augie thing? You and Ben okay with just letting it go?"

"No," I said. "But we'll swallow it to get my daughter out of harm's way and to end it once and for all."

"That's a reasonable position, I must say. More reasonable than I thought you'd be. I thought you'd come in and shoot me in the fucking head." He laughed, that insane overhearty laugh that made my teeth ache.

"I'm a businessman, not a killer," I said.

"Me, too. Funny how that is." He looked at me, gave a lopsided smile, reached out his hand. "Let's go talk to Clevenger."

"And you'll tell Clevenger what we agreed to?"

"'Course I will. That's what this was all about, right?"

"Okay," I said, and I took hold of his hand, took hold as if it was a lifeline of sorts, which it was. I took hold and I shook the thing like it mattered. "Okay, yes. We have a deal."

"Ben said you're a mortgage broker."

"I was."

"I bet you were good. You got the touch. Too bad that business went to shit, too. But a guy who can cut a deal like you won't ever have trouble making a living."

And he was right, I could feel it in my bones. I had just saved my daughter, saved my family, created for all of us the possibility of a future. If I could negotiate this, I could negotiate anything. I felt, just then, like a powerhouse. Suddenly I wasn't upset about my lost job, or my dire finances. Or even my wife kicking me out. I'd just negotiate her back. My life was ready for a refi and I was just the guy to pull it off. I couldn't contain my smile.

Derek looked for a bit at his glass. "And you can get the cash to me right away?"

"The hundred's already stacked."

"Confident, were you?"

"Making deals is what I do," I said, with a touch of false humility. "Ben will bring the money just as soon as my daughter is free."

"Good old Ben."

"So that's it?"

"That's it," he said. "We'll drive out to Clevenger, tell him what we agreed."

"Why not just call him?"

"A deal like this, it's best to deliver the terms in person. And I got something I want to discuss with you on the way. You might be wondering why I've been so agreeable."

"Yes, actually."

"It's because I got bigger fish to fry than small fry like you and Ben. I'll show you on the way out."

"And my daughter?"

"She'll be taken care of as soon as we see Clevenger. Is that good enough?"

"Do I have a choice?"

"Not really." He lifted the bottle with his good hand, gave me his warmest smile. "One for the road?"

45. Oceanfront, Nebraska

I NEED TO ASK YOUR OPINION," SAID MY NEW BEST FRIEND Derek Grubbins in his blue Corvette, much like the one he had parked on Henrietta Road all those years ago. We were speeding due west from his house, a straight shot beneath Interstate 75 and past the high walls of development after development, until the developments petered out into great swaths of lakes and swamp. "You might have ideas, seeing as you're in the business. Or you was in the business."

"Sure," I said, not really interested.

"You know, I got me this property I'm developing," said Derek.

"Ben told me," I said. "Everfair."

"An upscale golf community, first class all the way. My buyers are going to need mortgages, and I was wondering what was the best way to go about giving them so that most of the fees don't get sucked up by some fucking bank."

"Sell them yourself," I said.

"How?"

"Open your own brokerage, provide the mortgages, and then offload them. Since you'll in effect be paying yourself for the houses, it shouldn't even require too much of an investment on your part."

"Really? I mean, you can do that?"

"Sure, it's a snap. Everfair Financing."

"Something like that, it's kosher?"

"Not much isn't kosher in the mortgage-broker game."

"Son of a bitch, how do you like that?"

"I could set it up for you," I said, feeling suddenly magnanimous. And why shouldn't I be? After a quarter century of fear and caution, after a quarter century of running from what the three of us had done, it was finally over. I had gambled on the one possible way to get my daughter back and myself out of hock, I had reached beyond Clevenger into my past to find Derek Grubbins, and then I had negotiated everyone out of the deep crap. Just like I had planned. When the hell does that ever happen, really now? I had even picked the exact right number for the payoff, and have no doubt, there was always going to be a payoff—nothing seals a deal like cash.

So I leaned back with confidence as Derek rambled on about Everfair: the golf course, the clubhouse, the huge homes with high ceilings and infinity pools, built-in barbecues, three-car garages. And the more he talked, the better I felt, because the more he had to lose, the more solid was my deal. Maybe it was still the buzz from the Scotch or the getting out from under all that had been keeping me down for so long, but I felt my sense of security build as he kept up his patter.

"Here we go," said Derek, as we turned off onto a wide construction road that led toward the open gate of a great stone wall. "My baby."

"What are we doing here?"

"Clevenger's inside, waiting for us."

"Why here?"

"He wanted to be put up in style, and you know our motto: in Fort Lauderdale, if you want style, you want Everfair."

On the stone wall, the name of the development was formed in stylized letters of gold, surrounded by green enameled mangrove trees. It was a lovely entrance designed for a lovely development, a Patriots Landing of the Everglades. But that was just the entrance—what was beyond the entrance was something else entirely. In the whole of my life I had never seen anything more terrifying than what I spied behind those walls.

"That's the fourth fairway over there," said Derek Grubbins, pointing to a wide plot of mud and weeds just to the side of the road. "The lake we're going to build will stretch to the front of the green and will be stocked with fish to bring in the hawks and herons, ospreys. The PGA guy what's designing the course says it's going to be our signature hole."

The only bird I saw was a crow, pecking at a dead piece of gristle on the guttered road.

"These are the townhouse units," he said, pointing at a stretch of uneven ground not far from the entrance. "For those who ain't so flush. Upper-class amenities for the upper-middle class."

The ground he pointed to was pocked with uneven, half-finished cinder-block walls rising from poured foundations and looking like the teeth on a scurvy old sailor begging for rum.

"The clubhouse will go right up there," he said as he drove farther into the huge property, pointing at an artificial rise formed of rock, rusting twists of discarded metal, blocks of chewed-up cement. "It will overlook the lake. People in the know who have looked at the plans already say it will be one of the top four golf courses in Broward County."

One thing I had learned in the real-estate business is that people in the know always know nothing.

"And this here," he said, waving toward a completely undeveloped patch of marsh choked with weeds and scrub trees, "the part of the property that overlooks the lake and the holes leading back to the clubhouse, this is where the super-premium houses will be built."

"There's nothing there," I said.

"Not yet. These houses are going for two mil plus. You don't buy a super-premium suit off the rack, you get it tailor-made.

This is Rodeo Drive, baby. This is all custom. You pick the plans, you add your extras, we build to your exact specs."

I looked around. As far as I could see along the blighted fairways, the silent half-built ruins, the mud-spattered roads, there was no one. It was late in the day, sure, but still there was no one. "And your builder?"

"Ready to go."

"Why isn't he building now? The townhouses at least, or the other, less exclusive properties."

"He's waiting, we're all waiting."

"For what?"

"The third wave of financing."

I nodded like it was all in the bag, and I suppose in a way, just then, for him, it was. These days, waiting for that third wave of financing for a real-estate development was like waiting for that first wave of ocean in Nebraska.

But really, as soon as we drove through the gates I knew. Even before I saw the weedy fairways, or the unfinished townhouses, or the swamp with delusions of Rodeo Drive grandeur, I knew. You're in the business long enough, you can smell it. There was no profit here, this was real-estate desolation, as if a twister had ripped through the landscape, smashing every hope, the same tornado that had touched down in Augie's Las Vegas development, the same tornado that had decimated developments from California to Virginia and cost me my job. I don't know if it had ever been a feasible project, but now Everfair was as dead as the roadkill being pecked at by that crow. And so was my newfound confidence in getting my daughter back in one piece.

"This is all lovely," I lied, "but we need to talk to Clevenger. Where is he?"

"At the model home. And it's a beaut. Trust me, you'll love it. One look and you'll be ready to sign a contract yourself."

I looked at Derek Grubbins as he drove me ever farther into the maw of his failed dream, and I grew ever more scared. Was he delusional about Everfair, or a liar, or maybe a delusional liar? It didn't matter which; my deal was falling apart like a tissue-paper banner in a hurricane. See, even in Derek's overdone Lauderdale McMansion with its Bayliner hitched to the private dock, I had thought a hundred thousand dollars was enough money to ensure my daughter's safety. But a hundred thousand dollars would disappear into the swamp that was Everfair without even making a ripple. I had assumed he had much to lose, but the landscape itself told me that everything he had to lose he had lost already.

"It's right up there," he said.

And there it was, just in front of us now, a single house rising out of a sea of weeds and hard-caked mud, a cobbled mash-up of a manse right out of the Patriots Landing handbook, something between a Patrick Henry and a George Washington, with a splash of Floridian stucco and a huge garage door staring at us like a fearsome mask.

"Our model home is the centerpiece of the entire show," said Derek as he pulled the car into the driveway and pressed a button on the keychain that started the garage door to rising. "Granite countertops in the kitchen, granite sinks in the bathrooms. We even put it on the toilets, for Christ's sake. One thing I learned in this business, you can never have too much granite."

"And Clevenger's inside?"

"Sure, just like I said. In fact, while you were blatting with Lucille at the front door, I gave him a call, told him I'd be bringing you on by."

"And you're going to tell him about our deal?"

"Just like I said I would. But I don't think what we agreed on is going to hold much weight with the big guy. See, here's the thing, Moretti, and I feel sort of bad about it and all, but I didn't tell you the truth."

"The truth about what?"

"About anything."

I tried to stay calm, tried to stay reasonable: keep closing, keep closing, keep cool and keep closing. "You know, Derek, those calls are going to be made."

"That's going to be a problem for me, no doubt about it."

"And the cash, forget about the cash, man."

"It's hard to give that up," said Derek, with genuine rue in his voice. "You don't know how hard."

"So I don't get it," I said, just as I caught some movement out of the corner of my eye.

My head swiveled like it had been slapped. A man, short and stocky with black pants and shiny black shoes, a thug man, pulling a gun out of his belt as he walked out of the garage.

"I'll sweeten your deal," I said. "You want more money? Get me my daughter and I can get you more. Plenty more. Let's talk, let's negotiate."

"I would, really, but see, your debt, it don't belong to me no more."

"What the hell does that mean?" I said.

"Clevenger don't work for me like you thought," said Derek. "He works for an outfit in Chicago what was hired by the boys that gave me my second wave of financing."

"You went to a loan shark to keep this place afloat?"

"The project wasn't progressing the way I had hoped."

I spun around in the seat and spied another man, tall and lugubrious, coming up from behind, a gun already in his hand. I locked the door and quickly grabbed for the car keys, but Derek swatted away my hand.

"The problem is, these guys I borrowed from," said Derek, "they're not like a bank. A bank you can walk away from, they ain't going to break your legs, right? But these guys, they don't foreclose, they send Clevenger. And Clevenger, unfortunately, he don't just break your legs neither. But he does like to make an impression."

"What the hell did you do, Derek?"

"When he came after me, first he cut off a finger, snip-snap, just to get my attention. Then he sat me down to give him an accounting of everything I had that was anything at all. But I had nothing, see. My house is underwater, the car is leased, the boat is worth a ton until you try to sell it. Even the deeds to Everfair are as valuable as mud, what with the bank secured on every square inch. What the hell was I going to give him? Lucille? Not that he wasn't interested in that."

"Give me the damn keys," I said, grabbing at them again.

Derek swung his good hand hard and slammed me in the throat with the back of his fist. I fell upon the door, grappling at my neck, gasping for air. Still struggling to breathe, I looked out my window and both men were standing there. The tall one tapped on the window with the muzzle of his gun and smiled. His smile was more terrifying than the gun.

And then, from out of the front door of the model home stepped a man in suit pants and a short-sleeved shirt. He was short and round, the arc from his neck to his groin was dented by his belt, and he squinted his pale fat face at me in the car. He was smoking a cigarette and bouncing slightly on the balls of his tiny feet in their black patent-leather loafers, bouncing with the air of a man who had just won a game of Skee-Ball.

"And as Clevenger was about to cut off something more valuable than my finger," said Derek, "I thought of Ben. I wasn't going to do nothing to you guys myself, it was a long time ago, and what the hell was going to be left after all these years? I mean, Ben had nothing, I figured you guys had nothing neither. But I gambled that a potential million plus in stolen cash might get Clevenger's attention. So I did what I had to do."

"You son of a bitch."

"Hey, you know the way it goes. Things is tough, we're all just struggling to get by."

"He has my daughter."

"Yeah, I still think he was wrong about that, and I told him so, but truth is it ain't my call no more. You guys owed me, I owed Clevenger's people, so I made a trade. I got two months' forgiveness; he got you."

46. A Cold Wind

S O," said Clevenger, pausing to take a drag of his cigarette, in no apparent rush, "here we are."

Yes, there we were. The "we" were me and Clevenger and
his two collection agents, short-and-stocky standing behind me,
tall-and-morose-with-yellow-teeth standing like a silent zombie
behind Clevenger. The "here" was the basement of the model
home at Everfair. While the upper floor I had been dragged across
was impeccably finished, a living iteration of the granite-swathed
American dream with brown leather couches and hardwood
accent pieces, the basement was empty except for the table where
Clevenger sat, two metal chairs, a white canvas bag, a lamp, a
car battery. And no matter how beautiful the upstairs was, it
appeared someone had skimped on the foundation; the concrete
walls were already cracking, swamp water was already oozing.

"This little gallop of yours," continued Clevenger as he
leaned his elbows on the table, the smoke from his cigarette rising through the beam of light aimed at my face, "this run from
Vegas, back to Virginia, and then up and down the coast, must
have been quite the adventure. But for us, it was just business as
usual. Do you think you are special? Do you think everyone else
just volunteers to pay their debts?"

The question was undoubtedly rhetorical, as I was in no condition to provide an answer, bound to one of the sturdy metal

chairs in the middle of the floor, with a rope wrapped around my bare chest, my arms and wrists tied behind me, my legs tied to the chair legs, and a rag of cloth stuck in my mouth, held there by strips of silver duct tape. I was ready to give up, I was ready to trade everything, even myself, for my daughter, but, trussed like a turkey as I was, Clevenger wasn't giving me the chance.

"No one wants to pay, but it all works out the same in the end. Because this is what we do: we find you and collect your debts. We file liens when we can, we garnish wages when we must, we play the telephone like a Stradivarius. We have whole warehouses filled with people making calls. And we are hired by the most reputable firms. You would be shocked at the names. If you don't make your car payment, we place a call. If you don't pay your MasterCard bill, we place a call. And the mortgages, we had to rent a whole other warehouse just to handle the mortgages. This is all quite legitimate, state inspected, state approved. As we like to say, we put the *done* in *dunning*."

In addition to my being bound and gagged, short-and-stocky bashed me in the head whenever I groaned or struggled too hard in my chair, which was hard to avoid, gagging as I was from the gag in my mouth. But the first time I had really squirmed, rattling the legs of the chair back and forth, the goon had bashed me one but good, knocking me straight to the floor, banging my shoulder into the cement. Since then I had refrained from making a show of it.

"I got my start making calls," said Clevenger. "This was a long time ago, during the Reagan recession in the early eighties. It seemed such a major event, yet it is but a drizzle compared to the monsoon that has overtaken us. Once I received a file, first I'd call the debtor, then I'd call his employer, then I'd call his mother, then I'd call his mistress, then I'd call his wife. And not just once, or once a week, or once a day. Every hour. Oh, if I got your file, suddenly I was in your life. Some people have an aptitude for science, or music, or art. I have an aptitude for this. In person I am not much to look at, I know, but on the phone I can curdle your blood, can't I? And the message is always the same: time to pay up."

I remembered what Derek had told me about Clevenger liking to make an impression before asking the hard questions. Which made the car battery, sitting on the floor in front of me, with starter cables snaking around it, quite the unwelcome sight. Especially the way my bare feet were bound together in a bucket of water.

"And even after I was promoted out of the warehouse to a hard-case unit, and then promoted even higher to the special-case unit, strictly off the books and with a very special clientele, the message I was sent to deliver, in ever more dramatic ways, remained the same. Time to pay up."

Clevenger took another deep draw from his cigarette, then he waved the glowing ember toward the battery. Tall-and-morose stepped around the table and started hooking up the cables. Red to positive, black to negative, just as if readying to start a dead car. Then he turned to face me, his yellow teeth bared, a clamp in each hand, faced me as if I were a stalled Buick. Short-and-stocky pressed down on my shoulders to keep me in place as the clamps came closer. The hands clasped on my shoulders were now sheathed with yellow rubber gloves.

"We've been headed for this, you and I, ever since that first phone conversation in Las Vegas," said Clevenger calmly. "It was only a matter of time before we'd be together. And I have no doubt that you will give me everything I need. But first, I have found, it helps the process move more smoothly if you know exactly what time it is."

Tall-and-morose stood over me, opening and closing the red clamp in his left hand, an alligator snapping its jaws. I struggled like a maniac against the rubberized grip on my shoulders.

"Oh, look," said Clevenger, glancing at his watch as the goon jabbed at my chest, the clamp snapped shut on my right breast, and I roared through my gag. "It's time to pay up."

When I startled awake with a sharp crease of pain in my face and a ringing in my ear, I was no longer gagged, though still bound. The bucket was lying on its side on the floor, water pooling about it on the cement. On my chest, just below the right nipple, was now a gaping sawtoothed wound leaking blood, much like one of the strange wounds I had seen on Augie's chest. My nerves still were jangled, my bones still ached, my heart still raced, my ears still rang, the dryly electric taste of metal still cloaked my tongue.

"I enjoyed that entirely too much," said Clevenger, wiping his forehead with a handkerchief as his post-torture cigarette dangled from his thick lips. Tall-and-morose was no longer standing behind him.

As I stared at Clevenger, the throbbing of my chest subsided. Is there a more brilliant analgesic than hate? "Did you enjoy it as much when you did it to Augie?" I said through clenched teeth.

"Yes, actually. I am one of those rare breeds, a man in love with his work. But don't be modest, I'm sure it was just as stimulating for you."

When the second clamp had been pressed against my side I could feel the charge move through me, as if in slow motion, muscle by muscle, not the jagged ripple of alternating current, but something hot and hard slipping directly beneath my skin, shards of lava boiling my blood, freezing my muscles, sending my heart into a furious lurch. Alarm bells rang that only I heard. Every breath burned my lungs and hammered my head. My toes clenched tight from the charge as my burning feet kicked at the bucket. I tried to scream even as my jaw slammed down so hard I would have bitten off my tongue if the cloth wasn't there. It lasted for ten seconds, it lasted for an hour, it was an instant, it was a lifetime. I could smell the sweet singe, and my eyes bulged with blood, and I was certain, the whole time, that I was going to burst into flames.

And all the while Clevenger smoked and watched as impassively as if he were watching paint dry on a wall.

That's all I remembered before short-and-stocky slapped me awake. I had no idea how long I had been out; all I knew was that the breaths I now gulped in were so cool and clear it was like I was breathing in air from the Arctic.

"In fact," continued Clevenger, "I'm almost hoping you'll force me to do it again. That's the way it was with your friend Augie. He gave up his sham hiding spot under the chair after the first shock, as if he was the first to think of such a thing, but then he clammed up. Not a word about what else he had. Not a word about you. He dared me to throw more his way."

"And so you took him up on the dare."

"He had a taste for punishment that his body couldn't handle. If you think you're tougher than you really are, like your friend Augie, sometimes the wrong person shows up on your doorstep. You can blame me for it, that's easy enough, but as far I'm concerned, his fate was his choice entirely. I merely stood by while he died. And then I waited for you."

Suddenly a minuet began to play, something soft and lovely, so lovely I thought it had to be a trick of my mind, as if the pain and the terror were sending me to some angelic place. But Clevenger heard it, too, lifted a finger telling me to wait, as if I had a choice, and pulled a BlackBerry out of his pocket.

"Clevenger...Okay, that's fine...Take your time, the rush is over. How is she?"

Clevenger lifted his eyes to stare at me as I struggled against the bindings. I shouted out, "Shelby. Shelby, it's Dad." Clevenger nodded and something slammed my head from behind and I almost blacked out again. Clevenger continued talking calmly into the phone.

"Good, let her sleep. I'm taking care of things here...Don't bother, just let me know when you get in...Right." Clevenger pressed END on his phone, laid it on the table, took a drag from his cigarette. "Your daughter is fine. She's taking a little nap. It won't be long before she joins us here."

I stared at the BlackBerry for a moment, hungry for it. "Let me talk to her."

"Not until after."

"After what?"

"Our accounting."

"Why don't you just let her go?" I said. "Just tell your man to let her off at the next rest stop. You've got me, you don't need her anymore."

"But you see, Frenchy, I don't want you."

"Then what do you want?"

"Your money."

"You can have it. I would have given it over even without your sadistic little demonstration. All the cash I have."

"The wan hundred thou you promised Derek?"

"I can get more."

"Okay, then, let's add the extra you took from your friend Augie's house. From the bag, beneath the kitchen floor. You didn't replace the grout quite perfectly enough to keep the spot hidden from us. I put the amount in the bag at another hundred thousand."

"There wasn't that much," I said.

Clevenger laughed. "Your lies, your meager attempts at obfuscation, it's all textbook. You promised Derek a hundred thousand cash. Everyone lies about cash. I've been in this game long enough to have developed a formula. Based on your age, your fear, your level of arrogance, your stupidity and greed, I figure you have more than twice as much at least. We're talking two twenty, minimum. Where is it now? You were ready to pay off Derek tonight, so it's in the city. With your friends, I suppose. Just tell us where they are."

"And no one gets hurt?"

"That's the idea."

"And I can trust you?"

"You don't have a choice. I have your daughter. Who are you going to trust if not me?"

"And then it's over."

He laughed, his fat face creased like a pillow with a gaping maw, and he laughed. "No, Frenchy, it's just beginning. Right now we're talking about cash. Next we start talking your fixed assets, the art, the car, the IRA and pensions. Your children intend to go to college, right? Then we'll talk about your college funds. And the house, especially the house."

"There's no equity in the house. And no one will buy our furniture after what your goons did to it."

"There are ways to extract the money. In fact, it's being taken care of as we speak."

"What the hell does that mean? And what about the deal you offered?"

"That was when you were still on the loose. Now that we have our hands on you and your daughter, the price is steeper."

"Fine. Whatever. You can have it all."

"Of course I can. And I will." He reached into the canvas bag, pulled out a yellow tablet and a pencil. "In these cases we always start with an accounting." He took a pair of reading glasses from his shirt pocket, put them on, jotted something on the pad, and then peered out at me over the rims. "Let's start with the cash. How much is there, exactly, and where is it hidden?"

"I'll tell you everything as soon as my daughter's free."

"You don't set the rules anymore, my friend. The battery was just an appetizer, a taste of where this can go. There is nothing I would like better than to give you the main course."

I didn't want to see what he meant by that. God, I really wanted to say yes, yes, please, anything, yes. But I also knew exactly where I was, smack in the middle of another stinking negotiation. I had botched my negotiation with Derek through gross overconfidence; this one, I could not afford to lose. All I had left to trade was my cooperation, and so that was the one thing I needed to withhold until my daughter was free.

"Look, you win, Clevenger. Congratulations. Your dick's bigger than mine. You want my money, take it. You want a complete accounting of my assets, I'll give it. You want my signature, I'll sign anything you put in front of me. It's that simple. Just let her go, let her call me and tell me she's free and she's safe, and you can get everything you want."

"I can get it anyway."

"Not without my say-so."

"Oh, you'll give me what I need, all right."

"Or I'll spit in your face."

"From that distance?"

I tried, I hawked up a gob and tried to shoot it out, but with my body bound it barely made it past my legs. He stared at me for a moment, at the ground where my spit had landed with a mealy splat, and back at me. Then he looked at short-and-squat and nodded.

I was slugged on the back of my head so hard I toppled like a domino. When the chair crashed to the floor, my shoulder and head hit the concrete at the same instant and my entire side was blinded by a white-hot pain. When my shout had subsided and I could see again, I was staring at Clevenger's tiny black shoes, as innocent as a pair of Mary Janes, and the white canvas bag beside them.

"You are so precious in your defiance," said Clevenger, as calm as ever. "You tried to get away with something, you've fallen in over your head, and suddenly you're the victim."

"You killed my friend, you kidnapped my daughter, you stuck a fucking electrode on my tit."

"All justified, my friend. You took money that wasn't yours, you used it to live a richer life than you otherwise would be able to, and when it was time to pay up you refused. You're no different than any other deadbeat whose file I've been given. Think of me as the cold wind that blows through your life, putting everything back into balance. You were living beyond your means, and now you're going to live below them until you catch up—it's that simple. And you should be grateful, you should build shrines. I'm showing you the truth of things, boy. In this life you never get away with anything. You were robbing your future to pay for your present and I'm just enforcing the arrangement. So don't go spitting at me. Spit at the kid who made the deal in the first place."

I closed my eyes for a moment and who I saw just then was J.J. Moretti, aged seventeen, staring ogle-eyed at the riches revealed in the beam of his flashlight. In the darkness of my vision I heard a voice, sharp and arrogant. "Pick him up." The chair, with me tied to it, was leveraged off the ground and jarred to standing. I opened my eyes into the present, slipping through a quarter century as one slips on a banana peel.

"Let's try to do this again without the grade-school histrionics," said Clevenger, before calmly lighting another cigarette. He reached down for the canvas bag and raised it to the table. "And take my advice, think before you speak, because keeping all your fingers might depend on it. Are you ready to give me an accounting?"

I struggled again against my ropes, but there wasn't enough give to get free. There had to be something I could do. There had always been something I could do. I could stall for time, I could find an opening, I could free myself, leap from my chair, fight my way out of the basement, past the collection agents with their guns, into the mangrove swamp, suddenly free to save my daughter. But instead of the notion of my valiant escape filling me with the adrenalized energy necessary to make at least an attempt, I felt only exhaustion. It might have been the futility of it all. Or the shock from my bout of electrifying torture. Or it might have been that Clevenger, in his own vile way, was right about so much. But I think it actually was something else.

"Are we ready?" said Clevenger.

"No," I said, my voice no longer spitting mad, but instead monotone and dead.

"Is this going to be like your friend Augie?"

"It will be what it will be," I said. "But I don't trust you. I have one thing left to bargain with and you can't have it until my daughter is free."

"Well, then," he said, "we'll have to take a different tack."

He rummaged a bit in the canvas bag before pulling out a large bolt cutter. The sight of the cutter, with its long wooden handles and hooked blades, a tool perfectly designed to snap metal and bone alike, filled me with an electric terror as powerful as the charge that had ripped through my body only moments before. But what was I going to do about it?

Nothing.

From the moment that seventeen-year-old kid had aimed his flashlight into that crawl space beneath the Grubbins kitchen, I had been playing the role of a secret agent. I stole the money, that's the right word, stole it like any common thief, and after that bold act I lied to my friends, lied to my family, hid out in plain sight, planned my escapes, kept track of the threats, switched identities like T-shirts, ran this way, ran that way, sought guns and rammed cars and made wild threats on the phone. And propelling everything was the secret: it was my motivation, my energy, my superpower. But whatever it was, this thing I had carried through more than half my life, it was no longer what it had been. Everyone who mattered now knew the truth. I was stripped of my powers, Samson with a buzz cut, Dillinger without his wooden gun.

"Go ahead and do it," I said. "You're right, I deserve it, I deserve everything."

"You bet you do, buddy boy."

And I did. For all I had done, for all I had failed to do. In my resignation I was opening my heart to the malignant indifference of Clevenger. And just then, as if it were an accompaniment to my sudden acceptance of my inevitable fate, that minuet began again to play. Clevenger put down the cutter and took up the BlackBerry.

"What?…Anyone else?…Keep them there. We'll be right up."

He looked at me like I was underwater before putting the phone into the front pocket of his pants. Then he raised the cutter to his man behind me.

"Take this," he said to the man, "and cut him loose. We have visitors."

47. Rumble, Rumble

WHEN SHORT-AND-STOCKY DRAGGED ME UPSTAIRS, MY feet still were bare and my hands had been retied in front of me, but I felt less exposed with my shirt on, even though blood was seeping through into the material over the right breast. Clevenger was talking with Derek Grubbins at the windows surrounding the front door. Tall-and-morose was standing behind them, gun drawn.

"They didn't ring the bell?" said Clevenger.

"They're just standing by the fucking truck," said Derek, with a drunken slur. He had a bottle in his hand, even though he was already thoroughly self-medicated, and he staggered a bit as he stood in place by the window. "Waiting. Like they know something we don't."

"Well, we know something they don't know," said Clevenger. "We're going to kill them. You see anyone else?"

"It's just the two of them," said Derek. "The black guy is Ben, the other member of J.J.'s crew. The old guy, I ain't got a clue."

"Anyone check the back of the house?"

"I did," said tall-and-morose. "Nothing."

"All righty, then," said Clevenger. "Go see what they want."

"Me?" said Derek."

"You."

"They want him," said Derek, nodding at me.

"Then bring him along." The fat man grabbed my arm.

"He'll run."

"No he won't. We've got his daughter. He's tied to us. Go ahead, Frenchy." Clevenger grabbed my head so that he could put his lips close and said in a tight whisper, "Don't ever forget, for the rest of your stinking life, I own you."

I was still digesting this, feeling the certainty that every syllable he had jabbed like a knife into my ear was the utter truth, when Derek put down the bottle, took hold of my arm, and yanked me outside the model house. It was late afternoon, the sun was low and directly across from us. I tried to shield my eyes from the sun, but still all I saw were silhouettes, silhouettes I recognized: Harry leaning forward in a fighter's crouch, like he was back in the ring. Ben standing straight, holding my father's metal toolbox in his hand.

The emotions coursing through me as I spied them there were as strong as anything I had ever felt before—fear, of course, but along with the fear were love, gratitude, hope. And I felt a charge of energy, too, enough to banish the overwhelming weariness that had settled into my bones. I've had three great friends in my life and two of them had come to save me. Imagine that.

"Ben, you fat hunk of crap," called out Derek, "what the hell are you doing here?"

"We came for J.J."

"Hello, boys," I said.

"I told you not to trust him," said Ben.

"Yes you did," I said. "After all these years I forgot to listen."

"You look like you been rode hard, Johnny," said Harry. "What happened to you, son?"

"I was overcharged," I said.

"You couldn't help yourself, hey, Derek?" said Ben. "Had to get your licks in?"

"It wasn't me," said Derek. "Clevenger's calling the shots now, and he's a beast. He's in the house with his men and his guns, so don't do anything stupid."

"Too late for that," said Harry.

"What do you got in the toolbox?"

"Money," said Ben.

"How much?"

"How much did he offer you?"

"A hundred thou."

"That's exactly what we got," said Harry. "Just like Johnny told us you would agree to."

"Where's the rest?" called out Clevenger from the house.

"Who's that?" said Ben.

"Clevenger."

"You're the one who killed Augie," shouted Ben to the house.

"We would have come for you first, boy," said Clevenger, "but the only thing you got of worth are your kidneys, and they're not in A-one shape anymore. So we went after your friend instead. How does that make you feel?"

"Cold," said Ben.

"Your hundred isn't enough," shouted Clevenger. "There's at least another hundred in cash somewhere. Leave us what you got, get me the rest, and then we'll talk about letting your friend go."

"We're not leaving here without Johnny," said Harry. "No, sir. That's just the way of it. And he's not leaving without his daughter, so there we are."

"Just do what he says," I said. "It's over, I've given up. Leave the money and get the hell out of here."

"Not without you."

"Ain't you nursemaids a little overmatched?" said Derek.

"Mebbe so," said Harry. "But there's a fight here to be had and I never sidesteps a fight. And when I'm in a fight..." He reached into his belt and pulled out a gun, Holmes's gun. "I'm in it to win."

As soon as he saw the gun, Derek yanked me in front of him and grabbed me around my neck with a sweaty forearm. I could smell the stink of the liquor floating on his breath and oozing out his pores.

"Calm down, old man," said Derek. "Put that little pistol away before someone gets hurt."

"Someone getting hurt is the point of it," said Harry.

"They have more firepower and fewer scruples," I said.

"Shut up, J.J.," said Ben.

"They're going to kill you."

"They're going to try," said Harry.

Suddenly Derek tightened his grip on my neck and yanked me back. "What's that?" he said.

I listened and didn't hear anything other than the ringing in my ears. Until I did. A soft rent in the drumming silence, a rumble from far off, an ever-louder growl rising from the swamp surrounding us. I looked up for a helicopter, saw nothing but the deep blue of the darkening sky, as the rumble grew sharper, deeper, more insistent. When my eyes snapped down I saw the lone motorcyclist leaning into the curve that led to the model home.

And then a second.

And then a fourth.

"What?" said Derek. "Wait. What did you do, Ben?"

"What did you think we were going to do if you acted like a fool?" said Ben.

"I saved your financial ass," said Derek.

"You beat the crap out of me, set Clevenger on my friend Augie, and took J.J.'s daughter."

"What's that noise?" called out Clevenger from the house.

"It's them," said Derek.

"Who?"

"Them," said Derek, and immediately, using me as a shield, he began dragging me back to the house.

"What the hell did you do, boy?" yelled Clevenger.

"We didn't trust Derek," said Ben, "and we sure as hell didn't trust you. So we called in backup."

"You know what you just did," called out Clevenger as Derek kept dragging me back to the house. "You just killed yourself a second friend."

I tried to break away. Out of that house was now the safest place to be. I struggled to loose my bonds and run toward Harry and Ben, but my hands still were tied and Derek's grip was iron as it dragged me back, dragged me back. My bare feet couldn't get purchase as he dragged me back, even as the rumble grew louder, grew deafening, even as by twos and threes and tens the roads of Everfair filled with Devil Rams.

48. Jacob and Esau

T HE DEVIL RAMS ALIGHTED ONTO THE STREET IN FRONT OF the model house like a murder of crows on an electric cable. Almost forty in all, they lined their bikes along the curb and stood in pecks of trouble, knives bared, chains wrapped around fists, shotguns unsheathed from saddlebags, waiting for something, anything, to happen.

What have you come to kill, Billie Flynn?

Whaddya got?

Inside, Derek took a double swig from his bottle while Clevenger and the two collection agents kept uneasy tabs on what was going on outside the broad picture windows. I had been thrown harshly on the leather couch and told to keep quiet while they figured out their next move. There was fear in that house, and a sweaty panic, and the sulfur scent of some inevitable betrayal, though no one yet knew which way it would turn. But in the midst of my violent captivity, I alone felt a decided calm as the motorcycle gang congregated outside the door. I was the one who had brought the Devil Rams to Fort Lauderdale, after all. This was my plan B, my nuclear option. Now all I had to do was figure out how to turn the fear and the sweat and the betrayal in that room toward my daughter's favor.

"How many bullets you got?" said Derek.

"Not enough," said Clevenger.

"Bad planning. Maybe we can scare them off."

"They don't look like the scare-off type, do they? Gaines, check and see if there's anyone out back."

Short-and-stocky shot out of the front room, through the dining room, and headed for the kitchen and great room at the back of the model house. "They're all over the place," he said when he returned. "Bikers leaning against the rear development wall, bikers on either side of the house. There's an army out there."

"I've seen less animals in a zoo," said tall-and-morose, standing at the front window, swishing the curtain with the muzzle of his automatic.

"What are we waiting for?" said Derek. "They're not here to look at the tract map, they're here for blood. Hell, give me a gun. If we don't start the shooting soon, they will."

"They're going to feed us to the crocs," said tall-and-morose.

"Quit your bellyaching," said Clevenger.

"It's a tight spot, boss," said short-and-squat. "You got to admit."

"I've been in tighter," said Clevenger calmly, before taking a slow drag from his cigarette. "So let's figure some things out before we go off half-cocked. In these kinds of situations, there are only two questions: What do they want, and how do we get it to them?"

"You want I should ask them?" said tall-and-morose.

"Don't need to," said Clevenger. "The answer to the first part is sitting right there on that couch."

"Him?" said tall-and-morose.

"Me?" I said.

"The money you stole all that time ago belonged to that gang out there. They want you and they want the money."

"And they want Derek," I said.

"Shut him up, please," said Derek.

"Your head should satisfy them, Frenchy," said Clevenger. "And we'll throw in your cash if we need to. Gaines, watch the rear."

Short-and-stocky headed back into the kitchen.

"Now, fire a shot," said Clevenger.

"Boss?" said the tall collection agent.

"Aim for the fat one," said Derek. "He seems to be in charge."

"It's a she," I said.

"That's just a tragedy," said Clevenger.

"It's Flynn's daughter," I said.

"Christ, she's as ugly as her father," said Derek. "Put it between her eyes."

"Over her head," said Clevenger, "but close enough to put a scare into her. She's having fun playing her little biker games. Let's let her know we're serious as a bullet in the head."

Tall-and-morose smashed a window with the butt of his gun and fired into the sky.

From the street, a harsh call fired back, like the mating cry of the Bornean orangutan. "You missed me," shouted Billie Flynn.

"It wasn't easy, the size of you," shouted back Clevenger. "And we won't miss again. Let's talk before this gets out of hand."

"That's not how we work," said Billie. "First we let it get out of hand, and then we talk. Is that fucking traitor Derek Grubbins in there?"

"Maybe."

"Tell him he murdered my daddy and it's time to pay the price."

"So it's Derek you're after," said Clevenger.

"We didn't come down for the mosquitoes."

"Give us a minute," said Clevenger, before turning from the window and looking at Derek. Derek backed away until he backed into tall-and-morose's gun.

"What did you do to them?" said Clevenger.

"Nothing."

"Don't lie to me, boy."

"I might have testified against some of them back in the day," said Derek. "But I only told the truth."

"Only the truth," said Clevenger with a sneer. "What do you think, Henry?"

"I'd trade my mother to get out of here," said tall-and-morose.

"I'd trade your mother, too," said Clevenger. He rubbed the back of his neck for a moment, gave a little shrug. "I guess we're going to have to give up Derek here along with Frenchy."

"You can't," said Derek. "They'll tear me apart."

"And that's my problem how?"

"Because, what? But…" Derek sputtered. "But then I won't be able to pay the rest of what I owe."

"You weren't going to pay anyway."

"I'm working on some things that—"

"You've got nothing," said Clevenger. "Other than the boat, you're worth less than a pile of manure. You're only still alive because of what you told me about Frenchy here and the stolen cash. That was a bargain I could keep off the books, keep for myself. But I don't see a reason to delay the inevitable regarding you any further."

"We had a deal," said Derek.

"And now I'm breaking it," said Clevenger, flicking his glowing cigarette right at Derek's face.

"You lay down with dogs, dude," I said to Derek.

"Shut up, pal," said Clevenger. "No matter what we do, you're already dead. Which is fine, because we don't need you anymore. With your daughter in hand, we can still get what we're owed from your wife."

"You were never going to give her up," I said, not a question but a statement of fact.

"You shouldn't have taken his daughter," said Derek.

Clevenger made a gesture with his hand and tall-and-morose pistol-whipped Derek so hard Derek fell to his knees and then collapsed to the floor, blood welling into his hair before leaking onto the Brazilian-cherry floor. Clevenger watched all this with satisfaction and then turned back to the window.

"You want to kill Grubbins or should we?" called out Clevenger.

"You're offering him up?" said Billie Flynn. "Just like that?"

"Sure we are," said Clevenger. "And we have something else to sweeten the package. J.J. Moretti. You want him, too?"

"Who the hell is Moretti?"

"The cluck who took your money all those years ago."

"What color are his pants?"

Clevenger gave me a quick once-over. "Tan."

"Christ, he deserves what he's getting just for them pants. What do you want in return for all your goodies?"

"All we want is a route out. And one other thing."

"Go ahead."

"The two guys who called you in? The big black guy and the old man? We want them dead and the toolbox they're carrying."

"You're negotiating for a toolbox?"

"They're good tools. Craftsman."

"Those two called us in. You want us to betray them for their tools?"

"Now you've got it."

"I like the way you think," shouted Billie. "Deal."

"Grand," said Clevenger.

"With one more condition."

"Go ahead."

"Is there a Clevenger in there?"

Pause. "Maybe. What about him?"

"We want him, too. The only way any of you get out of that house alive is with Clevenger's head on a pike and his prick stuffed in his mouth. How do you like them fucking apples?"

Clevenger stepped away from the window, turned to tall-and-morose. "Shoot the bitch," he said.

But before tall-and-morose could get back to the window, a howl arose from the rear of the house, followed by the sound

376

of something cracking, something like a thick tree branch or a bone. And then another howl.

Clevenger wheeled and fired three times through the dining room, into the swinging door to the kitchen. Something fell with a thud.

"Finish him off," said Clevenger.

With his gun leading, tall-and-morose made his way to the back of the house. Derek, still on the floor and only barely conscious, slowly turned his bloodied head toward the kitchen door, uncertain what was happening.

"They won't get him," I said softly to Derek.

"What?"

"They're not good enough."

Clevenger, while still staring at the back of the house, said, "Shut up, both of you," before taking a step into the dining room.

"Who's back there?" whispered Derek.

"Your brother."

Derek's dull eyes brightened. "Tony?"

"If anything happened to me," I said, "I told Ben to call your brother first. There's no way that gang is here and he's not. And there's no way he'd let someone like Clevenger threaten to kill you without his doing something about it."

"Tony hates my guts."

"Sure he does, but you're still his brother. How sweet is this, Derek? Even though you're an asshole, your brother has come to save your life."

There was a shot, two quick cracks, and a long, morose howl before Clevenger put two more bullets through the door.

"Come on out, friend," said Clevenger, stepping farther into the dining room, gun trained now on the door, waiting for it to swing open so he could kill whoever was standing behind it. "Show yourself and we'll do this right, mano a mano."

The door shivered, then opened just wide enough for someone to burst through the opening, and someone did, leaping through the gap as if hurled. Clevenger put two slugs into him. Quick as that, he ejected the clip, banged in another, and fired two more at the now-prone figure lying in a growing pool of blood.

He stepped up to it and kicked it over. Tall-and-morose stared dead up at him, blood smeared across his horrid yellow grimace.

"You're a clever one, aren't you?" called Clevenger into the dining room, backing up as he aimed once again at the door. "Don't be shy. Come out, come out, whoever you—"

He didn't finish his sentence because, like a dead man come to life, the bloodied body of Derek Grubbins rose off the floor, lifted the low coffee table with both hands, took two steps forward, and slammed the table flush into Clevenger's back. Clevenger dropped as if from a hangman's scaffold.

Derek, a whole side of his face smeared red, stood hunched and ruined over the still form of Clevenger. He turned his bloodied face to me. "He shouldn't have done what he done to your daughter," he said, before leaning over and picking up Clevenger's gun.

"Tony?" he called out. "Is that you?"

"Who's asking?" came Tony's hoarse voice from behind the door.

"It's me. It's Derek."

"He's got a gun," I said loudly.

"Are you going to shoot me?" said Tony.

"Why would I shoot you?"

"I don't know," said Tony. "Who the hell knows what you're going to do? You're a maniac."

"You're right," said Derek. "I am. The worst kind. But I ain't going to shoot you."

"Who else is out there?"

"Just Frenchy. You want me to shoot him?"

"No, he's all right, the same little dork as always, but all right. Okay, I'm coming out," he said, and the door swung open to show an empty entranceway before it swung shut again. Then it swung open once more and there, standing in the doorway, was Tony Grubbins.

They stared at each other for a moment, two brothers, long estranged. There was electricity between them, but I couldn't tell if it was violence or compassion, bitterness or love, I couldn't tell if they were contemplating warm family memories or great family slights. Whatever was between them was as much a mystery to me as had been the Grubbins house all those years ago.

"You got big," said Derek.

"You got old," said Tony. "What'd you do to Clevenger?"

"I clocked him with the coffee table."

"I ought to clock you."

"I know."

"What are you going to do with that gun?"

"I don't know." Derek looked at it for a bit and then dropped it.

Tony took a step forward and stared a bit more, before jumping and grabbing his brother by the neck, as if he were about to wrestle him to the ground. But he didn't wrestle him to the ground, instead he pulled his brother close and embraced him, hugging his brother tight, so tight the breath was forced out. Or was Derek gasping from something else? And were the tears from the pain of the brutal embrace or something else? I remembered the way Derek had thrown his brother out of the house that afternoon so long ago when we were flipping cards on my stoop, and Derek had kicked his brother in the side as if Tony were a mangy dog. There had been utter brutality between them then, and now there were tears as they hugged like two little boys still missing their dead mother and father.

And who among us ever knows the secrets of the heart?

While still holding his brother, Tony lifted his chin and stared at me, his own eyes wet. "Get the hell out of here," he said.

I was standing now, and I backed away, unsure of what I should do.

379

"Just get the hell out," he said.

"With you," I said.

"Alone. And fast, before it all goes to hell."

"They're going to kill Derek."

"They're going to try. Now go. Run. I'll take care of the rest."

"That's twice," I said to Tony.

"Two times too many."

I rushed forward, kneeled over the prostate Clevenger, reached around into his pockets with my tied hands until I found his BlackBerry, shoved it in a pocket of my own. Then I turned from the brothers and their embrace, ran like a frightened house cat through the front room, and scrabbled at the doorknob with my still-bound hands.

49. Spark

I RAN FROM THAT HOUSE WITH MY BOUND HANDS HIGH, LIKE A plucked turkey scuttling out of a Thanksgiving kitchen.

The sun now had set; the sky now was a dusky gray. The air was filled with bike exhaust, and under the exhaust the smell of something deeper and more acrid, as if the gasoline from the tanks had started spilling. Once I realized I wasn't going to be mowed down like Jim Brown in *The Dirty Dozen*, I slowed my step as I headed toward a singular presence in the middle of the gang, the unlikeliest savior I could ever have imagined.

Billie Flynn leaned insouciantly on her Harley, her arms crossed, her mien as fearsome as Grendel's mother. She was flanked on one side by her old man, Stoner, and on the other by Corky and his knife. "What happened to Clevenger?" she said.

"Tony took out his men," I said. "Derek did the rest."

"My daddy always said Derek Grubbins was as hardy as a cockroach. Where the hell are they?"

"Still inside."

"A little family reunion, is that it?"

"They hadn't seen each other in a while."

"They better catch up quick," said Billie, before pushing herself off her bike and lumbering over to me. "So it was you, hey, tan pants? That's what Tony told us. It was you that stole our money."

"I told him to tell you," I said. And then, out of habit, and without any conviction, I added, "And it was drug money, so it wasn't your money."

"Shut the fuck up."

I shut the fuck up.

She took another two steps until she was standing right in front of me. My God, she was something. So big, I could feel her gravitational pull. Her face was streaked with dirt from a hard ride, her pores were huge, her jaw solid as a fist, and she smelled like a bad day at the abattoir. She looked me up and down with a countenance as hard as a set of brass knuckles. And then she slugged me in the jaw.

"That felt fucking great," said Billie Flynn as I rolled on the ground in a strangely delicious sort of agony. "That felt almost as great as fucking."

I had been wondering what I would get when I finally faced my most deep-seated demons: a knife in the throat, a chain around the neck, a dragging across a graveled road with my legs tied to the frame of a Harley. Compared with all that, and after my bout of Clevenger torture, a sock on the jaw seemed almost neighborly.

"That's all," said Ben, who was suddenly standing between Billie and me.

"I don't have Derek's throat in my fist yet, you fat black bastard," said Billie.

"Not our fault," said Ben. "Tony brokered the deal and we're keeping to it. We were off the hook so long as we told you where Derek was. Well, he's in there, like we said. If you can't get hold of him with all these gearheads, that's your problem."

"Our problem is your problem, big stuff," said Billie.

I sat up on the ground, my legs in front of me, and thought of things for a moment. And then I said to Ben, "Give her the toolbox."

"What?"

"You were going to give it to Clevenger in exchange for me, now give it to her."

"What's this bullshit?" said Billie.

"You told Tony he could buy his brother's safety for a hundred thousand dollars. That's what's in the box. I'm buying Derek's life. Take the money and leave him be, like you promised."

"What the hell are you doing?" said Ben. "He set you up, he tried to kill you, and you're saving him."

"I'm not doing it for Derek, I'm doing it for Tony. He saved my life twice. I owe him. And I'm doing it for us, too. A hundred thousand to bury the past for good."

"But I don't want to bury the past," said Billie. "I want to fuck it hard and make its ears bleed."

"That's why you have Stoner," I said. "Ben, get her the tool-box."

Ben looked at me like I was the village idiot throwing dollar bills into the air, and then he shambled over to the truck bed and lifted out the rusted green metal box. When he offered it to Billie, she just stared at it for a moment.

"I sure would rather kill him," said Billie.

"The chase is over. A deal's a deal, even for you," I said. "You saved my life, even if you didn't intend to, for which I am grateful. And we took the money long ago, for which we don't offer any apologies. You take this offering, and all of us, for ever after, are square."

"We'll never be square."

"As soon as you take the money we are."

"Maybe we'll just take it anyway."

"And maybe we'll just take it back," I said. "We did it once, we can do it again."

She shook her head and blinked down at me as I sat on the ground, helpless as a chipmunk. She stared at me as if she was seeing me for the first time. Then she laughed, a laugh as big as her shoulders and as hearty as a keg of Guinness.

"A deal's a deal," she said as she took the box from Ben. "We're done chasing." She opened the toolbox on her bike. Ten bundles of bills, their wrappers browned and aged. "Hello, babies," she said. "I been looking for you."

"Gimme some of that," said Corky.

"When we split it with everyone else, you old cocksucker," she said as one by one she started stuffing the bundles into her saddlebag. "You're a hell of gutsy son of a bitch, tan pants, ain't you?"

"I was," I said.

"I underestimated your bony little ass." When she had emptied out the tool case, she tossed it to the ground behind her. It landed with a clank and a sputter, ending splayed open on the mud in a way that bothered me. "Can't imagine a guy with pants like that having the balls for it."

"I wore jeans when I was seventeen."

"And that scar on the neck?"

"Corky," I said, scrambling to stand with my hands still bound. "He came to my house with your father, looking for the money."

"I knowed I knowed him," said Corky.

"You want to use that knife again to cut me loose?"

Corky came over, started sawing at the ropes with that buck knife of his. "How much you guys really get all those years ago?"

"Over a mil."

"Shit," said Corky, as my hands suddenly burst free. "I could have gotten drunk and laid for a whole year with that much money."

"That would be a hell of a year." As I rubbed my wrists, I turned to Billie. "You mind if I take the toolbox back?"

"Take whatever the fuck you want, as long as you take them pants."

"The box was my dad's."

"Fuck your daddy," said Billie.

"Yeah, you said that already." I stepped over to the box, picked it up, closed it, and snapped the latches, gave it a little rub like it was a genie's lamp. Just then there was a great thump, like a huge foot stamping down on the earth, and suddenly everything in front of me was lit with a flickering light. A cheer rose up from the bikers all about me. I turned around and the Everfair model home was sheathed in great walls of orange-blue fire. I took a step forward, thought of Tony and Derek and that sad hug, thought of Clevenger lying unconscious on the floor, took another step, and was stopped by a wave of heat that slapped me smack in the face.

The flames blew out windows and chewed at the roof. And as the fire raged, one after another of the gang members started shooting at the burning house, pistols firing, assault rifles, sawed-off scatterguns unloading barrel after barrel, the whole orgy of violence speeding the destruction and sending sparks flying. Whatever was inside that house was a lost cause. And walking toward us in a slouch, outlined by the flames, was a skinny kid with lank blond hair flicking a lighter on and off, on and off.

"I guess that settles that," said Billie with a cackle before hopping on her Harley.

"But we had...had..." I stammered and sputtered at the unfairness of it all, and then, even as I remembered something Tony had said inside, I kept the sputtering, for effect if for nothing else. "But we had a deal. You weren't going to kill Derek."

"I just said I wasn't going to chase him no more. And I'm not. It's over, like I promised. I won't dig up his charred dead body just to piss on it. So at least you got that out of it. Now it's quitting time. It won't be long before someone calls in the fire and the cops show."

"You're a nasty piece of work," I said.

"Don't start sweet-talking me, tan pants," she said. "I'd rut you into dust, but you sure as hell would enjoy it."

She let out a yelp that would have made a rebel wilt, hopped her Harley to a start, and charged out of Everfair. The Devil

Rams holstered their guns, revved their engines, and, like a pack of dragons roaring and belching, followed.

With the toolbox in my hand, I walked over to Ben and Harry, standing now by the truck. "Let's go."

"Where's that Clevenger?" said Harry.

"Inside," I said, gesturing toward the burning house. "Out cold."

"He ain't cold no more," said Harry, with a crotchety laugh. "How about that Derek?"

"Last I saw he was inside, too. With his brother."

"Shame about the brother," said Harry. "And what about your daughter, Johnny?"

"She's on her way down." I reached in my pocket, pulled out Clevenger's phone. "They're going to give me a call when they get in."

50. Lurch

I BARELY FELT THE LURCH.

It happened when we slowed to make the sharp left out of the Everfair exit. We could already hear the sirens, it wouldn't be long before the fire trucks and the police poured into the failed development. In my hand I held Clevenger's BlackBerry, the simplest way for me to get in touch with my daughter. Back in the hotel room was the rest of the money, the simplest way for me to buy her safety from the bastards who had taken her in North Carolina. Anything that complicated things endangered my daughter, and the police, with the remains of the model home still burning, were a complication I couldn't afford. So we were rushing the hell out of there. And the road was bumpy from the mud and the pits created by the construction vehicles. And I already mentioned that Harry's truck was a suspension-free zone, which meant every gully and rut was transmitted in vivid Technicolor to our bones. So when I felt the lurch it registered enough for me to turn around and check the rear window, but not enough for me to do anything when the cursory glance picked up nothing unusual in the bed. I just turned around again and let it pass. From such slight failures, corpses are made.

Back at the motel, we laid out the remaining cash on the bed, right next to the toolbox, the false floor, and the pile of tools. Ben had hidden the bills in a bag taped to the top of the toilet's tank.

That, two more days' advance in cash at the office, and a Do Not Disturb sign on the door had been the sum total of his precautions.

"The first spot they ever check," I said as I pulled off the duct tape, "is the toilet tank."

"We didn't have much time," said Ben. "When we got nervous at not hearing from you, we called you at Derek's house and got no answer. I knew something was rotten then. I figured he'd taken you to Everfair since it's all he ever talks about, so we made our call to Tony. By then it was hide it in the tank or take it with us."

"Good choice," I said.

Laid out on the bedspread now was $140,000, give or take a few hundred snapped out of the bundles for expenses. I took four of the bundles and tossed them to Ben.

"What's that for?" he said.

"Half of what I found at Augie's place."

"What about your daughter?"

"What I have left is more than enough."

"But over the years I borrowed more than forty from you."

"Keep it," I said. "That was between you and me, this is between you and Augie. It cost him his life not giving this up. He would have wanted you to have half."

Ben looked at the money for a long moment, and then his face slowly collapsed into a death mask of misery.

"Stop it," I said. "That's not what Augie would have wanted. Augie would have wanted you to laugh at his grave and then blow his money on booze and girls."

"That's what he would have done, all right."

"He just would have done it better than us. But don't ever forget that when I was in trouble you came for me. When I saw you and Harry out there with the truck, it felt as good as coming home."

"Still here, right?" said Ben.

"Still here," I said.

The rest of the money I put in the tool case, a cool hundred thou. All that was left for me from my brutal misadventure of a quarter century ago, and now all of it earmarked to buy Shelby's freedom. As I thought of her, lying in the back of the car, barreling south, scared and vulnerable, my teeth ached. And I knew the number of the bastards who took her, it was clear as neon on the BlackBerry's recent call list, but it wasn't the right thing to call them. They were bringing her here, to me; there was no reason to stop them. When they arrived they'd place a call and tell me where they were. If I played it right, I could show up without their being any the wiser.

I was just putting the false floor and tools back into the case when we heard a knock at the door. And I remembered the lurch.

I closed the case and latched it shut.

Harry pulled out Holmes's gun.

Ben jammed his bundles into his pockets and slid over to the door.

"What do you want?" called out Ben.

"I need to piss," came a voice, harsh and low.

"Get lost," said Ben.

"Open up, you pisshead, or I'll piss on your head."

"Let him in," I said, the smile threatening to break my face in two. "It's Tony Grubbins."

And Tony wasn't lying about having to pee. As soon as the door opened, with barely a nod in either of our directions, he stomped straight for the piss pot. It sounded like there was a sturgeon splashing around in there.

"How'd he find us?" whispered Ben.

"He jumped into the truck when we left Everfair," I said. "I thought I felt something lurch."

"I just supposed he was burned to a crisp with his brother."

"The way he spoke inside, it sounded like he knew something bad was going to happen and he had a way of getting out. I suppose while I went out the front, keeping everyone busy, he found a way out the back with Derek. Those Grubbinses are like genital herpes—nothing gets rid of them."

"Is he going to beat us up like old times?" said Ben.

"He never beat you up."

"True."

Tony let out a relieved "Ahhhhh" as he came back into the room, fastening up his pants. "I needed that." He stopped, looked around. "What?"

"We're just glad to see you still alive," I said.

"There you stand, Moretti, lying straight to my face. At least some things don't change." Tony dropped down on one of the beds, his hands beneath his head, making himself perfectly at home.

"Tony, not that I'm not glad to see you alive and all," I said, "but what the hell are you doing here?"

"I need a ride north," he said.

"How'd you get down?"

"My bike. But when we were out of the house, I gave it to Derek. He needed it more than I did."

"Not really," I said. "I gave Billie the hundred thousand she wanted. I bought your brother's life."

"Why the hell would you do something like that?"

"I figured I owed you."

"Then you should have given the money to me," said Tony. "I would have taken it and let the bastard fend for himself. He's on the run from Clevenger's people anyway, and I could sure use a new truck."

"Too late." Pause. "So how was it, seeing him again?"

"It was full, man, that's all I can tell you. Full. And you want to know what I did?"

"What?"

"I apologized. Just like I said I wanted to in that bar. I apologized—I don't even know what for—but I felt suddenly lighter. Like I had let go of another one. You ought to try it, man."

"Apologize to Derek?"

"To whoever."

"But I don't have anyone left to apologize to."

"Find someone."

"I'm sorry."

"See, is that so hard?"

"Sure, you can hitch a ride with us. We'll take you as far as Virginia. And maybe on the way up you can apologize to me for throwing that football in my face."

"Are you sure I did that?"

"I've been carrying it a long time."

"Let it go, dude, that's my advice. Let it go." Tony looked around a bit. "So this is what it's like to hang out with you guys. I always wondered. Pretty damn lame."

"It was better when we were sixteen," said Ben. "And when Augie was still around. And when we were getting high."

"So what *are* we doing, actually?" said Tony.

"We're waiting for a call," I said, and just then the minuet began to play.

I motioned to Tony to stay quiet and then, with shaking hands, gently handed the phone to Ben.

Ben closed his eyes for a moment like he was slipping into something and then opened them again as he answered the phone.

"Clevenger," he said in a sharp Midwestern patter that was surprisingly close to the original. "Good. Stay put…Is she okay?…Make sure she stays that way…Twenty minutes…Right."

When he hung up he dropped onto a bed like he had just run a marathon.

"Well?"

"She's okay. They're waiting for you."

"Where?"

"Where we should have expected them to take her all along."

51. The Piper

I HADN'T DARED DRIVE FROM THE MOTEL. I WAS TOO HOPPED UP, too angry, too frightened, too nervous, too distracted. So I told Harry to get behind the wheel and situated Ben next to him to give directions, which left Tony and me sitting in the bed like migrant workers, the wind rushing over us with a terrifying roar. And all the while I was running scenarios in my head.

What would she look like? How scared would she be? What would I say to her? Was she mad at me? God, I hoped she wasn't mad at me. I couldn't handle it if she was mad at me. How would I play it with the sons of bitches who had taken her? What kind of deal could I make? The key to her safety, I knew, was to keep it low key and nonconfrontational. No police with their bullhorns and SWAT teams ready to turn the night into *Dog Day Afternoon*, no guns, no hysteria or acrimony. Just some reasonable men trying to find a win-win for everyone. I needed to let them know that Clevenger was dead, that the game was over, and that if they released Shelby with a minimum of fuss, they could each leave Florida rich enough to start over again. Probably fifty would be enough, but I'd offer whatever was necessary to make it happen. It would be tricky, sure, but I could handle it. Life and death is every day in the mortgage business.

But when we arrived at Derek's overbuilt house, where my daughter was waiting, there it was, sitting right in front like a slap in the face. And as soon as I saw it I knew with a thumping certainty that all my best-laid plans had been laid once again to waste. A blue Corvette—*the* blue Corvette—its perfect paint job blackened and shredded, its hawk nose badly broken, as if smashed with a baseball bat, its windshield peppered with shot.

"Whose wreck is that?" said Tony, pointing toward the battered Corvette after we had descended from the truck's bed onto the street.

"Your brother's," I said, "though it was pristine when he parked it in the garage that went up in flames. You don't think he went back for it, do you?"

"He was grateful enough to get the hell out of there with his life and my bike. He wasn't going back for a car, even one that was once as nice as this one."

I turned to look at the wide front door and said, "I should have known the son of a bitch wasn't going to die so easily."

"What is it, Johnny?" said Harry, coming from the front of the truck.

"Complications," I said. "Go around back, Harry, and check out the boat. Make sure it's empty, and if it is, make sure no one gets on it."

"What are you fixing to do?" said Harry.

"I'm going inside the house to get my daughter."

"You have a plan?"

"I did, but that's been blown to hell. Now it's all about figuring it out on the fly."

"Then you might want this," said Harry, taking the gun from his belt.

"What the hell am I going to do with that?" I said.

"Shoot it," said Harry, "just not at your foot."

I went back to the truck, opened the door, took the toolbox from behind the seat. "All I'm going to need is this. Give the gun to Ben."

"Here you go, youngster," said Harry as he handed the gun over to Ben. "Don't you fire it at your foot neither."

We watched as Harry skipped around the house with his gimpy crooked lean.

"Handy guy to have around," said Tony.

"You don't know the half of it," I said. "Stay out here with Ben. Anyone but Clevenger tries to leave, let him."

"Clevenger?" said Ben.

"That's right."

"That rabid dog is in there and you're going in alone?"

"You need backup," said Tony.

"If he sees an army there's no telling what he'll do to Shelby. But he's got me pegged for the coward that I am. He's not worried about me, so we can work something out without the gunplay. In fact, the only reason he's still here is that he's waiting for me. Stay outside unless you hear me screaming in horrible agony, then maybe you two might want to join the party."

"Good luck, J.J.," said Ben.

"Yeah," I said before I slid over to the heavy wooden door, pressed the front latch slowly, pressed the door open softly, stepped inside. The foyer was dark, the whole house was dimly lit except for light bleeding through the living room from the back room with the bar and the flatscreen and the pool table. Something was going on in there; I could hear the tinkle of ice in a glass, smell the noxious scent of a cigar.

I slammed the door closed behind me and called out, "Honey, I'm home."

When I stepped down into the back room, I saw her immediately and my heart seized. There was nothing else in the room besides her. She was sitting demurely, her legs together, her arms crossed. Her beautiful face was wiped clean of its makeup, her eyes were small and red and wet, her mouth was tight with fear. And she seemed so young, Christ, a little girl again, my little girl. I was so captured by the sight of her, I even wondered why she didn't run right to me when she saw me enter; I was worried that she might be so angry at what I had done to her that she couldn't bear to touch me.

And then I noticed the guy next to her on the couch. With a gun jammed into her side. My old buddy Holmes. Out of the hospital and now in Florida, his face bruised, his left arm in a sling. So they had let him go, and he was the one who had picked her up. It kept on getting better and better, the mess I had created for my daughter. And the best treat of all was at the bar, with a drink in his hand and cigar in his teeth, his clothes blackened and singed but aside from that looking none the worse for the blow he took from the coffee table. Clevenger.

"Hey, Shelbs," I said as calmly as I could muster. I think I might have even winked. "How you holding up?"

"I'm sorry, Daddy," she said with a trembling jaw. "I'm so sorry."

"It's not your fault, it's mine. All of it is mine. Are you okay? Did Holmes hurt you?"

"No, I'm okay."

"Was it just him?"

"Just me," said Holmes.

"And he didn't…"

"No," said Shelby. "Nothing."

"That's good." I looked at Holmes. "For you and for him."

Holmes sneered at me out of that bruise of a face.

"I love you, Shelbs," I said.

"I know you do, Daddy."

"I'm going to take care of everything, okay?"

"Okay," she said, forcing out a sorry excuse for a smile.

"This is quite the touching reunion," said Clevenger, looking at the lit cigar he had taken from his mouth. "I'd be weeping if I was the kind of guy who wept. We've been waiting for you, Moretti."

"And here I am."

"Except you took your time getting here. We've been here too long, it's time for us to clear out. So let's get down to business, shall we? Who was it who decked me in the house?"

"Derek."

"He'll pay for that."

"If you ever find him, which I doubt. I brought in the case."

"Come to pay the piper, is that it?"

"Something like that," I said.

"It's good to see you wised up. The piper always gets paid. How much is in there?"

"All that was left of the cash we took. A hundred thousand dollars."

"There's twice that much."

"Was, but I gave a hundred to the motorcycle gang."

"Why the hell?"

"You don't think they earned it for saving our lives? This is all that's left. I'm sick of it anyway, it hasn't brought me anything but loss. It's cursed. You deserve it."

"You bet I do. It isn't enough to clean the books, but it will do for now. Bring it over."

"Not until you let Shelby go. Just let her leave out the front door and the case is yours, it's as simple as that."

"I'll set the terms, my friend, and you'll accept them. You don't have much choice, do you?"

I looked at Holmes on the couch, the gun still pointed at Shelby even as his attention was fixed on the box.

"No," I said. "You've got me in a vise, all right."

"So let's cut out the chatter and cut right to it. Show me what you have, boy."

I brought the case over to the bar. Clevenger put the cigar back in his teeth and swiveled to watch as I grabbed one side of the case with my right hand and reached down with my left to unlock the latch. As I lifted my hand to snap it open, in one smooth motion I missed the latch, grabbed hold of the handle, lifted the case, and drove it like a battering ram smack into Clevenger's face.

The fat man hit the floor like a sack of gravy.

"Here's how it's going down," I said to Holmes as I stared at the muzzle of his gun, now aimed straight at my heart. "You can bet I didn't come alone. You shoot, you die, it is that simple. But there's a way out. Put the gun down, walk out the front door, and it's over for you."

"What about him?" said Holmes.

"What do you care? Consider your employment terminated. The severance you get is your life. I'll even throw in the cash if you just do it without any lip or back-and-forth. If I have another negotiation I'll scream. Now put down the gun, take the money, walk out the front door, be something other than a mindless thug."

"Go to hell," he said, snapping his gun so it jammed right into Shelby's torso, causing her to gasp. "Get up."

"Daddy?"

"Do what he says, Shelby," I said.

She stood and he struggled to stand with her. There was something wrong with his leg; the accident had done a job on him, all right, but not enough of one to put him out of commission. I should have sprung for the bigger engine in the 3 Series. When he was finally off the couch, he jammed his gun again into Shelby's side.

"I am getting out of here," said Holmes, "just like you said, and with the money, too, but not like you said. It's going to be sweet Shelby and me together. And we're going out the back, not the front, where your little trap is waiting."

"You'll never get away."

"Sure I will. On the boat. Clevenger swiped the keys. Now slide the case over, low and slow."

"It's good to see a dumb lug like you taking some initiative," I said as I put the case on the floor and kicked it over to him. "Too bad you're a dumb lug."

He gestured for Shelby to take the case, and when she looked at me, I gave her a signal to do just as he wanted her to do. She reached down and heaved it up. While still pressing the gun into her side, he gave her a tug, and the two backed away, slowly, Holmes limping all the while, slowly backed away toward the sliding door that led to the pool and then to the dock.

"I hear a shout, a call, anything," he said, "and your daughter gets a hole in her gut. Understand?"

"I understand," I said. "And don't worry, you won't hear a peep out of me."

He turned briefly, opened the sliding door, and then continued backing out slowly, his gun still jabbed into Shelby, his eyes still on me as he stepped backward into shadow.

It happened so fast it barely registered. A flash of something, quick as a dart.

Holmes's face snapped back and he reeled around, his arms rising as he did.

And then two more just like the first, two quick jabs that pummeled his nose, leaving him teetering before a swift left hook to the jaw sent him down, down for the count, the gun sliding across the flat pale stones that surrounded the pool.

A bent figure now stood over his prostrate body. Like Ali over Liston. You bet it was. And as my daughter rushed back inside and pressed her wet face into my neck, I suddenly knew just how good a fighter Sugar Ray Robinson had been.

52. Slim Chance

THIRTY MINUTES LATER I STOOD WITH HARRY ON THE DECK of Derek's Bayliner as the engines churned the water and the boat slid backward into the waterway.

The boat lights were lit, red and green beaming from the front, a bright white on a post rising from the rear, and Harry was at the wheel, gently fingering the throttle. I turned and surveyed the scene to my right, the grotesque house bright and welcoming even though it was empty, the pool lit from below like a kidney-shaped jewel. It all would stay lit like a party of light until the power company turned off the juice and the bank repossessed the thing.

"You hear that?" said Harry.

"Yeah, I hear it."

"Let's hope no one else does."

"I'll take care of it," I said.

Before throwing off the ropes and hopping on the boat, I had done one of the most difficult things I had ever done in my life. In front of Derek's house I had said good-bye to my daughter. It was just until the morning, but still.

"Dad, no. I want to stay with you. Dad." There was fear in her voice, a panicky fear, completely understandable after what she had gone through, and it cut me that I was forced to ignore it. But there was nothing to be done.

"I'm going to leave you with Ben," I said. "He's one of my oldest friends. He'll take care of you. You'll go to his house and you'll call Mom. She already knows you're safe, but she needs to talk to you, to hear your voice. We'll be together again tomorrow."

"I'll stay with you. Let me stay with you."

"You can't," I said. "I don't want you involved when I take care of these guys. After tomorrow we'll be together long enough for you to be sick to death of me, okay? But I've got to make sure these people stay out of our lives for good."

"What are you going to do with them?"

"I'm going to take care of them."

"Dad?"

"With the authorities, sweetie. I'm going to take them to the authorities, where they're going to pay for their crimes."

"Okay."

"But you don't need to be in the middle of it. What they did to my friend in Las Vegas is enough to put them away for a long enough time. We can keep you out of it that way, so that's the way I'm going to play it. Go with Ben."

"I want to be with you."

I want to be with you. When was the last time she had said such a thing? "Go with Ben, call your mother, be as sweet to her as you've been to me. I'll see you tomorrow."

"I guess."

"No guessing," I said. "I love you, Shelby. It will all be okay. Now go on." And it would be okay, I knew, but still my heart cracked as I watched Shelby slowly leave my side and climb into Harry's truck.

Tony and Ben were standing to my right, surveying the scene as I sent my daughter away. "I won't forget what you did for my brother," said Tony.

"He sold me out, he sold out Augie."

"He's a bastard, I agree, he always has been."

"And yet you apologized to him. Maybe I'll figure it out sometime."

"I'll leave Harry's truck at the dock in Virginia where you told me and hitch a ride north."

"I guess that's it, then. I'll see you around."

"You coming up to Pitchford again?"

"Never."

"Then you won't be seeing me around."

There was a moment when I thought I ought to hug Tony Grubbins, a moment when the nascent embrace sort of hung in the air between us, but thankfully the impulse died.

"You were an asshole growing up, J.J.," said Tony. "I just wanted you to know that."

"You were a bully."

"We deserved each other."

"Keep an eye on Madeline for me," I said, before I took the hug that had been hanging around Tony and gave it to Ben, hard. And he hugged me back, just as hard.

"We'll keep in touch this time," I said while still grabbing tight to my oldest living friend.

"Sure we will," said Ben. "We'll check in every week."

"No, for real now. Not just still here, but how's it going, how can I help, the whole thing. Like friends should."

"Okay."

"I don't have many people left in my life. I'm not going to lose you again. We'll meet up in Las Vegas, all right."

"Sure."

"Sooner rather than later."

"Okay, yeah," he said, catching on. "Vegas."

I let go and watched Ben and Tony climb into either side of the cab. It was a comforting sight, like a security sandwich from my past wrapping around my daughter. As the truck pulled away, my daughter turned and stared at me. I gave a little wave.

When they were gone, I headed back through the house toward Harry and the boat. On the way around the pool I passed Holmes, still lying where Harry had put him down. I didn't know what to do with the son of a bitch, so I decided to leave him where he fell. To bring him to the police would get my daughter involved in something she should never have been involved in. I had done a job on him with the car, Harry had battered him with his fists, he wasn't worth the further trouble of dealing with. Maybe he would learn something, stop being a dumb lug, though I doubted it.

When I reached the boat, the engines were already thrumming. And beneath the thrumming, like a low undertone of dread, there was a moan coming from the boat's cabin. I threw off the lines tying the boat to the dock and hopped aboard. Harry gave me a look as I wiped away a tear before he started maneuvering the boat away from the dock. And as we slowly motored away from Derek's former mansion, I thought of the three people in that truck, the old friend to whom I had remained loyal, the old enemy whom I had befriended, and the daughter whom I loved and had saved. And as I thought of them I could believe that whatever I had done twenty-five years ago, and whatever I had done to protect what I had done, all of it hadn't ruined me. I could think of those three and believe in my own innate goodness.

Then the moan started up again and Harry said, "Do you hear that?" and after a moment more I left his side, climbed down the steps into the cabin, and kicked Clevenger in the head to shut him the hell up.

Back on deck I gave a nod to Harry as he edged the boat down the canal. We were sailing away from the house, away from my past, toward the Intracoastal Waterway and the inlet that would lead us out to the dark roll of the sea.

Do you have something to say? Think twice.

We're Americans. We eat too much, we work too hard for too many hours, we buy houses that are too big for our families, televisions that are too big for our houses, we have too many wives, too many cars, we own so much stuff we need to rent sheds to store it all in. We drown ourselves in our surfeit. And to pay for all this wondrous excess we take on too much debt. Hallelujah. Which is Hebrew for *get used to it*.

There was a time in this country when pennies were banked, when socks were darned and shoes repaired, and we stayed together for the sake of the kids. But then there arose a generation that knew not Woody Guthrie and the great splurge was on. Hallelujah. Show me a country that lives within its means and I'll show you Finland.

My country 'tis a nation of excess and I love it, with all its contradictions, with all my heart. In the spirit of my native land, I grabbed my piece of the pineapple pie when I was seventeen and never looked back. And when it was time to find a profession, I ended up selling that same opportunity to anyone with the vision and fortitude to spit the future in the eye and take hold of what he couldn't yet afford. For tell me true: Who really wants to live within his means? Where is the imagination in that? America is the land of giants, not half soles.

But that doesn't mean the piper won't come knocking, as from hard experience I can attest. We had sat down together and had our accounting and in the end I had paid the piper his price, steeper than ever I had imagined. I had given up everything that ever mattered to me without even knowing it, and in the process I had given up the richest part of myself. Yet in the shadow of that loss I say still, hallelujah. For if you embrace the excess, and I surely did, you need to embrace the piper, too.

But that doesn't mean the piper always gets his way, at least not in this great country of ours. Titans stiff the piper with a bailout. Minnows, in a house underwater, swim away. We even have a trapdoor out of the piper's prison called the US Bankruptcy Code. You would think all of this would keep the piper humble enough to know his place. But sometimes still the piper oversteps his bounds. And when he kills your friend, and sticks electrodes on your breast, and kidnaps your daughter, and threatens to hound you and your family for the rest of your natural-born lives, you have no choice other than to drown the vile son of a bitch in a bathtub as big as the Atlantic. Any other way would be un-American, and don't ever say I'm not a patriot.

Didn't I tell you where I lived?

"When you was belowdecks, you see any gin?" said Harry as he piloted us through the ocean waves into the brightening day after passing through the dark of the night.

"Not that I noticed."

"I'm not complaining now. You do what you got to do in this life and I don't see what you had any choice. But I sure could use myself something that burns all the way down because I still got the taste in my mouth."

"Hence the need for gin."

"Or something stronger if you got it."

"Kerosene?"

"That would do, as long as you lit it first."

We left the ocean at the Boynton Inlet, motoring past the clot of fishermen at the end of the long cement pier. With the sun at our backs we headed into the wide Intracoastal Waterway and then north, to a series of long sturdy docks reaching out into the canal. And there, at the end of one of those docks, with his hand shading his eyes as we motored toward him, was Ben. And standing beside him, waiting to climb aboard the Bayliner, as thin and fragile as a river reed, was my daughter.

It took us a week to make it up north.

A few hours after we picked up Shelby, we stopped at a marina and spent a chunk of cash on a batch of supplies. Instead of the kerosene, we grabbed some gin for Harry, along with vodka, rum, a couple of cases of beer. And once the necessities were taken care of we loaded up on the luxuries: gasoline, food, toilet paper, navigational charts.

"Charts?" I said. "You need charts, Harry? I'm disappointed."

"You're just showing off your ignorance there, Johnny. I haven't done the ditch in a while and them engineers, they're always changing things. You take a wrong turn, and before you know it, you're floating like an oil-soaked gull in the Gulf."

The final thing I bought was a cell phone, prepaid. Only one now, since I wasn't anymore on the run. And a cheap one, without all kinds of spaces for all kinds of stored contacts, because there was only one number I cared about.

It was a slow sail through the gorgeous scenery, and all in all it was the most time in one stretch I had ever spent with my daughter. I thought we would talk all about it, the ordeal, the trauma, those hours and days of terror she spent in the backseat of Holmes's car, but we barely mentioned it. In fact, we barely talked about anything deeper than the color of the sunset or the coolness of the breeze. At first it was frustrating, like there was this great gap between us that we both were afraid to fill, but then the frustration eased as I realized this was how it was between us, and probably how it always would be. Sometimes you say all you need to say with your very presence.

But once I did push her for an answer. I wanted to know, I needed to know, what she felt when she realized I had come to Derek's house to rescue her. It was selfish of me, of course, I wanted some acknowledgment of my hero moment. Was she surprised? Was she pissed at me? Was she thrilled to her bones?

"The whole time, I knew you would come," said Shelby, when I finally prodded her hard enough. "And then you did. Eric says you're the Batman."

"He reads too many comic books."

"Uh, yeah, he does, and you should do something about that. But still, because of him I wasn't surprised when you appeared. I was just a little pissed that it took you so long."

"I got hung up," I said.

"What's going to happen to those men?"

"Something bad, I hope."

"What did the police say?"

"That they'd take care of it."

"I hope they never get out," she said with a note of bitterness that stopped me from asking anything more.

And that was it, the sum total of our chat about her abduction and rescue. She wasn't going to say anything more to me, I was just her daddy. That's why they invented therapists. But she often leaned her head on my shoulder as we sat on the bow, admiring the sunset, and that said enough for me. Which was a good thing, because on the ride up she spent more time talking with Harry than with her father. Harry let her fuss around the boat, happy to have someone to whom he could explain all the ins and outs of the maritime arts, all the stuff I couldn't care about in the least. Harry taught her how to drive the boat, how to read the gauges and charts. He turned her into his navigator, and she loved it. And I think she grew to love him, too, which touched me in a way I hadn't expected and made me think again about my dad.

We relaxed and sunned ourselves and ate like kings on what Harry cooked on the cookstove in the galley: tugboat scampi, ragtime catfish stew. Shelby's skin darkened from the sun and she eschewed her overwrought eyeliner and every day, to my eyes, she grew more beautiful. In South Carolina, we stayed an extra night at one of the marinas because Harry knew someone who knew someone in the Department of Natural Resources. We arrived in Beaufort on the *Second Chance* out of Fort Lauderdale and left on the *Slim Chance* out of Port Royal, the boat now legally registered and fully titled to one Harry Conahan of Newport News, Virginia.

"What are you going to do with it, Harry?" I said.

"A boat this slick don't really fit me."

"Why not? You're a man of the world."

"But not this world. Fiberglass is like a woman I fell in with from New Orleans, nimble and quick when you first gets hold of her, sure, but when she goes, she goes fast. Wood's like my first wife, dependable. This time I'll keep what I got. My boat upstate is homey."

"It's a clunker."

"But it's my clunker. And if I can sell this for near what it's worth, I can get out of that debt I was telling you about and have enough leftover for a party."

"A hell of a party."

"Sure will be," he said. "Me and them Koreans, we'll be playing dominoes till dawn."

All the time Shelby spent with Harry gave me plenty of time to think, and plenty of time to talk on the phone, and who I was talking to was Caitlin. We spoke at length, multiple times a day, we talked about our lives together, about the kids, the house, the lies.

There was something about talking on the phone with my wife as we churned up the waterway that was addictive. It was as if she were a different person entirely, one with whom I had never talked before. It felt vaguely illicit. Outside of her physical presence, with her intimidating beauty and her disapproving eyes, I felt brave enough to open all my truths to her, all but one. And she, assured now of the safety of her daughter, and with the distance loosing her natural reticence, seemed to feel the same. We talked more on that trip up the ditch, and talked about more, than through the whole of our married life together.

And this is what we determined, both of us, with sadness and regret, but not without a touch of optimism for the future: our marriage was finished, was irrevocably over, our marriage was dead. Like a salmon washed up on shore, its belly bloated, its eyes pecked out by a crow, dead.

And yet, still we talked.

Even after we agreed that our past had been more barren than we had ever imagined, that our present was based on quicksand, and that our future together would revolve around shuffling Shelby and Eric back and forth between us until they graduated into their own lives, we continued to talk. Each morning while I drank my coffee as the sun rose full of promise on our right, I could barely wait to place my first call of the day to her. And each evening, as the sun died to our left and I digested another of Harry's feasts, I looked forward to opening a beer and making that final call of the day. The relationship I was creating with the woman on the phone was nothing like what I had developed with my wife, and I couldn't get enough of it. It was maybe the truest thing I had ever held in my life.

But it was over before it even started. And the closer we got to home, the more bereft I felt. It was as if all I had to grab on to anymore was this thing we had created for ourselves over the phone, this fragile beautiful thing with the lifespan of a copper butterfly. And our week was just about up.

"I'm confused, Harry," I said on the final afternoon of our trip north, as Shelby piloted us up the James River. "And I'm scared, and I'm confused about why I'm scared."

"I'm always confused there, Johnny. Confusion for me is like water to a fish, I wouldn't know how to breathe without it. My theory's always been, if you ain't confused about something, then you're living wrong."

"Is that why you drink?"

"That's why I fish. Fishing calms the nerves, eases doubts. Fishing makes sense. I drink because I like it."

"I owe you, Harry."

"No, you don't. I made out fine, and had an adventure to boot."

"You've been a good friend."

"We been good friends is more like it."

"I'm going to miss you."

"I ain't dead yet, sonny. You know what that thing is jutting out there?"

"Yes I do."

"I like that wife of yours."

"So do I."

"Good," he said. "About time you knowed it."

In the distance was the long stone jetty that led to the Patriots Landing marina. As Shelby drove us closer, I made my way around to the bow of the motorboat and stood, leaning forward on the guardrail, shielding my eyes from the sun as I searched the docks. We were already sliding into the inlet when I saw them, two figures, a woman and a boy, both peering out at us just as I was peering in at them.

And I wasn't confused one bit about what I felt.

53. The Dentist

It was a sunny day in Vegas when I said good-bye to Augie one last time.

Three of us stood in front of the tombstone, Ben and Selma and I. The stone was a simple rectangle, carved with the applicable dates, the inscription: A Good Son and a Good Friend, and the name: Augie Iannucci, D.D.S.

"Nice touch," I said to Selma. "Somewhere his mother's smiling."

"I should have put something snazzier on it," said Selma, leaning heavily on her cane. "He would have liked something snazzier."

"You did fine," I said.

"Truth is, I didn't know much about him."

"He was a good son," said Ben. "Instead of going to college, he took care of his dad when his dad was sick."

"That's sweet," said Selma.

"He didn't make much of a deal of it," I said, "but it was bigger than he wanted to admit. He was that kind of kid."

"And he was a good friend," said Ben.

I kneeled down and said softly to the stone, "I followed your advice the whole way, bub. They paid and we're still here. Thanks." I reached into my pocket and pulled out an old twenty-dollar bill, three pieces taped together. I put it right on top of the grass, spread it out as best I could. When it curled up, I spread it out again. That's when the words on the headstone got fuzzy.

"You can't leave it there," said Selma. "Someone will take it."

"I hope so," I said. "Maybe it will end up buying one last drink."

When I stood and turned around, I tried to hide my tears with a smile. Shelby was there, and Eric. And Caitlin, too. Imagine that.

We didn't fly into Vegas, we drove. It wasn't quite on the way, but it was close enough. The family had decided to make the trip on the spot, all of us. And the spot on which we made the decision was at Patriots Landing, right in front of our house, or what was left of it.

After hugs and tears of greetings, the four of us had walked together from the dock to the house. And as we made our way up the hill, my father's rusted green toolbox was still in my hand. I had thought of giving its contents away, tossing it to some charity to be free of the burden, but just as quick as the idea came I strangled it until its eyes bulged. A hundred thou, free and clear, finally. Not as much as I expected to move on with, but still something. And for a lot of reasons I needed something. At the end of our walk we stood before the blackened shell of what had been our George Washington, now a charred pit of refuse and rubble wrapped in yellow police tape. Clevenger had said he was going to help me extract whatever equity I had in the place, and this was his way. There was never anything subtle about Clevenger. If he had any charm at all, that was it.

"I have a contractor coming out tomorrow to level it," said Caitlin.

"Good."

"The neighbors have been complaining."

"I bet they have."

"We've been cited."

"I always wanted to be cited," I said. "But in the *New York Times*, not by the Patriots Landing Homeowners Association." Eric laughed at that, which I liked. "Did you guys find anything worth keeping?"

"I found my baseball glove halfway burned," said Eric. "I finished the job."

"Good boy."

"Everything was junk," said Caitlin.

"Before or after the fire?"

"Are you suddenly getting philosophical on us, Dad?" said my daughter, smiling.

"Hey, I've read Camus," I said.

"Dad."

"What?"

"The *s* is silent."

"Oh, those funny little French."

"The insurance company wants to know if we're going to rebuild," said Caitlin.

"I don't think so," I said. "Unless you..."

"No, that's fine," said Caitlin. "That's great. We can sell the lot, I'm sure. Someone will build something bigger, grander, some great monstrous house with a movie theater in the basement. They always do."

"So what are we going to do?" said Shelby. "I mean, living-wise?"

"Any ideas?" said Caitlin.

"Maybe we'll take the insurance proceeds and buy you that Patrick Henry you always wanted," I said, "while I get an apartment in Divorcé Estates."

"Sammy's dad lives there," said Eric, "and he says it smells like old socks dipped in pee."

"I think we're done with Patriots Landing," said Caitlin, "don't you?"

"God, yes," I said.

"Let's go someplace new," said Shelby.

"Are you sure?" I said. "What about Luke?"

"That's over," said Caitlin. "I think the police showing up and asking about Shelby was a bit too much for Luke's parents to take."

"He's a jerk anyway," said Shelby.

"Remember what I told you?" I said.

She looked at me, fresh faced and happy, and smiled like we were coconspirators, like we were suddenly in a league of our own. "Let's get out of Virginia. I'm sick of Virginia."

"You and me both," I said.

"And Eric will survive a move as long as he doesn't have to play Little League," said Caitlin.

"Just no winters," said Eric. "I already quit skiing."

"Someplace new, someplace warm," I said, nodding at the cleanliness of it all. "A house for you and the kids, an apartment for me."

"Sounds right, for now," said Caitlin. Was there a clue there? A hope?

"Where?" I said.

"California?"

"We're not that hip," said Shelby.

"And there's that whole earthquake thing," said Eric. "What about Florida?"

"I had enough Florida to last me," I said. "Arizona?"

"Real estate there is cheap enough these days," said Caitlin.

"Can we get a swimming pool?"

"It's up to your mom."

"Sure, why not?" said Caitlin. "Phoenix?"

"I hear it's all one big suburb," said Shelby.

"Perfect," I said.

Which was why we were on our way to Arizona. We had mapped the roundabout way together. On our journey we had already seen Chicago, and Mount Rushmore, and Yellowstone.

From Vegas we were heading to the Hoover Dam, then to the Grand Canyon, before dropping down to our new home. It was the best kind of adventure, on the fly and with people you love.

After our visit to the cemetery in Las Vegas, we headed back to Augie's neighborhood to take Selma home. For old times' sake we stopped off at the Applebee's for lunch. There were six of us, Ben and Selma, Caitlin and the kids and me. We sat around with our iced teas and hamburgers and riblets and talked about the old days.

"I still remember that first afternoon you showed up at the Bernstein house," said Ben, "with your little dog and your little tie."

"You had a tie?" said Shelby.

"You had a dog?" said Eric.

"I never told you about the old neighborhood, did I?" I said to my kids. "Pitchford, PA. But to understand the way I felt about Pitchford, you have to know about my dad. Did I ever tell you about my dad?"

"I didn't even know you had a dad," said Eric.

"Don't be a moron," said Shelby.

"I thought he was hatched."

"You told us something about your mom dying in Florida," said Shelby, "but nothing about your dad."

"There's a reason for that," I said. "My father left when I was nine. To say he fled would be more honest, but who wants honesty when dealing with family, right?"

Caitlin leaned forward and smiled.

"Certainly not my mother," I said.

And that's how I began telling my kids about what we had been, the three of us, Augie, Ben, and I, and what we had done, and how it had impacted all our lives. They deserved to know, because they were impacted, too, maybe most of all, and they listened, rapt for once at something I was saying. But I wasn't telling it only for them.

Caitlin stared at me with a bemused smile, like she was wondering who this person was who sat at the head of the table and talked so freely about his past. I had seen that same expression many times in the past few weeks. Our marriage was dead, thank God, it deserved to die for all it hadn't been, but that didn't mean we couldn't build something new, something better, built on a trust that we had never truly shared before. That didn't mean I couldn't try to seduce her all over again, this time with honesty.

What a novel concept. Seduction through honesty. Maybe I could write a book, maybe I could turn it into a self-help lecture, maybe I could sell it on late-night infomercials. I could be the Tony Robbins of honesty. Though not total honesty. I wasn't ever going to tell Caitlin what I did with Harry in the darkness after we sailed out of Fort Lauderdale. Just like Caitlin wasn't ever going to tell me what she did with Thad. But that was okay with me.

Hell, we all need our secrets.

Acknowledgments

I PICKED THE SMALL LAS VEGAS DEVELOPMENT IN WHICH I SET the opening of this novel from satellite images on the Internet. Through the screen, I could examine the precise houses that would be used, note the conditions of the lawns, pick the routes in which the hair-raising chase would occur. Such images are an amazing resource for writers, but you can get only so much from a photograph. I don't write about anyplace I haven't been, and so in the middle of the writing of this book I paid that very development a visit.

On the East Coast we were certainly hit hard by the Great Recession, but if you drove through our neighborhoods and squinted just a bit, things looked pretty much normal. This was definitely not true in that Las Vegas development. In the book I tried to express the emotions I felt as I walked through its deserted streets. Of all the things I saw during that visit, the street sign caked with dust remains the most memorable, as if a tragic storm had ripped through the landscape, blowing away not just budgets and dreams but also the very name of things.

When I returned to the manuscript, I started again on page one and let what I had seen and felt in that devastated neighborhood bleed into the book. And suddenly, Jon Willing was no longer a successful lawyer with money in the bank, he was an unemployed mortgage broker facing economic, as well as corporeal, calamity. This is how a novel is written, not just word by word, but emotion by emotion, memory by memory, and by a thousand pieces of advice.

I want to thank my son Michael and my great friend Pete Hendley for accompanying me to Vegas before we all headed down the Grand Canyon. I also want to thank Rex Morgan for showing me what would become Patriots Landing. I received amazing advice on this book from so many people, including from my agent, Wendy Sherman, the book's first reader and greatest advocate; from Mark Tavani, who gave trenchant advice; and from the fearless David Downing, who pointed out the manuscript's flaws with vision, gentleness, and just the right amount of snark. I especially want to thank Andy Bartlett and Daphne Durham at Thomas & Mercer for their advice, encouragement, and support in getting this manuscript to print. Working with Andy and Daphne and the entire Thomas & Mercer team has reenergized the whole enterprise of my writing.

My children, Nora, Jack, and Michael, gave me the courage to write about kids and what it means to love and be loved by them. And I remain forever grateful to my wife, Pam, because everything I do is part of our love and partnership. Finally, I grew up in Pitchford (not its real name), flipping baseball cards, riding a red bike bought at Sears, hanging in the woods at the end of the road. My siblings, Bret, Jane, and Suzy, are the only ones with whom I can reminisce about those days and our small split-level house, but I can tell you I loved being a kid in the suburbs and am grateful that my late parents settled there. It is too bad that Jon never understood how great a place Pitchford was in which to be a kid.

About the Author

WILLIAM LASHNER IS THE *New York Times*–bestselling creator of Victor Carl, who has been praised by *Booklist* as one of mystery's "most compelling, most morally ambiguous characters." His crime novels include *Blood and Bone*, *Killer's Kiss*, *Marked Man*, *Fatal Flaw*, and *Hostile Witness*. His novel *Kockroach*, published under the name Tyler Knox, was a *New York Times Book Review* Editors' Choice for fiction. Lashner is a former prosecutor with the Department of Justice and a graduate of the Iowa Writers' Workshop; his work has sold worldwide and been translated into more than a dozen languages.

Made in the USA
Charleston, SC
27 April 2013